Cristina Alger is a graduate of Harvard College and NYU Law School. She worked as a financial analyst and a corporate attorney before becoming a writer. She lives in New York with her husband and children.

You can discover more about the author at cristinaalger.com

THE BANKER'S WIFE

Annabel's seemingly perfect expatriate life in Geneva is shattered when her husband Matthew's plane crashes in the Alps. Clues emerge that suggest his death may not have been as accidental as it seems, however, and as Annabel investigates, she puts herself in the crosshairs of formidable enemies, forced to question whether she ever really knew Matthew at all. Meanwhile, journalist Marina is investigating Swiss United, the bank where Matthew worked. She uncovers proof of a shocking financial scandal that implicates some of the world's most rich and powerful, and knows she must expose it — whatever the cost. Possessing evidence so explosive that someone is willing to kill to keep it hidden, the two women find themselves caught up in an international conspiracy. Yet the real threat might just lie closer to home . . .

CRISTINA ALGER

THE
BANKER'S
WIFE

Complete and Unabridged

CHARNWOOD
Leicester

First published in Great Britain in 2018 by
Mulholland Books
An imprint of Hodder & Stoughton
London

First Charnwood Edition
published 2020
by arrangement with
Hodder & Stoughton
An Hachette UK company
London

The moral right of the author has been asserted

All characters in this publication are fictitious and any resemblance to real persons, living or dead is purely coincidental.

A catalogue record for this book is available from the British Library.

ISBN 978–1–4448–4384–2

Published by
F. A. Thorpe (Publishing)
Anstey, Leicestershire

Set by Words & Graphics Ltd.
Anstey, Leicestershire
Printed and bound in Great Britain by
T. J. International Ltd., Padstow, Cornwall

This book is printed on acid-free paper

For Jonathan.

Prologue

At London RAF Northolt airport, very few planes were cleared for takeoff. The crosswinds were strong; the downpour of sleet reduced visibility to nil. There was only one runway at Northolt, and a congestion of private jets looking to use it. It was six a.m. The crowd of passengers in the waiting area was small but impatient. Most were businessmen who had morning meetings in Paris, Luxembourg, Berlin. Some were booked on flights chartered by their corporations; a few owned their jets outright. These were not men who liked to wait.

A Russian named Popov was making a scene. He yelled alternately at the woman behind the front desk and at someone on the other end of his phone. Neither person was giving him the answer that he was looking for, so he toggled between them, the volume of his voice rising until he could be heard clear across the terminal. His female companion, a bored, willowy blonde in a fox-fur coat and sneakers, stared at her phone. She seemed accustomed to his rages. Everyone else was looking at Popov. Papers lowered; passengers turned to stare. At six feet four and at least 280 pounds, Alexei Popov was hard to miss, particularly when he was angry.

'I understand, sir,' the woman at the front desk said again, trying to remain professional in the face of his verbal barrage. 'And I'm sorry for

1

the inconvenience. But for safety reasons, we must advise — '

Popov cursed in Russian and threw his phone. The woman behind the desk ducked; two security guards walked briskly over to see about the fuss. Even the blonde was paying attention now. She took Popov by the arm and whispered something in his ear, attempting to calm him.

Thomas Jensen sat in the corner of the terminal, watched the scene with mild interest from behind a fresh copy of the *Financial Times*. Like the other passengers present that morning, Jensen wore a well-tailored suit and carried a briefcase. With his neatly combed silver hair and expensive loafers, Jensen looked like what he was: an Oxford graduate with a background in finance and a robust bank account. Unlike most of the other passengers, however, Jensen was not a financier or captain of industry. Though he was at Northolt on business, it was of a very different sort. He worked for a government agency in a capacity that few people knew existed. The only external indication that Jensen's work was not a desk job but rather a dangerous and occasionally violent enterprise was the distinctive crook in his nose from where it had once been broken. Though he had suffered worse injuries, Jensen's nose still gave him trouble. For that reason, he always kept a monogrammed handkerchief in his pocket. He removed it now and wiped his nose with it, while keeping a discreet eye on the other passengers in the waiting area.

Because of the fuss over Popov, Jensen was the only person who noticed when a man and

2

woman crossed the terminal quickly and slipped out the exit door onto the tarmac. Jensen stood, put his handkerchief back into his pocket, and ambled over to the window. He studied the woman's slight figure, her shoulders hunched against the wind, her hair wrapped up, Jackie Onassis-like, in a black scarf that protected it from the rain. The man was well built and a head taller than the woman. When the man turned, Jensen noted his tortoiseshell glasses and salt-and-pepper hair. The man put his hand protectively on the woman's shoulder as they boarded a Gulfstream G450. Theirs was the biggest and most expensive plane at Northolt on that particular morning. The news would later report that it was being flown by an exceptional pilot. Omar Khoury had spent a decade in the Royal Saudi Air Force before going into private employ. He was a true, seasoned professional, unlikely to be phased by the sub-optimal flying conditions. Almost as soon as the plane's doors had shut, it was cleared for takeoff. Popov was still yelling about the delay when the G450 taxied down the runway and disappeared into the sky.

Once the plane was in the air, Jensen folded his paper in half and tucked it beneath his arm. He walked past Popov, past the front desk, and out of the terminal. A town car was waiting for him at the curb.

His phone rang as soon as the car turned onto the A40 toward London.

'It's done,' Jensen said. 'Only one flight departed and they were on it.' He hung up, unfolded his paper, and read it in silence for the duration of the ride.

Less than one hour later, the G450 lost contact. Somewhere over the French Alps, it simply fell off the radar, as though it had never existed at all.

Marina

Marina stood on the balcony of her suite at Le Meurice and looked out at the glistening lights of Paris. The view was spectacular, particularly at night. To the west, the Eiffel Tower and Roue de Paris stood illuminated against the night sky. Across the rue de Rivoli, les Jardin des Tuileries glowed, as if lit from within. Marina considered waking up her fiancé, Grant, so he could enjoy the view with her. But there would be time for that. Their trip had just begun. Instead, Marina sat down at the table. She sparked a cigarette, inhaled. It felt good to have no work to do, no functions to attend, no emails begging response. She could read a book. She could do her nails. She could do nothing at all. The night was hers. Here in Paris, it was just beginning.

Her phone rang, jarring her. Marina felt a prick of irritation when she saw who was calling.

'Duncan,' she said, her voice curt. 'It's past midnight here.'

'Were you sleeping?'

'No.'

'Of course not. You're still on New York time. You don't sleep, anyway.'

'That doesn't mean you're allowed to call me during my first vacation in almost ten years.'

'I need you to do something for me.'

Marina cringed. This was exactly the reason that Grant wanted her to leave *Press* magazine.

5

In the near decade she'd worked for Duncan, she'd never once taken a vacation. She worked most weekends, countless holidays. She answered her phone at all hours of the night. She had begun her career as Duncan's assistant. Now, nine and a half years later, despite her senior status on the magazine masthead, he still occasionally treated her as such. Twenty-four hours into this trip, and already, he was tasking her with something. It was unbelievable, really, though not entirely surprising.

Marina intended to quit. She'd promised Grant she would, right after the wedding. The rumors that Grant's father, James Ellis, was going to run for president were true. The campaign would move into high gear in a matter of weeks. He had already assembled a team of campaign advisors and publicists. He would need it. A hotheaded billionaire from New York, he wasn't exactly the people's candidate. But once the spin doctors had done their magic, James Ellis would be transformed into a hardworking success story, a professional deal maker, a fresh alternative to the presumed Democratic nominee — and consummate DC insider — Senator Hayden Murphy. That was the plan, anyway. Murphy, who had been dogged for years by rumors of corruption and cronyism, was a formidable but flawed candidate. Ellis knew this; he was banking on it.

Quietly, Marina had her doubts that her future father-in-law was fit to be the leader of the free world. She'd seen him lose his temper at kind people who made the smallest of errors: at a new housekeeper who stocked the wrong kind of bottled water at the Southampton house, for example, or at a driver who missed the turnoff for Teterboro Airport, She also knew that Grant was a calming influence on his father. Grant would resign from his investment banking job and take over the family business while his father was out on the campaign trail. In his new capacity as president of Ellis Enterprises, Grant would travel constantly, and he would expect Marina to accompany him. There were things one had to do as the wife of a CEO of a multinational corporation. Not to mention the wife of the president's son, should it come to that. She couldn't work and be Mrs. Grant Ellis. At least, not at the same time. There was no question what was more important to her. She had to quit. That was part of the deal, and on some level, she'd always known it.

For a moment, Marina considered quitting right then, over the phone. It was justified, certainly. People at *Press* quit all the time. Duncan was a famously difficult editor in chief, and he paid his staff below the paltry industry standard. But it didn't feel right. After everything Duncan had done for her — and everything they'd done together — she wanted to resign the right way: in person, at a time that made sense not just for her, but for the magazine, too.

'You're unbelievable,' Marina said. She stubbed out her cigarette and slipped back inside to find a pencil. 'Aren't you supposed to be on a sabbatical?'

Duncan didn't answer the question. The topic of his sabbatical was a sore one. It was not

7

something he had agreed to voluntarily. Rather, it was mandated by Philip Brancusi, the CEO of *Press*'s parent company, who insisted that Duncan use the six weeks to dry out, once and for all. The drinking had become a problem, and everyone in publishing knew it. Everyone except Duncan himself.

'Are you writing this down?' he said.

'Of course I am.'

'I need you to meet someone. He's coming from Luxembourg. I don't know how long he'll be free, so make yourself available. He's going to give you a USB to bring to me. Be very careful with it. And tell no one.'

'What am I supposed to say to Grant? I have a date with a mysterious European?'

'Who's Grant?'

'You're joking.'

'Tell him you're going for a run. Or you need to meet an old friend. He's a big boy. He'll survive without you for forty-five minutes.' Duncan sounded irritated, which irritated Marina. She pressed hard on her pencil, snapping the tip.

'Damn it,' she muttered, and reached for a pen.

'Look, I know you're frustrated,' Duncan said. 'I know what I'm asking is annoying. But it's important, Marina. This material is highly sensitive. My source doesn't trust email, even encrypted email. He wants to hand over the data directly. I was going to fly to Geneva last week to meet him myself, but I believe I'm being followed.'

Marina stifled an eyeroll. 'By who?'

Duncan ignored her. 'I told him you're the

only person I trust.'

'Stop buttering me up, Duncan. I suppose I don't get to know what this is about?'

Duncan paused. In the background, Marina could hear what sounded like a snowplow. She wondered if Duncan was out of the city, holed up at his weekend house, where he was beginning to spend more and more of his time. She worried about him out there. He drank too much and socialized too little. When Duncan drank, he became dramatic and paranoid. When he got dramatic and paranoid, he usually called Marina.

'We'll talk when you're back,' he said. 'But, Marina . . . this is it. After all these years, I think we finally found him.'

Marina stopped writing. 'Him?'

'Morty Reiss.'

'Alive?'

'Very much so.'

Marina paused, absorbing the enormity of what Duncan was saying. It had been eight years since Morty Reiss's suicide. Almost to the day. Or rather, it had been eight years since Morty Reiss's car was found on the Tappan Zee Bridge, a suicide note taped to the windshield. Days after his alleged suicide, Morty's hedge fund, RCM, was uncovered as one of the largest Ponzi schemes of all time. Reiss saw the writing on the wall and jumped, or so the story went. His body, however, was never found. At the beginning, Marina and Duncan harbored the same suspicion as many: that Reiss faked his own death and disappeared with his ill-gotten gains to

9

some sun-washed country without an extradition treaty. Of all the people Marina had written stories about during her tenure at *Press* magazine, Reiss was perhaps the smartest, most ruthless con man she'd ever come across. Given that Marina wrote about New York society figures — Wall Street tycoons, real estate magnates, fashion designers, publicists — that was saying a lot. If anyone was smart enough to disappear along with his money, it was Reiss.

Reiss was brilliant — as brilliant as they come — but eventually all Ponzi schemes necessarily come to an end, and that was the one thing that had always niggled at Marina about the RCM story. Insider trading, embezzlement: anyone could get away with these crimes if they were clever enough. Just steal the money and ride off into the sunset. But a Ponzi scheme required an unending supply of investors. Without new investors, the whole scheme collapsed like a house of cards. So why would Reiss opt into a crime with no end? He seemed too smart for that. That is, unless he'd planned on faking his death all along.

If that was the case, Marina had to hand it to him: Reiss was potentially the most cunning financial criminal of all time.

As the years passed with no news or trace of Reiss, however, Marina's disbelief faded slowly into acceptance. Was it really possible for a man like Reiss — whose face flashed across television screens worldwide for months on end — to disappear? Marina didn't think so. It seemed too far-fetched — fantastical, even. A Hollywood plotline instead of a real news story. Reiss was smart, but he was also human. Perhaps his greed or hubris did end up getting the better of him.

While Marina's interest with Morty Reiss waned, Duncan Sander's blossomed into a full-blown obsession. After he and Marina co-wrote the original expose of RCM, Duncan went on to pen several more pieces about Reiss and his coconspirator, Carter Darling. His theories about Reiss's whereabouts became outlandish and unsubstantiated, and Marina feared that Duncan's fixation had irreparably damaged his reputation as a serious journalist. Six months ago, it had almost cost him his career. On a morning talk show, Duncan claimed Reiss had hundreds of millions stashed in an account at Caribbean International Bank in the Cayman Islands. US authorities looked the other way, Duncan said, because a ring of high-profile politicians, who also happened to have millions stashed away in numbered accounts, were protecting the bank. The interview caused a sensation, not only because of what Duncan said, but how he said it. His slurred speech and sweaty, unkempt appearance did not go unnoticed by viewers. Soon, there were rumors that Duncan Sander was headed for a public meltdown. Caribbean International Bank threatened to sue not only Duncan, but *Press* and its parent company, Merchant Publications. Under pressure from CEO Brancusi, Duncan issued a hasty retraction. Then he made a show of heading to a rehab facility in northern Connecticut, where he spent a few weeks drying out and nursing his ego. As far as Marina could tell, rehab hadn't helped much with Duncan's drinking. It bought him a reprieve at *Press*, however, and Duncan had returned to work a month later.

Now he was on his second attempt at rehab, and Marina knew it was the last chance with Brancusi. He had given Duncan an ultimatum: dry out for good and come back ready to work, or don't come back at all. Duncan couldn't afford another misstep. One more lapse in judgment, and Brancusi would have his head.

'Duncan, can you prove this? You'll need to. We can't have another — ' Marina stopped short, not wanting to finish that sentence. Duncan did not like being reminded of the interview, or his drinking problem, or frankly any mistake he'd ever made, ever. They'd never spoken of it, except in the vaguest of references.

'I can, this time. He's got more than seventy million at Swiss United.'

Marina wrote down *Swiss United* and underlined it. 'Swiss United. So not at Caribbean International,' she said, trying not to sound skeptical.

'No, that's the thing. It *was* there. I was right about that. And he moved it. Just before I gave that interview.'

'And you have proof. Account records or something?'

'My source does. Marina, this is the story of our careers.'

Marina jumped when she felt a hand on her shoulder. Behind her stood Grant, looking sheepish.

'Hi,' he whispered. 'I didn't mean to scare you.'

'I've got to go,' Marina said to Duncan. 'We'll talk later.'

'Is Grant there?'

'Yes.'

'Okay. I'll call you tomorrow when I have the details about the drop.'

'Fine. Good night, Duncan.'

'Sorry,' Grant said, kissing Marina on the head as she put down the phone. 'I heard your voice and hoped you were ordering room service. I'm starving.'

Marina laughed. 'I wasn't, but I can. What do you want?'

'Let's look.' Grant reached over her and picked up the menu.

'Who were you talking to?'

'Duncan.'

'What did he want?'

'He's working on a story. Wanted me to help.'

Grant glanced up from the menu. 'I hope you said no.'

'Of course I did.'

'Isn't he supposed to be in rehab?'

'Sabbatical.'

'Whatever. It's totally inappropriate for him to call you in the middle of the night during your vacation.'

'I think he was just excited about the story.'

Grant shook his head. 'He has no boundaries, Marina.'

Marina sighed. 'I know. He frustrates me, too. But you have to understand: Duncan is the reason I'm a journalist. When I started at *Press*, I honestly just wanted to work at a fashion

13

magazine because I thought it sounded cool. I thought I'd go to great parties and try on couture clothes and meet interesting people. But Duncan saw something more in me. And he expected more from me. When we worked on the story about the Darlings, he treated me like his colleague instead of his twenty-two-year-old assistant. He really let me run with it. And when it was over, he listed me as his cowriter. So yes, he drives me insane sometimes. A lot of the time. But I also owe him my career.'

Grant reached for Marina's hand. They interlaced their fingers and smiled at each other. 'I'm sorry,' he said. 'I'm just protective of you.'

'And I think you're very sweet.'

Grant cocked one eyebrow. 'And sexy?'

'Very sexy.'

'Is it sexy if I order myself a double bacon cheeseburger with fries now?'

'Incredibly.'

'It won't be here for at least thirty minutes. Join me in the bedroom while I wait for my midnight snack?'

'Order me fries, too, all right? I'm an only child. I don't share well.'

'I don't, either. So promise me something.'

'Anything.' Marina wrapped her arms around Grant's neck and smiled up at him.

'Promise I won't have to share you on this trip. It's just a few days. I want us to unplug and enjoy each other.'

Marina nodded. 'Mm-hmm,' she said. She reached up for a kiss. She felt Grant's hands on her backside and suddenly she was in the air, her legs wrapped around his waist. 'I promise,' she murmured, as he carried her to bed.

Annabel

Matthew Werner was late. His wife, Annabel, sat alone on the veranda of their Geneva flat, wearing a black cocktail dress and the long sable coat that Matthew bought for her when they first moved to Switzerland. A hairdresser on the Cours de Rive had coaxed her auburn hair into a twist. Her shoes, five-inch pumps that a sales-girl in a boutique on rue du Rhône convinced her to buy against her better judgment, pinched at the balls of her feet. In the dressing room mirror, the shoes had made Annabel's legs look impossibly long and slim. Two black satin ribbons extended from each heel and laced up around her ankles and lower calves, giving the impression of a ballerina en pointe. Back in New York, she might have lingered by a window display of shoes like these. But she wouldn't have gone into the store. She wouldn't have bought them. Too impractical, too expensive. In New York, Annabel wore mostly flats or wedge heels, with rounded toes suited to days spent on her feet. In New York, Annabel had worked. She had taken the subway, not a car with a driver. She didn't spend her money on shoes that cost a week's salary. Here in Geneva, she'd sign the receipt before bothering to glance at the price tag.

At home, she found she could hardly walk in them. In the harsh lighting of her closet, the lacing at the ankle looked theatrical. She wasn't sure if she looked like a banker's wife or a courtesan. All the other wives shopped at the boutique where she'd bought the shoes. They all looked the same, dressed the same, played tennis together. Sometimes Annabel felt as though she missed a memo when she had arrived in Geneva: How to Be a Banker's Wife. Most of the others were polite but distant. After an initial spate of lunch invitations, Annabel stopped hearing from them. They were polite enough at firm events, of course, but they seemed to understand, as she did, that she was different from them. Annabel had decided this was fine with her. Most of the other wives just wanted to talk about the Paris fashion shows and their country houses and their latest weekend jaunt to Sardinia. And they dressed up for everything, even a casual brunch on the weekends. Of course, it would be nice to be included some of the time. But most days, Annabel was content to wander a museum by herself, sit in a café with a book, and go to bed early. Charity balls and black-tie dinners held no appeal for her. And she had always hated tennis.

The shoes had been so expensive that she couldn't bear not to wear them. Once, at least. Annabel hoped they looked as expensive as they were. Matthew loved to see her in expensive things. It was the reason he worked as hard as he did, he said. He liked to show her off.

For now, though, Annabel unlaced the shoes and released her feet from their bondage. She tucked them up against her slender thighs to keep them warm. She was tempted to light a cigarette to take the edge off but stopped herself.

Matthew would be angry. For all Matthew knew, Annabel hadn't touched a cigarette since New York. She kept a pack hidden behind her art books in the living room. Matthew never looked at them, so Annabel was in no risk of being found out. Art had never interested Matthew, unless it was a client's investment, and then it was just that: an investment. Annabel allowed herself one cigarette — occasionally two — at a time, but only when Matthew was away for the night. Lately, that was often.

From the veranda, Annabel could hear the gentle roll of the trams below and the *clop-clop-clop* of tourist carriages on the cobblestones. Usually, she found these sounds soothing. Not today. She was too nervous. She glanced up at the steel-gray sky and wondered when it would start to snow. They'd been predicting a storm for days now. She wanted Matthew home. Without him, their flat felt like a hotel instead of a home. A luxury hotel, but a hotel nonetheless. It was still furnished with the same charcoal-colored sofas, ikat-patterned silk pillows, and glass-topped tables that had come with it. Chic but corporate. It was, after all, corporate housing, belonging to Swiss United and rented to them at well below the market price. One of the many perks of Matthew's job. Annabel had added a few personal touches over the past two years — a painting of hers hung in the living room, an impressionistic cityscape of Florence she'd given to Matthew to remind him of their honeymoon. Her books filled the shelves. Though Matthew told her it was unnecessary, she'd brought their

18

linens from New York: crisp white sheets with dove-gray borders, a *W* embroidered on each of the pillows, towels to match. They made her feel more at home. At first, she had put out photographs everywhere: on side tables, tucked in the bookshelves, on the mantel. Annabel and Matthew kissing in the back of the old checkered cab they'd hired to whisk them away from their wedding in Tribeca. The two of them cooking lobsters in the rickety Montauk beach house they had rented the summer before they left. Annabel at her first gallery opening, surrounded by friends. She'd put most of them away now. She'd thought, at the beginning, that photographs would make her feel less homesick. The opposite had been true. When she looked at them, she felt horribly lonely. So one night while Matthew was at the office, she'd drunk a bottle of wine and wrapped all the photographs up in bubble wrap and stashed them on a high shelf in her closet.

She tried to replace them with more current pictures from their life here in Geneva, but she didn't have many. Matthew traveled so much during the week that by Friday, he'd just as soon stay home, catch up on rest, hit the gym. Occasionally Matthew would visit a client somewhere exciting — Madrid or Berlin or the South of France — and Annabel would tag along. Those were work trips, though, and Annabel never saw much of Matthew during them. They'd gone to Venice for Annabel's thirtieth birthday, but Matthew had spent most of that trip on the phone with a hysterical client in the middle of a nasty divorce. Annabel had wandered the city alone, and the only pictures she'd taken were of a *gelateria* her friend Julian told her to visit and a flock of pigeons in Piazza San Marco. They'd gone skiing several times, usually in Zermatt, where Swiss United kept a chalet for the senior bankers to use, but Matthew's colleagues were always there. Most were expert skiers, who, like Matthew, were eager to hit the black diamonds or try off-piste or heli-skiing. Not wanting to be a stick in the mud, Annabel always waved Matthew off, booking herself a lesson on the bunny slope or just curling up with a book in front of the fire. No point in taking a photograph of that.

When they'd first come to Geneva, they'd planned on two years. Two years to amass some money, and then they'd return to New York, buy an apartment, think about trying again to start a family. Annabel was only twenty-eight when they'd arrived; Matthew, thirty-three. They had time. It would be an adventure, he said. An extended vacation. Venice, Prague, Paris, Bruges: so many romantic places, just a short flight or train ride away. The best art in the world would be at their doorstep. Annabel could brush up on her language skills. Her French was good but rusty. Her German — a useful language in the art business — was middling and in need of improvement. Matthew would teach her how to ski. They could take cooking lessons or a wine class. They'd eat fondue. Because it was for only two years, Annabel hadn't gotten a job. Getting a work permit could take months. It was a complicated process for someone who didn't work for a global corporation. Anyway, Matthew would be working hard enough for the both of them. He preferred her not to work. He wanted her to be free when he was free. It wasn't like he was asking her to quit her job forever. Only temporarily. All of it was temporary.

It hadn't been all bad, of course. Some of it was lovely. The grand apartment. The beauty of the Swiss countryside. Sometimes, Matthew would come home happy, and Annabel would remember why she'd fallen in love with him so quickly in the first place. He would whisk her away for dinner somewhere special. He'd be attentive and caring. He'd make her laugh. They'd watch the sunset over Lake Geneva and talk about an art show she wanted to see, a book she was reading. They'd reminisce about their friends back in New York. They'd light candles on their terrace and drink wine and play Scrabble. On nights like that, when Matthew was not just present but really *there*, Annabel thought she could learn to love Geneva. Her homesickness would drift away, replaced by a sense of calm and deep appreciation for the beauty and history of the place.

And there was the money. Annabel hadn't wanted for anything in New York; Matthew made more there than Annabel ever dreamed she'd have, growing up as she did in a small, blue-collar town in upstate New York. But here, their bank accounts swelled remarkably fast. Every month there was more. The money made Matthew proud, and, in turn, Annabel was proud of him. And she found that she liked having money. Suddenly, things that Annabel never considered buying were available to her. The shoes, for example. A decadent lunch, alone, on a Wednesday. Getting her hair done whenever she wanted. There was an ease to having money that Annabel had never experienced. She no longer studied price tags or cringed over credit card bills. There was more than enough.

With more money came more gifts. Matthew had always been wonderful at gift-giving; it was one of the things that Annabel loved about him. It wasn't about the extravagance. Matthew was thoughtful. He remembered things. Most mornings, he wrote her notes and tucked them in places she was sure to find them. It had become a little game between them. She'd find them in her purse, next to the coffeemaker, inside her compact mirror, taped to the creamer in the fridge. Once, she'd found a pair of tickets for the Metropolitan Opera tucked inside her wallet. They were for the next night's performance; Matthew would be out of town. *Take Marcus*, read the attached Post-it note, referring to Annabel's favorite coworker at the gallery, who loved opera more than anything. 'He's a keeper,' Marcus had said, when Annabel showed him.

Recently, the gifts had become lavish. A handbag she'd stopped to stare at in a store window. A pair of earrings she'd noticed on a colleague's wife. Last week, a painting that Annabel had admired at Art Basel. It was a smallish piece by Marshall Cleve, a little-known artist from Maine. Annabel had spent a good ten minutes staring at it in meditative silence. It was a series of looping blue lines that conjured up Brice Marden, one of Annabel's favorite painters. Brice Marden at the sea. It was the kind of thing she'd tried to paint herself at her small studio in Montauk, with only moderate success.

'You remembered,' she said, when Matthew gave it to her. Her breath caught in her chest.

'You should own this,' Matthew said. 'You love it. I could see it in your eyes when you first looked at it.'

'I can't explain why. I don't know much about the artist. I was just drawn to it.'

'That's love, then, isn't it? A connection. Electricity. You feel it in your gut. I felt it when I first saw you. I still feel it when I see you.'

Annabel pulled Matthew to her. 'Yes. That's love.'

'Do you remember how I used to walk by your gallery every morning, just to look at you through the glass?'

Annabel laughed. 'Marcus used to think you were looking at him.'

'It took me weeks to get up the confidence to go in and talk to you. And I studied first. About the artists you represented. I was smooth, right?'

'You knocked over the catalogs at the front desk and spilled coffee on the receptionist. But yes, you were smooth.'

'I keep hoping you'll forget that part.'

'It's the part I like best. It's sweet to see a handsome man get so nervous.'

'You were awfully intimidating back then. With

that short hair and the all-black wardrobe and the tattoo on your wrist, right under those bangles you used to wear. God, you were hot.'

'And I'm not now? Watch it, mister.'

'Hotter now. Hotter every day.'

'Do you miss the short hair?'

Matthew cocked his head, appraising her. 'Sometimes,' he said with a small smile. 'But I like it this way, too. It's elegant long. It suits you now.'

He kissed her then but pulled away more quickly than she would have liked. 'I want you to have this painting,' he said, his voice serious. 'I know how much you've given up to be with me here. I know you miss being surrounded by beautiful art. Part of the reason I took this job was so that I could buy you art. So you could own the pieces you loved. Your own private gallery.'

Annabel paused. Something about this pronouncement struck her wrong. She loved being a gallerist. Owning art was nice, of course, but it wasn't a substitute for work.

'That's very thoughtful, but I don't need it in our home. Really. I hope this wasn't terribly expensive.'

'It wasn't,' he said, though Annabel suspected he was lying. 'Honestly, the frame is the most valuable thing about this. I want you to remember that. If ever anything happens to me — '

'Don't say things like that.'

'I just want you to know. The frame. There's value in the frame. Okay?'

'It's stunning,' Annabel said, because it was. She appreciated a good frame. She ran her finger along its edge. It was a thick wood, gilted in silver leaf. Simultaneously modern and rustic, it drew out the bluish-grays of the painting. 'Let's hang it over the bed,' she said, her face softening. 'That way, we can go to bed each night and dream about love.'

The painting marked the beginning of their second year in Geneva. Annabel let the anniversary slide without comment. In the past few weeks, she'd wondered more than once if the painting was a bribe, a payment of some kind. Because they were staying. Matthew had started saying that he needed more time. For what, she wasn't sure. There was so much money. Not enough to retire on, or to buy that beach house in Montauk they always talked about, the one with the wraparound porches and the barn out back that had been turned into an art studio. But there was more than either of them ever dreamed possible. So more time for what, then? How much would be enough?

Annabel told herself that a little more time in Geneva didn't matter; home was wherever Matthew was. But the truth was, it was beginning to matter. It had always mattered. Geneva would never be home. Annabel was bored, listless. She missed work. She wanted children. She wanted her life back. She couldn't exist in this state of suspended reality forever. At least, not without going mad.

* * *

To bide the time until Matthew came home, Annabel pretended to read a novel in the waning afternoon light, but her eyes kept dancing over the words and straying toward her phone. It was a domestic thriller, about a wife who disappears on her commute home from work. It felt like the kind of book she'd read a million times before, a book with 'Girl' in the title and an unreliable narrator, and she kept forgetting all the characters' names. Why hadn't Matthew called? It wasn't like him. If it got too much later, she would have to leave for the Klauser party alone. Annabel never felt comfortable at the Klausers', with their uniformed staff and stiff friends, most of whom were decades older than Annabel. Matthew knew that. Matthew was mindful when it came to things like that. He wouldn't ask her to walk into that party alone. 'If Jonas wasn't my boss . . . ,' he always said with an apologetic smile. He never finished that sentence. Jonas Klauser wasn't just Matthew's boss. He was the head of Swiss United, the biggest bank in Switzerland. He was Matthew's godfather. He was the reason they were in Geneva to begin with. As long as they were there, the Werners had to make nice with the Klausers. 'It's just business,' Matthew said. But everything with Matthew had become business.

The church bells rang. Annabel put down her novel. The wife had been missing for ten days, but Annabel didn't care what happened to her. She didn't bother to mark her page. She hadn't finished a book in ages. The verandas off the neighboring apartments were empty; it was too cold now for most people to sit outside the way Annabel did, even with heat lamps. She liked the cold. It made her feel awake, alive. A brisk wind picked up, causing her eyes to water. Snow began to drift down from the darkening sky. The party was beginning. If there was a miscommunication and Annabel was meant to meet Matthew at the Klausers, she would embarrass him if she were late. Annabel hated embarrassing Matthew. Her lateness was something he found charming back in the States, part of the bohemian allure of dating a downtown gallerist instead of one of those Upper East Side socialites Matthew dated before Annabel. Bonfire Blondes, Annabel called them, after the X-ray-thin women in *Bonfire of the Vanities*. Matthew, having grown up on the Upper East Side, seemed to know them all. The Lindseys and Bitsies and Kicks. The ones with fancy last names for first names: Lennox and Merrill and Kennedy. Girls who had been raised to write thank-you notes on engraved stationery and arrive fashionably late, but not forgetfully late, as Annabel often did. Here in Geneva, her lateness bothered Matthew, especially when it happened in front of someone from the bank. It wasn't as though she had a reason to be late. She had no job. No children. No friends, except for Julian. She couldn't chance it. Back on went the heels.

The Klausers lived in Cologny, a suburb northeast of the city with winding roads and open fields. They kept a flat in town, too, for the nights that Jonas worked late (or, Annabel suspected, for holing himself up with his

27

mistress, a B-list French actress Jonas had met in Cannes, and whom he squired about openly while his wife was off riding horses or shopping the Paris fashion shows), but they never entertained there. Why would they, when their chalet — château, really — had a nine-hole golf course, a tennis court, a pool, a ten-car garage for Jonas's car collection? The art was not Annabel's style — it was all flashy, recognizable stuff, the sort of collection that an art advisor would foist onto a client with no taste and no budget to speak of — but it was outrageously, jaw-droppingly expensive. More impressive than the best galleries in New York on a good day, Annabel thought. Most of the rooms in the Klauser house had at least one major piece: a Damien Hirst, a Jasper Johns. A hideous Botero sculpture of an obese woman on a chaise, dead-smack in the middle of the living room. 'They might as well wallpaper the house in money,' Annabel had said to Matthew, the first time they went there. 'They must be richer than God, to have a collection like that.'

More impressive to Annabel than the Klausers' art collection were their unobstructed views of the Alps and the peak of Mont Blanc. She'd been to their home a dozen times, but those snow-capped mountains in the background never ceased to strike her into awed silence. It looked like a postcard, a fairy tale. She just couldn't believe a view like that was real. The sky was so blue and the snow was so crystalline and the lines of the mountains were so precisely drawn, it looked as though it had all been digitally enhanced somehow. Everything about the Klausers felt that way. Elsa Klauser, for example. She claimed to be the daughter of a minor Austrian royal, a viscount maybe, or something similarly ridiculous. Annabel suspected this was made up, part of a carefully curated pedigree that Elsa had adopted once she'd landed Jonas Klauser as a husband. It didn't jibe with her slightly too-large breasts, her shock of white-blond hair, or her accent, which was muddled and unplaceable. She wore all the right clothes — Loro Piana and Chanel and Brunello Cucinelli — but her leather pants were ever so slightly too tight, her hemlines too short, her necklines alluringly low, for a woman of supposedly noble birth. She draped herself in fur all year long, even in the summer. 'Like a character from *Game of Thrones*,' Matthew had joked one night after too much wine. It didn't matter now, anyway. The Klausers were royalty of a different kind. In this world of hidden bank accounts and secret money, Jonas Klauser was king.

Unlike his wife, Jonas carried himself like a true aristocrat. He remembered the names of everyone's children and parents and spouses and mistresses, even if he'd met them only once, years ago, during a cocktail party at which they were the least important person in the room. He could chatter on about art or wine or parasailing or stamp collecting — anything, really — and he could do it in five languages. He was a true gentleman's banker, Matthew said about him. Whenever he talked about Jonas, his voice was steeped in reverence. During their first week in Geneva, the Klausers arranged a welcome party for Matthew and Annabel at Skopia, a gallery known for promoting Swiss artists. Jonas took Annabel by the arm and introduced her to a mix of local curators, gallerists, and artists. He wanted her to feel welcome, he said. Matthew was family to him, and now so was she. If there was anything he could do to make Geneva feel more like home, all she had to do was ask.

★ ★ ★

Annabel called Armand, the driver. She jotted a note on a napkin and left it on the foyer table, where Matthew was sure to find it. Matthew kept all their notes in a box in his closet. Even the throw-away ones, written on receipts or napkins or old movie ticket stubs that Annabel had dug up from the bottom of her purse. Annabel discovered this after they were married and still found it terribly romantic. She was more careful with her handwriting now that she knew the notes would be preserved. Sometimes she drew little sketches for him, knowing it would make him smile. She had, over the past few years, cultivated a talent for naughty drawings.

Today there would be no sketch. She signed it, x, A. Less affectionate than *Love you, A.*, which she wrote sometimes, but warmer than simply *A. He'd better have a good excuse*, Annabel thought. *He'd better not be with Zoe.*

When she opened her front door, Annabel inhaled sharply. Two men stood in the vestibule outside her apartment. One held a briefcase. Both wore suits, overcoats, somber expressions. Their cheeks were red from the cold. Their hair was damp from the snow.

'Annabel Werner?' the one with the briefcase said. He pronounced her name *Verner*, with a hint of a Germanic lilt. His dark eyes blinked at her from behind clear-rimmed glasses.

'Yes?'

'Sorry to have startled you.'

He reached into the breast pocket of his overcoat and withdrew a badge, which he held up for her. His partner did the same.

'My name is Konrad Bloch, I'm with the Fedpol. This is my colleague, Phillip Vogel. May we come in? We have a personal matter to discuss with you.'

Before she could reply, Annabel's phone buzzed.

'I need to get this,' she said. 'Could you excuse me for a moment?'

Bloch nodded but didn't move aside. Instead, she could feel his eyes on her as she fished about in her purse, searching for the phone.

It wasn't Matthew.

'Hello? Yes, Armand. I'm on my way down. Could you wait just a moment . . . ' She cupped her hand over the phone. 'It's the driver. I'm on my way out. Perhaps you could come back at a different time — '

'Mrs. Werner, it's urgent that we speak to you. I suggest you let the car go.'

★   ★   ★

31

In the Apartment, Annabel gestured for the men to sit. She thought to offer them water or coffee but didn't; she wanted them to leave as soon as possible. Outside, the sky was dark. Snow collected on the window ledges. The roads to Cologny would be slow. The men removed their coats. Annabel left hers on as she perched at the edge of the sofa. It was too hot to be inside in a fur coat, and she felt herself growing light-headed.

'Mrs. Werner,' Bloch started. 'Your husband's plane from London did not land as scheduled. We believe it crashed in the Alps.'

Annabel stared at him, blank.

'A search has commenced in the Bauges Mountains, just east of Chambéry. There is a storm there, which is making the search difficult. But wreckage from what we believe was the plane was spotted atop Mont Trélod.'

Annabel frowned, processing this.

'No,' she said, after a long moment. She shook her head. 'That's not right. My husband has been in Zürich, on business. There's been a mistake.'

'Your husband is Matthew Steven Werner?'

'Yes.'

'An employee of Swiss United Bank.'

A siren shrieked by, piercing the air. Annabel waited until it passed before answering. She was unnerved by the sound of sirens here. They weren't like the ones in New York. Here, they were eerie instead of merely loud, like a howling dog, a cry for help.

'Yes, that's where he works.'

'He was listed as the second passenger aboard a private plane that departed from Northolt Airport in London this morning. It was scheduled to land at Genève Aéroport at 8:20 a.m. The other passenger was a woman named Fatima Amir. The plane belonged to her.'

Annabel shook her head. She had never heard of Fatima Amir.

'It's not possible,' she said. 'Matthew was in Zürich. For a bank off site. They hold them once a quarter. I spoke to him last night.'

After saying this, she realized it was not true. It was two nights ago that she had spoken to Matthew. He was at the office. He was scheduled to take a train to Zürich after a meeting, he had said. He'd be home in time for the Klausers' party. He sounded rushed, brusque, even. She could hear voices in the background and she knew she did not have his full attention. He had been reticent to set up a time later that evening when they could talk and say good night, and this had upset her. She had grown snappish, said something about how it felt as though he was never home anymore. He said that he hated being apart, more than she knew. That he'd be home soon, that he'd always come home to her. He'd made her repeat that back: *You know I always come back, don't you? As soon as I possibly can? Tell me you know.*

Yes, of course, she'd said. *I know you always will.* This had lessened the sting, though only slightly. She had not heard from Matthew since.

Annabel said none of this to Bloch. She was not wrong about the essential point, which was

33

that Matthew was in Zürich, not London. Annabel was certain of this. Matthew had flaws, but dishonesty was not among them. She felt suddenly protective of her husband. She did not want these men to think Matthew was the sort of person who didn't call his wife when he was away on business. A typical American banker who cared only about making money and not a lick about his family. Matthew was not that.

'Perhaps there was a miscommunication. Or a last-minute change of plans. I am very sorry, Mrs. Werner.' Agent Bloch spoke with finality, as though there was no possibility for error on his part. Annabel looked at his partner, Vogel. He, too, looked at her with sympathy. For the first time, she understood what was happening. These men were here to tell her that Matthew was dead.

'There's been a mistake,' Annabel repeated. She had to force the words out of her mouth. Her throat was tightening, making it hard to talk or breathe. 'Isn't that right? You've made a mistake?'

'Mrs. Werner, the likelihood that anyone might survive a crash such as this is extremely low. We do not expect it in this case. We understand this is a very difficult thing to hear. Is there someone we can call for you? A family member, perhaps?'

'Matthew's my family. I have no one else.'

Later, Annabel would not remember what happened next. Only that she began to scream as she fell to her knees on the floor.

Marina

Ditching Grant proved to be surprisingly easy. Marina felt a flicker of guilt when she lied to him — they were going to be married, after all — but it was fleeting. It wasn't really a lie, she told herself. She *was* going for a run. She just happened to be meeting Duncan's source halfway through it. As she laced up her sneakers, her heart pounded with nervous excitement. There was no high like the one Marina got when she was on the tail of a good story.

The late November air stung her cheeks as she set off across rue de Rivoli. Her breath crystalized in front of her; the sun had yet to rise above the trees. She lamented the fact that she hadn't brought her running hat or her polar fleece jacket. Running hadn't been on her agenda. She had planned to spend her vacation eating cheese and drinking wine. And yet, here she was, working and running like always.

Marina picked up her pace to a near sprint in order to stay warm. She usually ran to music, but not today. She needed to have her wits about her. The exchange would happen quickly and, if all went well, it wouldn't attract so much as a glance from passersby. Even at this early hour, Marina was aware of a handful of others in the Tuileries. To her right, there was an older woman walking her dogs. A man in an overcoat and a thick gray scarf cut in front of her, as though too much in a hurry to slow for a jogger. A pair of teenagers kissed by a gate. A security guard walked toward the entrance of the Louvre.

As she neared L'Orangerie museum, Marina's breath quickened. As planned, a man in a black windbreaker and running sneakers stood by the entrance, stretching out his quads. He was taller than she expected and in excellent shape. He looked to be in his late thirties and, like her, a seasoned runner. Marina knew she would learn nothing more about him. She suspected he was not the real source, but someone sent by the source as a middleman, a go-between. The source had already taken extreme measures in transmitting this data safely, a fact Marina found simultaneously reassuring and thrilling. After nine years in the field, Marina had developed a keen sense for sources. She could feel it in her gut when someone had a hidden agenda or was peddling false information. Everything about this felt right. According to Duncan, the source had not asked for money. He insisted on transmitting the data in person. He communicated via encrypted messages. He had done his due diligence on both of them and seemed as wary of them as they were of him. Most interestingly, he hinted at a wealth of information, beyond the data on Morty Reiss, which he promised to transmit at a later date, should they be interested. So far so good. This source seemed like the real deal.

The man turned and they made eye contact. Marina slowed her pace to a walk and stopped beside him. She pulled her ankle to her glutes, imitating his stretch. They both glanced around to ensure they were alone.

'Marina?' He spoke with a touch of an accent that she couldn't place.

'And you're Mark.' This was the name she'd been given via text.

He nodded. 'I have something for you,' he said, his voice low. 'How long are you in Paris?'

'Three more days. You?'

'A little while longer. You can reach me at the number on the bottom of this card if you run into any trouble.' He pulled a business card from the pocket of his windbreaker. With a second glance over his shoulder, he handed it to her. Her fingers curled around it and the small USB hidden beneath.

She tucked both into the zippered pocket of her running pants.

'There is a password, I assume.'

'The external password is your mother's maiden name, followed by the number one: russell1. No caps.'

'How did you know my mother's maiden name?'

'If you are detained at the airport, refuse to give the password. Say that the USB contains personal data, photographs and such. But if you are pushed to do so, it will be all right. The information of real consequence is hidden beneath the photos, in a secret section of the hard drive. The password for that section is forty-eight characters long. For your safety, I will send that password to Duncan Sander via encrypted message. That way, even if you wanted to, you will not be able to grant US Customs or anyone else access to that data.'

'Of course,' Marina said, trying to sound calm. In fact, she felt dizzy from excitement. It hadn't occurred to her that she might be detained or that the government might want this information. 'What sort of photos? In case someone asks.'

'Generic pictures of Paris. Photos you might have taken on vacation.'

Marina nodded. 'Is this everything?'

'This is nothing. It's the tip of a very large iceberg of data. But it's the data Duncan Sander was interested in receiving. I understand that he has been looking for Mr. Reiss for quite some time.'

'He has. But you're willing to give us more.'

'Yes. Enough to keep you and a team of journalists busy for months. Years, even. Mr. Sander was interested in the Reiss story. But there are others.'

Marina's lips parted. She had so many questions, she didn't know where to start.

'Do you know how much money is stored in offshore accounts, Ms. Tourneau?'

'Tens of billions, I imagine.'

'Thirty-two trillion. More than the GDP of the US and Japan combined.'

'Jesus Christ.'

'There's a whole world offshore, Ms. Tourneau. A world of dirty money, hidden away in shadow accounts, and it belongs to some very powerful and dangerous people. Imagine if you could see their bank balances. Their transactions.

Their network. I'm talking about cartel kings. Terrorists. World leaders. Even people you know, people you went to school with, people who live across the street. And yes, Morty Reiss, too, who is alive and well and living off nearly seventy million dollars he has stashed at Swiss United Bank.'

'And you have this data? Bank balances? Emails? Tangible proof that this money exists — and who it belongs to?'

Mark nodded toward her pocket. 'And now you do, too. The world needs to know — '

The sound of voices turned both their heads. A pair of joggers moved toward them, chattering in French.

'I should go.'

Marina nodded. 'I'll get this to Duncan as soon as I return to the States. I imagine he'll be in touch.'

Mark's dark eyes darted from left to right, then back at her. 'Ms. Tourneau,' he said. 'You must understand: several people have risked their lives to get this information to you. Tell no one, trust no one. I have trusted you only because Duncan Sander asked me to, and time is of the essence. The sooner this information comes out to the public, the better. We will all be safer once it does.'

'We won't let you down. This is what Duncan and I do. You can trust us.'

'We have bet our lives on that.' He nodded good-bye. Marina watched him disappear between the trees. Then she turned and sprinted back toward Le Meurice.

Grant was still in bed when Marina returned to the room. His thick brown hair was tousled and his glasses sat askew on his nose. A pot of coffee sat on the bedside table; the New York Times was spread across the sheets. He didn't look up when Marina opened the door. For a moment, Marina stood still, admiring her fiancé. Six years out of the navy, he still had the same lean and well-muscled body as the day they met. His eyelashes fluttered when he slept; his thick, brooding eyebrows were knit together as though he was deep in thought. He wore his hair a little longer now, not in the crew cut he'd sported for his first few years out of the military, but still cropped close around the ears. Every four weeks, he went to the barbershop around the corner. Marina loved to run her fingers through it right after a cut. There was a practicality to Grant that she found incredibly sexy, a disinterest in his own handsomeness that made him more handsome. Grant had the kind of good looks that turned women's heads on the street, though he never seemed to know it. If anything, he was shy around women. Marina had made the first move and asked him out. Twice. The first time he declined, something she still liked to occasionally tease him about.

'He turned me down once. So when I saw him in Starbucks six years later, I demanded a date from him. I was not taking no for an answer again,' Marina declared during her toast at their engagement party. This statement was met with wild applause from their friends. 'I walked right up and introduced myself and he remembered me. We went on our first date that weekend. And when he held the cab door open for me at the end of the night, I just knew he was it. I wasn't going to let this gentleman get away twice.'

It was a good story, one she knew they'd tell again over the course of their life together. But the truth of it was that if Grant had said yes the first time, it never would have worked. Marina was a young, hungry society reporter living the high life in Manhattan. Grant was a Navy SEAL who was about to return to Fallujah on his second tour of duty. Their initial spark was intense, but it would have fizzled out over time and distance and the sheer differences in their lives. Anyway, she had needed time to grow up. By their second chance encounter, Marina was old enough to know a good thing when she saw one.

★ ★ ★

Not for the first time, Marina thought how lucky she was to fall asleep beside this man every night and to wake up next to him in the morning. She felt a pang of regret for having left him, if only for an hour.

'Good morning, husband-to-be.' Marina smiled as she said the word. Reflexively, she reached for her engagement ring, which she'd left on the nightstand. It was a massive five-carat emerald-cut diamond set between trapezoidal sapphires. A breathtaking ring, the kind she had always hoped to wear. But once she had it, she found she was almost afraid of it. She couldn't imagine wearing it on the subway to work, or to interview a source, or even while sitting at her desk at *Press*. Most mornings, she left it in a small dish on her bedside table. She knew it bothered Grant that she didn't wear it all the time, but he seemed to understand her desire to not risk losing something so expensive and irreplaceable. Once they were married, once she had quit her job, she promised to wear it all the time.

'How long have you been up?' she asked.

When Grant looked at her, Marina's smile faded.

'What's wrong?'

Grant shook his head. Without a word, he handed her the paper. It was folded to a page in the Metro section. Marina took it and scanned its contents.

''From the Penthouse to the White House.'' She glanced at the picture of Grant's father. She skimmed the article — it seemed neutral, raising only the vague specter of Ellis family ties to Middle Eastern money. Nothing that hadn't been printed before.

'It's not terrible,' she said. 'Your dad looks handsome in this picture. He looks like you, actually. Just with less hair.'

'No. Not that.' Grant took the paper from her and flipped it over. 'Here,' he said, tapping the page. 'Look at this. He was a Harvard classmate of mine. Matthew Werner. Only thirty-five.'

Marina scanned the page. 'Oh, that's sad. Was he married?'

'Yes. You met them once.'

'I don't remember.'

'At a party at the Whitney. The wife worked at a gallery in Chelsea.'

Marina remembered the wife. In a room filled with beautiful women, Annabel Werner stood out. She wasn't exactly beautiful, but she was striking. She had worn something very avant-garde, white and asymmetrical, a dress that very few women could pull off. A distilled calm emanated from her face. Her high cheekbones were accentuated by boyishly short hair. Bright blue eyes that shone with a serene, watchful intelligence. Marina liked her immediately. They had spoken briefly, as their husbands chattered on about old classmates. They had even exchanged contact information, but neither had followed up. Months later, Marina heard that the Werners had moved to Europe. She had felt a twinge of disappointment. There weren't many women who Marina thought she might like to try to be friends with. Annabel Werner had been one of them.

'He was a nice guy. Well liked. He took a job at Swiss United working for — ' Grant kept talking but Marina had stopped listening. Her eyes had fallen to a small article at the bottom of the page, beneath the clip about Matthew Werner.

''Society Journalist Found Dead in Connecticut Home,'' she read aloud.

Beneath the headline was a photograph of a picturesque white Colonial with black shutters, its window boxes covered in snow. The front door of the house was open; emerging from it was a paramedic who appeared to be wheeling out a body on a gurney. Police tape cordoned off a section of the front porch. Through a window, Marina could see an antique grandfather clock that looked instantly familiar.

'Oh God,' Marina whispered, her voice hoarse.

She knew that house. She'd been at that house just last month.

'What is it?'

'It's Duncan. Duncan Sander. He's dead.'

Annabel

For forty-eight hours, Annabel held out hope that Matthew would be found alive. When she wasn't on the phone with the airport officials, search party personnel, or Agents Bloch and Vogel, she was frantically researching private plane crash statistics. She found a newspaper article about a Gulfstream G450 that had crashed in the Canadian Rockies during an electrical storm. Three of its passengers had survived. They were found thirty hours after the plane went down, several miles from where the plane's fuselage had landed. Starving and injured, but alive. She memorized their names: Paul Gagnon, John Leblanc, Alec Roy. At night, after taking a cocktail of sleeping medications, Annabel repeated their names to herself, like an incantation, a mantra. Survivors gave her hope.

She found another article about another G450, a Dutch plane that had crashed in the Alps. It had happened twelve months ago, also during a storm. The facts were not good. There had been no survivors. Almost nothing was recovered; just the black box and small fragments of the body and wing. Annabel read it again and again. Finally she deleted her search history, banishing it to the internet ether.

Annabel looked up Fatima Amir, too. How could she not? Matthew had died with her, aboard her plane. A woman she'd never heard of before Fedpol came knocking on her door.

There was remarkably little information about Fatima Amir online. More than one article commented on how publicity-shy she was; a recent article in the *Financial Times* referred to her as a 'reclusive financial wunderkind.' In a way, Annabel was relieved there wasn't much to read. Fatima Amir was wildly wealthy, successful, well educated, beautiful. Scrolling through photographs of her felt like an act of self-flagellation. It served no purpose and sent Annabel spiraling further into despair.

The day before, a search team had located the plane's black box on the summit of Mont Trélod. According to Agent Bloch, who delivered this news to Annabel in person, it showed that the ice protection system failed midflight. This caused ice to build up on the plane's wings, unbeknownst to the pilot. A relatively common problem with private jets, Bloch said. He said this matter-of-factly, as though he was talking about a minor design flaw. Seats that didn't fully recline. Crooked tray tables.

'An accident,' he said, in conclusion. 'A tragic accident.'

'You're certain? There's no concern that . . . ' Annabel trailed off. On the BBC, an anchor had wondered aloud about a potential terrorist link to Fatima Amir and her pilot, Omar Khoury. Annabel had switched off the television right away, unwilling to consider that possibility. Still, suspicion gnawed at her. She was ashamed to admit it, but the fact that both were Middle Eastern gave her pause.

'That it was an intentional act?'

'Yes.'

'It was considered, of course. In today's political climate, it always is, especially when a family like the Amirs are involved. But as of now, that doesn't seem to be the prevailing theory. Black boxes contain a good deal of information, Mrs. Werner. The data and voice recordings from the cockpit both indicate a system malfunction.'

''A family like the Amirs?''

'Fatima Amir. The owner of the plane. She was the other passenger.'

'Yes, I know,' Annabel said curtly. It bothered her that Bloch spoke about Fatima Amir in the past tense, as though he already assumed she was dead. It was so cold, so clinical. She wanted to correct him but hadn't found the nerve. She was too tired to pick fights. 'As I told you, I'd never heard of her before — ' She stopped. 'Before this.'

Annabel looked over at Julian. He had come to see her every day since the crash. He was the first person Annabel had called after Agents Bloch and Vogel left her apartment. The only person. He was, she realized, the one person she'd met in Geneva who she truly cared about, and who she knew cared about her.

Like Matthew, Julian White was a trained tax lawyer. He'd come to Geneva seven years earlier for the same reason Matthew had: to make money, and lots of it. When he left London, Julian was an overworked and underpaid agent for HMRC, the British equivalent of the IRS. Here in Geneva, he was a private banker with a thick wallet and an even thicker Rolodex.

Annabel hated Julian when she first met him. She found him pompous and extravagant, everything she feared Matthew might become if he hung around too long at a private bank in Switzerland. Three months into their relocation, Annabel had accompanied Matthew on a business trip to Zürich. While Matthew was in meetings, Annabel took the train to the Museum Oskar Reinhart, a private villa that housed one of the most exquisite collections of French nineteenth-century art in the world. It was what Annabel did most days in Switzerland. She walked through museums and galleries alone and looked at art. Not so different from her life in New York, she told herself. Though, of course, here she wasn't paid for it.

When she emerged from the railway station in Winterthur, it had begun to rain. Annabel sat down on the bench and laced her boots tighter, bracing herself for an unpleasant walk to the museum. She had no umbrella and hadn't thought to wear a rain jacket. When she felt the rain stop, she looked up. Julian was standing over her, sheltering her beneath a Swiss United umbrella.

'I imagine you're going to the same place I am,' he said. 'May I walk you?'

'Shouldn't you be at the offsite? I thought it was a firm-wide thing.'

'It is.' He smiled agreeably. 'Which is why they won't notice that one of us decided to play hooky.'

'And you've decided to spend your spare day

with Renoir and Cézanne instead of with —
Forgive me, I can't remember the name of the
young woman you introduced us to when we saw
you last.' Annabel knew she was being snarky,
but she couldn't help herself. They had bumped
into Julian a few weeks earlier at a restaurant,
sitting with a woman in a shockingly short dress.
If she was of age, she had only very recently
become so.

Julian didn't seem to mind. 'Oh, Natasha? Very
smart woman. She discarded me almost
immediately.'

'She does sound smart.'

'I'm really more of a Daumier man myself.
Such a sense of humor. Do you know him? I can
tell you all about him if not.'

'Yes, of course!' Annabel said, surprised. 'I
wrote my graduate thesis on Daumier when I
was at Yale.'

'Then you must know just slightly less about
him than I do. Come. Let's go educate each
other.' Julian extended his elbow. Annabel stuck
her arm through his and pulled herself close to
Julian's side as the skies opened up and the
thunder cracked angrily over their heads.

By the time they returned to Zürich, Julian
and Annabel were friends. He seemed to sense
how lonely she was. He invited her to gallery
openings. He introduced her to artists and
collectors and curators. He encouraged her to
find work. He had connections to clients who
needed art advisors, he said, and friends at
auction houses who would happily hire an
experienced appraiser. Matthew didn't seem to

mind that Annabel spent so much time with Julian. If anything, he was happy that Annabel finally seemed more settled in Geneva. Never once did Matthew seem threatened by their relationship. Annabel wished she could say the same about herself. In New York, it hadn't occurred to her to be jealous. Or maybe she just hadn't had the time. In Geneva, she had too much time. Matthew was always gone. He ate dinner in the office. He traveled for work. He had a beautiful young assistant, a French girl named Zoe, who went with him everywhere. Annabel found that when she was alone, her imagination took over. She began to have terrible dreams about Matthew cheating or leaving her. When she was with Julian, at least, she didn't think about such things. Being with Julian made her feel like herself again: a human being with friends and interests. A person with an identity beyond being an expat, a banker's wife.

Julian cleared his throat. He stood by the window, hands stuffed in his pockets. He looked exhausted. Circles ringed his pale blue eyes; worry lines creased his forehead. His thinning blond hair, usually combed neatly in place, looked unkempt. Annabel realized that he hadn't changed his clothes since yesterday. Had he gone home to sleep? She couldn't remember. Days had begun to blur together. She slept in snatches. An hour here, an hour there, with only a vague sense of day or night. The pills Julian gave her did little to help. She washed them down with wine, hoping for rest. A sense of deep fatigue permeated her bones. She was tired all the time, but an electric fear coursed through her veins, forcing her brain and nerves to work in overdrive.

Julian had something to say. Annabel could sense it by the way he pursed his lips, as though he was trying to keep himself from sharing something he knew she wouldn't want to hear.

'Who is she, Julian?' she prompted. 'Tell me. I need to know.'

'Fatima is one of Matthew's clients,' Julian said quietly. 'My understanding is that she's a distant cousin of Bashar al-Assad.'

'A direct cousin,' Bloch corrected.

'She's not a terrorist.' Julian shook his head. 'She's a hedge fund investor. She lives in London. She was born and raised there; her father is a doctor. They have no relationship with the Syrian side of their family. Swiss United wouldn't do business with them if they did. I promise you.'

Annabel frowned, considering this. 'How did she know Matthew?'

'I imagine Jonas introduced them. Her brother's been a client of the bank for years.'

'Is that why Matthew was in London, then? To see her?' She almost said *To be with her*, but caught herself.

'I don't know, Annabel. Really, I don't. Our business is built on confidentiality. Matthew and I never speak about the people in our books. It's just not something you do.'

'But you know she's his client.'

'He never told me that. I just assumed. I saw them together a few times.'

Annabel raised her eyebrows.

'In a professional context, I mean,' he added hastily. 'At the bank. You know, coming and going from meetings.'

'I just don't know why he'd lie to me. If he said he was going to London to see a client, it wouldn't have bothered me. Even if it was a beautiful woman like Fatima Amir.'

Bloch and Julian exchanged glances. Annabel realized she sounded jealous. She *was* jealous. Fatima Amir was beautiful. Objectively, intimidatingly so. In the few photos Annabel found of her, she appeared to be in her late thirties. She had striking, photogenic features: a strong Romanesque nose; pronounced cheekbones; full, sensual lips. Her coffee-colored skin was luminous and her thick hair was so black it shone blue in sunlight. In every photograph, she was elegantly dressed, always in slacks and turtlenecks and blazers. Fatima Amir was the sort of woman who did not need to flaunt her exceptional looks. She was, by all accounts, a woman of substance. This was worse. Zoe, Matthew's assistant, seemed like a potential mistress, a fling, a regrettable mistake that Matthew might make on a business trip after an extra glass of scotch. But Fatima was not a mistake. She was not a fling. She was the kind of woman for whom a man would leave his wife.

'Was he having an affair? Would you tell me if he was?'

'Annabel, stop. He adored you. You know that. You're just tired.'

'She died with my husband. He was on a trip I

didn't know about, to a country I didn't know he was in. How could I not know these things?' Her voice was reaching a hysterical pitch. She knew she needed to calm down, to control herself, but she couldn't. She wanted to stand out on the veranda and scream at the sky as loud as she could, for as long as she could, until she couldn't anymore.

'I'll see what I can find out. I'm sure there's a perfectly reasonable explanation for his trip to London.' Julian went to her and put a hand on her shoulder. He looked at Bloch. 'Perhaps Annabel could speak to whoever is conducting the investigation? It might put her mind at ease.'

'Of course. She can call me anytime. And she's welcome to speak to the tech who examined the black box. He can tell her more about the system malfunction.'

'I think that would be helpful. Thank you. And what about the search teams? They are continuing to look, are they not?'

'They are, yes,' Bloch said. 'Standard protocol is that the search will continue for another twenty-four hours.'

Twenty-four hours. Annabel's heart seized. It hadn't occurred to her that they'd stop looking. At least, not so soon.

'That seems hasty.' Julian frowned. 'I'll talk with Jonas. With private funding perhaps we can continue the search.'

'Maybe I should lie down now. I don't feel well, I'm sorry.'

Bloch stood, recognizing his cue to leave.

'I think that would do you good, love,' Julian

said. 'Get some rest. I'll show Agent Bloch out.'

Annabel paused outside her bedroom. She could hear their muffled voices in the foyer. She craned her neck to listen.

'The search will likely end tomorrow. Is Mrs. Werner prepared for that?' There was concern in Bloch's voice. She could picture his stern expression: the furrowed brow, the crossed arms. He adjusted his glasses when he was nervous, she had noticed. She imagined he was doing this now.

'Is anyone ever prepared for this kind of thing?' Julian responded. 'She's thirty years old, for God's sake.'

'Of course. I'm sorry. I didn't mean to be insensitive. I just meant — '

'So you don't think his body will be recovered? I thought perhaps that might bring some closure.'

'We don't expect that. Typically, in these sort of malfunction cases, the planes are largely consumed by fuel fires midair.'

'If it's an issue of money . . . '

'It isn't. Personally, I find that it's in the best interest of the families to close the investigation as expeditiously as possible. A prolonged investigation can be very hard on them. It plants a seed of doubt where none should exist.'

'So your office is confident this was just a system malfunction? No foul play? You're certain of it?'

'Yes. We were lucky to retrieve the black box intact. This was a tragic accident, nothing more. I know that doesn't change the outcome for Mrs.

Werner. But at least she can take comfort in knowing that no one intentionally brought harm to her husband.'

Julian said something that Annabel could not hear. She tiptoed farther down the hallway, until she was standing fewer than ten feet from Julian and Agent Bloch.

'The Amir family is making arrangements for a memorial service. Do you know if Mrs. Werner is doing the same?'

'I'll speak to Annabel about it after she's had some rest.'

'Thank you. There is one other thing. This is a bit of a delicate matter.'

'You can tell me.'

'Some of Mr. Werner's personal effects were found at Ms. Amir's home in London. Should I arrange to have them sent? I don't want to upset her.'

Annabel inhaled sharply. Bloch's words felt like a punch to the gut. It hadn't occurred to her that Matthew was staying at Fatima Amir's home in London instead of a hotel. That seemed so intimate, so familiar. Irrefutable evidence of an affair.

'I can take care of it,' Julian said. 'Just let me know who to contact.'

'I will. Thank you for your help.'

'Of course. If you get any further information, please reach out to me. Annabel is in a very fragile state. If you discover anything suspicious or have any reason to doubt that this was more than an accident, let me know first. This has been an enormous shock to her. To all of us, of course, but particularly Annabel. She was so devoted to Matthew. I think she will handle news better if it comes from someone she trusts.'

'She is lucky to have a friend like you, Mr. White. She will need you now.'

Annabel heard the front door click closed. She slipped back down the hallway and disappeared into her bedroom before Julian caught sight of her. From inside her closet, Annabel pulled out the box of notes.

She set them out in neat rows on the bed, like a quilt made of small scraps of paper. Concert tickets from their third date. A Polaroid photograph of Matthew sleeping, which he had placed on the pillow beside her one morning before leaving for an early flight. A matchbook from their honeymoon. A page torn from a day planner on the day Matthew proposed. She looked at each one until her eyes blurred with tears. She lay down on top of them. For a long time, she stared at the blank white of the ceiling. Eventually she drifted into a deep and dreamless sleep.

★ ★ ★

Hours later, Annabel jolted awake. She had been in the middle of a terrible dream, and her heart was racing. The street outside was quiet, and a full moon gleamed through her window. She glanced around her bedroom, orienting herself. A sweater of Matthew's hung over the back of the desk chair. The novel she'd been reading lay on the ottoman. For a moment, she wondered if the past few days had been some kind of hellish nightmare from which she'd finally awoken. Maybe Matthew was in Zürich. Maybe he was on his way home. Maybe it was all just a horrible mistake.

Annabel sat up. She could hear a voice in the living room. A man's voice. She was awake now, alert. Could it be Matthew? Her heart leapt at the thought. *That's absurd*, she told herself. *Stop it.* Still, she hopped out of bed and stumbled toward the bedroom door.

When she opened it, the voice became clear. Annabel paused in the hallway, listening.

'There's something not right about this,' Julian said, his voice low. 'I have a bad feeling.'

Annabel tiptoed closer and peered around the corner. Julian was standing by the bookshelves in the living room. His back was to her. His cell phone was cocked between his shoulder and his left ear. He held a picture frame in his hands.

'I don't know,' he said. 'It just feels to me that the investigation is being rushed . . . yes. Exactly. That was my sense, too. I mean, two people are dead. Two important people.'

Julian turned then and replaced the photograph to its place on the bookshelf. Annabel bit her lip when she saw it. The photograph was of the three of them. Arms interlinked in front of a chairlift in Zermatt. Matthew was in the middle. His head was tilted back, his mouth in an open grin. Annabel loved that photo of him. One of their happiest times since they'd left New York. They had stayed at Julian's chalet, just the three of them. Matthew had been so carefree that weekend, so relaxed. In the photo, he was laughing at something Julian had said. A joke, Annabel remembered, about Jonas. Julian did a pitch-perfect Jonas impression, especially after a few drinks.

Annabel watched as Julian picked up the picture again. He rubbed his thumb gently across it. 'Jonas is as shocked as I am,' he said to the person on the other end of the line. 'Yes, he agrees. Just do me a favor. Look into Agent Bloch at Fedpol. Find out what you can about him and let me know.' He paused, nodding his head as the person on the other end of the phone spoke. 'Thank you. That would be quite helpful. And of course, this is between us.'

Annabel leaned forward and the floorboard groaned beneath her weight. Julian looked up. 'I'll talk to you soon,' he said. He set the photograph back and hung up the phone.

'I'm sorry. I didn't mean to eavesdrop. I was just getting a glass of water.'

'Don't be silly. This is your apartment. I hope I didn't disturb you?'

'No. I was up anyway. I'm glad you're still here.'

'I wasn't going to leave you alone. I thought I'd sleep on the sofa, eventually.'

'I don't think either of us is going to do much sleeping tonight.' Annabel took a seat on the couch and patted the cushion beside her.

'I love that photo,' she said.

'Me, too. What a weekend that was.'

'It was the first time I felt at home here. Actually, it's one of the only times I've ever felt at home here.'

'Really? It doesn't show.'

'When I moved to Greenwich Village, I felt like I was home, right away. But here . . . '

Julian nodded, as though he understood. He patted her knee. 'It's not easy to be an expat. Especially in Geneva. But you've handled it well.'

'I don't know. I don't exactly fit in with the other bankers' wives.'

'Maybe that's the reason I like you so much.'

'Because I'm a scrappy upstart from a blue-collar town?'

Julian laughed. 'Because you're smart and tough and interesting.'

'I don't know. That weekend in Zermatt was the first time I felt like myself. Like I wasn't just putting on a show. Honestly, I felt lost before I found you.'

'You have no idea how many women have said that to me.'

Annabel smiled.

'Who were you talking to?' Annabel asked then, her voice serious again.

'A friend. Who has connections at Fedpol.'

'Why?'

'Do you really want to know?'

'Yes.'

'I'm not sure I trust Agent Bloch. Or at least, I'm not sure he's doing his job.'

'You don't think the crash was an accident.'

'I think they're being hasty in concluding that it was an accident. I don't want to scare you, Annabel. But Matthew was my friend. And if someone caused this, I want to know who it was.'

'Me, too. And I don't trust him, either.'

For a moment, they sat together in silence. Then Julian's arm dropped around Annabel's shoulder and she rested her head against it. She squeezed her eyes shut, but tears welled up anyway, and began to slip down her cheeks.

'Everything about this feels wrong,' she whispered. 'Why would anyone — ' She stopped, unable to finish the sentence.

'I don't know,' Julian said, kissing the top of her head. 'But trust me, if someone did, I'm going to find out.'

'Let me help.'

'No. You've got enough to deal with. Please. Just let me make some inquiries. I know the right people to talk to. If anyone can get to the bottom of this . . . I promise I'll tell you anything the moment I hear it.'

Annabel frowned. She didn't like the dismissive tone in Julian's voice, but she could sense this wasn't an argument she was going to win. 'All right,' she said. 'Thank you. I don't know what I'd do without you.'

'Just get some rest, all right?' Julian patted her thigh. 'You need it.'

'We both do. Will you be all right on the couch? I'll bring you some sheets and a pillow.'

'I'm fine. I can sleep anywhere. I have some calls to make.'

Annabel stifled a yawn. 'Don't stay up all night,' she said, and kissed him on the temple. 'Good night.' Then she rose and padded off toward the bedroom. For a long time, she stayed awake, listening to the faint sound of Julian on his phone. From her bedroom, Annabel couldn't hear what he was saying. That was fine. She had her own work to do. She stayed on her computer until the room grew light and her eyelids grew heavy. But she pushed on, even when she heard the living room fall silent. When Julian slept, Annabel rose, showered, and headed out to catch the first train to Bern.

Marina

Sander is dead. We have a serious problem now.

The ping of the email woke Marina up. She hadn't really been sleeping. She had dozed off after going nearly blind from staring at her phone in the dark while Grant slept beside her. After reading the article about Duncan's death, she'd emailed every journalist she knew in New York. No one knew anything. They were saying it was a robbery gone wrong. They were saying it was a scorned lover. They were saying there had been a rash of break-ins in Duncan's typically quiet corner of Connecticut. Some reports said that valuable antiques and a painting had been stolen. Others heard that nothing had been taken. The police thought Duncan might have startled an intruder and ended up dead.

The email was from a Mark Felt. In a groggy haze, Marina racked her brain for the name. It sounded familiar. Mark was the name she'd been given for her contact in the Tuileries. Was this him?

Then it clicked: Mark Felt was the FBI agent who helped Bob Woodward and Carl Bernstein break the Watergate scandal in the 1970s.

Mark Felt was Deep Throat.

Marina felt the hairs on her arms stand on end.

This person — these people — whomever they

were — were Duncan's Deep Throat. Now they were hers.

I know. How can we talk? she typed back.

Encrypted channels only.

Marina hesitated. She wanted to do this right. *Goddammit, Duncan,* she thought. *Where are you when I need you?*

She could wait until she returned to New York. There she at least could consult another journalist about how best to communicate safely. Owen Barry at the *Wall Street Journal*, maybe. Another one of Duncan's protégés and known to be something of a tech whiz. She could trust Owen. But she wasn't scheduled to return to New York until next week. This could hardly wait that long. Given that she had a USB of data stuffed in the toe of her running sneaker in the back of the hotel closet — a USB loaded with information so sensitive that her boss was now dead — Marina didn't know if this could wait until tomorrow, much less next week. She had to get home, as soon as possible.

'Fuck it,' she murmured aloud, and typed out contact details for further encrypted communications. She hit send.

'Hey there.'

Marina turned. Grant was sitting up, looking at her. He was shirtless, the sheet covering him only from the waist down. In the semi-darkness, he gave her a sleepy smile. 'Are you okay?'

'Sorry,' she said. 'Didn't mean to wake you. I couldn't sleep.'

Grant reached out and cradled her face with his hand. 'I know. It's awful.'

'I can't believe he's gone.'

'Listen, I'll do whatever you want to do here. It's your call. But I think we should go back to New York. In the morning, if possible.'

She winced. 'This trip. You put so much work into it and — '

'Paris will be here. We'll come back another time.'

'But the expense . . . '

Grant shrugged. 'Forget the expense.'

Marina covered her face with her hands and let out a small sob.

'Oh, don't do that,' Grant said. 'Please, I don't want you to be sad.'

'You're just such a good man,' she said. 'How did I get so lucky?'

Grant's face relaxed. 'I'm the lucky one.'

'You really wouldn't be upset if we left?'

Grant shook his head. 'I'd prefer it,' he said, his voice firm. 'Duncan was family to you, Marina. And family is the most important thing in the world. Everything else is just collateral damage. Don't worry about the trip.'

Marina pulled his hand to her lips and kissed it. 'Thank you,' she whispered. 'Thank you for understanding.'

'Of course.' Grant pulled her in and wrapped his arms around her body. He held her for a long time in silence. Eventually he pulled back, picked up the phone, and called the airline.

Annabel

It was snowing in Bern. Annabel stared out the window of the conference room at the Fedpol headquarters, watching a drift collect on the sill. A flat-screen television flickered on the wall across from her, the sound muted. Annabel glanced at it, then back out the window. A BBC journalist was walking through a dusty street in Aleppo, between the bombed-out shells of what had once been apartment buildings. A handkerchief shielded her nose; a bulletproof vest, her torso. What good would those things do, Annabel thought, if they dropped another bomb on that godforsaken place? Annabel could see her reflection in the windowpane. The thought of Aleppo made her even queasier.

In front of her sat a cold cup of weak coffee, brewed for her by Agent Bloch's assistant. There was no milk in it and no sugar. Annabel had abandoned it after just one sip. A clock ticked overhead. She had been there for more than an hour. That was fine. She had expected to wait; after all, she hadn't called to say she was coming.

'Agent Bloch is in a meeting,' the assistant had said, when Annabel turned up at the front desk.

'That's all right,' Annabel said.

The assistant looked irritated but said nothing. Only a polite nod, an offer of coffee. Then she whisked out of the conference room, leaving Annabel alone. She didn't mention how to find her or where the bathroom was or how long Annabel could expect to wait.

Finally, at noon, a knock came at the door. Agent Bloch entered, an accordion file beneath one arm. He'd cut his hair, Annabel noticed. She wondered how he'd had the time to do that in the middle of an investigation. But then, maybe he'd done it himself. His hair was cropped close to the skull now, a military cut. He could have done it over the bathroom sink with an electric razor. He seemed like the type who might cut his own hair. His clothes, his mannerisms, his glasses: all of it was utilitarian. She wondered what his apartment looked like. Blank white walls, she suspected. No feeling of home.

Annabel rose to her feet. She tried to smile.

'Thank you for seeing me,' she said. 'Perhaps I should have called first. I just knew if I didn't come today, I'd lose my nerve.'

Bloch nodded. He gestured for her to sit. 'I'm sorry you had to wait. Julian White mentioned you might have some questions about the investigation.'

'Yes.' Annabel paused. Now that she was here, she wasn't sure why she had come. This morning it had seemed urgent, so much so that she had run through the Genève-Cornavin train station as though her life depended on it. She stared at the file under Bloch's arm. 'Are those photos?' she asked. 'Of the plane?'

'Photos, yes. Black box recordings. Interviews with airport personnel and the report from the plane manufacturer. You're welcome to look at any of it. We want you to feel satisfied that the investigation was thorough.'

'I'm sure it was. I just — '

'You needn't explain yourself, Mrs. Werner. It's natural to have questions.'

'Thank you. I don't know why I want to see the photos, really. I suppose it doesn't feel real to me yet.'

'There's no right way to approach this kind of loss.'

'Have they stopped looking? The search parties, I mean?'

'Yes. Earlier this morning. I'm sorry.'

Annabel managed a nod. Though it was what she expected, hearing it aloud knocked the wind out of her.

'The search was extensive. Jonas Klauser insisted upon it. In fact, he offered to fund a continued search himself.'

'I didn't know that. That was kind of him.'

'We would have continued looking if we thought there was anything more to find.'

'May I?' Annabel gestured at the file.

'Yes, of course.'

Bloch produced a thin stack of images. He slid them across the conference room table to Annabel.

She ran her hand over the top image. It was an aerial view of a ridged mountaintop, covered in snow. She peered closer. The ridges were debris, she realized. A wing, broken in half. The round barrel of plane fuselage. Twisted pieces of metal lay on the pristine white snow like sculptures, like an art instillation. The sun glinted off the edges. It was almost beautiful, she thought. If you didn't know what you were looking at. The final resting place of her husband. She felt bile rising in the back of her throat. She closed her eyes for a second, steadying herself.

The next few photos showed the debris in greater detail. A catalog of broken plane bits. Some of the images were pixelated and dark, hard to interpret. Like Rorschach inkblots. Annabel stared at one, her eyes tracing the curve of what at first looked like a human skull, a body curled in the fetal position. But the longer she looked, the less human it appeared.

'That's a window,' Bloch offered. 'Of the plane. We look closely at where the damage occurred to the body of the jet. It helps us determine the cause of the crash.'

'What's this?' Annabel pointed at a white piece of metal. She picked up the photograph, narrowed her eyes. Letters were barely visible at the upper edge. They disappeared on the curve of the plane, in the reflection of the snow. Something about it struck her as familiar. 'JKE,' she murmured aloud.

'You have a good eye. That's hard to read, even for me.'

'I'm a curator. Or I was in a past life. I spent a lot of time looking at small details in photographs and paintings.'

'Where did you work?'

'At Christie's, for a while. In the Impressionist department. Then later at a gallery. I got my master's at Yale.' Annabel blushed. She didn't know why she felt compelled to give this man her resume. To be taken seriously, she supposed.

She did that more often now. In New York, she didn't feel the need to credential herself. But then, in New York, she had an answer to the question: What is it you do?

'You don't work here in Geneva?'

'No.'

Bloch nodded. 'Most of the expat wives don't.'

Annabel tried not to read into that statement.

'Here is one of the search team.' Bloch pushed another photo in front of her. A group of men in bright orange suits, surrounding the side of the plane. A few held ice axes, most wore helmets. The sky behind them shone like an iron curtain. 'As you can see, this is a challenging area to excavate. The plane crashed into the western face of the mountain, below which is a sheer drop of several hundred meters. Particularly in adverse weather conditions, it can prove difficult even for the most seasoned search team to reach the site and to recover wreckage.'

'They were able to find the black box, though.'

'Yes. Here, just below the wing. I can explain to you its contents, if you like.'

Annabel scanned the photograph. Her mind whirred as she processed it. Something about it felt not quite right. Her eyes fell again to the lettering on the plane. Then it clicked.

Annabel stood up. 'That's all right. Can I keep these?' she said, picking up the photographs.

'Well, technically those aren't — '

'Matthew had a life insurance policy. And they've asked for a death certificate and all these other documents and I just want to make sure I'm giving them everything they need. It's really quite overwhelming, all the paperwork.' Annabel was lying and she hoped Agent Bloch couldn't tell. She stared nervously at the table, waiting for a response. She didn't know why she'd said that, about the life insurance. It was just the first thing she'd thought of. And she needed to leave this room with those pictures.

Agent Bloch hesitated. 'That's fine.'

'Thank you so much.' Annabel slipped the photos into her bag and extended her hand.

As she turned to leave, Annabel paused. 'May I ask one last question?'

'Yes, of course.'

'Do you happen to have a picture of the plane? Before the crash, I mean.'

Agent Bloch frowned. 'No, I don't think so. Would you like me to try to locate one?'

'No, it's all right. I was just wondering. I appreciate your help.'

'You're welcome, Mrs. Werner. They say a storm is coming in from the north. The snow is picking up already. You didn't drive here, did you?'

'I took the train. I'll be fine, but thank you.'

'Get home safely, Mrs. Werner.'

Annabel nodded and mumbled something in thanks. She checked her watch as she made her way down the hall. If she caught the next train, she could make it to the research library in Geneva before it closed.

⋆ ⋆ ⋆

Annabel sat alone in the microfilm room. Two students had been there for most of the

70

afternoon, but they had left around dinnertime. Now her head throbbed from fatigue and hunger, and her eyes ached from staring at a lit screen. Annabel didn't care. She was used to studying images down to the pixel. She had an eye for it, a natural ability to assess minute detail, which had been honed over her years in the art business. Today, it had paid off. After hours of fruitless searching, she had found what she was looking for. It was there in front of her, in black and white.

She turned the knob, enlarging the image. Then she held up one of the photographs that she had retrieved from Agent Bloch. It was not the same photo, as she had originally suspected. The image on the screen appeared to have been taken later in the day. The mountain face was dappled in long, dark shadows, and there were fewer rescue workers around the site. In the first image, the one given to her by Agent Bloch, Annabel counted twenty-three men in orange suits. In the image on the screen, only nine. But it was the same plane. She was sure of it. The crack down the middle of the plane's midsection had the same ridged edge; a dismembered wing lay on the glistening snow, sheared cleanly from the body of the plane. The angle of the camera in the second image showed the lettering on the side of the plane more clearly: *JKE*.

It was an act of sheer willpower that Annabel was able to translate the newspaper article from German. The version she had read on the internet, before her meeting with Agent Bloch, was abbreviated, translated into English for the

Daily Mail. She already knew the depressing statistics: the plane was a Gulfstream G450, which had flown out of the Netherlands and crashed in the Alps, almost exactly one year to the day before Matthew's plane went down. There were no survivors. At the time she'd read it, she hadn't wanted to know more.

But now, she wanted to know everything. The plane, she read, had crashed in the Bauges Mountains, just east of Chambery.

The wreckage was spotted atop Mont Trélod.

The plane was part of the Royal Netherlands Air Force. Koninklijke Luchtmacht in Dutch. That explained the *JKE* emblazoned on what was left of the plane's body. The last three letters of *KONINKLIJKE*.

After an intensive search, the black box of the plane had been recovered. It indicated a failure in the ice protection system. A common occurrence, the article said, in private jets of this size.

Annabel felt her hands shake as she hit print. In the corner of the microfilm room, the printer whirred to life. Annabel hurried over, snatched the papers off the printer as they came out. They were still warm as she tucked them away in her bag.

'*Arrête ça, madam.*' A voice behind Annabel stopped her in her tracks.

'I'm sorry?'

A man with a mustache and ink-stained fingers glared at her from the doorway.

'You cannot print items from the microfilm without a library ID card or a university pass.'

'I'm sorry, I didn't realize. How can I get one?'

The man gestured impatiently at the clock overhead. 'It's too late now. The circulation desk closes at five p.m. You'll have to come back tomorrow.'

'No, no. I'm happy to pay for it, but I need this article tonight.'

He pursed his lips. Finally, he held out his hand. 'Let me see, please.'

Reluctantly, Annabel handed over the article.

The man licked the tip of his finger and counted out the pages. 'Five pages. Fifty cents, please.'

Annabel dug through her purse, hoping to God she had fifty cents. At the bottom of her bag, next to her ChapStick, she found a single euro. She handed it over to the man. 'Keep the change,' she said, and took the article out of his hand before he could protest.

'For the future, please get a printing pass,' the man called after her, as she hurried down the hall.

She turned into the stairwell and collided with a man wearing a backpack.

She fell backward, landing squarely on her behind. The strap of her handbag slipped from her shoulder, and its contents scattered across the floor.

'*Je suis vraiment désolé.*' The young man knelt down and began to collect the photographs off the floor.

'*C'est bien.*' Though her lower back smarted from the fall, Annabel popped up. She snatched the photos out of the man's hands and shoved them back into her bag. He glanced up, eyes wide. Annabel felt a twinge of embarrassment at the sharpness in her voice. '*Merci beaucoup*,' she said. '*C'est ma faute.*'

'No, I was rushing,' the man offered in English. He gestured down the hall. 'Is that the microfilm room?'

'Yes. They're closing now.'

'I should hurry, then.'

'I hope you find what you're looking for,' Annabel said, and began to descend the stairs.

★   ★   ★

Twenty minutes later, the young man emerged on the front steps of the library. It was dark outside, and the landscaped grounds were silent. He looked both ways. Annabel Werner was gone.

As he crossed rue De-Candolle, he pulled out his phone. 'She had quite a busy day,' he said to the man on the other end of the line. 'First she was in Bern, visiting Agent Bloch at Fedpol. He gave her photographs of the crash. A whole stack. She has them in her bag. Then she spent several hours at the library.'

'Looking for what, exactly?'

'She left with a printout of an article. About a plane crash from last year. Similar statistics. G450. Crashed in the Alps, no survivors.'

'Why, do you think?'

'Maybe she suspects that Agent Bloch hasn't been entirely forthcoming about the details of the accident.'

'There's something off about Agent Bloch,'

Jonas Klauser said. 'I'll have someone look into it. Do you have a copy of the article?'

'Yes, sir.'

'Bring it to me. And keep following her. I want to know her every move. Where she goes, who she talks to. I want to know what she's thinking.' Then: 'Any update on Matthew's computer?'

'No, sir. It hasn't turned up.'

'Perhaps it was on the plane with him, then.'

'I don't think so. According to Amir security, he didn't have it with him when he left for the airport.'

'All right. Keep looking. And stay on top of the wife.'

With that, Jonas hung up the phone. Andre Lamont hopped onto his moped and sped off into the night.

Marina

There was more security at Charles de Gaulle Airport than Marina remembered seeing. Everywhere she looked, there were police in blue berets. There were soldiers in fatigues, too, patrolling in pairs with intimidatingly large firearms.

'What do you think is going on?' Marina whispered to Grant as they waited in line to have their carry-on luggage scanned. 'This place looks like a military base.'

Grant shrugged. 'I find it reassuring. At least they take security seriously.'

Marina nodded, but she couldn't shake the feeling that something was off. There was a tension in the air that crackled like electricity.

'This line hasn't moved in ten minutes.' Marina nodded at the queue ahead of them. She went up onto her tiptoes, trying to determine the source of the holdup.

'You need to relax.' Grant put his hand on her shoulder and dug his thumb into a pressure point. 'You're tired. I'm sorry this flight is so late. It's the best I could do.'

Marina groaned. 'Oh my God. That feels so good.'

'I had us scheduled for a couples massage at the hotel tomorrow. But since we're missing it, I had Rachel book us one in the city instead. I thought it might be nice for you after the flight.'

Marina narrowed her eyes in mock suspicion.

'What's wrong with you?'

'What's wrong with me?'

'I'm serious. There has to be a catch. You're handsome and smart and funny and possibly the most thoughtful man on earth. There has to be a catch.'

Grant chuckled. 'I have plenty of flaws.'

'Name one.'

'I'm a very hairy person.'

'I think that's cute. You're like a pet.'

'I eat a pint of ice cream basically every night.'

'Also cute.'

'I work too much.'

'Preaching to the choir.'

'I should work out more.'

Marina shook her head. 'Guys that work out all the time are boring. You're in great shape. Perfect. Best butt I've ever seen.'

'You should have seen it when I was in the navy.'

'I did. Once. I asked you out. Remember?'

'Go.' Grant patted her on the behind. 'The line is moving. You're up.'

Marina patted him back and winked. She felt lighter now. Happy, even. Grant had that effect on her. She slipped her bag off her shoulder and put it onto the scanner's conveyor belt.

Grant's bag came through the scanner first. Marina watched as he slipped on his shoes, put his laptop back into the bag. The couple behind them retrieved their belongings, too, and headed toward their gate. Marina frowned. The line was moving efficiently now, but there was no sign of her bag.

'*Excusez-moi,*' she called out to the guard behind the scanner. '*Ou est mon sac?*'

'I'm sure it will just be a minute,' Grant said, putting his arm around her waist.

Marina ignored him. She stepped closer to the scanner. '*J'ai besoin mon sac,*' she said, louder this time.

Marina felt a tap on her shoulder. A stern-looking police officer stood behind her. 'Madam,' he said, flashing a Police Nationale badge, 'please come with me.'

Grant stepped forward. 'What is the problem here?'

The officer looked directly at Marina. 'You need to come with me.'

Marina took a deep breath. People around them were staring. 'It's all right,' she said to Grant. 'I'm sure it's nothing.'

'I'm going with you,' Grant said.

'If you like,' the officer replied.

Grant took Marina's hand. Wordlessly, they followed the officer through a discreet white door. He gestured to a bench. 'You may wait here,' he said to Grant. To Marina, he said, 'Follow me, please.'

Grant squeezed Marina's hand three times: *I love you.*

She squeezed back twice: *So much.*

'Don't worry,' she said to him.

'Our flight starts boarding in forty minutes,' Grant said, more to the officer than to Marina. Marina smiled at him, trying to appear calm. As she followed the officer into a small room, she ran through all the possible scenarios in her head. It could be a mix-up of some kind, or perhaps she had been randomly selected for some additional security screening. Maybe she had mistakenly put something in her carry-on that alarmed security. A nail clipper. An aerosol can.

The more alarming possibility was that this had to do with the USB. Marina tried to remember exactly what her contact had told her to say. The password was russell1. The USB contained personal information. Photos. Nothing work related.

'Please have a seat,' the officer said, gesturing at the small table with metal chairs. 'Someone will be in shortly.' With that, he left the room. Marina sat in a chair and crossed her hands in front of her on the table. Overhead, a clock ticked away the seconds. *Thirty-seven minutes until boarding*, Marina thought. She closed her eyes and took a deep breath, trying to relax.

'*Bonsoir*, Ms. Tourneau.' Marina's eyes popped open. A slight man in wire-rimmed glasses and an ill-fitting blazer entered the room. He carried a notebook under one arm, and in his hand, he held her carry-on bag. He placed it on the table between them and extended his hand. 'Antoine Fournier. Police Nationale.'

Marina stood and smiled as she shook his hand.

'I'm sure you are wondering why you are here.'

'Yes.'

'Ms. Tourneau, what was the purpose of your trip here to Paris?'

'I'm celebrating my engagement.'

'No work?'

'No.'

'When was the last time, Ms. Tourneau, that you spoke to Duncan Sander?'

'He called me a few days ago, but we spoke only for a few minutes.'

'About what?'

'He wanted to wish me a good trip.'

'You didn't speak about work?'

'No. I'm on vacation. And Duncan is on a sabbatical.'

'You're aware, of course, that Mr. Sander was murdered shortly after that call.'

'Yes. That's why I'm returning home. For the funeral. Are you investigating Mr. Sander's murder?'

'No, madam. He's an American citizen. However, we have reason to believe that Mr. Sander was planning a trip to Geneva and may have been trying to illegally obtain information from inside a Swiss bank.'

Marina frowned. 'That doesn't make sense to me. Duncan wasn't working. As I said, he was on sabbatical.'

'People work on sabbaticals, Ms. Tourneau.'

'Maybe. I don't understand what this has to do with me. Or you, for that matter.'

'It involves the theft of confidential information from French citizens. So it does concern me.'

'I'm sorry, but I can't help you. I haven't spoken to Duncan about work in weeks.'

'Did you meet anyone while you were in Paris, Ms. Tourneau?'

'We had dinner with a college friend of my fiancé.'

'No one else?'

'No.'

'Did anyone leave anything at your hotel or ask you to bring anything back to Mr. Sander?'

'No. I'd say you could search my bag, but I imagine you already have.'

Fournier smiled and wrote something down in his notebook.

'Did you purchase anything while in Paris?'

'I took some photographs. And I bought my mother an Hermes scarf.' Marina glanced at the clock. 'My flight will be boarding soon.'

'I'm aware.' Fournier didn't glance up from his notebook. Marina watched him write. She realized he had produced no identification. She wondered who he was and who he worked for. *Duncan, what did you get yourself into?* she thought, as she shifted nervously in her seat.

'All right, Ms. Tourneau. Thank you for your assistance. I just have one last question.'

'All right.'

'Did Mr. Sander ever speak to you about Swiss United Bank?'

'Not that I can recall.'

'You don't believe he was working on a story at present?'

'That's two questions.'

Fournier smiled again.

'No, I don't,' she said. 'To be frank with you, Duncan had a drinking problem. It had become quite severe. He was on medical leave from the magazine. I truly do not believe that Duncan had either the time or the capacity to be working.'

Fournier nodded. He rose to his feet. Marina did the same.

81

'Thank you for your time, Ms. Tourneau,' he said, extending his hand.

'My pleasure. May I take my bag?'

'Yes, of course.' Marina picked up her carry-on and slung it over her shoulder. She couldn't help but notice that the zipper was fully closed. It had not been when she placed it on the X-ray machine's conveyor belt. As discreetly as she could, she opened the bag and slipped her hand inside. She felt around for the inner pocket, which held the USB. When her fingers closed around it, she breathed a small sigh of relief.

Outside, Grant was pacing nervously in the hallway. 'There you are,' he said, when Marina emerged. 'I was starting to worry.'

'No need.' Marina forced a smile. Inside, her heart was racing. 'Sorry to hold us up.'

'We're good. We'll make it.'

As they hurried toward the gate, Marina reached for Grant's hand.

'What did they want?' he asked.

'I don't really know. I think it was just a mix-up.'

'That's odd.'

'It was, a little.'

At the gate, boarding had not yet begun. In fact, there were no airline personnel behind the desk. Marina looked around, surveying the scene. A large crowd was standing around a television in the corner.

'What's going on?' Marina whispered to Grant. 'This doesn't feel right.'

'There's a terrorist attack at Stade de France,'

a woman beside them said. 'Suicide bombers, they're saying. At a football match. President Hollande is there.'

'Oh my God,' Annabel whispered. 'Is anyone hurt?'

'They don't know yet.' The woman nodded at the television. 'They're reporting live.'

'That explains the security,' Grant said. He put his arm around Marina and pulled her close.

Marina nodded, unable to speak. She couldn't take her eyes off the screen. It was too small and too far away for her to make out much, except for smoke and what looked like people fleeing in all directions.

'What a world we live in,' Grant said quietly, shaking his head.

'Horrible.' Marina leaned her head against Grant. To the right, she noticed a group of soldiers in fatigues circling the perimeter of the gate. Though she now understood why they were there, she couldn't shake the feeling that her own interrogation had nothing to do with the terrorist attack. Hers was not a random screening Antoine Fournier, whomever he was, had been waiting for her. He suspected, correctly so, that she was trying to leave the country with highly valuable information. Either he had not thought to check her USB, or he had and was unable to uncover the hidden data. Marina suspected it was the latter. If he had been able to, she would still be in the small white room with the metal chairs. It was possible they would be handcuffing her and telling her to contact a lawyer. The thought of it caused her body to shiver in fear.

Grant felt it and wrapped his arms around her. He kissed the top of her head.

'I'm here,' he whispered. 'I've got you.'

'I know,' Marina answered. She was lying, of course. Grant couldn't protect her now. Maybe no one could. If Antoine Fournier had found her this quickly, there would be others. And they would be more forceful in their interrogation than he had been.

Annabel

Six days after the crash, a memorial service was held for Matthew Werner at the Klausers' home in Cologny. Annabel did not plan it. Julian handled the logistics. Jonas Klauser made sure to invite all the members of the firm and their most important clients. Elsa Klauser arranged for flowers and programs and catering for the reception afterward. The morning of the service, it snowed again, and the Klauser estate was coated with white. The sky was gray and clear, but another storm would arrive by evening. Dark clouds loomed over the mountains in the distance. Annabel stared at them as Father Moreau, a priest whom she met for the first time only the day before, delivered Matthew's eulogy. He talked mostly about God and very little about Matthew. Annabel stopped listening early on. It all felt surreal to her, as though she were watching a movie about a memorial service and not an actual memorial service, for a man she'd married just four years earlier. Others around her were crying, but she felt surprisingly, unsettlingly numb.

At the reception afterward, everyone quietly agreed that the service was beautiful and elegant and flawlessly organized. A fitting tribute to Matthew Werner. When they said so, Annabel nodded in assent but could hardly speak. For her, it was all a waking nightmare.

'She's hardly said a word,' she heard someone say to someone else.

'I can't imagine,' was the reply.

'Is she alone here?'

'I think so. I'm sure she'll go back to New York soon enough.'

The women passed by her on the way to the table where drinks were being served. They didn't see her. She didn't know most of these people anyway. They were almost all Swiss United people, employees or clients. A few Geneva acquaintances. Matthew's aunt and cousins had flown over from New York, but Annabel had met them only a handful of times before today. Annabel's sister, Jeannine, still lived in upstate New York. A single mom of two young kids, Jeannine couldn't afford to fly over, and Annabel didn't want her to. The sisters had never been close. The cracks between them had widened into a chasm after Annabel settled in New York City, married a lawyer. If Jeannine was resentful of Annabel's life in Manhattan, Annabel couldn't imagine what she'd think of her life in Geneva. She felt only relief when Jeannine apologized for not coming, and she could sense Jeannine's relief when Annabel said she understood.

The Klausers hadn't asked for contact information for their New York friends, and Annabel hadn't volunteered. She just wanted the whole ordeal over with, as quickly and as painlessly as possible. She couldn't handle the idea of lingering houseguests. Or the people who would stay in some five-star hotel in Geneva and expect to take her out for dinner the following evening and look into her eyes and tell her that she could call them for anything, anything at all. She'd known those people. They'd pick up the dinner bill and disappear again. They would check in with her once a month or so, then even less often, just to feel as though they'd done something for her, that they'd really been there. And at home they'd talk about how sad it had all been, but how they were happy they went, because really, it was the right thing to do.

'Who are these people?' Annabel asked Julian. 'Why don't I know them?'

'A lot of banking clients. It's quite amazing, really, how many people flew in to pay their respects.' Julian pointed to a cluster of men by the bar. 'That's Vitaly Abramovich. He owns the largest oil company in Russia. He's speaking to Clive Currie, the record label owner. Clive recently sold Vitaly his interest in Chelsea.'

'The place?'

'The soccer team.'

'And who is that?' Annabel pointed toward a man she'd met once before. She wasn't sure he remembered her, however, and she wanted Julian to introduce them.

'The man with Jonas? That's Rohan Agarwal. Steel magnate. Lives in Monaco.'

'No. Him, there. Talking to Zoe.'

'Ah. Lorenzo Mora. He's a client of the bank. Heir to the largest sugar fortune in the world.'

'Matthew's client?'

'Jonas's, I think.'

'Introduce me.'

Julian raised his eyebrows but said nothing. Annabel knew what Julian was thinking. Lorenzo Mora was shockingly handsome. He was built like Matthew, tall and broad-shouldered, and had thick black wavy hair. He had the kind of smile that was perfectly imperfect. His two front teeth overlapped slightly and he had a dimple in just one cheek. Even though the day was overcast, he wore dark sunglasses and a scarf wrapped up to his chin, as though he'd rather not be recognized, even at a private, high-profile gathering such as this. As the heir apparent to the Mora sugar fortune, Annabel had no doubt that a great many women asked to be introduced to Lorenzo Mora. But she was not interested in his looks or his money. She wanted to talk to him about Matthew.

Julian nodded and ushered Annabel over to where Zoe and Lorenzo were sharing a cigarette. Not for the first time, Annabel thought how pretty Zoe was, and how young. Her pale skin and translucent blue eyes appeared even more ethereal against the slate sky. Her blond hair was pulled back into a low bun; tendrils escaped around her hairline, framing her face. She did not appear to be wearing makeup, but she hardly needed any. Annabel knew she was young, maybe twenty-four or -five, just a year or so out of university. All the assistants at Swiss United looked like Zoe. Elegant, young, thin enough to disappear as they slipped silently in and out of conference rooms filled with men. Annabel had mentioned this to Matthew after her first visit to his office. He shrugged, dismissed it as optics.

Optics. A word Annabel had thought a lot about over the past six days. A word she should have thought more about over the past two years. How much of what happened at Swiss United was just optics?

'Hello, Zoe.' Annabel leaned in to kiss Zoe on the cheek and found herself trapped in an unexpected embrace.

'Oh, Annabel, I've been so worried about you,' Zoe breathed into her ear. Annabel felt the crush of Zoe's slight frame against her own. When she pulled back, Zoe held on to Annabel's arm. From her worried expression, Annabel could tell that Zoe's concern was genuine. She felt a wave of regret. She'd always been a bit cold toward Zoe. Even though the girl seemed professional and kind, Annabel couldn't help but be bothered by the idea of her husband spending endless hours with such an attractive young assistant. They even traveled together, and this was what bothered Annabel the most.

'I assume you get separate rooms,' Annabel sometimes joked, 'or does the concierge think Zoe is your daughter?' But her jokes came across as insecure and childish instead of lighthearted, and Annabel always regretted making them afterward.

Matthew had remarked on a few occasions that Zoe had a boyfriend, a French lawyer who he claimed was 'brilliant' and 'charming' but who may or may not have left his wife for Zoe. Matthew said he was worried that Zoe would get her heart broken. She spent every weekend now traveling around Europe with him, sometimes even sneaking out early on Fridays to catch a flight, thinking Matthew didn't notice. But Matthew said others at the bank had noticed, and her performance was suffering, and he was worried she would be fired. Even Jonas had said something to him about it.

Annabel assumed Matthew didn't really care about Zoe's absences. He talked about Zoe's boyfriend to make Annabel feel more comfortable around Zoe. It didn't work. Did that ever work? Was any wife anywhere made more comfortable by her husband's frequent chattering about an attractive colleague? In fact, the boyfriend, in Annabel's opinion, was a strike against Zoe. It made Annabel uneasy that Zoe was dating someone she met through work, someone who appeared to have been married until very recently. Wasn't that how most affairs started? Annabel suspected this sort of thing happened all the time at Swiss United. These men worked such long hours. Most nights, they ate dinner at the office. They were on calls all weekend, and when they weren't, they were distracted, unable to hold a sustained conversation about anything other than exchange rates and tax loopholes and the world price of gold. They skipped birthday parties and other social engagements. They showered and dressed in the dark, slipped out of the house before the sun was up without so much as a goodbye to their wives. The pretty assistants at Swiss United were more than just optics. They were a work perk, an enticement, salve for the sixteen-hour days the men spent huddled in conference rooms over a pile of trust agreements and tax forms. Men like Zoe's French lawyer left their wives every day. It could have just as easily been Matthew. Maybe it had been Matthew. Annabel was determined to find out.

'I'm sorry I haven't called,' Annabel said to Zoe.

'Please, you needn't explain. I can't imagine. I just wanted you to know that I'm here for you, that I'm thinking of you.'

'Of course. You're kind.'

'I'd like to come visit you, if that's all right.' Zoe was staring at Annabel with such intensity that Annabel glanced away. She murmured something affirmative to Zoe and turned to Lorenzo.

'I'm Annabel Werner,' she said. 'Matthew's wife.'

'Yes, of course.' Lorenzo extended his hand. 'Lorenzo Mora. I'm so sorry for your loss, Mrs. Werner.'

'We met once before, Mr. Mora. You probably don't remember.'

'Of course, yes. And it's Lorenzo, please.' He removed his sunglasses and blinked uncomfortably in the afternoon light. Annabel wondered if he did remember their meeting or if he was merely being polite. It had lasted only five minutes, maybe less. She had run into Matthew with Mora on Boulevard Helvetique one evening around nine. It had stunned her when she caught Matthew's eye from across the street. She was coming from a theater, where she'd watched a movie alone. Matthew was with a man and a woman, and they were laughing. The man was opening the door to the Griffin's Club, a posh member's-only restaurant and nightclub where celebrities and the ultrawealthy hobnobbed to the beat of internationally known DJs. For a minute Annabel thought Matthew was going to duck into the club and pretend not to have seen her. Instead, he waved her over. She crossed the street, her heart pounding in her chest as she steeled herself for an unpleasant marital confrontation.

Matthew grinned as though nothing at all was wrong. Either he was a very smooth liar or he didn't think he had misled her. Was he working late? Did work happen at the Griffin's Club? Annabel wondered.

'What a surprise,' he said. 'This is my wife, Annabel. Annabel, these are clients of Jonas's. He's under the weather and asked that I show them a good time tonight.'

Annabel smiled, a tight smile that was the best she could manage given the circumstances. She noticed that Matthew didn't ask her to join them, and so the four of them stood awkwardly outside the club, listening to the reverberation of the bass from within.

'I should get home,' she said, nodding briskly. 'It's been a long day and I'm tired.' She thought she saw Matthew's guests exchange a look of relief when she said it, but perhaps she was simply being paranoid.

'I'll be home soon,' Matthew said. He kissed her on the cheek — a chaste, dismissive sort of kiss — before opening the door for his guests.

Annabel realized now that Matthew had never said their names. But now she recognized them both: Lorenzo Mora and Fatima Amir.

'Could I chat with you, Lorenzo? Privately, please.'

'Perhaps I can offer you a ride home? Once you're ready to go, of course.'

'Thank you.' Annabel nodded. 'In fact, I'm exhausted. I think I would like to go home now, if that's all right.'

'Annabel, there are so many people here who want to speak with you,' Julian said. He put his hand on her shoulder. 'And the Klausers — '

'Jonas and Elsa will understand. It's been a long day for me.'

'Of course they will,' Zoe interjected. 'Go rest, Annabel. I'll let them know that you left.'

'Please thank them for everything.'

'I will.' Zoe gave Annabel a hug. 'I'll come see you soon,' she whispered, before letting go.

Annabel kissed Julian on both cheeks and followed Lorenzo to the driveway. A silver Mercedes pulled up and Lorenzo held open the door. Annabel felt a flutter of nerves; she didn't want anyone — even the driver — to hear their conversation. But once she'd given the driver her address, Lorenzo pressed a button and a tinted glass window slid up, separating them. Finally, they were alone.

'Thank you,' she said. 'You have no idea how much I wanted to get out of there.'

'It's my pleasure. You remember me, don't you? From that night in front of the Griffin's Club. I was with your husband and Fatima Amir.'

'Yes.'

'And you want to know about Fatima, no?

93

That's why you came over to talk to me.'

'I . . . ' Annabel hesitated. 'I just recognized you at first. But I wasn't sure from where.'

'Do you know who my family is, Mrs. Werner?'

'Call me Annabel, please. And no. Well, yes. Just what Julian said, when I asked him who you were.'

'He told you my uncle was the head of the Mora Cartel?'

Annabel's eyes widened in surprise. 'No!' she exclaimed. 'No, no. Nothing like that. He said your family runs the largest sugar business in the world.'

Lorenzo laughed. 'We do that, too,' he said. Annabel couldn't tell if he was joking. She forced a smile. Here in Geneva, she'd learned to be discreet about money. There was so much of it here, and not all of it clean. It was always better not to ask.

'Our family does many things. Mora International has become a many-headed beast. I run Mora Crystals, the sugar business. Have you been to the Dominican Republic?'

'No, I haven't.'

'I live on a very small island off its southern coast. Isla Alma. It's the most beautiful place on earth. We have a private club there, Cane Bay. I'm away much of the time. Miami, New York, Paris, Panama. But that is where I think of when I think of home. Our sugar plantations are on the main island.'

'It sounds lovely.'

'Well, Isla Alma is. The sugar fields are brutal places. It takes a very specific kind of person to

94

work in the sugar business. Someone who is comfortable running things with an iron hand.'

Annabel didn't know what to say, so she just nodded. It occurred to her that perhaps she'd made a mistake. She was alone in a car with a dangerous man, and for what? To ask him about a chance encounter on the street?

'You're welcome to visit my island anytime. My door is always open to you. I came to Geneva to tell you that. I wanted you to know that you have a friend in me.'

'That's very kind of you. Where does the rest of your family live?'

'My brother runs another subsidiary of our family business in Miami. My sister is in New York. My father lives mostly in Palm Beach. I have one uncle in Paris and another in Venezuela. It is not easy for all of us to agree when it comes to running our various businesses. This is why we came to Swiss United. Jonas is known for being good at navigating complicated family structures. And Jonas trusted Matthew's judgment, especially when it comes to tax matters.'

'Matthew was a tax lawyer in New York. One of the best.'

'I came to rely a great deal on Matthew's counsel. He had a very calming way about him. Particularly as conflicts have arisen between the older and younger generations in our family.'

'I always said Matthew should have been a psychologist. People tell Matthew things, private things. It happens all the time. On our first date, I told him about my parents dying when I was young. He has — he had — just the warmest way about him. I'm sorry. I keep using the present tense. It hasn't sunk in yet. I keep thinking he'll just walk through the door.'

Lorenzo patted her hand. 'I know exactly what you mean.'

They were quiet for a minute. Annabel thought she might cry, but her eyes remained dry. She had run out of tears. She had cried them all out. Instead she looked out the window and felt achingly empty.

'I don't know why we came here,' she said. 'It all feels like a bad dream.'

'You came to make money. Matthew wanted to buy a big town house in London or Paris or maybe a mansion on the beach in Malibu, retire at forty-five, spend his days with you. No?'

'I suppose that was the idea. Nothing so grand as a town house in London. Maybe a little house with a wraparound porch and a view of the ocean.' Annabel looked away, cringing with discomfort. What else could she say? That at five months pregnant, she'd miscarried their baby? And then, just two weeks later, Matthew's father had died of a heart attack? They had been devastated, twice over. They had needed a fresh start.

After one phone call with his father's old friend Jonas Klauser, Matthew decided that private banking was the perfect fit for him. With his background in tax law, his Ivy League pedigree, his prep school connections, and his immense charm, he'd be a natural. Jonas promised him that he'd spend most of his days flying first class to New York, London, Paris, Madrid, Hong Kong, where he'd hobnob with CEOs and sultans. No more sad takeout dinners at his desk; at Swiss United, he'd be expected to wine and dine his clients at Michelin-starred restaurants all over the world. He'd ski with them in Gstaad, he'd sunbathe with them on their yachts off the coast of France. Private banking was a business built on trust, Jonas said. It was about gaining the client's confidence. It was about making them feel like you were their best friend in the world, and that no matter what, you'd take care of them — and more important, their money. All this for three times the salary he'd been making at Skadden, plus a healthy bonus each time he brought in a client of his own. And the perks, which included a lease on a 500-series Mercedes, a 2,000-square-foot flat in Old Town, access to the firm's ski chalet in Zermatt, and a Corporate Amex with no fixed spending limit. It all seemed so romantic, so exotic, so new. Matthew was hesitant, but Annabel had pushed him to accept. It was exactly what they needed, she said.

Try it for a few years, Jonas said. If you don't like it, we'll find you something in New York. And in the meantime, you'll be making good money. You'll clear your head. You'll get to experience Europe. What could be better?

'Did Matthew talk to you about his work? His clients?' Lorenzo asked.

'Never. He worked all the time. I hardly ever saw him. And he told me everything he did was confidential, so I tried not to ask.'

'Did you see Fatima Amir after that night?'

'No. That was the only time. He never mentioned her name.'

'She was a client of his.'

'I gathered that.'

'You didn't know he was going to London to see her?'

'He told me he was in Zürich.'

'They weren't having an affair, if that's what you think.'

Annabel frowned. 'How could you know that?'

'I knew them both reasonably well. That night at the Griffin's Club wasn't the first time we met. Matthew introduced us about a year ago. Fatima and I had much in common. Matthew thought I could help her. And I did. I tried to, at least.'

'I'm sorry. I don't understand.'

'Fatima's family is in the oil business in the way mine is in the sugar business. The Amirs have legitimate business pursuits and not so legitimate. Understand?'

'Yes.'

'Fatima ran her own hedge fund. She wanted nothing to do with the illegitimate side of the family finances. But it's hard to keep your hands clean when the pot is dirty.'

'Ah. I see.'

'Matthew was helping her do that. But it was complicated. And dangerous. Between us, Fatima's second cousin is Assad. Her brother works for him. They are dangerous people, with many, many enemies. And they take family loyalty quite seriously. They don't like to think they are being betrayed, even in the smallest way. Especially by a woman.'

Annabel felt a chill run through her body. She pulled her jacket closer around her shoulders, hugging herself. Why had Matthew involved himself with these people?

'Julian told me the Amir family weren't terrorists. That Swiss United wouldn't do business with them if they were.'

'They aren't terrorists. They're money launderers. Their cousins are the terrorists.'

Annabel shot Lorenzo a look of exasperation.

'Anyway, Swiss United will bank with anyone. Terrorists. Dictators. Drug dealers. If they didn't they'd be out of business. Who do you think keeps their money in Swiss bank accounts? Accountants? Housewives from Tulsa?'

Lorenzo laughed. Annabel felt her cheeks beginning to burn. Of course she'd heard stories about Swiss banks. She'd even met a few clients of Matthew's here and there — mostly old college friends of his who had made money in New York or London and wanted to tuck a few dollars away in a numbered account. Annabel knew they were doing it to avoid taxes, or maybe a wife who might one day try to take it all in a divorce. She knew that was a gray area, legally speaking. But it also seemed relatively harmless, like a crime without a victim. And Matthew was a lawyer. A tax lawyer! Wasn't that why they'd hired him? To make sure it was all technically within the bounds of the law? Wasn't that what he spent all day doing? Finding loopholes and mechanisms that saved money without triggering any tax implications?

'If your friend Julian told you that, he is lying. He knows better than that. Be careful who you trust, Annabel. You are in Wonderland, my friend. Here in Geneva, criminals can be your friends and your friends can be criminals. Do you understand me?'

Annabel nodded. 'Which are you?'

The car hit a bump in the road, and Annabel let out a small scream. Lorenzo's arm shot out, protectively pinning her back against the seat. The driver lowered the partition.

'*Lo siento, Señor Mora,*' he said. '*Hay hielo en la carretera.*'

'*¿Es el plano de los neumáticos?*'

'*No, no.*'

Lorenzo nodded. He leaned forward, pressed the button to put the partition back up. As he leaned forward, she glimpsed a black strap beneath his jacket. At first she thought it was a suspender. But then she realized what it was. Lorenzo Mora was wearing a gun.

'Just ice on the road,' he said. 'The tire's fine.'

'I speak Spanish,' Annabel whispered.

Lorenzo raised his eyebrows. 'Smart woman. Any other languages?'

'French. A bit of German. You didn't answer my question.'

Lorenzo nodded. 'Annabel,' he said, with an unreadable smile. 'Right now, I'm the best friend you have. So listen to me when I tell you: don't trust a soul from Swiss United. Do not trust Julian White. Do not trust Jonas Klauser. They are not your friends. You have no friends here in

Geneva. You should go back to New York. Or visit your sister. You can come to Isla Alma, if you like. It doesn't matter where. But if I were you, I'd leave as soon as possible, and I wouldn't ever look back.'

Marina

Duncan Sander's funeral was held at St. James' Episcopal Church on the Upper East Side, an unusual choice given that Duncan was neither an Episcopalian nor an Upper East Sider. But St. James' was the de rigueur house of worship for the fashionable ladies with whom Duncan kept company, and it was *the* place for a high-society Manhattan funeral. Even if he'd met his end eating a sandwich alone at his desk, his head blown apart by a .45-caliber gun fired at close range, Duncan Sander would make damn sure he'd have a dignified, elegant good-bye. Apparently, he'd left an extensive list of demands and directions for his funeral with his attorney for when the time came, specifying everything from the music to be played to the color of the urn that would hold his ashes. It was exactly the way he would have wanted it. In this, Marina took comfort.

The pews were nearly filled when Marina arrived, and so she took a seat toward the back of the church. At the front, on the left-hand side by the pulpit, Marina saw the staff of *Press* magazine, all kissing one another hello with great solemnity as they subtly vied for positioning near Philip Brancusi or, at least, toward the center aisle so that they might be seen. On the right-hand side of the church, the socialites were doing the same. Marina smiled. Duncan would have loved it all. Everyone who was anyone was here. It was the best-dressed crowd she'd ever seen outside of Fashion Week. All in black, of course, but in the latest collections off the runways in Paris. Marina had never seen so many black Birkin bags in one room at one time. The altar was festooned with lilies and white roses and potted arrangements of giant Dutch tulips that bowed their petals to the ground as though the very flowers themselves were in mourning. Marina wondered if they had been styled by society florist Jerome Cotillard, with whom Duncan once had a brief, tempestuous affair. She hoped so. He was, after all, the best.

Marina herself was dressed simply in a black dress with three-quarter-length sleeves, and over it, a vintage Lanvin coat that Duncan had once told her was 'perfection.' She wore little makeup and no jewelry but for her engagement ring. Her black hair was pulled back in a ponytail. Her porcelain skin was nearly translucent from lack of sleep, and deep blueish circles were stamped under her eyes like bruises. She looked like hell, but she didn't care. Unlike the other staffers from *Press*, Marina was there to mourn, not to be seen mourning. Though she was having trouble focusing; her eyes kept darting around the room, wondering if she was being watched or followed. She kept her hands tightly wrapped around her small black clutch. In it, she had sunglasses, a package of tissues, and the heart-shaped key ring Grant had given her when she first moved in with him. On the key ring was her house key and, more important, the USB.

The USB had not left Marina's body since the airport. She was terrified to have it and even more terrified to lose it. She hadn't dared open it on her computer, though she desperately wanted to. What if someone hacked into her laptop? She knew anything with an internet connection was vulnerable. These days, hackers could spy on anyone through their cell phones, their laptop cameras. She had to be sure the information remained secure. She needed help from someone with far greater tech skills than her own, but it had to be someone whom she could trust. There was only one man she could think of for the job, and with any luck, she'd find him there.

'Is this seat taken?'

Marina heard the familiar voice and looked up. There he was.

She slid down the pew, making room for Owen Barry. He looked much the same, though it had been at least a year since they'd seen each other. He was still as tall and lanky as she remembered, his thinness accentuated by an ill-fitting suit. His strawberry-blond hair had a touch of gray around the ears, and he wore it short now, which she thought made him look more sophisticated than usual. Even though Owen's fiftieth birthday had come and gone, he had a boyish charm about him. When he smiled, Marina couldn't help but smile back.

'I was hoping to see you here,' she said.

'How are you, gorgeous?' Owen kissed Marina on both cheeks. 'You look smoking hot, as always.'

An older woman in the pew in front of them

turned around and glared.

'Sorry,' Owen whispered in Marina's ear. 'You do look incredible, though.'

Marina stifled a laugh. Duncan had always loved Owen and it was easy to see why. When Owen wasn't hitting on her — and even when he was — he was terribly charming. He was also a damn good journalist. He was one of the few who Duncan considered a peer. He had helped them break the Morty Reiss story years ago; since then, he'd won two Pulitzers — one for a story about arms dealers in the Middle East; the other, about the water crisis in Flint, Michigan. Marina had heard a rumor that he'd left the *Wall Street Journal* to become the head of a website called the *Deliverable* but had not had confirmation of this from Owen himself. They had kept in only loose touch over the years, occasionally trading emails or bumping into each other at industry events or at Duncan's annual Christmas party. Though she enjoyed his company, Marina had made a point to keep Owen at an arm's length once she was engaged. He was just flirtatious enough to make her nervous.

'Thank you,' she mouthed, and then nodded her chin toward the front, where an organist had begun to play a somber strain of processional music.

'We need to speak after this,' Owen whispered, his shoulder knocking against hers. 'Somewhere private.'

Marina nodded, glancing around to make sure no one could hear them. 'I was thinking the same thing.'

'My place or yours?'

She shot him a look.

'What?' Owen blinked his eyes innocently. 'We're both uptown now. That's all I meant.'

'Owen, I'm engaged! I can't come home with you in the middle of the day.'

'What am I supposed to suggest? The Carlyle? We can't exactly go sit in a coffee shop. And my office is down in Tribeca. I can come to your place.'

'My fiancé will not be thrilled.'

'Oh, the fiancé.' Owen rolled his eyes. 'Where is he now? Off swimming laps in a pool of money?'

Marina turned and scanned the back of the church. 'There he is.' Grant stood behind a cluster of mourners who had aggregated behind the pews. When he saw Marina, he smiled and waved and made a gesture that indicated that he was trying his best to make his way to her.

'Would you *please* be quiet,' the woman in the pew in front of them hissed. 'This is a *funeral*.'

Owen and Marina dropped their heads in prayer.

'We'll talk after,' Marina whispered, in the faintest voice she could muster. 'We'll find somewhere.'

'Good. Because there's something I need to show you. It's from him.'

'From *him*?' Marina nodded her head toward the altar.

'Yep.'

'For us.'

'Yes.'

'Jesus Christ.'

'Jesus Christ indeed,' Owen said, and crossed himself as the congregation stood and the processional began down the aisle.

★ ★ ★

After the funeral, Grant headed back to his office. Marina waved good-bye as his car pulled away from the curb. Once he was around the corner, she and Owen quietly agreed to meet at his apartment. Marina said hello to colleagues while Owen disappeared. If anyone had seen them leave together, they probably wouldn't have thought much of it. But still, it was better to be safe than sorry.

Owen Barry lived on the upper floor of an old town house on East Sixty-ninth Street. As they rode the rickety elevator up to his apartment, Marina wondered why they had never run into each other. She and Grant lived just one block away. Their apartment, a sprawling three-bedroom in a fancy Park Avenue building, was far grander than Owen's. But that was the funny thing about New York. Cramped studios were available for rent across the street from $50 million penthouses. Marina and Grant might live in a different world than Owen Barry, but they still probably shared a dry cleaner. They took the same subway stop. They bought their groceries from the same small bodega on the corner of Lexington and Sixty-eighth.

'Sorry about the mess,' Owen said, as he opened the door. He offered Marina a hand as she stepped over a stack of old newspapers. 'I wasn't expecting company.'

Marina surveyed the apartment. It looked to her as though Owen had had company, as recently as last night. An empty bottle of wine sat on the coffee table. Two glasses — one with a stain of lipstick on the rim — had found their way to the floor in front of the fireplace. Marina pretended not to notice. For a moment, she wondered if Owen was actually living with someone. But she dismissed the idea quickly. The Owen Barry she knew wasn't exactly a believer in commitment. And no woman she could imagine would live in such a pigsty.

'You want a beer or something? Or coffee?'

'Coffee would be great,' she said. 'Thanks.'

Owen nodded and disappeared into the kitchen. 'Have a seat anywhere,' he called out. 'Or if you want, take the stairs up to the roof. I'll meet you up there.'

Marina opted for the roof. She followed the twisty metal stairs up to what looked like a trap-door in the ceiling. When she pushed it open, she felt a rush of cold air and heard the sounds of traffic from the street below. After Owen's apartment, she wasn't expecting the roof deck to look like much. But instead, she found herself in what felt like a secret garden, filled with potted plants and enough wrought iron furniture to host a small dinner party. A panoramic view of Central Park unfolded in front of her.

'Wow,' Marina murmured to herself. The leaves were mostly off the trees, but there was something elegant about the muted color palette of browns and grays set off against the West Side skyline and the roofs of the other town houses along Sixty-ninth Street. It wasn't quite the view from the balcony of Le Meurice, but it wasn't too far off.

'It's nice up here, right?' Owen emerged. He had a laptop under his arm and was gripping two mugs of coffee in one hand. 'The apartment is kind of a shitbox, but it's worth it for this view. I work up here whenever I can. It's where I do my best thinking.'

'This is all yours?'

'Yep. The only way to access it is through my apartment. Nice trade-off for the crappy air-conditioning and the crazy landlady, who lives on the first floor. She's a piece of work. She has a shih tzu named Zsa Zsa Gabor.'

Marina snorted.

'She's always pissed at me for one reason or another. I think I'm the resident problem child in this building.'

'One too many overnight guests?'

Owen laughed. 'Something like that.' He took a seat at the table and opened up his laptop. 'Okay. So here it is. About a month ago, Duncan called me up out of the blue. He said he needed my help with a story. He made me drive all the way out to Connecticut to see him. He was holed up out there, said he wasn't sure when he'd be back in the city. Thought he was being followed or something crazy. Honestly, you know I love the guy, but he could be kind of a drama queen.'

'Tell me about it.'

'So I get out there and my first thought is that

109

he's off the wagon. The shades were all drawn, the house was a mess. He looked like shit. Unshaven, exhausted. Fat.'

Marina frowned. 'That's not good. He usually stops drinking when he's on a story.'

'He wasn't drunk while I was there. Just looked like hell. He said this was his big break. Claimed to have a source inside a financial institution with access to mountains of confidential data. He wanted me to show him how to set up encrypted channels so they could communicate.'

'So did you?'

'Yeah, but the source freaked out. Said he wasn't sure it was safe. Wanted to hand over the information to Duncan personally.'

Marina nodded. 'I think that's where I come in. I met a source when I was in Paris. He gave me a USB to give to Duncan.'

'What's on it?'

'I have no idea. I've been too scared to open it. Anyway, I don't have the password.'

'Well, then, I've got the key to your lock, babe.'

'God, you're such a child.'

'I'm serious.'

Marina raised an eyebrow. 'Do you really have the password? How?'

'The day before Duncan died, he called me. He told me he was going to send me something, and that you had the other half of it, and that if anything happened to him, I needed to find you and give this to you. A few minutes later, he sends me a string of numbers and letters over BlackBerry messenger. Honestly, at this point I didn't know if the guy was losing it or what. But then, less than twenty-four hours later, he's dead.'

Marina shivered. 'It could be a coincidence,' she said, pulling her coat tighter around her. 'It *is* possible it was a home invasion. Right?'

Owen shot her a look.

'Right.' She dug into her purse. 'Here,' she said, producing the USB. 'Let's do this.'

'You sure? I can just give you the password if you want. It's your story.'

'Are you scared?'

Owen laughed. 'I feel like if your life isn't in danger, you aren't reporting the right story.'

Marina stuck the USB into Owen's computer and typed in the password Mark had given her. A few nondescript folders appeared on the screen. 'Okay,' she said. 'Here we go. He said that there's more information, buried somewhere. But damned if I know how to find it.'

'You're in the right place.' Owen pulled the laptop toward him, and after maneuvering around the screen, a second window popped up, prompting him to enter another password. From off his BlackBerry, he entered the series of letters and numbers Duncan had sent to him.

The screen went black.

'Uh-oh,' Marina said, biting her lip.

'Just wait. It's thinking.'

Suddenly, a folder appeared. It was labeled 'Morton Reiss.'

Owen clicked it open. The first document was a bank statement from Caribbean International Bank.

Marina gasped when she saw the balance: $73,542,980.11.

Owen let out a whistle. 'I don't know who Client 437-65-9881 is, but damn,' he said. 'He's done well for himself.'

Marina frowned at the screen. 'That's weird. There's no name attached. It's just a statement from a numbered account. There must be something else on here that proves that Reiss is Client 437-65-9881. Maybe that's his Social Security number?'

Owen shook his head. 'No way. These accounts are set up so that no one can trace them back to their actual owners. What do you know about offshore accounts?'

'Not much.'

'Well, here's how it works, more or less. Morton Reiss takes his money to some shady law firm. The shady law firm acts as an intermediary between him and a global bank. It sets up a shell company — let's call it Dinero & Co. Then, the shady law firm makes sure there is a protective screen around the Dinero & Co.'s real owner. They appoint nominee directors to Dinero & Co. — who are really just straw men, paid by the law firm — who just sign anything the law firm puts in front of them. The law firm goes to the bank — in this case, CIB — and says, We represent Dinero & Co., here are the company's directors, and they'd like to open a numbered account. And so this account exists in the CIB system — but there's no link to Morty Reiss.'

'But then how does Morty Reiss access his money? He must need to make periodic withdrawals, no?'

'Usually the real owner gets a power of

attorney from these nominee directors so that he can access the bank account or safe that Dinero & Co. sets up. Or the law firm does it for him.'

'And that's legal?'

'It's a gray area. In the case of someone like Reiss, no. It's illegal for a law firm to deal with Reiss. They can't knowingly assist a criminal in hiding his assets. But in the case of your run-of-the-mill CEO? It's not exactly kosher, but it's not illegal, either.'

'And the bank? They're comfortable doing business with companies that just have these fake directors? Aren't they required to know who their clients are?'

'Yes. In theory. But banks like CIB do business with criminals all the time. It doesn't bother them, as long as they are making a healthy fee to do it. They just want there to be a protective screen in place so that if the authorities come knocking on their door, they can pretend they didn't know who was on the other side of the shell company.'

'But *someone* at the bank must know. When Morty Reiss shows up with a power of attorney to access Dinero & Co.'s bank account — someone at CIB must be interfacing with him, right?'

'Right. Yes. Typically a private banker.'

'So Duncan must have found a banker at CIB who was willing to talk.'

'If he did, my hat's off to him. I've been trying to get into the pants of an offshore bank — or a banker — for years. So far, no luck.' Owen rocked back on his chair, far enough to make Marina nervous. 'Hey!' he said, snapping back suddenly. 'CIB sued Duncan, right? Because he

113

said they were housing Reiss's money?'

'I think they just threatened to sue. He issued a retraction and they backed off.'

'Do you remember when that was?'

'Six months ago?' Marina frowned, thinking. Then she nodded. 'Yeah, that sounds right. Duncan spent a few weeks at Silver Hill. You know, the rehab place in Connecticut. It was part of his mea culpa. He was supposed to go back there, but now I'm wondering if he ever did, or if he was using his sabbatical to work on this story.'

'Look at this.' Owen tapped the corner of the document. Marina focused on the date: April 1, 2015. 'So if this *is* Morty Reiss's account, Duncan was right. He did have money stashed at CIB.'

He clicked it closed and opened the next document. 'Here's an email chain, from inside some firm called Schmit & Muller. Any idea who they are?'

Marina shook her head. 'Sounds like a law firm. But I've never heard of them.'

They both looked at the screen, reading through the emails in silence.

April 2, 2015
From: Peter Weber
To: Hans Hoffman
Subject: CONFIDENTIAL: Internal Use Only

CIB is no longer comfortable holding assets for Mr. Reiss. We need to find another bank for him. CIB has requested that he transfer all of his holdings out of the bank by the end of the month.

April 2, 2015
From: Hans Hoffman
To: Peter Weber
Subject: Re: CONFIDENTIAL: Internal Use Only

Understood. I will speak to my contact at Swiss United. I think it's best not to use Mr. Reiss's name in external communications. Tell Swiss United this is a valuable client of ours who will bank with them only in complete anonymity. When they see the size of his account, I imagine they will be flexible.

April 4, 2015
From: Peter Weber
To: Hans Hoffman
Subject: Re: CONFIDENTIAL: Internal Use Only

I've spoken to Julian White at Swiss United. He is quite pleased to take on a new client. He understands the condition of anonymity and is comfortable with it. I assured him that we did our due diligence before banking with this client. He has set up a numbered account at Swiss United and it will be ready to receive a transfer from CIB by Close of Business on Thursday. Please inform Mr. Reiss of Swiss United's rates for this size account, and our commission for this transfer. If he is comfortable, we should proceed immediately.

April 4, 2015
From: Hans Hoffman
To: Peter Weber
Subject: Re: CONFIDENTIAL: Internal Use
Only

I've spoken to Mr. Reiss. He is comfortable with both the rate and the commission.

There is an American journalist named Duncan Sander who arrived in the Cayman Islands last night. Apparently, he has been trying to track down Mr. Reiss for years. There is concern that he has a source within CIB who is feeding him information on Mr. Reiss and potentially other clients of the bank as well.

Mr. Reiss asks that the funds be transferred tomorrow. I have assured him that this will be done and that once it is, there will be no record of him ever banking at CIB. As far as CIB is concerned, client 437-65-9881 is a Panamanian widow named Alicia Marcos. As of tomorrow, her account will be closed.

April 5, 2015
From: Hans Hoffman
To: Peter Weber
Subject: Re: CONFIDENTIAL: Internal Use
Only

Is something being done about this leak inside of CIB? That would be bad for business, for them and for us.

April 6, 2015
From: Peter Weber
To: Hans Hoffman
Subject: Re: CONFIDENTIAL: Internal Use
Only

The leak has been contained.

'Holy shit,' Owen murmured when he reached the end of the email. He clicked it closed and opened the next document. There it was: a numbered account at Swiss United, with the same amount: $73,542,980.11.

Owen tapped the screen. 'A couple of weeks after this, Duncan did that interview, claiming that Morty Reiss was storing his money at CIB. But by then, Reiss had already transferred his money to Swiss United.'

'Right. So the bank threatened to sue and Duncan came off looking like a crazy conspiracy theorist. What do you think he means when he says, 'The leak has been contained'? That's ominous.'

'I don't know, but my guess is if we start digging, we'll turn up a CIB banker who died under mysterious circumstances right around that time.'

Marina stood up and started pacing. Grant's friend, Matthew Werner, had died in a plane crash the same day as Duncan. He was a private banker, wasn't he? But not at CIB. A Swiss bank, she thought. Had it been Swiss United? She couldn't remember. She stopped and looked up. 'You think bankers go around murdering one another in cold blood?'

'Offshore banking is a dirty business. These guys aren't bankers; they're cowboys. They operate by a completely different set of rules.'

'So do you think it's possible they killed Duncan? These people at CIB?'

'I don't know who killed Duncan. Maybe CIB. Maybe Schmit & Muller. Maybe some monkey who works for Morty Reiss. Your guess is as good as mine. But we're going to do our best to find out.'

'I think we're in over our heads,' Marina said, and sat back down in her chair.

'Sweetheart, you were in over your head the day you accepted that USB.'

'But if I just don't do anything with it.'

'Whoever killed Duncan will find you. If they were willing to kill him in order to ensure this information didn't get out, you better believe they'll kill you, too.'

'So what do I do?'

'You find them first.'

'And then what?' Marina snapped, exasperated. 'Give them the USB and tell them I'm sorry and that I just want to go be a stay-at-home mom now, so no worries? I don't think that's going to assuage their concerns.'

'You want to be a stay-at-home mom now? Seriously? Oh, fuck. Don't tell me you're pregnant.'

'Jesus, Owen. Focus. I'm freaking out here.'

'I know, I know. I'm sorry. I joke when I get nervous.'

'Well, stop. I think I should go to the police.'

118

'I think we find Duncan's source and get as much information as we can. Then we put it all out there on the *Deliverable* website, as fast as possible. They can't hurt you once this all goes public.'

Marina narrowed her eyes. 'You just think this is the story of the year.'

'Well, yes. I can't deny that. But I also think this is bigger than the police. The police can't protect you from the world's largest bank. The police can't protect you from all the heads of state who bank there, and the cartel leaders, and the terrorists, and the dictators. All these people have a vested interest in making sure there are no information leaks. So as long as you have the USB and the information isn't in the public domain, I think your life is in danger. And I think you know I'm right.'

Marina bit her lip. She was the keeper of highly valuable, dangerous information. Information that had gotten Duncan killed. As long as she had it, it was very likely that it would get her killed, too. Maybe she could just go home and pretend to be Mrs. Grant Ellis for the rest of her life. Quit her job, join the Christmas Committee at the Colony Club, dedicate herself to throwing charity lunches for the Red Cross and redecorating their house in Southampton. She could destroy the USB and its contents and pretend that Paris had been nothing more than a lovely vacation, cut short by the death of an old friend and colleague.

But could it ever be that simple? Marina doubted it. Someone would always be looking for her, hot on the trail of the information that went missing somewhere between Paris and New York. Even if they weren't, she'd wonder if they were. She'd always be looking over her shoulder, taking note of dark cars that idled too long in front of her apartment building, or strangers who came just a little too close on the street.

'If we do this,' she said, 'we have to act fast.'

'Of course. Clock's already running.'

'And if something happens and I decide this is getting too dangerous, we go straight to the police.'

'Fair enough.'

'And bylines. I get to decide the bylines,' Marina said, thinking about Duncan. She wanted him to get credit for finding Reiss, if, in fact, they ever did.

'You're the boss. It's your story.'

'Well, it's Duncan's story. I'm just making sure it goes to print.' It would be their last story together, she thought. She would make sure it was their best.

'So you're in?'

'In,' she said, and turned back to the keyboard.

Annabel

Annabel was sleeping when her phone rang. It jolted her upright, and for a moment, she sat very still, wondering if she was dreaming. She ran her hand over Matthew's side of the bed. It was cold and empty. She picked up the phone just before it went to voicemail.

'I'm sorry for calling so late,' the voice on the other end said. 'I wanted to catch you when you were alone.'

'Who is this?' Annabel stifled a yawn. The clock on her bedside table blinked the time: 11:45 p.m.

'Sorry, it's Zoe. Can I come up?'

'Where are you?'

'I'm outside your building. I wanted to make sure you were by yourself before ringing the bell.'

'I'm alone. I'll buzz you in.'

Annabel was fully awake when she opened the front door. She wore Matthew's bathrobe over her nightgown, and in a moment of last-minute vanity, she'd run a brush through her hair. Even in the middle of the night, Zoe looked fresh-faced and chic in black jeans, high-top sneakers, and a fur vest. Her skin glowed in the dark hallway, the moonlight glinting off her high cheek-bones. Annabel wished she hadn't answered the phone.

At Zoe's feet was a brown cardboard box, which she picked up. She followed Annabel into the living room and handed it to her.

121

'What is this?' Annabel asked.

'It's Matthew's laptop. From work. They've already taken his desktop. They will come looking for this. It has everything on it. All his clients. All their financial data. Everything.'

Annabel stared. 'Why do you have it?'

'He gave it to me. Before the plane crash. He told me to hide it. It's only a matter of time before they realize I have it.'

'Who are they?'

'The bank. The security people questioned me about it yesterday. I was hiding it in my apartment, but I can't do it anymore. I need to leave, Annabel. Things are not safe for me.'

'Who at the bank? Why can't they have Matthew's files?'

'Because he was leaking them. And they know there's a leak. They just don't know who it is. Or was. If they find this — '

'Wait.' Annabel put her hand on Zoe's shoulder. 'What are you saying?'

Zoe sighed. 'He really didn't tell you anything, did he?'

'Matthew was my husband,' she said, her voice curt. 'He told me everything.'

'I'm sorry. I didn't mean it like that. I meant he didn't tell you anything about his work. That's good. He was protecting you. The less you know, the safer you are.'

'The less I know about what?'

Zoe sighed. 'It's safer for you if you just turn over this laptop when they come looking for it. Just put it in his home office. Tell them you don't know the password. Then leave. Go back to New

York. Get away from here.'

'I don't know the password.'

'Great, so then they'll believe you.' Zoe couldn't hide her exasperation. 'If you don't know anything, they won't hurt you.'

'But you think they hurt Matthew?'

'I think someone did, yes. That plane crash was no accident.'

Annabel frowned. Zoe seemed so certain. The uncomfortable feeling that Matthew and Zoe had been closer than he had let on descended on her. It wasn't the first time. 'What do you know, Zoe?' Annabel said. 'If you know what happened to my husband, you need to tell me. Now.'

Zoe got up, walked over to the window, scanned the street. She pulled the curtains closed and turned around.

'You're sure you want to hear this?'

'Why don't you sit,' Annabel said. She put the box down on the coffee table. 'Would you like some coffee or tea? Or something to eat?'

'Perhaps some water. I can get it.'

Annabel waved her off. 'Please. Sit. I'll be right back. Then we'll talk.'

In the kitchen, Annabel set the teakettle on the stove. A wave of light-headedness overtook her. She steadied herself on the counter, her hands gripping the cool marble. She shut her eyes and willed herself to breathe. For a moment, she considered her options. If Zoe was right — Matthew was involved in some dangerous or illegal bank dealings — did she really want to know? Would it put her at risk to know? Perhaps she ought to turn over his laptop to Swiss United and take the next plane back to New York. She could put this whole nightmare behind her.

But would she ever be able to start over? Or would she always wonder what really happened to Matthew? Would it haunt her, never knowing what he'd been willing to risk his life to reveal to the world? Would she revisit the facts as she knew them again and again, looking for signs and clues that she might have previously missed?

Zoe had information. At the very least, she ought to hear it. She would never forgive herself if she didn't.

The teakettle began to whistle. Annabel lifted her head. She took a final, resolute breath before pouring the steaming water into two cups. She placed the cups on a tray, beside tea bags and a box of cookies sent the previous day by some vice president at Swiss United she had never met.

Zoe smiled gratefully when she saw the tray. She reached for the cookies the moment Annabel placed them on the coffee table.

'Thank you,' she said. 'I haven't been eating, really. I didn't realize how hungry I am.'

Annabel nodded. 'Me, either,' she admitted, and though she hadn't planned to, she took a cookie for herself, too. 'Help yourself.'

After Zoe had finished the cookie, she took another. Then she wiped her mouth and began to speak. 'Matthew and I started at Swiss United the same month,' she said. 'I liked him right away. He was kind to everyone, even the assistants. And he loved you so much. He talked about you all the time. He was one of the few men who had a picture of his wife on his desk, where everyone could see it. Not like some of the others, who stared at anything in a skirt that passed them.

'I knew he was being groomed by Jonas for a senior position at the bank. Everyone said so. Matthew was smart and hardworking. And Jonas trusted him. It takes Jonas a long time to trust anyone, but Matthew was different, I guess, because Jonas had such a close relationship with Matthew's father.

'I was happy to be assigned to Matthew. I knew that he'd treat me well and that, if I was good enough, my star would rise along with his. Jonas's assistant, Therese, has been with him for seventeen years. She makes more money than some of the senior bankers. I thought maybe I could be like that, if I worked hard enough for Matthew. I made sure I was always available to him and went out of my way to do everything he asked.

'Right away, Swiss United seemed like a dream to me. I was making so much more money than any of my friends from university. And the perks were good. When we traveled, we always stayed in the best hotels and ate in the nicest restaurants. I grew up in a small town in the South of France. No one ever goes anywhere. Most of my friends are still there. So for me, flying to Monaco and New York and Paris was exciting. That probably sounds silly to you, I know.'

'Not at all. I grew up in a small town, too. And part of the reason I agreed to come to Geneva with Matthew was the travel. It's a romantic life. At least, it sounded romantic.'

Zoe nodded. She seemed relieved that Annabel wasn't judging her. 'The hours were terrible, of course. I worked all the time. You know. Matthew did, too. And no one in my position ever takes a vacation. We're supposed to be on call whenever the bankers need us. Nights, weekends, anything. But I didn't mind. I knew that's why we got paid so much.

'A few months ago, I walked into Matthew's office and Jonas was in there. And they were angry with each other. They stopped talking when I walked in, so I ran out as quickly as I could. But afterward, Matthew was upset. So I took him out for a drink after work. He got a little drunk, which wasn't usual for him. That's when I knew something was wrong.'

Annabel shifted, crossing and uncrossing her legs. She didn't like the idea of Matthew confiding in Zoe over drinks. But she nodded and said nothing.

'He told me he was worried about some of Jonas's clients. Look, a lot of our clients aren't exactly — how do you say this in English? I'm sorry, my English fails me when I'm tired. On the up-and-up? I mean, they come to us to hide their money. From the government, from spouses, whatever. That's what we do. We hide money in numbered accounts so no one knows who it belongs to. You understand?'

'I think I do,' Annabel said slowly. 'Do you mean to say that what you do is illegal?'

Zoe shrugged. 'We're not breaking Swiss law.

If a US client comes to us, for example, and puts ten million into one of our numbered accounts and doesn't pay taxes on that money, he's the criminal, not us.'

'Okay. So you may be helping someone violate tax rules elsewhere, but here in Geneva, what you do is legal?'

'Technically, yes. But there are exceptions. And that's where Matthew started disagreeing with Jonas.'

'What are the exceptions?'

'There are people that the bank isn't supposed to do business with at all. People on sanctions lists. Terrorists. Arms dealers. Dictators. Swiss United can't do business with these people. No bank can. There's a whole Compliance wing of the firm that is supposed to make sure of it.'

'But Jonas would ignore those rules?'

'Yes. If it was lucrative enough to do so. Bashar al-Assad, for example.'

'The Syrian dictator?'

'Yes. Assad, everyone in his family, all his ministers and officials, they're all on sanctions lists. Sanctions lists are one way the UN, the EU, the US crack down on people like this. They're telling you: if you do business with anyone on this list, that will mean trouble for you.'

'And so if Swiss United does bank with them, they're violating international law.'

'Yes. But Swiss United does it anyway. Not officially. Unofficially, Jonas is the Assad family's personal banker.'

Annabel shuddered. The videos and photographs coming out of Syria were horrifying.

Chemical attacks. Cities reduced to rubble. Heaps of bodies, starved and burned and hanged, piled up in prisons. How could anyone do business with a man like Assad? How could Jonas sleep at night?

'Did Matthew . . . ,' she started, but her voice faltered. 'Was Matthew . . . '

Zoe shook her head. 'No. They don't give clients like that to junior bankers. But Jonas was grooming him. He was drawing him in. He wanted Matthew to take on Fatima Amir, a cousin of the Assads, first. She isn't on the sanctions lists. She runs a legitimate business. But once Matthew knew who she was, he got uncomfortable. And he didn't like the way Jonas was dealing with Compliance. It made Matthew nervous that Jonas was flouting the sanctions. It's illegal and Jonas knows it.'

'So then why did Matthew agree to take Fatima on as a client?'

Zoe gave a tight smile. 'If Jonas tells you to do something, you do it.'

'He could have quit.'

'Maybe. But it's not that simple. Jonas has ways. He could make sure that Matthew never worked in the US again.'

'You can't be serious. Jonas treated Matthew like a son.'

Zoe frowned. 'Do you know how Matthew's father died?'

'He had a heart attack,' Annabel said stiffly.

'He killed himself.'

'How do you know that?' Annabel snapped. Matthew had rarely spoken about his father.

Until this moment, Annabel thought she was the only living person who knew that Tom Werner had committed suicide. To the outside world, Tom had been a highly successful, well-liked, philanthropic man. He had homes in Manhattan, Southampton, and Palm Beach. He sat on the boards of several corporations and had been, at one time, the president of the Knickerbocker Club in New York City. Only Matthew knew that his father had, in the end, run into financial troubles. The idea of dying penniless had, apparently, been too much for him to bear. And so he had hanged himself in his Fifth Avenue apartment. It was Matthew who found the body. He told Annabel what had happened, but to everyone else, Matthew claimed his father had died of a heart attack. It was a story that had been repeated so often that Annabel occasionally forgot it was a lie.

'Jonas told me.'

'Jonas?' Annabel said, stunned. 'How does Jonas know?'

'Tom Werner was one of Jonas's clients. He stole millions of dollars skimming off the top of his mutual fund. Then he gave it to Jonas to hide at Swiss United. He killed himself after the IRS investigated him for tax fraud.'

'Oh my God,' Annabel whispered. 'I knew he had financial troubles, but nothing like that.'

'No one in the US ever found out. Everyone thought he died of a heart attack. Jonas made sure of that. Otherwise, Swiss United would have come under investigation. And Matthew's family would have been horribly embarrassed. So

Matthew was indebted to Jonas.'

'I just knew that Tom and Jonas were friends. That's all.'

'When Matthew and Jonas argued about the Assad family, Jonas became enraged. I could hear them yelling at each other, even from the hall. Jonas said he could destroy Matthew and ruin his father's legacy. He threatened to go public with details about Matthew's father's suicide.'

'That's horrible.'

'Yes. But that's the way Jonas works. He has a team of private detectives who dig up dirt on all the bankers who work for him. The detectives follow them everywhere at the beginning. Nothing they do is private. Jonas learns their secrets. He uses them as leverage. That way they stay loyal to him. And if there are no secrets . . . '

'If there are no secrets?'

'He sets his people up. He finds weaknesses and exploits them.'

'How do you mean?'

Zoe closed her eyes and winced. 'He tempts them. He's like the devil, Annabel. Truly.'

'You know this for sure?'

'I've helped him do it.'

'How?'

Zoe squirmed uncomfortably. Her eyes shifted to the floor. 'I'm not proud of this. But when I started at the firm, Jonas brought some of us to Monte Carlo for a retreat. We all drank too much. Some of the bankers were doing coke, too. Jonas knew it. He provided it, I think. I was new and I didn't want to seem like I wasn't having fun. The next thing I knew, I couldn't see straight. I could barely stand. They drugged me. And Jonas insisted that one of the bankers help me upstairs. I remember only a little, but we ended up in bed together. He didn't want to be there. He was married. But he was as out of it as I was. They drugged him, too, I think. I don't really remember what happened. But someone was taking pictures — '

'Oh my God. I'm so sorry.'

'It's not your fault. It's mine. I should have quit after that. I don't know why I didn't. It's a horrible place.' Zoe blinked back tears.

'Do you know who was taking pictures of you?'

Zoe shook her head. 'I don't remember much. I just — I've always wanted to apologize to that man's wife. I've never had the guts.'

Annabel nodded. 'Maybe it's best that you didn't. It would hurt her. It would cast doubts.'

'Yes. And she shouldn't have any. It meant nothing, to either of us, It was a situation that Jonas created. He used a lot of the assistants that way. Some of us were asked to sleep with clients, too.'

'I just can't believe Matthew would work for someone like that. It's not the Matthew I knew.'

'Well, he didn't want to. I told him to go to the authorities, but he said that Jonas has the Swiss government in his back pocket. Which, I imagine, is true. Swiss United is the biggest bank in Switzerland, you know.'

Annabel shivered, thinking of Agents Bloch and Vogel and the speed with which they had

131

closed the investigation. She thought about the photographs they had given her, and the explanation about the ice protection system. A cover-up, but until now she hadn't been sure who they were covering up for.

'I thought we should go to the press. But Matthew said that was too risky. Journalists can't protect you from people like Assad. That's what he thought, anyway.'

'Did he change his mind? Someone killed him, Zoe. I'm sure of it.'

Zoe shook her head. 'A few weeks later, he told me that someone at the US Department of Justice contacted him. I think his name was Morse. He had been investigating Swiss United for years, looking for a way into the bank. Matthew met him in New York. He never told me so, but I think he agreed to cooperate with him.'

'Why do you think that?'

'Because when he came back from New York, he was like a different person. He apologized to Jonas. He started working twice as hard. Suddenly, he was in meetings with the Assad family. Jonas was happy. He seemed to think Matthew had come around to see things from his point of view. But I had my doubts. He refused to talk to me about anything. He was so tight-lipped, doing all his work himself. He just didn't seem like Matthew anymore.'

'I know what you mean,' Annabel said. 'He hardly spoke to me anymore, either. He worked all the time, never told me what he was doing. Honestly, I started wondering if he was having an affair.'

Zoe shook her head. 'No. He loved you so much. You must believe that.'

Annabel nodded but didn't respond.

'Sometimes I worried that you might think we were having an affair. I was so scared of you when we first met.'

Annabel glanced up, surprised. 'No, no,' she began, but stopped herself. 'Well, all right. Yes. The thought did cross my mind. But not because of anything you did. It's just hard — maybe one day you'll understand this — to see your husband work with someone who is beautiful, and younger — '

'I understand.'

'Matthew said you were in a relationship with someone, though.'

'I am. A lawyer in Luxembourg. We met through Swiss United, actually. He is the love of my life.'

'Matthew told me he's married.'

Zoe's face crumpled. Annabel filled with regret. 'I'm sorry,' she said, placing a hand on Zoe's. 'I don't know why I said that. It doesn't matter.'

'He's separated. He was before I met him.'

'Really, it doesn't matter.'

'He hates the work we do, too. We both want to get out of it, to get away from this whole world. I was tempted by the money at first, but now I can't stand money. It makes people do terrible things. It makes people terrible people.'

'And you think Matthew was the same? That he wanted out?'

Zoe nodded. 'Sometimes I'd find him at the

office late at night, after he had told me to go home. He would shut his door, pretend he hadn't seen me. And he was always using this laptop, even at his desk. He was working on something. I think he was gathering evidence for Agent Morse.'

'So why don't you contact Agent Morse? Give this laptop to him?'

'Because I don't want to end up like Matthew.'

Annabel inhaled sharply. 'Where will you go?'

Zoe didn't answer. 'Annabel, you need to leave, too. It's dangerous for us both here. If the bank thinks either of us knows anything, I promise you, they will kill us.'

'What do I do?'

'Someone from the bank will come looking for Matthew's laptop. Give it to them. Pretend you know nothing, you heard nothing, you saw nothing. Make them believe that you are not a risk. You don't need to be involved in this. Matthew didn't want you to be involved. Go to New York and never look back.'

'And you?'

'I'll take care of myself. But do me a favor. If anyone asks about me, tell them we spoke after the funeral. Tell them that my mother is sick, and I was returning home to France to care for her. Hopefully they won't come looking for me. If they do . . . well, I can't think about that.'

'All right. Don't worry, I'll make sure they know. You can trust me.'

'I should go.'

They both stood and embraced.

'Zoe, are you sure you'll be safe?' Annabel

said, as they headed toward the door.

Zoe stopped and gave Annabel a wan smile. 'No,' she said. 'I'm not sure I will ever be safe. You, either. So take care of yourself, Annabel. We both have powerful enemies now.'

Annabel lingered at the door, reluctant to let Zoe go. But Zoe needed to leave Geneva, and the sooner, the better. She had taken a risk by coming here, Annabel knew, and she was grateful for it. Before tonight, Annabel felt as though she was staring at a large jumble of puzzle pieces, none of which fit together.

After Zoe left, Annabel went out onto the veranda. She peered out over the balcony at the street below. She saw Zoe emerge from the building's lobby and hurry down the block. She was dressed all in black, and her slender form was barely visible as it slipped in and out of the shadows.

Zoe darted across the street and then alighted into a dark SUV parked just at the corner. A moment later, its headlights went on and it pulled away from the curb. Annabel was about to turn away, when she noticed the lights of a second car, a hundred meters back, turn on its lights and pull into the street. She watched as it followed the SUV, creeping slowly down the emptied street like a predator stalking its prey.

Marina

We are running out of time. The company I work for is aware there is a leak.

Marina was pulling up to Duncan's house when the email lit up her phone. She turned off the engine and chewed her lip, debating how to respond. On one hand, she wanted her source to know that she was working with Owen, who was far more tech savvy and had experience with large-scale, global investigations. He had already set up a secure channel for them to receive more data. He had access to a computer capable of handling a vast inflow of information. Without his help, there would be no way for Marina to effectively sort through the data that her source claimed to have access to.

She was worried, though, that the mention of a colleague would spook her source. It was an understandable concern. The fewer people involved, the safer they would be. Clearly Duncan had not been able to keep his investigation under wraps; otherwise he'd still be alive. Every new person who gained access to their information was a potential leak. And a potential leak in an investigation like this was a risk they couldn't afford to take.

Marina had no way to prove to her source that Owen Barry was trustworthy. She wasn't entirely sure why she trusted him. He wasn't exactly the type she'd set up with a friend. He had never had a sustained relationship with any woman as far as Marina could tell, and she knew a few who hated his guts. He was a true adrenaline junkie, the kind of guy who thought it would be fun to sneak into North Korea just because he could, and that made him inherently unpredictable. He had run afoul of enough rules and regulations to get himself either fired or arrested several times over. In fact, Marina had heard rumors that he had been fired from the *Wall Street Journal*, despite the array of awards he'd accumulated while working there. The editor in chief didn't trust him anymore, people said. He had bailed Owen Barry out one too many times. He was more trouble than he was worth.

But Marina had worked with Owen over enough years to know that Owen's integrity when it came to a story was unimpeachable. He could not be bought or swayed or corrupted, and he would die before revealing the identity of a source. He was a journalist's journalist. To Owen Barry, truth was everything.

I have a colleague who can help us, Marina typed.

He can create a multi-level security database and has the technical ability to sort through vast quantities of data quickly. He's done this before for investigations of this scale. His name is Owen Barry; he worked for the *Wall Street Journal* for many years and now is the head of a website called the *Deliverable*. I have worked with him before and I trust him.

137

Marina hit send and waited. Her car was cold and her breath was visible. She rubbed her hands together to keep them warm. Seconds ticked by, then minutes. If the source got spooked, he might evaporate, disappearing like a ghost. He might go to another journalist; he might go underground. She hoped she had not made a vital mistake.

With your life?

Yes, she replied. I trust Owen with my life.

All right. Are you ready to receive the data? There's a lot. More than a terabyte.

We are ready.

You will begin to receive it in the next few hours. Have you been able to determine who Duncan Sander spoke to before his death? We must be very careful not to make the same mistake that he did.

Working on it now, Marina wrote. And trust me, we will not. We both know the stakes here. She thought about Matthew Werner. She couldn't shake the feeling that he was somehow a part of this. It seemed too coincidental to her that he had died the same day as Duncan, especially in a plane crash with a high-profile client of the biggest bank in Switzerland, and of Schmit & Muller's. Someone at Schmit & Muller had been looking for a mole. What if they thought it was Matthew Werner?

Marina thought better than to ask the source. She didn't want him to feel as though she was trying to figure out who — and where — he was. She would have to research Matthew's death on her own. She made a mental note to do it later that evening.

The sooner this information is public, the better off we will be.

Agreed. We are on it.

Stay safe.

You, too.

A rap on Marina's window startled her. Marina looked up; a young guy in a Somerset County Police Department jacket was peering at her through the glass.

Marina rolled down the car window.

'Marina?' he asked, with a tentative grin.

Marina smiled back. Though she hadn't seen Miles Leonard since middle school, she recognized him immediately. His thatch of red hair had mellowed to a strawberry blond over the years, and he had grown from a skinny, gangly kid into an imposing man with broad shoulders and a bit of a belly. He had the same warm smile and light blue eyes that she remembered from her days at Lakeville Elementary. For a time, Miles and Marina had lived across the street from each other. His mother, Sandra Leonard, drove Marina to and from school twice a week, when Marina's mother was at work. As she looked up at Miles's face, Marina remembered the scent of his mother's vanilla perfume and the taste of the peanut butter cookies they would eat in the back of the car on the way home from school. The summer before they were supposed to enter the sixth grade, Sandra filed for divorce from Miles's father. Miles moved with her to Somerset, just a few towns over, where Sandra took a job as a secretary at the local precinct. Thanks to Facebook, Marina knew Miles was a newly minted detective in Somerset County. It never occurred to her that they would ever see each other again or that he would one day help her as he was about to now.

'Miles Leonard,' she said. 'My God. It's been years.'

'About twenty.' Miles laughed. He opened the door, and Marina stepped out of the car. He extended his hand, but Marina hugged him instead.

'Thank you for calling me back,' she said. 'And for meeting me here. I know this isn't exactly protocol.'

Miles shrugged. 'I think you might be able to help me. I'm the only one around here who seems to think this wasn't just a random break-in gone wrong.'

'That seems to be the prevailing theory.'

Miles cleared his throat. 'Listen, Marina,' he said in a low voice. 'Everything we talk about now is off the record, right?'

'Of course. You have my word.'

Miles nodded. 'Chief Dobbs wants this case wrapped up. This isn't the kind of community where people get murdered, you know? Hell, before the burglaries started, no one even locked their doors. People leave their keys in the car when they go into town. You remember. You grew up around here.'

'Somerset is a quiet place,' Marina agreed. 'It's one of the things Duncan loved about it. Any leads on the burglaries?'

'Nope. This case doesn't fit that profile, but Dobbs keeps insisting it's the same guys.'

'Why, do you think?'

Miles shook his head. 'Not sure. Maybe he doesn't want the town to go crazy thinking there's now a killer on the loose. People are nervous enough.'

'So why doesn't it fit the profile?'

'I'll show you.' Miles gestured for her to follow him up to the house. The front door was still sealed with yellow tape reading 'Crime Scene — Do Not Cross.' Miles walked up the steps to a side door and ushered Marina into the kitchen.

She stepped inside. Everything was as she remembered it: the large aproned farmhouse sink, still filled with dishes. The blue-and-white-tiled backsplash behind the stove and the upholstered breakfast nook and the quaint, exposed beams running lengthwise across the ceiling. This house had been Duncan's sanctuary. He had restored it lovingly, making it both stylish and homey. In the months leading up to his death, he had all but relocated here, returning to the city only when absolutely necessary.

A pile of mail sat on the counter, and the coffeepot was half full. It was as though Duncan had just stepped out to run an errand. Only the air felt strange. It was cold in the house, too cold for habitation. Marina shivered and buttoned up the collar of her coat.

She had been to crime scenes before, some quite gruesome. But this was the first one involving a friend. Owen had offered to take the lead on investigating Duncan's death, but Marina had insisted. She didn't like the implicit suggestion that she wasn't able to control her emotions. After all, they had both been close to Duncan. Just because she was a woman didn't mean she was any less capable of handling a violent crime scene, she said. Anyway, she was the one with the connection at the Somerset Police Department. Owen's time was better spent setting up a secure database. That was something Marina couldn't do. So off she went to Connecticut while he focused on the data they'd already been given. They planned to reconvene the following morning to compare notes.

'You okay?' Miles asked.

'Fine,' Marina replied. 'Sorry. It's just — I was here last month.'

Miles nodded. He understood.

'Where was he? When he died, I mean.'

'In his office. I'll show you. Don't touch anything.' They walked down the hall, through the living room. Miles ducked beneath more crime scene tape and held it up for Marina to do the same. Marina stared at Duncan's desk and the chair, which lay on the floor behind it.

'It looks like the killer let himself in through those doors there.' Miles pointed to French doors leading out to the patio. 'They were locked, but he picked them. Very skillfully, I might add. Then he walked here' — Miles strode across the room to an alarm touch pad — 'and entered the code. Or I assume he must have, because the alarm system was off when we found the body. The neighbor said the vic — I'm sorry, Mr. Sander — was a little paranoid about security. She said he turned it on every time he left the house. The housekeeper confirmed that.'

Marina nodded. 'He was,' she said. 'Especially lately.'

'So the killer — or killers — disarmed the security system and waited for Mr. Sander to return home. He was patient about it, because Duncan entered through the kitchen with groceries, unloaded them, and made himself a sandwich. Then he came in here and sat down at his desk.'

Marina wasn't listening. She was staring at a burst of dark red on the wall behind the desk. It was Duncan's blood, she realized. It was splattered all over the wall, the floor, the chair, the desk. The body itself was gone, of course, and it seemed as though someone had cleaned up most of the gore that came with it: the bits of brain and skull and skin that had, no doubt, exploded upon impact. But the stains remained, as did a neat hole where the bullet had lodged itself after tearing straight through Duncan's head. Marina swallowed hard.

'The bullet was removed from the wall,' Miles said. 'It was a clean shot, judging from the height of it, straight between the eyes. I'm guessing a .45 caliber.'

'Professional?'

'That would be my guess. I'm assuming he hid there' — Miles pointed at an open closet door — 'and when Duncan was sitting at the desk, he came out and shot him. It's about eight feet from the desk, so a less assured shooter would have gone for a body shot first, then moved in for a head shot. But here, there was only one shot and it was a bull's-eye.'

Marina grimaced.

'The neighbor was home and she didn't hear a thing, so I assume he used a silencer,' Miles added.

'Did she see anything unusual? Any cars out front, that kind of thing?'

Miles shook his head. 'Not that evening. But she did say she'd seen a bright blue sedan circle the block a few times earlier that day. She claims to be a birdwatcher, but I think she actually likes to spy on her neighbors. She's older. I think she's basically homebound.'

'Did she happen to get a make or model?'

'She said it was a boxy-looking car, maybe a Kia. She got a partial plate.'

'Have you run it?'

'She got only the last three numbers: 434. Said it was a yellow plate. New York, maybe.'

'Or Maine. Was anything taken?'

'Not sure. You knew Duncan. Anything leap out at you as missing?'

Marina surveyed the room. Bookshelves held Duncan's collection of first editions, some quite valuable. There was an antique gold clock on the mantelpiece and several rare maps on the walls. She stepped forward toward the desk. 'May I?' she said.

Miles fumbled in his pocket and pulled out a pair of latex gloves. 'Put these on.'

Marina pulled on the gloves. She was careful to avoid the bloodstains on the carpet as she made her way over to the desk.

'Did you find his computer?' she asked, examining the desktop. There was nothing on it except for a leather cup of pens and a box of paper clips.

'No.'

'He had a computer up here. Also, he liked to handwrite notes on legal pads.'

'There are some blank ones in the top drawer.'

Marina shook her head. 'Look here,' she said, pointing to a small but crisp L-shaped bloodstain on the desktop. Miles joined her, stooping to get a close look. 'See that? It looks like blood splattered on a notepad. Or something with a corner, anyway. A book, maybe.'

Marina squatted down beside the chair. She pointed to a pen on the floor. 'Maybe this dropped when he was shot. So that means he was taking notes. But the notepad on the desk was gone.'

'It could have been there before.'

'No. Duncan was a neat freak about his office.'

Marina pointed to a pair of loafers, neatly lined up by the door. 'He didn't wear shoes in here. And look at the books. Organized by genre, and then alphabetically. He wouldn't have left a stray pen on the floor, especially on such an expensive rug. He was writing when he died.'

'You'd be a good detective.' Miles nodded approvingly.

'I just happen to know a lot about this particular victim.' Marina pulled open the top desk drawer. Behind the stack of blank legal pads, she saw what she was looking for. A small, navy blue leather-bound diary. She pulled it out and held it up. In the lower right-hand corner, Duncan's monogram, *DST*, was embossed in gold.

'He used this for everything. All his appointments. Notes on interviews,' she said. 'I used to buy him a new one every year. His Christmas gift.'

Miles's eyes lit up. He reached for the planner. 'I assumed his calendar was on his computer.'

'No. Duncan was something of a technophobe. Always thought he was going to get his identity stolen or something.' *Or hacked*, she thought to herself. Now that she knew what Duncan had been working on, his obsessive concern about phone taps and email surveillance seemed justified.

'Do you know a Hunter Morse?' Miles asked. He pointed to a page in Duncan's diary. 'He had a call with him right before he died and was supposed to meet him in DC the next day. Look, he underlined his name twice.'

Marina frowned. 'Doesn't ring a bell.'

'Was he working on a story? I thought he was on a sabbatical. That's what the nosy neighbor told me, anyway.'

'He was technically on leave from *Press*. But Duncan was always working on a story.'

'Do you know what this one was about?'

Marina hesitated. On one hand, Miles had been completely forthcoming with her. He'd even let her see the crime scene. And the more people looking for Duncan's killer, the more likely they were to catch a break.

But Marina didn't like the sound of Chief Dobbs, Miles's boss. It didn't make sense to her that he would be lumping Duncan's murder in with the recent slew of break-ins, unless he was either exceedingly lazy or attempting to cover up something. Miles might trust him, but Marina didn't.

Anyway, Marina didn't want anything to happen to Miles. He was just a local detective. This whole investigation was way above his pay grade. If Miles started poking around an offshore bank like CIB or Swiss United, he would most likely end up with a bullet between the eyes, just like Duncan.

'I don't know. I can ask around. But listen, Duncan had a lot of enemies. He wrote stories that pissed people off. Off the top of my head, I could come up with a page-long list of people that might have wanted him dead.'

Miles sighed. 'Yeah, I figured as much. The nosy neighbor hated him, too, by the way. Said on sunny days, he liked to read the paper on the porch in his underpants.'

'How would she know?' Marina laughed.

'Told you. She's a 'birdwatcher,'' Miles said, using air quotes.

'Talk to her again. Maybe she'll remember some more details about that night. Or the Kia.'

Miles nodded. 'On my list.'

'And let me see what I can find out about Hunter Morse.'

'Sounds good. Let me know.' He checked his watch. 'Listen, I should head back to the station.'

'Thanks, Miles. I really appreciate your help.'

'Likewise. Let's stay in touch, all right?'

Marina followed Miles out of the house and onto the driveway. The temperature had dropped and the sky was a threatening gray. Miles walked Marina to her car.

'Say hi to your mom for me,' Marina said, and reached up to give him a hug.

'Will do. How are your parents doing?'

'Okay. Getting older.'

Miles smiled. 'Send them my best. They're good folks.'

'The best,' Marina agreed. She watched as Miles loped off toward his pickup. She let him pull out of the driveway first. He turned to wave one last time before making a left onto Walnut Street.

Marina eased out of the driveway. Across the street, three houses down, she noticed a dark sedan parked by the side of the road. She turned right, driving as slowly as she could so that she could scope out the neighbor's property. It was an old Victorian house, with a widow's walk and wraparound porches. In the front window, she thought she saw the figure of a woman through gauzy white curtains.

She sped up after passing the house. She shot a glance at the sedan. In the front seat was a man in a Red Sox cap, reading a paper. When she reached the end of Walnut Street, she clicked on her blinker. The sedan, she noticed, was gone.

It wasn't until she reached the highway exit that Marina saw the sedan again. It was two cars behind her, waiting at a red light. The driver's baseball cap was unmistakable, as was the gold casing around the license plate. Marina sat up tall, trying to read the plate number in the rearview mirror. A New York plate, starting with *FBY*. Marina turned around, trying to catch the last few digits, but the light turned green and the driver behind her leaned on his horn.

As she pulled onto Route 44, the sedan followed suit. It remained two or three cars behind her, but Marina knew she was being followed. Her heart began to pound in her chest. When she saw the exit for Lakeville approaching on the left, she shifted into the right lane. The sedan did the same. She revved her engine as though she was going to fly by the exit, but instead she made a sharp left, cutting past two rows of traffic. An SUV honked angrily at her as it slammed on its brakes. Marina sailed past it, barely making the exit, and the sedan continued down the freeway. As she pulled up to the light at the end of the turnoff, she closed her eyes and took a deep breath. A close call, but there was no one behind her. The sedan was gone.

Ten minutes later, Marina pulled into her

parents' driveway. She hadn't planned on visiting them, and she didn't really have time to do so now. But at least she had lost her tail for the time being.

Marina hadn't seen Richard and Alice since her engagement party. She kept saying she'd visit, but between the wedding plans and her job and the social demands of the Ellis family, Marina felt as though she never had a minute's rest. She half-heartedly invited them into the city for various events — the Ellis Foundation's annual gala, *The Nutcracker* at the New York City Ballet — but she knew that they'd never come. Her parents hated the city. Ever since her father's stroke, they had been less mobile than ever. As she walked to the front door, she noticed, with sadness, how their once manicured hedgerow looked decrepit, and the jaunty Persian blue paint that her mother so loved was peeling from the front door. Richard Tourneau was a man who prided himself on self-sufficiency. He hardly ever hired a handyman. The garage was filled with tools and paint and lawn equipment and fertilizer. Marina knew how much it must've bothered him to see the ragged edges of the hedgerow, the bare patches of dirt at the borders of the lawn. His health must have declined since she'd seen him last.

The joyous barking of her parents' dog cheered her, though, and when her mother opened the door, the look on her face was one of sheer delight.

'Richard!' her mother shouted into the house. 'Guess who's here!'

Marina's smile faded as her father appeared in the doorway. He was seated in a wheelchair, his left leg bound in a cast, and what appeared to be a nasty gash on his cheek was covered by surgical tape.

'Dad,' Marina gasped. 'What happened?'

Her father waved her off. 'Oh, nothing. It was silly. Come here! It's so good to see you.'

'He fell in the shower,' Alice said. 'Thank God I was home.'

'Is your leg broken? Oh, Dad. How do you get upstairs to the bedroom?'

'We're sleeping in the den for now. It's fine. It's quite comfortable, really. And the morning light is lovely.'

'Why didn't you call me?'

'Because you were in Paris, dear. We weren't going to interrupt your trip. And then everything that happened with Duncan — '

'He could have hit his head or — '

'Well, he didn't. Will you look at Henry? He's so happy to see you. He's such a good dog, Marina. After Tucker died, I never thought we'd adopt another dog, but this guy has really stolen my heart. Are you hungry? I can make lunch. Or maybe you'll stay for dinner?'

'I can't stay. I was just in Somerset and thought I'd come by and say hi.'

Marina noticed her parents exchange looks of disappointment. In the car, she had thought that a short visit was better than no visit at all. Perhaps that was a mistake. At least she'd shaken the sedan that had been trailing her. For that reason alone, the visit home had been worthwhile.

'Well, you're here now,' Alice said. 'So tell us — what were you doing in Somerset? Looking at wedding venues? They have that beautiful old estate over there — what's it called, Richard? The Snowden House?'

'Why would she get married in Somerset?' Richard shifted uncomfortably in his wheelchair. 'Lakeville's prettier. If you're going to do a Connecticut wedding, why not right here at home?'

'At our house!' Alice exclaimed. 'Oh, Richard, we can't handle that kind of event here. The Ellises must have a million friends! I'm certain this is not what they were thinking for the wedding of their oldest son.'

'Not *here*, Alice. Just in Lakeville. The Interlochen Inn is nice. Or what about at Hotchkiss? That would be great. I can talk to the dean about it tomorrow.'

'The chapel *is* lovely,' Alice agreed. 'Where would the reception be? The Boathouse, maybe? Or — '

'You guys.' Marina's parents looked up, as though they had forgotten she was there. 'It's already decided. We're getting married at the Ellises' house in Southampton.'

The silence was brief but deadening.

'I see,' Alice said finally, her voice prim. Marina knew exactly what she was thinking: *In my day, it was the bride's family who hosted the wedding.* 'Have you picked a date?'

'Well, originally we were thinking this summer, but I think the summer following is probably more realistic.'

'What?' her parents exclaimed together.

'Marina! That's nearly two years away!'

'A long engagement isn't healthy, Marina,' Alice chided. 'Your father and I were engaged for eight months and it was far too long, in my opinion.'

'Is one of you having cold feet? What is this about?' Richard peered at her over the top of his reading glasses.

'There's still ample time to get married this summer, dear. We'd have to get started now, of course, but — '

'Stop!' Marina took a deep breath. 'It's not cold feet or anything like that. It's just . . . ' She trailed off for a moment. She hadn't wanted to go down this rabbit hole with her parents, but it seemed inevitable now. 'Grant's father is running for office,' she said finally. 'He's going to declare his candidacy soon. And if he wins the Democratic nomination — '

'For *president*?' Alice looked aghast.

'Yes, Mother. For president.'

'But, but — he's a developer! He's a billionaire! I heard rumors, of course, but I really didn't think he would go through with it. Why on earth — '

'Because he's a smart man and he's not in the pocket of special interests. He's consulted a number of advisors and there's a lot of momentum behind him at this point. Frankly, everyone he's talked to thinks he has a decent shot to win.'

For a moment, they all stared at the floor. Marina knew her parents loved Grant. How could they not? He was articulate, thoughtful, well educated. He doted on her. He was everything one could hope for in a son-in-law. His parents, however, were another story. Her parents had never said one negative word about the Ellises. But she knew Richard and Alice, and Richard and Alice were not fans of showy people. And the Ellises, tasteful as they were, were about as showy as people could be.

'Are they even really Democrats?' Alice whispered. To be anything but was, in Alice's book, a great failing of character.

'Yes, they're really Democrats. Look, I didn't come here to fight with you. Certainly not about politics. Or the wedding.'

'Of course not.' Alice ran a hand through her sensibly short silver hair. 'I'm sorry. Let's go sit in the den. Your father is more comfortable in his armchair.'

After they were settled — Marina on the old tweed sofa with a Hotchkiss blanket over her lap, her father in front of the fire with his leg propped up on an ottoman — her mother bustled off into the kitchen to fetch a snack. Whenever Marina came home, Alice saw to it that she ate. Alice always clucked disapprovingly that Marina was 'wasting away' or that she 'looked thinner than usual' at least once during every visit. Marina was surprised she hadn't said something yet. Ever since Duncan's death, she had lost her appetite. Her jeans hung loose on her frame; her cheekbones were razor-sharp. For the first time in her life, Marina had lost weight without trying at all.

'Here we are,' Alice said, bearing a platter of brownies. 'Just a little something. You're looking awfully skinny for someone who was just in Paris.'

'I was only there for a few days.'

'Honey, we're so sorry about Duncan Sander's passing,' her father said. 'I know you two were close. That must've been very hard to hear.'

'Tragic story.' Alice shook her head. 'One of several break-ins in the area, you know. We've never locked the door before, but we do now. Can't be too careful these days.'

'Did you go to the funeral, sweetheart?'

'Yes, of course. I cut the trip short so I could be there.'

'Was everyone from the magazine there?'

'Yes, everyone.'

'Was Duncan still working there? I didn't realize that. For some reason I thought he'd left.'

'He was on a sabbatical.'

'I remember chatting with him at your engagement party,' Alice said. 'Remember that, Richard? What was that story he said he was working on?'

'I don't know. I think he'd been overserved.'

'Well, that's not a nice thing to say,' Alice reprimanded.

Richard sighed. 'I'm just being honest. I never liked the guy. I didn't like the way he treated Marina. The way he treated anyone, really. He was very entitled.'

'He was a great mentor and a terrific journalist, Dad.'

'Well, I thought he was very rude at your engagement party.'

Marina frowned. She was aware of her father's dislike for Duncan Sander, but she didn't really feel like discussing it now that he was dead. 'What did he do at my engagement party?' She did vaguely remember a scene toward the end

155

that resulted in James Ellis calling Duncan a cab.

'He was drunk as a skunk!' Richard said, his eyes wide. 'Don't you remember? And he was chewing James Ellis's ear off about Morty Reiss, and how the guy had his money stashed in a Swiss bank, and how he finally was going to prove it.'

Marina tried to contain her surprise. 'Are you sure it was a Swiss bank?' she said carefully. 'Or was he talking about that interview he did six months ago, when he tried to prove that Reiss had his money at a Cayman Islands bank?'

Richard shook his head. 'No, no. He wasn't talking about that interview. Though, good God, you would have thought the man would have stopped drinking after *that*. No. He was saying the money was at a Swiss bank now. It sounded like nonsense, honestly. The Ellises were embarrassed.'

Marina closed her eyes and took a deep breath. *Jesus Christ, Duncan*, she thought to herself. *You were talking about it at my engagement party? Whatever happened to discretion?*

'Are you all right, dear?' Marina blinked her eyes open. Her parents were staring at her, concerned. 'You look tired.'

'I'm sorry. I have a horrible headache. I should probably get on the road soon.'

'You should eat a brownie. Have you eaten anything today?'

Marina stood up. She folded the blanket quickly, draping it over the sofa's arm where she had found it. She was itching to get back to the city and, more important, back to Owen Barry's apartment.

'Thanks, Mom. Maybe I could take some home? I'm sure Grant would love some.'

Alice pursed her lips, disappointed. 'All right. I'll just get a Ziploc from the kitchen. Maybe you could bring him up here for dinner sometime.'

Marina nodded. She leaned in and embraced her mother, for longer than either of them expected. 'I would love that,' she said. She felt the words catch in her throat. 'I really miss you both. It was good to see you.'

'We miss you, too, Marina.'

'Be careful out there, sweetheart,' her father said. 'It gets dark so quickly this time of year. And it's a Saturday night. You never know who's out there on the road.'

You're not kidding, Marina thought to herself. 'I'll be safe, Dad. I promise.'

Annabel

Khalid Nasser stood at the arrivals gate at Heathrow Airport, looking for Annabel. Though it was technically morning, it was still dark outside. Everyone in the airport, Khalid included, looked bleary-eyed and in need of coffee. Annabel's flight was practically empty. As Khalid watched what appeared to be the last of the passengers deplane and head toward the baggage claim, he grew worried. Had Annabel missed her flight? Had she lost her nerve? Or had he misunderstood when she was supposed to arrive? Her phone call the previous night had woken him up, and admittedly, he'd had a few drinks. Several, in fact. He might have still been drunk when he spoke to her. Somehow, he'd managed to understand that he needed to set an alarm before passing out again, so that he could be there to pick her up at the airport. She'd seemed skittish — scared, even. She needed to leave Geneva immediately, she said. She was going to take the next flight out. Could she stay with him? *Of course*, he had said. *I'll pick you up.*

When his alarm had gone off five hours later, he had considered snoozing it for only half a moment before snapping upright, heart racing, head throbbing. He hadn't left himself time for a shower. He'd thrown on track pants and his glasses — no time for contact lenses — and headed to the airport, teeth unbrushed, mass of wavy black hair unkempt. There were few people he would do this for, he thought, as he had pulled onto the M4. Annabel Werner was one of them.

An older woman with a set of monogrammed Louis Vuitton luggage was eyeing him. Khalid was familiar with the look: it was one of suspicious concern, of heightened awareness. He got that look everywhere, but especially at the airport. When he was traveling on business, he made a point to wear one of his Savile Row suits and to comb his hair neatly to the side, like a proper banker. He booked seats in first class. He was gratuitously courteous to anyone who spoke to him. Otherwise, he kept to himself. This didn't stop the looks — nothing would. But mostly, it kept them shorter.

He ran a hand through his hair, trying to tame it a little. The woman was considering reporting him, he could tell. There was a sign overhead about suspicious packages. 'If You See Something, Say Something,' it read. She was looking around for a security guard. He regretted the decision to wear his 'Bad and Boujee' sweatshirt, which a friend had gotten him as a gag gift when he took the gig at Goldman Sachs. He thought it might make Annabel laugh, and God knew she needed to laugh right now. But in retrospect, he could see how a six-feet-three, unshaven Syrian guy in a hoodie at the airport might set a granny on edge.

'Annabel?' Khalid saw her just as she was about to walk into the baggage claim. In jeans and a backpack, she looked so young that he hardly recognized her. When they had first met, back in New York, he'd found her stunning. Back then, she wore her hair cropped in a pixie, a cut that ordinarily he didn't care for on women but found sultry on Annabel. It showed off her delicate neck, her large, watchful eyes with their incredible fringe of dark lashes, which she highlighted with smudged, kohl-black eyeliner. Even on the weekend, she wore cool, streamlined clothes that were never overtly sexy. Khalid had been impressed — and yes, jealous — that his college buddy had done so well for himself. Mostly, though, he was happy that he would never have to suffer through another dinner with one of Matthew's dull country club girlfriends. The woman Matthew had dated seriously before Annabel — Kelly, was it? Casey? Khalid could hardly remember — was an interior decorator who lived at home with her mother on the Upper East Side. If Matthew had married her, it was only a matter of time before he was out in Darien carpooling his three kids to their tennis lessons on the weekends. Khalid would never hear from him again.

Annabel turned, her ponytail flying over one shoulder, and her face lit up with relief.

'Khalid! Thank God.' Annabel ran to him and buried her head into his chest. Khalid noted, with satisfaction, that the suspicious woman had witnessed the whole encounter. He smiled at her over the top of Annabel's head. She looked away, pretending she hadn't been staring at him.

'You didn't have to come pick me up,' Annabel said.

'I figured you wouldn't take such a bloody early flight if it wasn't important.'

'I'm sorry. I know I'm asking a lot of you.'

'Annabel.' Khalid shook his head. 'I'd do anything for you. You know that. And God, I'm so sorry. There's really nothing I can say. It's horrible, what happened. Heartbreaking.'

'You're kind. Matthew loved you. Even though we hadn't seen you in a while, I know he considered you one of his closest friends.'

'Likewise.' Khalid gave her a squeeze around the shoulders. 'Check anything?' He nodded his head toward the baggage carousel.

Annabel tapped her backpack. 'This is it.'

Khalid nodded. He had a lot of questions, but he figured they could wait until they were home. He would need coffee first. He imagined she would, too.

★   ★   ★

Khalid lived in an oversize loft off Brick Lane in Shoreditch, an artsy, edgy neighborhood in London's East End. His building was once a warehouse that was now primarily used as live/work studios for artists. Khalid was the only suit in his building and he liked it that way. He liked having interesting neighbors. George, the celebrity tattoo artist, who occasionally supplied him with shatter, an intense weed concentrate that blew his socks off. Natalia, the leggy model who Khalid guessed moonlighted as an escort between gigs. He liked the Brick Lane bars and the street art and the pop-ups, which nestled themselves in railway arches and old warehouses, and the galleries that all kept their doors open late on the first Thursday of every month. Sure, the neighborhood was gentrifying, and this was both good and bad. There were a lot of man-buns now and over-priced coffee and girls with blown-out hair on their way to lunch at Soho House. But to Khalid, Shoreditch still felt alive and humming, a swatch of color in a mostly black-and-white city. It was where he felt most at home.

Brick Lane was also a nice counterpoint to what Khalid saw as his daylight life. He was a tech geek who had, for the moment, sold out to Goldman Sachs. Technically, Khalid was a freelance programmer. He occasionally took on finite and highly lucrative gigs at banks and law firms to help them beef up their cyber security. Then he would take off several months and travel. This gig at Goldman, though, had gone on for two years and had no foreseeable end in sight. Khalid didn't particularly mind, since the pay was so good. But the idea of working for a big bank in perpetuity chafed on him, and he was beginning to feel restless. Annabel's arrival gave him a nice excuse to call in sick, a break he sorely needed.

'There's only one bedroom,' he said apologetically when they arrived at his flat. 'But you take it. I'm happy enough on the couch.'

'Oh, no, I couldn't,' Annabel said. 'Please. I'm sorry to drop in on you like this. To be honest, I didn't feel safe in a hotel. And I didn't know who else to go to in London.'

Khalid bit his lip. He knew she'd reveal everything soon enough. He took her backpack and coat from her and tucked them away in the coat closet. 'Don't apologize to me. And you are staying in the bedroom.' Before she could persist, he asked, 'Do you want coffee? A shower? A nap?'

'All three?' Annabel laughed.

'Which one first?'

'Coffee. And maybe a quick shower. And then let's talk.'

Khalid nodded. He pointed toward the bedroom. 'Back there. There should be fresh towels. I'll get some breakfast going. I only know how to scramble eggs and toast bread, so if you want anything else, we'll need to go out.'

'Eggs are perfect,' Annabel said. 'Thank you. For everything.'

'Don't thank me. It's good to see your face, old friend.'

★　★　★

A half hour later, Annabel sat at Khalid's kitchen counter, sipping coffee and shoveling eggs into her mouth as quickly as she could move the fork. Khalid tried not to stare — it seemed as though she hadn't eaten in weeks — but instead refilled her mug and kept busy cleaning up the kitchen. Her auburn hair was damp from the shower, and her lovely, delicate face was free of makeup. She was exhausted: Khalid could tell from her eyes. And she'd lost weight, if that was physically possible. But other than that, she looked as beautiful as he remembered. Her hair was longer now, and she had a few lines on her forehead, but she was the same Annabel from his days in New York.

'I'm sorry I didn't call you about the service,' she said, finally. 'I should have. It all happened so fast. The firm arranged it.'

Khalid waved her off. 'I can't imagine what you've been through. I called you when I heard, a few times, actually. But a fellow named Julian answered the phone. I wasn't sure the messages got to you.'

'He told me. You were kind to call. Thank you. It was all just so overwhelming. I shut down, I think. I'm still shut down.'

'Of course.'

'Did you know he was here before he died? In London?'

Khalid turned on the water in the sink and began scrubbing the egg pan. 'Yes, I think I heard that,' he said, not looking at her. In truth, he had heard a good deal more. The London tabloids had reported that Matthew had been staying at the home of Fatima Amir, a well-known hedge fund mogul, and that he had died aboard her private plane. The papers hadn't gone so far as to say they were having an affair, but they certainly had suggested it. Khalid didn't want to believe it. He knew Matthew, and he knew the way Matthew felt about Annabel. Or at least, he knew the way Matthew had felt about Annabel years ago, when they were all in the same city. But even he had to admit that Fatima Amir was sensationally beautiful, and that the

164

one photo that had emerged of the two together — huddled over a candlelit dinner at a restaurant in Soho — made them look like more than banker and client. He wondered if Annabel had seen that photo. He hoped she hadn't.

'His client lived here. Fatima Amir. Have you heard of her?'

Khalid nodded. 'She's Syrian. Syrians in London are like New Yorkers in Geneva. We all mostly know one another. She grew up in Saint John's Wood, too. Not far from my parents.'

'Matthew was her banker. Or so they tell me. I'd never heard of her before . . . ' She trailed off.

'She ran a hedge fund, no?'

'Yes. Apparently she was quite successful. Matthew left some things at her house. I wanted to retrieve them myself. Now that I'm here, though, I'm not sure I can handle it.'

'I can do that for you.'

Annabel gave him a weary smile. 'Thank you. Maybe. Let me think about it. I have something else that I need you to help me with. Am I officially the most annoying houseguest you've ever had?'

'You're the best, actually. And look, I'm charging you a thousand pounds a night, so you should get your money's worth.'

Annabel laughed. She glanced around his loft. 'I hope that's the friends-and-family rate.'

'Of course. This is a posh area, despite what my mother thinks.'

'Are your parents still in Saint John's Wood?'

'Yes.'

'Did you know the Amirs? Personally, I mean?'

'No, not personally. But I know who they are.' Khalid paused. He could sense where this conversation was going, and it made him nervous. The Amirs — and particularly their cousins, the Assads — were not people to be trifled with. From everything he had heard, Fatima Amir was a legitimate financier. But when he read that Matthew was her personal banker, alarm bells had gone off. Any business with a family like that was dangerous business.

'Swiss United does the banking for the whole family. They have billions of dollars stashed in offshore accounts.'

Khalid couldn't conceal his surprise. 'Do you mean Fatima? Or her cousins?'

'Both.'

'But the cousins — the Assads — are on sanctions lists. Goldman wouldn't touch their money with a ten-foot pole. And don't get me wrong. Goldman does business with some shady characters. But not like that. Bashar al-Assad is a dictator. A war criminal. It's illegal to do business with a man like that. Not to mention, immoral as hell.'

'I know. And Jonas, Matthew's boss, is his private banker.'

Khalid let out a low whistle. For a moment, they were both silent. 'I hope this isn't out of line,' Khalid said slowly. 'If it is, tell me to shut the hell up. But was there an investigation into Matthew's death?'

'There was. It was an accident. Or so they tell me. Something about an ice protection system.'

'They found the black box?'

166

'So they say.'

'But you have your doubts.' He studied her face. She looked up at him, her green eyes meeting his.

'Yes,' she said, her voice a whisper. 'Wouldn't you?'

Khalid hesitated. 'I would.'

'I went to meet with the agent in charge of the investigation. Agent Bloch at Fedpol. He gave me photographs of the crash site. Or, at least, he told me it was the crash site. But it wasn't Fatima's plane.'

'What do you mean, it wasn't her plane?'

'The photographs were of a different plane. A Dutch plane that crashed a year earlier.'

'How did you figure that out?'

'I did some research. Everything they told me about the crash — the failure of the ice protection system, the location of the crash, everything — it lines up exactly with this crash from last year. It's either a very eerie coincidence or they are lying to me.'

'But why? Why would a Fedpol agent lie to you?'

'I imagine someone paid him off. He wanted me to believe that the crash was an accident. So he showed me the black box data and the photographs from another crash, which was an accident, and hoped I didn't ask any more questions.'

Khalid nodded slowly, considering this. 'Who do you think paid him off?'

'Fatima, allegedly, was trying to cut ties with her family.'

'So you think they had her killed?'

'Maybe. Or maybe it was Matthew who was murdered, and she just happened to be with him.'

'Why would anyone murder Matthew?'

Annabel closed her eyes and took a breath. 'You must promise this stays between us. I've told no one but you.'

'Of course.'

'Someone Matthew worked with told me she thought Matthew was cooperating with someone at the US Department of Justice. That he was a whistle-blower. A mole.'

'Oh God.'

'She didn't know for sure. But he was in contact with someone at the DOJ. He even flew to the States to meet him. And then his plane went down a few weeks later.'

'Do you have access to his email?'

Annabel shook her head. 'No. But I have his laptop. It's encrypted, though.'

Khalid smiled. 'Well, I can help you with that. That's kind of my thing, you know. Not to brag or anything, but I'm really quite good at it. I imagine I'm better than whoever they've got over there at Swiss United, anyway.'

'That's what I hoped.'

'The bank didn't come looking for it?'

'His colleague — the one who told me he was cooperating with the Feds — she said he asked her to hide this one. She gave it to me. That's why I flew here this morning. It's only a matter of time before they come looking for it.'

Khalid rubbed his hands together. His eyes gleamed with excitement. 'Well, before they do, let's find out what's on it.'

* ★ ★ ★

Across the river Thames, Thomas Jensen sat in his office at MI6 headquarters, folding a stack of his monogrammed handkerchiefs neatly into squares. Though Jensen detested the exterior of the building, which, in his opinion, looked like a stack of giant Legos, he did enjoy the view from his desk. On clear mornings, he liked to watch the sculls gliding silently beneath the Hammersmith Bridge. Jensen himself had rowed for Oxford some years ago. Indeed, he'd captained the team to victory at Henley. These days, he rowed when he could, but it was usually on a machine in some foreign hotel gym, and it wasn't nearly the same as being out on the river. Watching the rowers on the Thames felt nostalgic and meditative, and he liked to do so in silence for a few minutes before attending to the business of the day.

This morning, it was not to be. His phone rang just as his assistant, Letty, was placing his espresso on his desk. He had arrived the previous evening from Baghdad, and his head was still swimming from too many nights of travel with little sleep. When he saw who was calling, however, he snapped up the phone immediately. Letty, who had been with Jensen for more years than either of them cared to count, was well trained in the art of making a quick and graceful exit. One had to be to work for a man like Thomas Jensen. She scurried to the door and closed it behind her.

'Jensen here.' He took a deep draught from the

espresso and braced himself for more bad news.

'Annabel Werner is in London,' said the voice on the other end. 'She arrived this morning. She appears to be staying with a friend in Shoreditch.'

'That's interesting,' Jensen said, because it was.

'It's a problem, I think. What happens if she starts poking around, asking questions?'

'Perhaps she's here to collect his things. He left some personal effects at the Amir house.'

'I thought Bloch was supposed to return those to her.'

'She declined, apparently. Said she'd come get them herself.'

'That's not good. Not good at all. This is the last thing we need, Thomas. We're so close to the finish line. We can't have Annabel Werner stirring up the hornet's nest. If she reaches out to a member of the Amir family — '

'She's a grieving widow. It would be natural for her to have questions.'

'She's a liability, is what she is.'

'Perhaps she's simply visiting an old friend.'

'An old friend who happens to be Syrian? I don't like it, Thomas. It doesn't sit right.'

Jensen sighed and drained the last of his espresso. He'd need another to make it through the morning, which was already proving to be something of a train wreck. 'I'll look into it,' he said. 'What's the friend's name?'

'Khalid Nasser. Went to college with Matthew Werner. Works at Goldman Sachs now, doing some sort of security work.'

Jensen scribbled down Khalid's name and next to it wrote *Goldman Sachs* and *Shoreditch*.

'I'll see what I can find out. Leave Annabel Werner to me. You focus on our friend Mr. Morse at the Department of Justice. He's the bigger concern.'

'I'm aware. We've got him under surveillance.'

'We need to move forward soon. The longer this drags on — '

'No one wants this to drag on. But in the meantime, make sure Annabel Werner isn't running around playing Nancy Drew.'

'I understand. She won't. I'll make sure of it.'

And with that, Thomas Jensen hung up the phone. He took his overcoat off the hook by the door and headed out in the direction of Shoreditch.

Marina

At some point during the night, Owen had fallen asleep at the computer. When the intercom buzzed, he heard it through the fog of a dream and didn't budge. But the noise grew louder and more persistent, and eventually he sat up and wiped the drool from the corner of his mouth.

'Fuck,' he said, and dug his thumbs into the sides of his neck, which felt as though it might be permanently crooked from sleeping facedown on his dining room table.

The buzzer blared again. This time it sounded as if someone was leaning on it.

'Coming!' he shouted. 'I'm fucking coming!'

'Good morning to you, too,' Marina said, when he opened the door. She looked fresh-faced, as though she'd just gone for a run in Central Park. Her glossy hair was pulled back into a ponytail, and she wore black spandex pants and a tight-fitting windbreaker that was unzipped just enough to reveal a slice of tank top beneath. Owen tried his best to maintain eye contact.

Marina held out two large coffees. 'Rough night?'

'Long night,' he said, and reached for the coffee before ushering her inside. 'What time is it?'

'It's eight a.m. I was going to come over at seven, but I figured I'd let you sleep a little. Or, you know, bid adieu to any overnight guests.'

172

'Thanks.' Owen yawned. He hadn't been out of bed at eight a.m. on a Sunday in a very long time. He nodded his head in the direction of his bedroom. 'I think she's in the shower.'

'Funny. Do you want me to come back later?'

'No. We have too much work to do. I was up all night and barely scratched the surface.'

Marina glanced around. The window shades were drawn throughout the apartment. Three laptops sat open on the dining room table, and from each, a jumble of cables extended, like a multiheaded medusa. Strewn about were coffee cups, a pizza box, USBs, and stacks of paper. Owen was wearing glasses, which meant he'd spent the better part of the past twenty-four hours staring at a screen. Marina hadn't seen him in glasses since the Darlings investigation eight years earlier. His were thick and slightly off-center on his nose. He looked nerdier in them, but sweeter, too. She wondered why he didn't wear them more often.

'This place looks like a scene from *Snowden*,' she said.

'This is bigger than Snowden. You have no idea.' Owen moved a stack of files off a chair and offered her a place to sit. 'How was Connecticut?'

'Well, for starters, I think I was being followed. There was a sedan lingering around Duncan's house while I was there, and it followed me most of the way home.'

Owen frowned. 'Most?'

'I pulled out into the Lakeville exit and lost him.'

'Make?'

'I think it was a town car. You know, like from a limo company.'

'Did you get a plate?'

'Partial.'

'Give it to me. I'll have a cop friend run it. Speaking of cop friends, what's up with the investigation?'

'Seems like a professional job. Clean shot to the head, .45 with a silencer. Neighbor saw a Kia casing the block earlier in the day, so Miles is going to try to track that down. Duncan's notebooks were missing, as was his laptop.'

'Bet that's the first time the Somerset Police Department has come across a hit man.'

'Well, the chief of police thinks it was just a break-in gone wrong. I think it's a matter of time before he tries to close the case.'

Owen shrugged, unsurprised. 'I'm pretty sure those guys aren't going to be cracking this case, anyway. Did you get the Kia's plate number? I can run that, too.'

'The last digits were 434. A yellow plate, so probably New York. Could also be Maine, maybe? One other interesting thing. I got a peek at Duncan's calendar for the last few weeks. He'd been calling someone at the Department of Justice. Hunter Morse. And then he had it penciled into his calendar to go down to DC. He wrote *Morse* next to it and underlined it.'

'He had an actual calendar? Like a Filofax or something?'

'So do I. Don't judge. I think it's nice. Did you know you retain information twice as well if you write it down by hand? Duncan taught me that. And look, you can't hack into it.' Marina pulled a pink leather day planner from her purse and pushed it across Owen's dining room table.

'What if you lose it?'

'I'd die. But I haven't yet.'

Owen snorted. He pulled Marina's day planner over to his side of the table and inspected it. 'Jesus, who even makes these anymore?' He ran his finger over her initials, *MT*, which were embossed in gold on the lower right-hand corner of the leather cover. 'What happens when you get married? Won't you need to change this? Will it say 'Mrs. Grant Ellis' instead?'

Marina ignored his mocking tone. 'Maybe I won't need one at all,' she shot back. 'Since I won't be working after the wedding. Maybe I'll just have my social secretary give me my schedule every morning. Like Letitia Baldrige and Jackie Kennedy.'

'Touché. You aren't really going to quit though, are you?'

'I really am.'

Owen frowned, suddenly serious. 'You're a good writer. Duncan was grooming you to take over for him. Did you know that? I always thought you should go over to the *Journal*, though.'

'You're not even at the *Journal*!'

'You know what I mean. To a serious news outlet. *Press* is too much of a society magazine for you. You like hard-hitting stories, you always have. I saw the spark in your eye during the Darlings investigation. You loved it. It's in your blood, Marina.'

'You make it sound like I have a disease.'

'You do. I've got it, too. The truth bug. No cure, unfortunately.' Owen locked his hands behind his head and tipped his chair back, looking smug.

'At least we agree that I shouldn't stay at *Press*. I can't imagine the place without Duncan.'

'I can get you a job at the *Deliverable*, if you want. It might be too edgy for you now that you live on Park Avenue.'

Marina shook her head. 'I'm out, Owen. Grant's going to be running the family business soon. We can't both be traveling all the time. Especially not if we're going to start a family. I always knew I was going to quit. I thought I'd wait until after the wedding. But now that Duncan's gone . . . '

'So Papa Ellis is running for president, huh? The rumors are true?'

'He'll announce his candidacy any day now. Don't give me that look.'

'What look? No look.'

'I know you well enough to know when there's a look.'

Owen raised his hands. 'I'm just surprised, that's all. I don't see you as a Park Avenue housewife. That's a compliment, by the way, not a criticism.'

'Well, maybe I'll be a Beltway housewife instead.'

'You've got my vote. He's a Democrat at least, right? Hard to tell with billionaires. Or does he prefer the term 'limousine liberal'?'

'Who's a Democrat?' Marina almost levitated

off her chair when she heard a female voice behind her. She spun around and found herself facing a sultry brunette with olive skin, almond-shaped eyes, and a body that would put a swimsuit model to shame. The woman was barefoot, and her jeans were rolled up at the cuff. Marina couldn't help but notice the intricate mosaic pattern tattooed around her left ankle that seemed to extend up her leg. God knew how far it went.

'I'm Yael,' the woman said, extending her hand. 'You must be Marina.'

Marina nodded and shook her hand. For once in her life, she was speechless.

'You should have woken me up,' Owen said to Yael. 'I was drooling on myself like an asshole.'

Yael laughed. 'You needed the rest.' She had a light accent that Marina thought sounded Israeli, but she couldn't be sure.

'I was joking about the overnight guest,' Marina said.

Owen grinned. 'I know.'

She stood up and started collecting her things. 'I'll go. I'm sorry. I thought we said — '

'Whoa, where are you going? We're here to work. You going to join us?'

Marina glanced at Owen, then at Yael, then back again. She felt dizzy with embarrassment.

'Yael's a programmer,' Owen said. 'I keep trying to hire her, but she's too expensive for me. Anyway, she's going to help us out. And fuck, we're going to need it.'

Marina's embarrassment turned to frustration. 'What? Owen, no. You can't just — May I speak with you? Alone, please?'

Yael gave Owen a wide-eyed 'oh boy' glance.

'Marina, look,' Owen said, 'I understand your hesitation. But I trust Yael. She's the best. And we can't do this alone. Just let me show you what we've been doing and I think you'll understand. Okay?'

Marina hesitated. On one hand, she was furious with Owen for bringing in a partner without asking her first. The source was skittish enough; what if he found out she had a whole team of people looking at his data? He could disappear without so much as a word. He could go to another journalist. Worst of all, he could turn himself in and take his chances with the authorities.

On the other, she knew the volume of data they had to work through was enormous. Every minute they wasted was a minute lost; the sooner this information went public, the better off they all would be. Owen tended to be a lone ranger when it came to his work; his inability to play nicely with others when it came to team investigations was a well-documented flaw of his. So if Owen said they needed help, chances were, they did. And if Owen said Yael was the best, she probably was. Even if she did look like Jessica Alba.

'Okay.' Marina nodded. She slid back into her seat. 'Sorry. I just — '

Yael waved her off. 'I get it. This material is as sensitive as it gets.'

'Wake up, Maestra, baby,' Owen said to the computer. He typed in a password and the screen whirred to life. 'Time to rise and shine.'

'Maestra?'

Yael laughed. 'That's what I call her. She's mine, by the way.'

'And she's a beaut,' Owen said.

'I thought we were using your computer,' Marina said to Owen. 'I thought we agreed.'

'Do you know what an air gap is?' Yael asked. Marina shook her head.

'This computer has never been connected to the internet,' Yael explained, pointing to Maestra. 'Its WLAN — that's wireless local area network — is deactivated, so no LAN cable will ever penetrate its casing.'

Marina stared at her.

'Basically a computer is only safe if an air gap separates it from other systems. So this ensures that no one will be able to hack us. Also, it has five hundred gigs of memory. So it can handle the amount of data the source has sent. So far, anyway.'

Owen shot Marina a look, as if to say, *See? This is why we need her.*

'Basically, what I'm doing here is setting up a secure database for all the documents. Right now, they're just indexed. Eventually, I'd like to construct visualizations so that every company and its related entities will appear, along with their shareholders. Like an org chart. That way, we can see who is connected to whom. But we're not there yet.'

'How are you indexing them? The documents, I mean. There must be millions.'

'I've been using Nuix Investigator. Nuix is a company that makes forensic IT software. Basically, it's a program that helps you sort and sift through vast quantities of data. It can even search unsearchable stuff, like PDFs and scanned documents. It's super cool.' Marina was impressed that Yael didn't seem annoyed with her questions. In fact, she seemed excited to have someone to talk to about the project.

'It's crazy expensive,' Owen said. 'It's not like a new version of Adobe Acrobat or something. You can't just go out and buy it.'

'It's basically only used by police forces and law firms,' Yael said. 'The SEC. Places like that. But Christophe Martin hooked me up with a license. So we're off and running.'

Marina frowned. 'The head of the ICIJ?' She didn't love the idea of the head of the International Consortium of Investigative Journalists getting looped into this. The ICIJ was a global network of more than 150 reporters who collaborated on in-depth, cross-border stories. While Marina had nothing but respect for their work, she couldn't imagine getting 150 reporters from across the world involved in this story. How could they possibly operate with that many cooks in the kitchen? And could they tell the source they had gone from a team of two to a team of 150 in fewer than twenty-four hours? Surely, if the source wanted to have that many journalists involved, he would have taken it to the ICIJ in the first place.

'Christophe's a friend. Don't worry. He doesn't know what it's for. He trusts me,' Yael said.

'Think of it as super-Google,' Owen explained. 'Basically, the files you want to search are uploaded into the program as evidence. Nuix automatically indexes them. Once the index is created, we can search anything. You can type in a name, a company name, whatever. And Nuix will bring up all the documents related to that search. It's totally wild.'

'Wow. Even if it's a PDF? Or a fax?'

'Yeah, that's the cool part.' Yael's eyes gleamed. 'Nuix is sophisticated. It has optical character recognition. So like, if there's a photo file that has me standing in front of a law firm, and in the background, you can see that it says 'Schmit & Muller' on the door, Nuix will pick that up. Normal search tools can't do that.'

'So is the index done?' Marina asked incredulously. She thought it would take days — weeks, maybe — for them to manually click through everything. But instead, they were light-years ahead. Now they could get to the fun part — writing the story.

'Yup.' Yael nodded. 'We were up all night, but it's done.'

'He's still sending more,' Owen said. 'It comes in batches. Even Maestra may not be able to handle what this guy's got.'

Yael shrugged. 'We're caught up now. We have a secure database in place. Now we just need to start searching it. We can add data as it comes.'

'So where is the data coming from? Any thoughts?'

'At first we assumed the source was someone inside a big offshore bank — CIB maybe, or Swiss United. But now it looks like it's coming from inside a law firm in Luxembourg. Schmit &

181

Muller. They seem to be the go-to law firm for all these offshore banks, like CIB and Swiss United. They are the middleman, so to speak. They help the clients set up these shell entities with fake directors. And then they take the shell entities' money to the banks. How on earth they are still in business is a mystery to me. If these people have time to do legitimate business, I'd be amazed.'

'Wow. Who do you think the source is? Maybe a disgruntled ex-employee or something?'

Yael shook her head. 'The data is recent. We're getting emails from yesterday. Whoever our source is, he is very much alive and still working at Schmit & Muller. And he has access to its entire database. It's like we bugged their computers. We're watching what happens inside as it happens. A fly on the wall of a deeply corrupt law firm.'

'That's a crazy risk.'

Owen nodded. 'Insane. Honest to God, we should be checking in with this guy regularly to make sure he's still alive. It takes serious cojones to steal data in real time. Most sources steal it and bolt. This guy is just stealing it, sending it to us, and stealing some more.'

'Stealing isn't the right word,' Yael argued. 'He's doing the right thing. This guy is whistle-blower of the year. Maybe the decade.'

'Fine. You're right. He's like the Robin Hood of data. Stealing from the corrupt rich. Distributing to us, the noble poor. Sorry, Marina. I know you're no longer a member of the proletariat now that you're engaged to Grant Ellis.'

Marina ignored him. 'Did you look up Morty Reiss?'

Owen and Yael exchanged glances.

'So Yael and I were talking about the best way to do this,' Owen said. 'Both of us think it might be time to call in the cavalry. If we bring it to the ICIJ, we can get a team of reporters working on it. Only the best. We'll work together with Christophe to determine who will be pulled in. Each reporter we bring covers a region — Russia, China, the UK. You and I can pick which US stories we want to work on, dole the rest out to other reporters here — maybe folks at the *Times*, the *Journal*, the *Post*. We can discuss. Then we all publish simultaneously. Same hour, same day. It will be incredible. The biggest data leak in history.'

Marina shook her head. 'I think it's too risky.'

'This story is bigger than Morty Reiss, Marina. Morty Reiss is a small fish in a very big, dirty, illegal pond.'

'What about Matthew Werner?'

'We looked. And you were definitely onto something. Matthew Werner isn't all that interesting, but Fatima Amir, the woman he died with, sure was. Come check this out.'

Marina moved her chair over next to Owen's. Yael stood behind them, her arms crossed. He typed in 'Fares Amir.'

A glossy head shot from a London-based hedge fund, the Amir Group, appeared on the screen. Smiling and handsome, with thinning but perfectly groomed hair, horn-rimmed glasses, and a bright blue Hermes tie that popped against his dark skin, Fares Amir looked like the quintessential British banker.

'Meet Fares Amir, Fatima Amir's brother.'

'Fares Amir is a managing director in charge of Client Services at the Amir Group, a hedge fund founded by his sister, Fatima Amir, in 2009,' Marina read. 'Fares holds degrees from Oxford and Cambridge, and prior to working at the Amir Group, he spent several years in the Real Estate Principal Investment Area (REPIA) at Goldman Sachs.'

'Impressive résumé, right? He forgets to mention that his biggest 'client' is his cousin Bashar al-Assad. Who, publically, he claims to have no relationship with. Otherwise he'd end up on sanctions lists. But in private, he's been doing the guy's money laundering for years.'

With another click, Owen pulled up a grainy photograph of two dark-haired men in suits. They were walking shoulder to shoulder, their heads turned in caucus. Marina squinted at the screen. One was unquestionably Assad. The other bore a remarkable resemblance to Fares Amir.

'Fares is a client of our friends Schmit & Muller. Through them, he sets up a series of shell companies, with innocuous names like 'UK Land Corp' and 'Island Properties Inc.' Assad deposits money into UK Land Corp, typically in gold bars that have been purchased with dirty money, made from arms sales or payoffs from corrupt officials. UK Land Corp turns around and uses the gold to buy property, which is then sold to Island Properties. This continues down a

184

chain of shell companies, until the original source of the funds is so obscure that it would be impossible to trace. Eventually, the property gets sold back to one of Fares Amir's clients at Amir Group. The client is thrilled because they pick the property up at a significant discount. And Assad doesn't care that he's losing a bit of money, because now it's clean, sitting in a bank account at Swiss United, ready to be withdrawn for him by one of his minions.'

Marina stared, wide-eyed at the computer. 'And you have proof of all this?' she asked Owen. 'A full paper trail?'

'Full paper trail. Emails — very explicit emails. It's actually kind of awesome how crooked these guys are. They literally just talk about what they're doing like its business as usual. 'Mr. Al-Assad would like to transfer ten million US dollars into four new companies. He understands that the fee for this transaction will be five hundred thousand US dollars. He would like this done by close of business on Friday.' Stuff like that. And then there are the bank accounts, the wire transfer confirmations, the formation documents for the shell companies. All in neatly labeled folders from inside Schmit & Muller's internal database.'

'It never occurred to these people that they might be hacked? Or that this data might leak in some way?' Marina said.

'They have an incredibly sophisticated security system in place,' Yael explained. 'Schmit & Muller is like Fort Knox. The only way the information would get out is through an inside leak. I guess they have their ways of preventing those, too.'

Marina frowned. 'They weren't able to prevent this leak.'

'No. But I think they tried.' Owen clicked open an email between Hans Hoffman and Julian White. 'Remember these guys? From the Morty Reiss emails? Hoffman's one of the heads of Schmit & Muller. White is a private banker at Swiss United. He reports directly to Jonas Klauser, the bank's CEO.'

'I remember.'

Marina skimmed the email. She shivered, her arms crossing her body reflexively. The content was short and the words were chilling.

October 20, 2015
From: Julian White
To: Hans Hoffman
Subject: HIGHLY CONFIDENTIAL: see attached

We have confirmed that on at least three separate occasions over the past month and a half, Fatima Amir met with an agent from MI6. At the second meeting, her banker from Swiss United, Matthew Werner, was present. We believe that they have and will continue to provide confidential financial information regarding Fares Amir, Bashar al-Assad, and his associates to the authorities. Photos are attached.

Marina clicked open the photos. They were grainy and shot from above. They showed two men and a woman, sitting on a private balcony of what appeared to be a hotel. They sat at a table, and the woman's face was partially obscured by the table's umbrella. She was leaning forward, her hand atop a manila envelope. One of the men had a briefcase. In the subsequent photos, he could be seen examining the contents of the manila envelope and then placing it into his briefcase.

'So Fatima Amir was giving incriminating information about her own family to MI6?'

'Her brother is a money launderer. Her cousin's a war criminal. Anyone who thinks their family is fucked up should meet the Amirs.'

'But our mole is from inside Schmit & Muller,' Marina pressed. 'And our mole is, as far as we know, alive. So Fatima Amir and Matthew Werner were not the ones feeding information to Duncan. But it just seems like too much of a coincidence, right? That they were all killed on the same day? Something about it doesn't sit right with me.'

'But maybe Schmit & Muller didn't know where the leak was coming from. All they know is someone is feeding information to the authorities. And these two appear to be doing just that.'

'So she was a mole, but not our mole.'

Yael opened another screen. It showed the wreckage of a plane, its parts strewn about a glistening mountaintop. 'And this is how they deal with moles.'

'Christ.'

'Plane crashed just forty-eight hours after these emails. Same day Duncan was murdered. Convenient, right?'

'If by convenient, you mean terrifying.'

'Oh, and remember Duncan's trip to the Caymans?'

Marina nodded. 'Yeah, the Schmit & Muller guys figured he had a source inside CIB.'

'Well, guess who turned up dead the day after Duncan left? Freak boating accident.'

'A CIB banker.'

'Bingo.'

'So we've got two dead private bankers, a dead private banking client, and a dead journalist,' Marina said, shaking her head.

'But one living mole,' Owen said, pulling up his computer. He pointed to the screen. 'He's sending us more data now. Let's get to work. If we're going to go to the ICIJ, we need a secure database first that can be accessed by users around the globe.'

'The source has to agree. We can't bring in a whole team without talking to him.'

'This guy is already on borrowed time, Marina. I think he'll come around to seeing the benefit of having the ICIJ behind him.'

'Is Christophe Martin ready to help us?'

Yael smiled. 'Are you kidding? This is the story of a lifetime. For him — for all of us.'

Annabel

Fares Amir lived in a stately Edwardian home on Lygon Place in Belgravia. All the homes on Lygon Place were immaculate and nearly uniform in construction. They had grand, redbricked facades, black wooden shutters, cross-hatched windows, and peaked roofs that reminded Annabel of the illustrations of London in *Peter Pan*. The central courtyard was pristinely kept, set behind a security gate with a porter's lodge. Annabel's hands shook as she opened the gate and let it click closed behind her. Though it was midmorning on a Sunday, the courtyard was as quiet as a library. The trees rustled in the breeze overhead, and in the distance, Annabel could hear only faintly the sounds of traffic on Ebury Street. London, particularly this corner of it, was so much more serene than New York. It struck Annabel as remarkable that a man who might be at least tangentially responsible for the mass destruction of whole cities in Syria could live in such a peaceful place.

Before she knocked on the front door, it opened. A man in a suit gestured for her to step inside. Annabel couldn't tell if he was a butler, a bodyguard, or a business associate. He, however, knew exactly who she was.

'Please come in, Mrs. Werner,' he said, taking her coat. 'I'll show you into the library. Mr. Amir is expecting you.'

Annabel followed him down a long hall to an

oak-paneled library overlooking the courtyard. At one end of the room, two leather armchairs sat around a coffee table heaped with books. Annabel didn't know whether or not to sit, so she stood uneasily by the fireplace. Over it hung an exquisite Monet. She moved closer, unable to resist.

'It's a wonderful work, isn't it?' Fares Amir said from behind her. 'He's a master of light and color. The way he depicts the sky here is exceptional. I bought it at auction just a few days ago. I think it looks lovely there.'

Annabel turned and extended her hand, embarrassed. 'Yes, lovely,' she said, her words catching in her throat. 'I'm Annabel Werner. Thank you for seeing me.'

'Of course.' Fares gestured for her to sit at one of the two armchairs by the fireplace. 'Would you like anything? Tea? Water?'

'I'm fine, thank you.' Fares nodded at his employee. He drew the library doors closed, leaving Fares and Annabel alone.

'I'm sorry for your loss, Mrs. Werner. I only met your husband once or twice, but Fatima always spoke highly of him.'

'Thank you. I'm sorry for your loss as well.'

'Did you ever meet my sister?'

Annabel shook her head. 'No. Matthew was very private about his work. He never mentioned her to me.'

'Discretion is perhaps the most important quality a private banker can have.'

Though it struck Annabel as an odd, possibly ominous thing to say, she nodded her head in agreement. 'Matthew believed that, too.'

'I have his things for you. You're probably wondering how they ended up at my sister's home. I know I would wonder that, if I were in your position. I assure you, contrary to what the tabloids here have suggested, their business relationship was just that, a business relationship. I didn't know your husband well, Mrs. Werner, but I did know my sister. She was a consummate professional and a very loyal person. She would have never crossed that ethical line. It's unthinkable to me, frankly.'

'I trusted my husband as well, Mr. Amir. Implicitly. I'm sure there was a good explanation for why he was staying at your sister's home instead of at a hotel.'

Fares nodded. He seemed pleased that she had reached this conclusion. 'There is, I'm afraid. And it's my fault. My sister, you see, was a powerful woman. She ran a twenty-billion-dollar fund. I worked for her, though she would have never said it. She was always kind enough to say that I worked with her.' He laughed, and Annabel did her best to smile with him. He was, she thought, remarkably at ease for a man who had just lost his sister in a plane crash.

'My sister had access to a great deal of confidential information. And as her banker, Matthew did as well. It was my job to ensure the security of that information. Recently, we'd had some concerns about data leaking outside our firm. So being the vigilant person that I am, I insisted that Matthew stay at Fatima's home instead of a hotel. I wanted to be sure that he

191

was using a secure network. With hotels, one never can tell. This was something we do with all of our bankers and lawyers. Jonas Klauser stayed here, with me, just last month. I can see how, at first blush, that might seem unusual or even inappropriate. But it really was just a security issue.'

Annabel nodded. She wanted to believe Fares. But his explanation struck her as too smooth. Practiced, even. Not unlike Agent Bloch's description of the plane crash itself. 'Thank you,' she said. 'I knew there was a reason for his stay, but you've put my mind at ease, now that I know what it is.'

'I'm glad to hear it.'

'You said there were security concerns at your firm? When you heard about the plane crash, did you wonder if . . . ' Annabel trailed off. She didn't want to risk offending him. But she was desperate to see if he flinched when she began to probe him about the plane crash.

'If there was foul play?'

'Yes.'

'Of course. I imagine you did, as well. But we have our own investigator. He concluded it was an accident. A tragedy, of course. But an accidental one.'

Annabel nodded. 'That's good to hear,' she said slowly. 'The idea that someone would want to harm Matthew . . . it's very painful to me.'

'I understand completely.'

They sat for a moment in silence. Then Annabel stood, hoping she wasn't making an offensively abrupt departure. The truth was, it

192

made her skin crawl to sit across from Fares Amir and allow him to continue to lie to her. 'I don't want to keep you from your work,' she said. 'Thank you for seeing me. And for returning me Matthew's things.'

Fares stood. 'It's my pleasure. My assistant, Emmet, will give them to you on the way out. It's nothing of consequence, really. Just his overcoat and a USB, which, for reasons I've already explained, we don't allow into our compound here. I hope I've given you some comfort about your husband's visit to London. If you have any other questions, or if I can do anything for you, please don't hesitate to be in touch.'

'I will, thank you.'

'Are you returning home to Geneva?'

'I'm staying with an old friend here in London for the next day or so. Then I thought I'd go home and pack up our flat in Geneva. I'd like to return to New York as soon as possible. New York is home to me. I think it's the best place for me now.'

'That sounds like a wise plan.'

'You've been very kind, Mr. Amir. I'm sorry again for your loss. My thoughts will be with you and your family.'

'And mine with yours.'

Annabel couldn't help but let her eyes linger over the Monet as she exited the room. 'This is truly magnificent,' she said, pausing for a moment in front of it. 'I love his later works. They're so elegant in their simplicity. Just the sky, the mountains, the light. He painted this during his time in Antibes, no? The quality of light is just extraordinary.'

'You have a good eye, Mrs. Werner.'

'I worked at a gallery back in New York.'

'You should again. There are few things in this world that offer solace like a good painting.'

'Indeed.'

She extended her hand, and their eyes met as he shook it.

'You've been very helpful, Mr. Amir.'

'Have a safe trip home, Mrs. Werner.'

★   ★   ★

Back in Shoreditch, the door to Khalid's apartment was ajar. Annabel hesitated, then stepped inside. The place was trashed. Clothes were strewn across the floor. Papers scattered across the dining room table. Rap music was booming so loudly from the speakers in his bookcase that the threshold pulsed beneath her feet. Annabel felt cold. The window, she noticed, was open. Should she run? What if someone had come after her — after the laptop — and found Khalid instead? If anything happened to him because of her, she could never forgive herself.

'Khalid?' she called out. No response.

'Khalid!' she called again, urgently this time. From the bedroom, she heard the faint sound of water running. She walked toward it, her pace quickening as she went. As her hand reached for the knob, the door flew open. Annabel let out a small scream.

'Christ, Annabel,' Khalid exclaimed. He was

194

dripping from the shower. A towel was slung around his neck, otherwise he was naked. He grabbed it quickly and wrapped it around his midsection, but not before Annabel's face turned crimson with embarrassment. 'You scared the hell out of me.'

'You scared me! When I came in, the front door was open and the music was blasting and there were clothes everywhere . . . I thought . . . '

'I went for a run. And yes, I'm a slob. I'm not used to having a roommate.'

'No, I don't care! I just — '

'Thought I'd been kidnapped?'

'Yes! Or something like that.' Annabel put her hand over her heart. 'Jesus, that was scary. I'm sorry. I guess I'm a little on edge.'

'I am, too. That's why I went for a run. We have to talk about Matthew's computer. But first — how was your visit with Fares Amir?'

'Maybe you should — ' Annabel gestured at Khalid's torso. 'I can give you a minute.'

'Oh Christ, sorry. Let me get dressed.'

Annabel closed the bedroom door behind her. She picked up Khalid's running clothes from the floor. Not knowing where else to put them, she left them in a tidy pile on an armchair. Matthew used to do that, too. After a workout, he'd shed his clothes into a pile on the floor and hop into the shower, not bothering to transfer them to the hamper. She wondered now why it had bothered her so much. Back in New York, she hadn't minded. But in Geneva, it felt like an insult. Like he assumed she was there to pick up after him. As though she had nothing better to do.

She began to straighten up the mess on Khalid's dining room table. She threw away an empty Starbucks cup, put a plate with sandwich crust in the sink. A loose pile of printed emails caught her eye. She picked them up, zeroing in on Matthew's name. It was a different email address, one she'd never seen before.

'I got into his computer,' Khalid said from behind her. 'Took a while. He did not fuck around when it came to security.'

Annabel held up the pile of emails. 'What are these?'

'His emails. To a guy at the Department of Justice, Hunter Morse. He was negotiating a deal with him. An immunity deal.'

'But he didn't do anything wrong.'

'Well, that's not exactly true.' Khalid pulled up a seat at the table and gestured for Annabel to sit. 'I mean, these guys — these private bankers — their job is to help their client hide money offshore. So at the very least, he was probably knowingly assisting people in avoiding taxes.'

'How did he get in touch with someone at the DOJ?'

'From what I can see, Hunter Morse approached him a few months ago. He was investigating Swiss United and was looking for an insider to talk. It seems like Matthew was fed up with the way Jonas Klauser was doing business, especially with people like Bashar al-Assad. Matthew flew to New York to meet with Morse. After, he was supposed to fly back to Geneva and start collecting backup data from inside the bank on USBS. The deal was that he

196

would FedEx the USBs to PO boxes in the US, where they would be picked up and delivered to Agent Morse. The information was to include the names and statements of any US citizens hiding assets at Swiss United, as well as any individuals on international sanctions lists.'

'He was supposed to. So did he?'

'Well, this string of emails occurred about a week before he died. He said he had sent some of the information but wanted a guarantee of immunity from prosecution before sending the rest of it. I think the remaining information pertained to clients of Matthew's. So my guess is, by sending it to Morse, he would be incriminating himself.'

'But — he was a whistle-blower! He was helping them voluntarily. Why would they turn around and prosecute him?'

'Morse said they wouldn't. That the DOJ wouldn't, anyway. But that he couldn't speak for the SEC or the IRS. Matthew seemed angry; he wanted a guarantee from the SEC and the IRS, too. But Morse thought it was too risky. Said the fewer people who knew about this, the better. He wanted Matthew to trust him.'

'And then? Did Matthew send him the data or not?'

'I don't know if he got the chance. He died two days later.'

Annabel slumped back in her chair. 'Oh God.'

'I know. I'm so sorry, Annabel.'

They sat in silence. Minutes ticked by. Finally, Annabel looked up. 'Is the data on this computer? The data he was sending to Morse?'

Khalid nodded. 'I don't know if it's everything. But there's a lot there. Annabel, it's terrifying stuff.'

'What do you mean?'

'On this laptop, he had client data for 117 people. About half of them are just run-of-the-mill tax evaders. You know, CEOs who stash money at Swiss United and use it to buy art or yachts or whatever. And don't pay any tax.'

'And the other half?'

'Not as nice. Your friend Fares Amir is on there, for example. He was acting as a go-between for Assad and all his henchmen. Through Amir, more than four billion dollars flowed into Swiss United and then disappeared into numbered accounts. That place is like a giant black hole of dirty money.'

'Was Fatima Amir aware of it? Was her money dirty, too?' Annabel winced. She couldn't bear the thought of Matthew helping a war criminal like Assad. It was one thing to show a CEO how to circumvent US tax law. It was another to help finance an endless, brutal war against innocent civilians.

'I don't think so. Matthew was trying to help her. He was asking Morse if he could get asylum for her in the US, in exchange for information about her brother and the Assad network.'

'And did Morse agree?'

'He didn't have the chance.'

Annabel closed her eyes. 'I'm scared, Khalid. I'm terrified.'

'I am, too, honestly. What did you think of Fares Amir?'

'There's something very wrong with him. If he wasn't the one who had them killed, he certainly isn't crying over it.'

Khalid grimaced. 'I'm far more afraid of Fares Amir than I am of Swiss United. And frankly, Swiss United is pretty fucking scary.'

'He bought a painting. A Monet. After she died.'

'That seems like an odd thing to do. I mean, right after losing your sister. Who grieves by spending millions on art?'

Annabel shook her head. 'It's not that he bought it. It's the painting itself that disturbs me.'

Khalid cocked his head, confused.

'It's of the Alps,' Annabel said. 'Mont Trélod. And it's hanging over his goddamn fireplace.'

Annabel watched as Khalid registered what she had just said. 'The plane — ' he said, his eyes widening. 'It crashed — '

Annabel nodded. 'I have to leave,' she whispered. 'I don't think I'm safe here. I don't think I'm safe anywhere, as long as I have that.' They both looked at the laptop.

'You have to get to Morse. He can help you.'

'I think so, too. I'd better go back to Geneva first. Pack up my things. Make it look as though I'm leaving for good. Then after I'm back in the States, I'll bring this to Morse. If I just disappear now, they'll know something's up. They'll come looking for me. And chances are, they'll find me.'

Khalid paused, considering. 'That's risky,' he said finally.

'I know.'

'But you might be right. If you go back, play dumb, and then leave, they might not suspect you. Even when people get arrested, they might assume it was Matthew who gave Morse the information.'

'Right. I have to go back. It's the only way.'

Khalid chewed his lip. 'Leave it here with me,' he said.

'The laptop? I can't ask you to keep it.'

'It's safer that way. Leave it here. Then on your way back to the States, connect through Heathrow. I'll meet you there and give this to you. Then go straight to Morse. All right?'

'Are you sure? I feel like I've put you in enough danger already.'

Khalid smiled. He took Annabel's hand, pressed it between his own. 'You can always come to me, old friend.'

'Thank you,' Annabel whispered. She used the back of her other hand to wipe away tears. 'For everything.'

'Don't thank me. Just come back. Come back to me in one piece. All right?'

Annabel nodded. 'I will,' she said. She thought about the last time she had spoken to Matthew, and how he'd made her repeat his words back to him.

You know I always come back, don't you? As soon as I possibly can? Tell me you know.

Yes, of course, she'd said. *I know you always will.*

Marina

Hey, it's Miles. Ran the partial on the Kia.
Came up with nothing. Fingerprint analysis
came back, too. Nothing there. I think we've hit
a dead end. Call when you get a chance.

Marina stood at the center of the ballroom of
the Mandarin Oriental hotel, beneath a crystal
chandelier so immense that it approximated a
starry night sky. Partygoers swirled around her.
They chatted and laughed, complimented one
another's dresses while criticizing those of others
who passed them by. Some networked; others
tried to catch the eyes of the society reporters
who roamed the party, in pursuit of the guests
worth photographing. Marina had been one of
those reporters not long ago. At the time, she
found benefits like this one — where tables cost
$50,000 and sold out before the invitations went
out — as exhilarating as a big-game hunt.

Now she was a guest. She was one of the
photographed. Tickets to these events appeared
in her mailbox without her having to lift a finger
— because of how much money Grant's family
gave to charity, because of who they were and
how much they were wanted at events just like
this. It was what she thought she wanted when
she had started at *Press*, nearly a decade ago.
Real access, not the kind that came with a press
pass around her neck.

Usually crowds exhilarated Marina. Especially well-dressed crowds of interesting and important people. Tonight, however, she was too skittish to enjoy a party. Ever since her run-in up in Connecticut, Marina was dogged by the feeling that she was being followed. She looked for him everywhere: on the street, buying groceries, at the gym. In a city as busy as New York, it was enough to drive a person mad. Too many unfamiliar faces; too many windows behind which he might be lurking. Just because she hadn't seen him since Connecticut didn't mean he wasn't there.

Any luck with either plate? Marina texted Owen.

Found the sedan, Owen texted back. Call me ASAP.

'Hi, Marina.' Marina closed her text messages and looked up. Her face lit up when she saw Leon Diaz, *Press*'s most sought-after photographer, smiling at her.

'Leon, hi,' she said gratefully, and moved in for a double kiss. 'You're a sight for sore eyes.'

'Oh please, I'm just one of the hoi polloi. Look at *you*.' Leon gestured at her dress, a navy shantung sheath held up by a single, dramatic ruffle over her left shoulder. It fit her perfectly because it had been custom-made to her slender frame. The color made her blue eyes pop and her pale skin glow. From each earlobe dangled a chandelier of brilliant sapphires. 'Valentino?'

Marina nodded.

'It's beyond. It looks like next season, but tweaked a bit. Custom?'

'Yes,' Marina said demurely. 'Thank you.'

'And the earrings, *Dios mío.*'

'Loaned!' Marina laughed. 'I'm honestly terrified to wear them around. I feel like I need a bodyguard.'

'Don't you have one?' Leon frowned. 'If you don't, you should.'

Marina bit her lip. Grant had suggested the idea of security before their trip to Paris, but Marina had dismissed it as extravagant and unnecessary. Now she had begun to regret that decision.

'A woman this beautiful should certainly have security.' Marina startled when she felt a hand at the small of her back. Beside her stood her future father-in-law, wearing a tuxedo and a generous smile. 'She's my son's prized possession,' he said to Leon. 'We can't have anyone stealing her from us.'

'You're too kind,' Marina said, forcing a smile. She bristled at the word 'possession' but tried not to show it. She shifted slightly, forcing James's hand to drift from her back. 'James, this is Leon Diaz. A friend from *Press.*'

'Any friend of Marina's,' Ellis said, extending his hand.

'It's an honor, sir,' Leon replied. Marina breathed deep, forcing herself to keep smiling. She found it absurd how people kowtowed to James now that he was expected to run for president. She wondered, not for the first time, if he really wanted the position itself, or if he merely wanted the celebrity and authority that came along with it.

'Could I get your picture?' Leon asked, his

eyes hungry. 'For the magazine?'

'Of course.' Marina felt James's hand grip her side. They stood, locked in their smiles. Passersby turned to gawk, a few didn't bother to disguise their whispers. Marina's pulse quickened. She wished Leon would get on with it.

'Thank you,' he said, after what felt like an eternity. 'These are terrific.'

James Ellis dismissed Leon with a short nod. Marina hoped that James would slip off into the crowd, to go mingle with people more important than his daughter-in-law-to-be. Owen's text lingered on the screen of her phone, tucked in the recesses of her jeweled clutch.

'Marina, we need to talk,' James said. His smile was gone, replaced instead with a look of concern. He gestured toward the eighteen-foot windows at the edge of the ballroom. 'Let's go look at the view.'

Marina followed James across the room. They stood by the glass, each one silently observing the panorama of Central Park and the gleaming buildings of Midtown. James's stern face glowed in profile from the city lights. In a tuxedo adorned with antique ebony studs and cufflinks and his silver hair neatly coiffed, he looked as presidential as they came.

'I wanted to thank you.'

'Thank me for what?' Marina said, genuinely surprised.

'For making my son so happy.'

Marina smiled. 'Oh my. I don't know what to say. He's made me so happy. I feel lucky that he wants me to be his wife.'

'Grant is a good man. Perhaps the best I've ever known.'

'I couldn't agree with you more.'

'This campaign — my campaign — it won't be easy on him. And I feel guilty about that. He didn't ask for it. All the publicity. The reporters — forgive me, I know you're a reporter — but all the reporters who will inevitably hound him. And for the position he'll have to assume at Ellis Enterprises. I've asked a lot of him. And he's been so gracious about it.'

'We're all very proud of you.'

'That's kind of you to say. But I think he's been amenable to it because he's so happy. And he's been happy because of you.'

'Well, I'm glad,' Marina murmured, her cheeks flushed.

'I'm asking a lot of you, too. It may be more than you bargained for. Being in the public spotlight is not easy. You're beautiful, of course, and very poised. Wonderful pedigree. Lovely family. You have all the things that make for a successful politician's wife. But I want to be sure you know what you're in for.'

'I wasn't aware I was marrying a politician.' Marina laughed lightly.

'Well, not yet. But if I win — and I think there's a good chance of it, Marina, I really do — I hope Grant might consider a run himself. Are you prepared for all that?'

Marina paused, considering how to answer. She wasn't sure she understood the question. Was he asking her if she was uncomfortable with celebrity? Or was he asking her if she had any

205

skeletons in her closet that would embarrass him and his family?

'I think I'm as prepared as one can be,' Marina said carefully. 'I love Grant, and I'll support whatever he decides to do with his career.'

'Good, good.'

'So, have you decided to announce your candidacy, then?' Marina asked. She realized she had never spoken to her future father-in-law alone for this long before.

He nodded. 'Tonight,' he replied. 'During my speech.'

'Tonight,' Marina replied, surprised.

'It was a last-minute decision. But I think it's a good time. I'm being honored by the NYPD. It's a friendly crowd. And tomorrow, every newspaper in America will be running a story about Senator Murphy and the illegitimate child he fathered ten years ago with his housekeeper. Who, by the way, is in the country illegally.'

Marina's mouth dropped open. 'Oh,' she said. 'My.'

'Oh my, indeed.'

'Well, congratulations, then. It's an exciting night.'

'For all of us.'

'For all of us. Yes.'

'Grant mentioned to me that you thought you were being followed.' James turned and looked Marina in the eye. 'You should have come to me, you know. Right away.'

'I'm sorry,' Marina stuttered. 'I didn't realize — '

'Don't apologize. I just want you to know you

can always come to me if you are having a problem. Of any kind.'

'Of course. Thank you.'

'Grant is worried about your safety. I told him it was likely just a reporter trying to dig up dirt on the family. They do that, you know. Once someone is in the public eye. They'll be watching you day and night.'

'I know. I'm ready for it.'

'But you were still worried, Grant said.'

'I just thought someone was following me when I went to Connecticut to visit my parents, and it spooked me a bit,' Marina said. She regretted having said anything to Grant now. It hadn't occurred to her that he'd tell his father.

James nodded. 'You both need to be wary now. For that reason, starting tomorrow, I want you both to start interviewing security teams. I have some excellent people lined up for you to speak to. You can choose whomever you feel most comfortable with. All ex-NYPD, all highly trained. They won't interfere in your daily life. But they'll be there to keep you safe. I'm doing the same for myself. I hope that will help ease your mind.'

'I'm not sure it's necessary, but thank you.'

'It's necessary. Trust me. I don't like to hear that my future daughter-in-law is being followed.'

'It could've been nothing.'

'Perhaps. Or maybe it was something.'

'I appreciate your concern.'

'We're family now, Marina.'

'I'm glad you think of me that way.'

'I hope you'll do something for me. Since we're discussing security.'

'Of course. Anything.'

'Grant mentioned you were working on a story for *Press*. He said he had hardly seen you since you returned from Paris.'

Marina looked away, unable to meet James's gaze. 'He's right,' she said. 'I've been quite busy.'

James frowned impatiently. 'My son needs you right now, Marina. And the last thing we need as a family is for you to put yourself in danger running after a story. Grant said that you were thinking of leaving *Press* after the wedding. I was hoping you might do it now. You'll be busier than you've ever been with campaign events. And it would mean a great deal to me — and to Grant, though I know he'd never say it to you — if you would be there to support our family during what will inevitably be a stressful time.'

'I, well — ' Marina stuttered.

'Don't answer now.' James held up a hand. 'Just consider it. Talk it over with Grant. After the election, you can think about returning to work. But I don't think you'll want to. I think you'll find that making the news is a lot more interesting than just writing about it.'

Marina smiled, tight-lipped. She knew him well enough to know that this wasn't a request. It was a command. If she wanted to be an Ellis, she would fall in line.

'I completely understand.'

'Excellent.' James put his hand on her shoulder and smiled, his face relaxing into his usual, jovial expression. 'Oh, I'm nervous,

Marina. I've given a lot of speeches in my day, but this is a big one.'

'You'll do wonderfully.'

'Thank you, my dear. I knew I could count on you.'

The crowd began to clap. Marina and James turned toward the stage. Grant was standing beside the chairman of the NYPD Foundation, a microphone in his hand. He smiled at the crowd. Finally the chairman gestured for everyone to quiet down, and Grant stepped forward with the mic.

'Thank you so much for this warm New York welcome,' Grant said. Marina was impressed by how relaxed Grant seemed. If he was at all nervous, he didn't show it. 'This has always been a special evening for my family. My father and I were both born and raised here in New York. This city is immensely important to us, and we both have spent our working lives trying to find ways to give back to the community that has given us both so much.'

'He's a natural,' James whispered to Marina. 'Just look at him.'

'I graduated from college in 2001,' Grant continued. 'I was one month into an internship at a bank when 9/11 happened. Three days later, I enlisted. I thought my father would be angry, or at least worried. But he understood why I wanted to serve. I will admit he was a little horrified when he found out my starting salary, but he was proud of me, too. He said there was no greater honor for him than to have his son serving the public good.'

Grant nodded gratefully as the room burst into applause. Several members of the NYPD, all in dress blues, stood up, leading the crowd in a standing ovation. Marina felt a swell of pride. Grant was so humble. He had no interest in celebrity or accolades. Even at dinner with their friends, he talked little about himself. He had an incredible way of turning questions back to his companions. Unlike so many New Yorkers, he listened far more than he spoke. It was one of the things that Marina loved and admired about him. It was a nice change to see him standing on stage in front of a thousand people, getting applauded for his service.

'Grant is what this country needs,' James whispered in her ear. 'He doesn't care about the applause. He genuinely cares about doing good. If I'm successful at this — and I hope I am — I want him to be next. He doesn't realize it now, but he was born to be a politician. I mean that in the best way possible.'

Marina looked at James. His eyes glowed; his lips curled into a small, contented smile. The clapping faded; Grant raised the mic again. 'In recent months, my father and I have talked a great deal about legacy. About the kind of mark we'd like to leave on this world. My father, as you all know, has achieved a great many things in his life. He's been immensely successful in business. He's been a patron of the arts and a generous philanthropist for decades. He's been a proud and loyal husband to my mother, Betsy, for thirty-nine years, and a terrific father and mentor to me. That's why it's with great enthusiasm that I take this opportunity to introduce my father, James Ellis.'

The crowd rose to its feet again, roaring its approval. Everyone around them turned to stare at James and Marina, who stood shoulder to shoulder at the edge of the room. Marina blinked as the cameras winked in her direction, momentarily blinding her with their flash.

She felt James's hand on her shoulder. 'Come on up with me,' he said, pushing her lightly in the direction of the stage.

'Are you sure?' In front of her, Grant stood waving at the crowd. When he made eye contact with her, he smiled. He gestured for her to join him. Betsy was already climbing the stairs.

'Yes. They'll want a photograph of the family.'

His fingers wrapped around her upper arm, his grip firm. In front of them, the crowd parted, opening up a path to the stage. At the front, Marina noticed a cluster of journalists. Some were taking notes; others, photographs. She recognized most of them. At the front was her old friend Leon. He winked at her as she passed. Marina paused and blew him a kiss. Then she turned and ascended the stage.

Annabel

Annabel was in Geneva for what she hoped was the last time. At Heathrow, she'd fought the urge to run. To board a plane bound for another destination and simply disappear. She could dye her hair. Change her name. Start over. A part of her thought that if she returned to Geneva, she'd never leave it alive. But she also knew that if she ran, whoever had killed Matthew would find her. Running made her look guilty.

Annabel found herself standing at her front door, key in hand. She remembered the first time she saw the apartment. It never occurred to her that she'd live somewhere so elegant, so spacious, so grand. The foyer itself was nearly the size of their entire apartment back home in New York. The views — of the cobblestone streets, the elegant Old Town buildings, the crystalline sky that turned slate gray in the snow — were better than any painting. After everything they had been through — the miscarriage, the death of Matthew's father — she'd felt like they deserved this. A new start. A beautiful life.

Before Annabel could turn the knob, the door creaked open on the hinge. Her heart seized up. The front door was unlocked. She had not left it that way.

She pushed the door with one palm, and it banged open against the foyer wall. Annabel didn't need to enter to know the place had been ransacked. Whoever had done it wanted her to know they had been there.

'Hello?' Annabel called out. Her voice trembled. 'Is anyone here?'

She heard only the rumble of the cable car on the street below and the rustling of the curtains. The windows, she realized, were open.

She shivered and drew her coat close. The room was freezing. Crisp November air streamed in though the open windows. She thought, perhaps, she ought to turn around and run. But in her gut she knew the apartment was empty. Whoever had done this must have come in the night. They were long gone now. Or maybe they were close by, lying in wait. Maybe they were watching her from across the street, observing her every move through long telephoto lenses.

Annabel walked through the apartment in silence, observing the damage. The cabinets had been emptied, their contents scattered on the floor. Her drawers, tossed. The safe in the closet — where she kept her good jewelry, their passports, their marriage certificate — gaped open. The jewelry was still inside. Nothing appeared to have been taken, except for the laptop Annabel had left in a locked drawer in the office. She had purchased the laptop right before she left for London; the same model as Matthew's. It had no information on it. She had locked it in the drawer as a kind of a test. Now, she was glad that she had.

The couches in the living room were slit open and gutted like fish. The paintings and mirrors had been removed from the walls, presumably to

213

check for hidden safes behind them. The one Annabel had painted herself — for Matthew as an anniversary gift — had been dissembled from its frame. It lay in tatters at her feet, the Florence skyline reduced to strips of gray and brown.

Annabel knelt beside it. As she collected the fragments of canvas, something inside her snapped. To lose this painting — worthless to everyone except for her and Matthew — was too much.

'Enough!' she screamed into the empty apartment. 'You've taken enough.'

Annabel stood. Pure fury burned away the fog of grief that had enveloped her since Matthew's death. For the first time in days, Annabel felt clearheaded and filled with purpose. If Jonas wanted a fight, she would give him one. She would not stop until every person responsible for Matthew's death was dead or in jail.

But first, she would give them what they wanted. She would wave the white flag. She would let them think that they had won.

She picked up the phone and dialed.

'Julian,' she cried when he answered. 'I've been robbed! The whole apartment — it's been torn apart!'

'Are you all right? You aren't hurt, are you?'

'No, thank God. I wasn't home. I was in London, collecting Matthew's things. But I came home just now, straight from the airport, and — ' Annabel let out a hysterical sob.

'I'll be right over. Have you telephoned the police?'

'No, no. You're the first person I called. I

214

should, shouldn't I? I'm sorry. I'm just so upset.'

'Of course you are, darling. Don't worry. I'll call them. And I'm on my way to you now. Are you safe there?'

'I think so. The apartment is empty.'

'Was anything taken? Anything of value?'

'I don't know. I haven't really checked. Please hurry, Julian. I need you.'

'Of course. Don't worry, Annabel. I'll take care of this. I'll take care of everything.'

No, Annabel thought to herself as she hung up the phone. *You won't. But I will.*

She went to the bathroom. She splashed water on her face, causing her mascara to run down her cheeks. She tousled her hair. The show was about to begin, and she was ready for it.

Before Julian arrived, Annabel made one last call.

'*Office de la Police,*' a female voice answered. 'Agent Du Pres.'

'Agent Bloch, please,' Annabel said. She glanced down at the card in her hand, double-checking the number that she had dialed. It was correct.

'I'm sorry,' the woman replied. 'Agent Bloch is no longer with Fedpol. May I help you?'

'Agent Vogel, then.'

'Ma'am, there is no Agent Vogel.'

'Thank you,' Annabel said, as coolly as possible. 'I must be mistaken.'

'Can I help — '

Annabel hung up the phone before the woman finished her question.

Marina

Where are you?? We're ready to go to press.
This is your story. Let's get it out there.

Marina was standing on the sidewalk outside Owen's apartment when she read his text message. She hated what she was about to do. Owen was going to hate it, too.

I'm outside your apartment, she wrote back. Ringing buzzer now.

Owen's face lit up when he opened the door. In his hand was a corkscrew.

'You came just in time,' he said, ushering her inside. 'About to open up something really special.'

'Isn't it a little early for celebratory toasts?'

'As my dad used to say, it's five o'clock somewhere in the world.'

'I mean, isn't it premature? Are we really publishing the story *now*?'

'Spoke to Christophe an hour ago. Everything will be ready to go by tomorrow night at midnight, New York time. Stories will be uploaded simultaneously. The following morning, we will be front-page news at basically every major source around the globe.'

'That's great.' Marina offered him a tight smile.

'Your enthusiasm is overwhelming.'

'I'm sorry. It's really amazing. Truly. I'm happy for you.'

216

'For me? How about for us?' Owen presented her with a bottle of Château Margaux. 'Does this look familiar?'

Marina studied the label. Her eyes widened when she remembered. 'Duncan sent that to you, didn't he?'

Owen nodded. 'As a thank-you for my help on the Darlings investigation.'

'And you've saved it all these years?'

'He told me to drink it with someone special.'

Marina met Owen's gaze. She felt a shiver of desire. His eyes changed colors according to his mood, and today they were a gold-flecked green. He leaned in, and for a moment, Marina thought Owen was going to kiss her.

I should pull away, she thought. Instead she stood transfixed, and her eyes fluttered closed.

They popped open when she felt the cork-screw in her hand.

'You do the honors,' Owen said.

'Where's Yael?' Marina replied, flustered. Suddenly, she was a flurry of action, removing her coat, glancing around the apartment.

'Sleeping.'

Marina craned her neck toward the bedroom.

'At her own apartment.'

'Are you two . . . ?'

'Nah.' Owen shook his head. 'We were. For a second. About three years ago. But now we're just friends.'

'Is that really a thing? Being friends with an ex?'

Owen chuckled. 'You don't think that men and women can be friends?'

'I don't think that men and women who sleep together can be friends.'

'I guess we shouldn't sleep together, then.' Owen's eyes twinkled, but in his voice there was a touch of seriousness.

'I guess not.'

Owen looked at her for another second before turning away. He gestured for her to give him the bottle. He inserted the corkscrew and twisted, pulling the cork from the bottle in one smooth movement. 'Good. Because I have a proposal for you.'

'I'm already engaged,' Marina said with a nervous laugh. 'Remember?'

'I want you to come work with me.'

'At the *Deliverable*?'

'Yes. I need a managing editor. You can still write, too. You pick your own projects. Though I'd suggest you start with the Morty Reiss story. There's plenty to go off of from the material we've looked at so far.'

'Wow.' Marina took a seat. 'That's a really generous offer.'

'You'd be my second-in-command. Right below me on the masthead.'

'Thank you, Owen. I'm honestly flattered.'

'But you're going to say no.'

Marina couldn't bear to look at him. She could hear the disappointment in his voice. A lump rose in her throat. 'I'm sorry,' she said, 'but I can't.'

Owen nodded. For a moment, they were both quiet. Then he picked up the bottle of Château Margaux and poured it into the two glasses he'd set out on his dining room table. 'Okay,' he said, 'well, if you change your mind, my door is always open.'

'Thanks. That's very kind.'

'Let's have a toast, anyway. To this story. From the two of us to Duncan.'

Marina picked up her glass and tipped it toward Owen. She felt her heart pounding hard in her chest. She'd been through plenty of breakups before — a few had been horrible. This felt worse.

'About this story,' she said, putting her glass back down on the table.

'What's wrong?'

'I want you to run it under your name.'

Owen looked genuinely perplexed. 'Why? It's your story. You broke it. It will be a career-maker for you, Marina.'

'I know. But I'm giving it to you. Okay?'

'Is this about the Ellises?'

Marina frowned. 'It's my decision. I just can't put myself in danger anymore. I don't like being followed. It's been really scary. And there's already enough media attention on Grant and his family. I don't need to stoke that fire.'

'Stoke it how? By doing your job?'

Marina shot him a look. 'Don't make this more difficult than it needs to be.'

'I'm confused. Does Grant want you to quit?'

'Grant is supportive either way. But I'm going to have obligations now, Owen. I'm going to have to travel with him. I'll be out on the campaign trail. My career is over, whether I publish this story or not. So why not give you the credit?'

'Because that's not what we do!' Owen banged his fist on the table.

Marina flinched, startled. 'You don't need to shout at me.'

'I'm sorry,' he said, lowering his voice. 'But our whole business is about truth. That's how I see it, anyway. I thought you did, too.'

'I do. Of course I do. I just — I want to protect Grant. I'm going to make plenty of enemies if I publish this piece. Some of them might be family friends, business associates. Some of them might even be world leaders. I just can't do that to Grant or his father. It could be devastating to their careers. And for what? So I can have a byline?'

'It's not about a damn byline. It's about being proud of the work you've done. These people are criminals, Marina. And you're worried about your husband maintaining a good relationship with them?'

'I just can't be associated with this investigation.'

'Well, in that case, I might as well tell you.' Owen glared at her. He crossed his arms, ready for a confrontation.

'Tell me what?'

'Yael dug up another story two days ago. I told her to shelve it out of respect to you, but since you're not a part of the team anymore, I guess we can run it.'

'What is it?'

'Your father-in-law hasn't exactly been forthcoming on his tax returns. Turns out Papa Ellis has a cool thirty million stashed at Swiss United.

Not in his name, of course. Under the creatively named shell company Offshore Properties.'

'No,' Marina shook her head. 'That can't be right. No way. James is a straight shooter. And he has so much money, it's not like he needs more. I don't believe he would cheat on his taxes.'

'Well, it's not just about saving a few tax dollars. It's about hiding money earned from illegal business transactions.'

'What illegal business transactions?'

'James Ellis has been doing big business with our old friend Assad.'

'That's absurd,' Marina said sharply. 'What business could James possibly have with Assad?'

'Back in 2007, Ellis went on a buying spree of high-end luxury hotels throughout Europe. He wanted to start his own brand, like Starwood or Hilton, and he leveraged himself to the hilt to do it. But then the financial crisis hit. Ellis was facing bankruptcy. At the last minute, a mysterious angel swooped in and, through a series of shell transactions, purchased the hotels from him practically overnight. He lost hundreds of millions, but not everything. In fact, after it was all said and done, he was still on the Forbes 400 list. He was lucky to walk away with the shirt on his back.'

'Someone would have noticed. There's no way — '

'Oh, people noticed. For a while, there was buzz at the *Wall Street Journal* that Ellis had been bailed out by a big Middle Eastern family. But no one knew for sure who it was. All anyone could prove was that a shell corporation called

Zara bought Ellis's hotels. Turns out the person behind Zara Corp is none other than Bashar al-Assad. And since Assad is on sanctions lists, Ellis is going to be in big trouble when that story gets out. He will definitely be rethinking his run for the White House.'

'I don't believe you.'

'Why would I make this up? You know I can prove it. I wouldn't tell you about it if I couldn't.'

Marina winced. She knew Owen was telling the truth. He had no reason to lie. And he had access to all the client files at Swiss United. She just couldn't believe that James had been able to hide this secret for so long. Did he really think he could continue to while running for president? The world was watching him now. It seemed like a crazy risk. She sank back in her chair.

'He hired people to vet him,' she said slowly. 'Why would they let him run for office if he's hiding piles of dirty money in offshore accounts?'

'They probably don't know. That's the thing about offshore accounts. No one can find them. Unless you have an inside source who is willing to blow the whistle.'

'Oh my God,' she said, closing her eyes. 'Out of everything, this is the biggest story you have.'

'It's certainly one of them.'

'Why didn't you tell me?'

'Because I was trying to protect you,' Owen snapped. 'This is your family we're talking about.'

'But now that I'm quitting the investigation, you're comfortable destroying my family.'

'Give me a fucking break, Marina. I didn't create this situation. James Ellis did.'

'You should have told me.'

'Maybe.' Owen sighed. 'I was worried . . . '

'You were worried that what? You were going to ruin my life?'

'I was worried that you would think I was trying to break up your engagement.'

'Why would you do that?'

Owen widened his eyes in surprise. 'Seriously?'

'Yes, seriously. Why — '

'Because I have feelings for you! Are you really unaware of that?'

Marina's lips parted.

'I'm sorry,' Marina said. 'I don't know what to say. I didn't expect that.'

'That I have feelings for you? Or that your fiancé is a tax-evading criminal?'

'My future father-in-law, not my fiancé. And no, I didn't expect any of it.'

'You're not much of an investigative journalist, are you?' Owen said. They stared at each other for a moment. Then they both laughed, breaking the tension.

'I guess you're lucky that I'm quitting, then,' Marina said, looking away. Inside, her heart was pounding. Owen's feelings for her weren't a surprise, she realized. Though she never would've admitted it before now, there had always been an undercurrent of electricity between them. What did surprise her was his willingness to admit it.

His vulnerability disarmed her, In that moment, Owen seemed sweeter and more mature than she ever imagined he could be.

'Are you really doing this?' he said softly. 'You're really walking away from this story?'

'Yes. I'm sorry, but my mind is made up. You can run it under your name, of course. It's your story, too.'

'And what about Ellis and his ties to Assad? What about that part of the story?'

Marina's jaw tensed. 'That's a choice you have to make.'

'The story will come out, sooner or later. It always does.'

'Maybe,' Marina said, meeting his gaze. She stood up and zipped up her coat. 'But it doesn't have to come from a friend.'

'He's a bad guy, Marina. You deserve better.'

She shook her head. 'You're wrong. Grant is the best guy I've ever met. Maybe his father has made mistakes. Maybe. But Grant doesn't deserve to lose everything because of them. If you try to take him down, just know that I'll be standing right next to him, holding his hand.'

Marina walked out. Owen called out her name, but she ignored him. She let the door slam behind her.

'Don't you want to know who's been following you for the past few days? You're not going to like it,' Owen shouted. But she was already out of earshot.

Annabel

Jonas Klauser. There he was, standing at Annabel's door. He was impeccably, if casually, dressed in jeans and a purple cashmere sweater that zipped at the neck. His silver hair was neatly combed and impervious to the wind that had been rattling Annabel's windows for the better part of the morning. Though it was snowing, Jonas wore a light suede jacket, no hat or scarf or gloves. He had on loafers, not snow boots. Jonas always dressed this way, as though he needn't bother to dress for the elements. Indeed, with his fleet of drivers and private jets to transport him from place to place, Jonas's feet hardly met the pavement unless he wanted them to. Annabel thought it was intentional. Everything about Jonas was intentional. He wanted you to know that he was above you. For God's sake, he was above the weather.

'Jonas!' she exclaimed, unable to mask her surprise. She couldn't avoid being pulled into an embrace. 'I wasn't expecting you.'

'Julian is on his way over,' Jonas said, after Annabel wriggled free. 'He called me about the break-in. I was so worried about you. I didn't like the thought of you here alone.'

'How did you get here so quickly?'

'I was in the neighborhood. You look pale. You should sit. Can I get you a drink? Some water, perhaps?'

Jonas swept past her, not waiting for an invitation. She followed him in. He rustled around the living room, picking up debris as he went as though it was his apartment, not hers. *It is his apartment*, Annabel thought, her stomach lurching uncomfortably. *It belongs to Swiss United*.

'My God,' Jonas said, stooping down to restore a stack of books on the coffee table. 'What happened here? This place is a wreck.'

'I don't know. I just got home from London and found it this way.'

'You didn't need to go to London alone, Annabel. We could have sent someone for you. That must have been very trying.'

'I wanted to. I stayed with a friend. I met with Fares Amir. He was very welcoming. I'm glad I went. I needed the closure.'

'I'm glad to hear that. Fares is brokenhearted, too.'

'Yes, he seemed that way.'

'Have you called the authorities?'

'Yes,' Annabel said, even though she hadn't. She wondered if Julian had bothered to, or if he'd just called Jonas instead. 'They should be here soon.'

Jonas nodded. 'Good. This is awful. I'm so sorry.'

'It's all right. It isn't your fault.' She met his gaze, and he held it. If he felt guilt, he was doing a masterful job concealing it. If anything, he appeared sad. Concerned. Genuinely so.

Optics, Annabel reminded herself sternly. *It's all optics*.

'Was anything taken?'

Annabel shook her head. 'It's the strangest thing. It doesn't seem like anything's missing. My jewelry's there. Some of the art was destroyed but none of it's gone. I even had an envelope filled with money in my top drawer and they left that, too. It's like they were looking for something specific.'

'What about Matthew's office?'

'It's been trashed as well. I never went in there, so I wouldn't be able to tell if something had been taken.'

'His computer, maybe? Or files?'

'I really don't know. Wouldn't his computer be at his office?'

'No, his laptop. The one he used for travel.'

Annabel shrugged. 'Oh, I don't know,' she said, as casually as possible. 'I assumed it was with him. On the plane, I mean.'

Jonas nodded. He turned away. Annabel thought she saw him blink back tears.

'Could you help me close the windows?' she said. 'It's so cold in here.'

'Of course.'

Silently, the two began to work. Jonas pushed his sweater up on his forearms and went about closing the windows until the sound of the street became muffled and the air in the apartment fell still. Annabel collected the papers that had blown off the coffee table and were scattered about the rug. She put the pillows, slit open and leaking feathers, back in their rightful positions on the sofa. She returned the books to the shelves. When they had finished in the living room, they moved to the dining room. There was less mess there and fewer windows. The kitchen was the most work. The cabinets had been emptied. The jars filled with sugar and coffee and flour had been dumped out onto the floor. Jonas asked where the laundry room was, and Annabel pointed to a door off the kitchen. He returned with a vacuum in one hand and a broom and dustpan in the other. Annabel watched as he went to work. When he was finished, he began on the countertops, spraying them down and wiping them up with wordless precision.

The office came next. Annabel tried not to stare as Jonas worked his way around Matthew's desk, pushing in drawers, righting the lamp, straightening the chair. He moved quickly and efficiently. If he was looking for anything — scraps of information, loose papers, USBs — he didn't show it. She felt almost guilty when he fell to his knees and began replacing shredded paper and old wrappers in the waste basket.

'You don't need to do that,' Annabel said.

'Nonsense. If we work together it will be done in no time. Not that I want you staying here tonight. But at least we can tidy up.'

'Do you think we should wait? For the police, I mean. Is this a crime scene?'

Jonas shrugged. 'If nothing was taken, I really don't know if there's anything to be done.'

'You're right. I don't think there's really any point in them coming at all, now that I think of it. Thank you for helping me straighten up. I'll pack up my things and leave, I think.'

'I'd like you to come stay with us, in Cologny,

Annabel. That way I know you'll be safe.'

'That's very kind. I may do that, just for the night, if that's all right.'

'You can stay as long as you'd like.'

Annabel smiled. 'I won't stay long. It's time for me to go back to New York. It's hard for me to be here in Geneva.'

'I understand. I'll make any arrangements you need.'

They went into the bedroom last. There was something disarmingly intimate, Annabel thought, about making another person's bed. Jonas did it with remarkable care. He pulled the duvet up and smoothed the wrinkles out with his hand. He fluffed the pillows. The tangled mess of sheets was restored to pristine arrangement within minutes.

'You're quite good at that,' Annabel said. She couldn't help herself — she smiled. 'Do you make your own bed at home?'

Jonas laughed. 'It's been a few years. You can take the man out of military school, but you can't take the military school out of the man.'

'I didn't know you went to military school.'

'Yes. At eleven. My parents died, and they shipped me off. A formative experience, to be sure.'

'My parents died then, too. When I was eleven.'

'Who cared for you?'

'My aunt. She sent me to boarding school as well. Though not at eleven. That's terribly young.'

Jonas shrugged. 'I grew up quickly that year.'

'And you learned to make an excellent bed.'

'Indeed. Elsa is a lucky woman.' Jonas

chuckled. He sat on the floor, leaning up against the bed. 'You and I have a lot in common, Annabel.'

'Do we?'

'Yes, I think so. Why we came to Geneva, for example.'

Annabel raised her eyebrows. 'Why did you come here?' she said. It was hard to picture Jonas living anywhere else but here. Of course, he must have come from somewhere. He hadn't always been the king of offshore banks.

'I came here to start over. After losing Charlotte. My first wife.'

'Oh, I'm so sorry.' Annabel took a seat on the floor beside Jonas without even thinking.

'Matthew never mentioned her to you?'

'No. I had no idea.'

'I told Matthew about Charlotte just once. When I offered him this job. I don't talk about her a lot. It's still hard for me to say her name, after all these years.'

'I'm sure.' Annabel felt her heart rising in her throat. Would she ever be able to speak of Matthew again, she wondered, without feeling as gutted as she felt right now?

'She was my college sweetheart. She went to Radcliffe and I was at Harvard. We met at the Harvard-Yale game, our sophomore year. The day we graduated, I proposed in Harvard Yard. We got married that August, at her parents' house in Maine. We settled in Boston. Charlotte grew up in Milton and she felt comfortable there, and a professor of mine got me a job in private banking. We lived in a little house in

Beacon Hill. There was no air-conditioning and it was hot as hell in the summer, but we were very happy there. I wanted a backyard, but Charlotte didn't want me to have to commute. She liked having me home for dinner. There were these little blue window boxes and Charlotte filled them with flowers in the spring. She called them our gardens. I think it was the happiest time of my life.'

Annabel nodded. She found herself interested to hear more.

'Back then, I traveled a lot for work. I was building my business. Meeting clients. Expanding my book. Charlotte's parents never liked me. They didn't think I was good enough for her. Her father was from an old New England family, a real Boston Brahmin. He thought I was a nobody, and even though he was right — I really was a nobody — I was desperate to prove him wrong. I went about it in the only way I knew how: making money. I thought if I grew rich enough, they would have to accept me. So that was my goal. I wanted to take over the bank. Anything less would have been a failure in my eyes.

'For the first year, I did quite well. Charlotte handled it all wonderfully. She never complained. Even when she got pregnant, she was always cheerful. Never said a word about all the missed dinners and the vacations that never happened. When she was physically uncomfortable — and I knew she was, as the pregnancy wore on — she never said so. Didn't want me to worry about her. She accepted everything with such grace.'

231

Annabel felt tears welling up in her eyes. She knew the trauma of a pregnancy gone wrong. It had been so long since she'd thought about her own. She'd tried to bury that loss in the darkest recesses of her mind. Every now and then, it bobbed back up to the surface, sharp and painful as ever. Now was one of those times.

'I was in Chicago when she died. Charlotte was about to enter her third trimester. She had been having fainting spells and her doctor put her on bed rest. It was supposed to be my last overnight trip. After that, I promised her I'd come home every night. Even if it meant leaving at the crack of dawn and returning that same day, I would do it. I wanted to sleep beside her. I knew she wasn't listening to her doctors. She would call me after she'd been out shopping or to the market. She was still gardening. She was never one to sit still. It wasn't in her nature. Frankly, it was one of the things I loved most about her.

'Her mother called when I was leaving for the airport. I'll never forget it. I remember everything about that day: what I was wearing, where I was standing, what the weather looked like outside. It was afternoon but the sky outside the hotel window was dark. I was worried I would miss my flight home. I ended up making the flight, but it didn't matter. Charlotte was already dead. She bled to death. A placental abruption, do you know what that is? The placenta separates from the uterus. Completely, in Charlotte's case. The baby didn't make it. They were both gone by the time I got home.'

'Oh, Jonas,' Annabel whispered. 'I can't imagine.'

Jonas patted her knee. 'I think you can, actually. Every loss is different, of course, but grief, I've found, is universal. We speak that language, you and me. We always will.'

Annabel nodded. She felt her cheeks grow hot with tears.

'After that, I wanted to get as far from Boston as I could. I couldn't bear to return to our little house with the window boxes. I called a client of mine who lived in Geneva and begged him to help me get a job. I started at Swiss United as an assistant, basically. They paid me half of what I was making back in the States and worked me twice as hard. But I didn't care. I was so grateful to escape. That's what I had hoped I could give to Matthew. After his father died, after the loss you two suffered, I knew he needed to start over. You both did. And that's why I brought him to Geneva.'

'It was my fault we came here. I pushed Matthew to take this job. I needed the fresh start more than he did. I begged him for it.'

'You can't blame yourself.'

'I know. But I do blame myself. Don't you?'

'Yes. I feel guilty every day. It is the cross we bear, Annabel. For losing someone we loved. For not being able to save them.' He smiled at her then, tight-lipped. For a moment, they stared at each other, his cool blue eyes meeting hers.

'And you still find the will to go on?' she said. 'To get up every day, even when you're weighed down by your conscience?'

'I do. You will, too. They could not be helped. That's what you and I must remember. Some things, no matter how tragic, cannot be helped.'

The doorbell rang. Annabel jumped.

'Excuse me,' she murmured, her voice hoarse. 'I think someone — '

'Ah, good. The police are here. We'll straighten it all out now.'

But of course the police hadn't arrived. No one had called them. It was Julian White. And Annabel was alone with them both in the apartment.

Marina

Marina was out of breath when she reached 5 East Sixty-fifth Street. As she skipped up the steps of James Ellis's limestone town house, her heart pounded in her chest. The wind off Central Park stung at her cheeks and ears and ankles. She hadn't planned on being out so late, or it being so cold, and she was woefully under-dressed. A part of her — the cowardly part — thought about going home, but she forced herself to ring the bell. She had business with James Ellis. Immediate business.

For a minute, no one answered. Marina felt a tiny shiver of relief. She was turning away when she heard the familiar skitter of dog paws on the marble floor. The locks clicked open. James Ellis, flanked by his two pointers, stood in the entryway. He was casually dressed in chinos and a plaid button-down rolled up at his forearms. On his feet, he wore the fleece-lined slippers Marina had bought him for Christmas last year. When she saw those, her heart softened. She wanted to turn and run. But there was no choice. No going back now. Owen would send the story to press in the next twenty-four hours. She forced a smile.

'Hi, James,' she said. 'I'm sorry to drop by unannounced.'

'You're always welcome here. Please, come in.'

Marina followed James inside. The first floor

was dark. A stack of hunter green luggage sat by the kitchen door. He was coming or going — she wasn't sure. He was traveling constantly now that he was officially on the trail. She was lucky to have caught him.

They walked down the hallway to the library. A small fire crackled in the fireplace. A stack of papers lay facedown on an ottoman. A tumbler of scotch, neat, sat beside it.

'I'm sorry it's so dark in here,' James said, flicking on the overhead lights. 'I just got back from DC a few hours ago. Betsy's in Long Island. Did you hear about the leak?'

'The leak?'

'Yes, in the basement. In Southampton. Did Grant tell you?'

'Oh, no. He didn't. Was it serious?'

'Not sure yet. Happened during that cold snap last week. A pipe burst and everything's flooded, apparently. These old houses are so much work, I can't tell you. I would have been happy with a new build myself, but you know Betsy. She thinks all those Hamptons spec houses have no charm. Anyway, she's dealing with it. So I'm alone tonight. Just me and the dogs and my security detail. But now I've got you. Lucky me. Can I get you a drink?'

'I'm all right.'

'Come on. I've already poured myself a scotch. How about a glass of wine? Keep an old man company. Red or white?'

'Red, please. Thanks.'

James nodded and headed to the bar in the corner of the room. 'Is Grant joining us?' he asked. He pulled out two bottles of red, examined both, settled on one. He opened it and poured her a generous glass.

'No, it's just me.'

'Well, this is a nice surprise, then. Cheers.'

'Cheers.' Marina took a small sip. It was an excellent red, full-bodied, rich. Definitely expensive. She felt guilty that he had wasted it on her, on a night like this.

'So,' James said, settling back in his armchair. 'I'm guessing this isn't just a friendly visit.'

Marina smiled. 'You're right. It's not.'

'What can I do for you?'

'Answer me honestly.'

'Of course.'

'How much money do you have stored in offshore accounts?'

James raised an eyebrow. He seemed amused. 'This is about money?'

'Isn't everything?'

'I didn't think *you* were. In fact, I was counting on it.'

'I'm not shaking you down, if that's what you think.'

'I don't know quite what to think.'

'There's a story being written about you. Not by me, but by someone I know. About your ties to Bashar al-Assad.'

'That old story.'

'Yes. Except this time, there's a paper trail.'

'That's not possible. I have no connection to Mr. Al-Assad, as I've said in the past. I plan on releasing my tax returns to prove that.'

Marina shook her head. 'That won't prove

anything. All your business dealings with him happened through shell companies. With money in accounts at Swiss United Bank. Not exactly the kind of accounts that show up on tax returns.'

'Sounds like the premise of a great novel.'

'Except it's fact, not fiction. And we both know that.'

James's face hardened. Marina had seen him lose his temper before, but never with her. She braced herself, her fingers curling around the arms of the chair.

'Let's get to the point, then,' he said, his voice cold. 'How long were you two working together? Was it before or after you met my son?'

Marina frowned, confused. 'How long have I been working with who?'

'With Duncan Sander. You think I didn't know he was writing a story about Swiss United? If that's the case, you're not much of an investigative journalist.'

'You know, you're the second person to say that to me today,' Marina said. She smiled, trying to keep her cool.

'Everyone at Swiss United knew about it. They warned me about him. Told me to stay away. Then Grant shows up with you on his arm. To be frank, I was certain you were a plant. It was an interesting plan. What better way for Sander to get the inside scoop on me than to send his pretty young assistant in to fuck my son?'

Marina's mouth dropped open. 'That's what you think? That all this time, I've been with Grant so I could spy on your family?'

238

'Listen, you're a terrific actress. You had me fooled for a while. I told Grant that I had my doubts about you. But he said he was madly in love, and you really did seem to care about him. About all of us. So I convinced myself that it was just an unfortunate coincidence.'

For a moment, Marina stared at James in stunned silence.

'Oh my God,' she whispered finally. 'You killed Duncan.'

James glared at her, indignant. 'Of course not. I was speaking at a real estate conference at NYU at the time. You can check. There are plenty of eyewitnesses. Anyway, the man had scores of enemies. I was hardly the only person whose life Duncan Sander tried to destroy.'

'But you had him killed.' Marina didn't need a response. She felt her voice rise with rage. 'And you don't even care.'

As she said the words, she remembered what Grant had said to her in Paris. *Focus on family*, he had said. *Everything else is just collateral damage.*

Suddenly her head was swimming. The room felt unpleasantly hot. Marina wiped her forehead with the edge of her sleeve.

'You're not looking well, Marina. Are you all right?'

James moved toward her. Reflexively, Marina threw her wine in his face. 'What did you do?' she screamed. 'Why did you do it?'

'Keep your voice down,' James snarled. 'I have security down the hall.' He lunged for her. She flinched, covering her face with her forearm. She

239

felt him snatch the dripping glass from her hand and pull away. She opened her eyes. He was walking away from her, toward the bar. He placed her glass in the sink. From a drawer, he withdrew a cocktail napkin and began to blot his face dry.

'You didn't need to kill him,' Marina said, her voice breaking into a sob. 'He was a good man.'

'He may have been good to you, but Duncan Sander was far from a good man. He was a drunk and a liar and a crook. I didn't kill him, but I don't mind telling you that I'm happy he's dead.'

'You can't seriously be calling Duncan a crook.'

'He was a crook. He would do anything for a story. He tried to blackmail the head of Swiss United, did you know that? Threatened to run some tawdry story about how he was having an affair with an actress if Jonas didn't give him information on some of his banking clients. He made a very powerful enemy that day.'

'He wasn't investigating you, you know,' Marina cried. 'He didn't care about you. He was trying to track down Morty Reiss. That's why he was poking around Swiss United.'

James scoffed. 'Maybe that's how it started. But Sander was a smart man. He knew how valuable it could be to have a source inside an offshore bank. Morty Reiss is a small fish compared to some of the other clients at Swiss United.'

'Like you.'

'Like me.'

'So you admit it, then. You have money there.'

James laughed. 'You want me to tell you the whole story? You may not like what you hear.'

'Yes, of course I do. That's why I came here.'

'Because you want the truth.'

Marina was aware that James was mocking her, but she didn't care. She could tell he was about to break. He wanted to tell her the story, she realized. Maybe he was planning to kill her afterward. Or blackmail her or bribe her into silence. But like so many other criminals she'd interviewed, she could tell he wasn't ashamed of what he'd done. He might even be proud of it.

'I do,' she said, her voice small. 'You may not believe this, James, and I have no way to prove it to you, but I love Grant very much. I came to you tonight because I am worried about you. And I wanted to warn you that this story is being written. Not by Duncan. Not by me. By a journalist at the *Wall Street Journal*.'

For a moment, they were both silent. James took a seat, his brow furrowed. Marina could tell he wasn't sure whether to believe her, but he was going to give her his ear.

'Why was Duncan fishing around Swiss United?'

'Duncan was obsessed with Morty Reiss. He's always wanted to prove that Reiss faked his own death, that he was still alive somewhere. That's why he started poking around offshore banks. He figured that the best way to find Reiss was to find his money.

'He never told me who his sources were. In fact, he was completely close-lipped about the

241

whole investigation. I do know that a source gave him quite a bit of information. Financial records, emails, everything. Just before he died, Duncan must have shared it with other journalists. It's a huge investigation now, involving a number of people at a number of publications. And the stories will come out. Soon.'

'And one of the stories is me.'

'Yes.'

'Involving my holdings at Swiss United.'

'Yes. And your business dealings with Assad.'

James sighed. Suddenly he seemed very tired. With his thumb and forefinger, he massaged the skin between his eyebrows. 'And you came here because you want to know if it's true.'

'Not as a journalist. As your daughter-in-law.'

James nodded, considering. 'You know I hired a team. To vet me, basically. Paid a small fortune. They didn't find a thing.'

'So you decided it was safe to run.'

'I'm hardly the first politician to have money stashed offshore.'

'I'm sure.'

'The Assad business was so long ago. It doesn't really matter now.'

'He's a dictator. Of course it matters.'

'He's a deal maker. Same as me. He bought me out of a bind, that's all. And it's been a very lucrative arrangement for him. He's made a killing off those hotels.'

'But optically — '

'Yes, optically, it's not good. Because of sanctions lists and what-have-you. What people don't understand is that sanctions lists aren't about justice. They're just leverage. A way for one country to exert power over another.'

'So you don't believe that sanctions lists should exist?'

'I think we live in a global economy. If we want the economy to operate efficiently, we should be able to trade freely, with whomever we please.'

'Even if that means doing business with criminals.'

James smiled. 'Who gets to decide who is a criminal? Just because the US doesn't like a foreign leader and slaps his name on a sanctions list, does that make him a criminal?'

'Assad is an extreme case.'

'Perhaps. But you can't trust everything you read in the papers, Marina. If you were to pick up a Syrian newspaper, I'm sure you'd find some scathing critiques of our current president. It's all a matter of perspective.'

'It's a matter of truthful reporting.'

'You know what I think is criminal? Illegally acquiring financial statements from inside a bank and publishing them.'

'Does Grant know about your holdings at Swiss United? Or your dealings with Assad? Does he know what happened to Duncan?'

'No.' James gave her a stern look. 'Keep Grant out of this, Marina.'

Marina nodded. She breathed a small sigh of relief. 'I will.'

'If this story comes out, it will destroy his career, you know. Mine, certainly. But his, too.'

'I know.'

'And you love him. Or you say you do.'

'I love him very much.'

'Then you must understand that I will do everything in my power to kill this story. I have, and I will.'

'I understand.'

'And you'll stand silently by as I do it.'

It wasn't a question. Marina nodded. She couldn't bring herself to speak.

'Good. We're family now, Marina. Every family has its secrets. This will be ours.' James rose from his chair. 'You'll have to excuse me,' he said. 'The dogs need their walk. And I have an early flight in the morning.'

'Of course. I can show myself out.'

'Don't be ridiculous. I'll have my driver take you home. It's dark out now. Can't be too careful.'

Marina followed James down the hall. From the foyer table, he removed two leashes. Upon hearing the jangling sound of the metal clips against the marble floor, the two dogs came running. They sat obediently at James's feet as he tightened their collars around their necks and clipped them into their leashes.

'Good boys,' James murmured beneath his breath, feeding each a treat from his pocket.

James opened the town house door. His Escalade idled at the curb. Marina looked to her right and left, scanning the street. She did this reflexively now, always aware that someone might be following her. Across the street, lights twinkled from inside a cozy French bistro. A neighbor's maid stood on the sidewalk, watering the topiary bushes that flanked the town house door. Otherwise, the block was empty. The cross streets between Fifth and Madison always felt eerily quiet after dusk. Marina began to descend the stairs.

She stopped halfway down and turned.

'James,' she said, just as he was beginning to close the door.

'Yes?'

'The man who has been following me. Was he sent by you?'

James smiled. From the look on his face, Marina knew the answer was yes.

'You know, this morning I had Betsy fire the caretaker out in Southampton,' he said.

'Why?'

'Because of the leak. These things start small, but if you don't watch them, they can destroy a whole house.'

'He should have been watching more closely, you think.' Marina shivered. A light rain had begun to fall and Marina felt her hair growing damp.

'With a house that valuable, he should have been watching it like a hawk. It's what I pay him for. Leaks can be deadly.'

Marina nodded. The dogs cowered beside James, unhappy but silent. The rain was coming down harder now. She couldn't pretend to ignore it.

'Go home, dear. Take care of yourself. Manuel will make sure you get there safely.'

James yanked on the leashes, and the dogs leapt to their feet. Marina watched as they descended the steps and headed in the diretion of the park. She turned and strode defiantly past James's car. She would rather walk home in the rain.

Annabel

'Darling.' Julian pulled Annabel to him, his arms locking behind her back. 'There you are. I was so worried.'

'I'm all right. Jonas is here. He helped me clean this place up a bit.'

'It was a mess,' Jonas said, from behind her. His face was grave. 'I'm glad you called me. Annabel shouldn't be alone right now. This is getting out of hand.'

The men exchanged a look. Annabel sensed how uneasy they both were, which made her uneasy. If they were the ones who did this, wouldn't they appear more confident? Menacing, even? Instead, Julian looked genuinely alarmed by the state of her apartment. Jonas, too, seemed shaken. If it was an act, it was a hell of a good one.

'What's getting out of hand?' she asked.

'Annabel, let's sit,' Jonas replied. 'I think we need to talk.'

Wordlessly, they filed into the living room. Though they had tidied up much of the mess, evidence of the break-in was everywhere. Pictures on the floor. The gutted couches. Piles of paper stacked on the coffee table. The air was still cold. Annabel perched uncomfortably on the arm of a chair.

For a moment, no one spoke. Then Julian looked to Jonas, who gave him a nod. Julian cleared his throat.

'Annabel, there's something we've been keeping from you,' he said gently. 'We haven't — hmm — we haven't wanted to trouble you, on top of everything that's happened. But now, I think, is the time for honesty.'

Annabel stiffened. 'Honesty,' she said, her voice curt. 'Yes, I'd appreciate that.'

'We know you saw Zoe Durand right before you left for London. She came to your apartment, stayed for around an hour. Had you had any contact with her prior to that?'

'How did you know I saw Zoe?'

'We've been tailing her for some time,' Jonas said. 'We believe she's been stealing client information and selling it. We weren't sure to who, so we had her followed. We wanted to see if we could catch her buyer. We suspect someone had an ax to grind with the Amir family. They have powerful enemies. Anyway, I believe whoever was buying the information from Zoe was responsible for Matthew's death.'

Annabel inhaled sharply. 'Why?'

'The client information we have is incredibly valuable,' Julian said. 'Think of our client base. Who they are, who they do business with. People will pay enormous sums to have access to that kind of information. For that reason, we're very selective about who we hire. Zoe was not a typical hire for us. Not well pedigreed. She's from a very small town in the South of France. Very little money. She's a smart girl and brilliant with languages. She speaks five, I think. And quite ambitious. But ultimately, I think the financial temptation proved to be too great for her.'

'What did you think of Zoe?' Julian asked Annabel. 'Did you spend much time with her?'

'No. I didn't know her, really. Just in passing.'

'Did Matthew speak about her at all?'

Annabel winced, thinking of the schoolboyish way Matthew would talk about Zoe. 'Not really,' she said.

'Why did she come to see you? The night of Matthew's funeral?'

Annabel looked up and met Jonas's eye. 'I don't really know,' she said. She chose her words slowly and deliberately. 'She brought me a box of Matthew's things. Nothing of consequence. Just personal items that had ended up in her desk, that kind of thing. I think she felt guilty that we hadn't really ever gotten to know each other.'

'Did you ever think they might be having an affair?'

Annabel turned and looked at Julian. 'Yes,' she said, as calmly as possible. 'The thought crossed my mind. But I dismissed it.'

'Why?'

'Because I trusted Matthew. I believed in what we had.'

'Zoe is a persuasive woman. We think she may have convinced Matthew to help her. We know he gave her access to client information that typically bankers do not grant to their assistants.'

'That doesn't mean they were having an affair. Or that Matthew was doing anything improper.'

Julian took a deep breath. He reached into the breast pocket of his jacket and pulled out an envelope. 'I didn't want to have to give this to you,' he said, as he handed it to Annabel.

Annabel stared at the envelope. Then she slid a finger inside the seal and pulled it open. Inside, there was a stack of photographs. The first was grainy and so dark she had to hold it up to make out its contents. She flipped quickly through them, stopping on the last one. The image was clear. Their faces were unmistakable. Matthew and Zoe, lying together in a bed Annabel didn't recognize. Zoe's eyes were closed. She wore only a bra, sheer enough that her nipples were visible through the fabric. Her hair splayed across the pillow. They weren't kissing or making love. It was worse. Zoe's head lay tenderly against Matthew's shoulder, her hand resting on his naked torso.

'I'm sorry,' Julian said. 'Really, I am.'

Annabel stuffed the photographs back into the envelope. 'Why did you show me these?'

'Because we're trying to make you understand how dangerous Zoe Durand can be.' Jonas reached across the table and put his hand on Annabel's knee. 'We think she came into Swiss United with the intention of stealing data. Seducing Matthew was part of her plan.'

'And you think he helped her.'

'We think he might have. But he came to his senses. He was going to turn her in. And it got him killed.'

'So what do you want from me?'

'Help us find Zoe.'

'I don't know where she is.'

'She disappeared after she visited you. She didn't tell you where she was going?'

Annabel sat back. She felt her bones settling

250

into the chair, a deep liquid fatigue flooding her body. She closed her eyes. She welcomed the silence, the momentary darkness. Then the image of Zoe's half-naked body next to her husband flickered on the backs of her eyelids, like a film projection her mind couldn't shut off. Her eyes popped open.

'She told me to tell you she was going home. To take care of her sick mother.'

'She told you that? Or she told you to tell us that?'

'She told me to tell you that.'

Julian looked at Jonas.

'And did she mention a computer? Matthew's laptop?'

'Zoe has it,' Annabel said. She looked Jonas in the eye. 'If you find her, she'll have it.'

Jonas nodded. 'Thank you, Annabel. You've been very helpful.'

'It's been a long day,' Annabel said. She stood. 'Would you mind if I showered, cleaned myself up a bit?'

'Of course.' Jonas and Julian rose to their feet.

'Annabel, you can't stay here tonight,' Julian said. His eyes shone with concern. 'It isn't safe.'

Jonas agreed. 'You'll stay with us. In Cologny.'

'Go with him, Annabel,' Julian said. 'You'll be safe there. We need to find Zoe. Once we do, we can figure out who her buyer was. Whoever they were, if they killed Matthew, they will come for you.' He gestured around the apartment. 'They already have.'

'All right. Just give me time to shower and pack up a few things.'

'Of course. Take all the time you need. We can wait downstairs in the lobby.' Jonas nodded at Julian. The two men turned and let themselves out. As soon as Annabel knew they were gone, she covered her face with her hands and began to weep.

Marina

Marina's apartment was dark when she entered. Her hands trembled as she unbuttoned her coat. She pulled off her heels. They were soaked through from the rain. She left them on the foyer floor and padded, barefoot, to the library bar.

She needed a drink. Not wine; something stronger. She pulled out a bottle of Macallan and poured herself an ounce. She swirled it, sniffed it, and then tossed it back. She closed her eyes, savoring the burn at the back of her throat.

'Celebrating something?'

Marina's eyes opened. She turned; Grant leaned against the library door, hands in his pockets. Though he looked handsome in a button-down, blazer, jeans, and loafers, she could tell he was tired.

'Jesus.' Marina put down the glass. 'You scared me. I didn't know anyone was here.'

'I just got home. Where were you?'

'Out.'

'I was waiting for you at Chat Noir.' Grant glanced at his watch. 'For over an hour. When it started getting awkward, I left.'

'Oh my God, Grant. Why didn't you text me?'

'I didn't think you needed a reminder about our anniversary.'

Marina's hand flew to her forehead. 'I'm so sorry. It's just been crazy at work.'

'I thought you wanted this to be a tradition.'

'I did. I do. I'm sorry, Grant. Can we sit and talk?'

'Of course.' Grant nodded toward the bar. 'Have a drink with me, at least? It's our anniversary, after all.'

She gave him a small smile. 'Neat?'

'Always.'

Marina handed Grant a tumbler. They both took a seat on the couch. Side by side but not close enough to touch.

Marina took a small sip. 'I was at your father's.'

'Why?'

'I wanted to ask him about his offshore holdings.'

Grant frowned. He put his tumbler down on the coffee table. 'His offshore holdings?'

'Yes.'

'I don't understand.'

'There's a journalist I know. He's writing about your father. His holdings at Swiss United Bank. His business ties to Assad. Don't bother defending him, Grant. He admitted it was all true.'

Grant's expression transformed from confusion to shock. 'He what?' He shook his head. 'I can't believe that.'

'He said you weren't involved.'

'I'm not.'

'I know. I believe you.'

'How do you know about this story?'

'It was Duncan's story. A friend picked it up after he died. I wanted your father to hear it from me, before it came out.'

'Duncan Sander?'

'Yes. Did you know that your father was having him followed?'

'I know he didn't trust Duncan,' Grant said after a pause. 'I didn't, either, to be honest.'

'He asked me if I fucked you as a way to get the inside track on your family.'

Grant looked up. 'Jesus Christ. I'm sorry. Dad can be crass when he's upset. He doesn't really think that about you. I hope you know that.'

'He didn't trust me, though. Do you? Did you ever wonder about me?'

Grant slid closer to her. He cupped her cheek in his hand. Gently, he turned her face so that they were looking at each other, eye to eye. 'Never,' he said firmly. 'Not once.'

She nodded.

'Look, I know the rumors about Dad. About the offshore business. I don't want to justify anything, but a lot of people do it. You know, for tax reasons. I'm not condoning it, but — '

'Do they do business with tyrannical terrorists, too?'

Grant took a deep breath before he answered. 'No matter what Duncan or anyone else may have told you, my father wouldn't do business with Assad.'

'He told me he did, Grant.'

He looked away. 'That's just not true.'

'That's not the end of it, either. He had Duncan killed. To cover the story.'

Grant turned back to her, his eyes blazing. 'No,' he said, his voice cold. 'You're wrong.' His jaw muscle flexed as he clenched his teeth. It struck Marina how much Grant looked like his father when he was angry.

He stood up and strode over to the window. 'Why would you say that?'

'He basically admitted it, Grant.'

'You can't be serious.'

Marina rose to her feet. They stood, staring at each other, from across the library. 'Your father is not the man you think he is,' she said, crossing her arms.

'My father is the best man I've ever met. Whatever you think you know is wrong.'

'I understand how hard this is to hear,' Marina said. She reminded herself to stay calm. 'Grant, you have to prepare yourself. He's running for president. The truth will come out. It always does.'

Grant snorted. 'Whatever my father has done pales in comparison to the behavior of many great men.'

'Maybe so.'

'He'll be an excellent leader. Better than Hayden Murphy, for God's sake. Dad's brilliant. He's unbiased. Whatever he's done, he's done for the greater good. You need to think about the big picture.'

'I'm sorry, but I don't believe that the ends always justify the means. Especially if the means involve murdering a friend of mine.'

'He didn't kill Duncan, Marina!' Grant's voice rose in frustration.

'Why don't you ask him yourself?'

Grant took a deep breath. For a moment, they stared at each other, silent. Marina could hear the distant rumble of traffic on Park Avenue and the steady drumbeat of the rain on the windowpanes. Grant shifted, and the light caught his hair. For the first time, Marina noticed a hint of silver around his ears. These past few weeks had taken a toll on all of them. Grant appeared leaner, too. He hadn't been sleeping well or going to the gym, and it showed. He looked, Marina thought, more like James than ever.

She felt a sharp pang of guilt. James was Grant's father. What would she do if it was her father? Richard, of course, would never so much as jaywalk. But Marina was lucky in that way. She'd never given much consideration to the moral character of her parents, except, perhaps, to measure herself against it.

How could she judge Grant? He believed in family. He believed in loyalty. It was those values that would make him a good husband. But they could be his downfall, too. He would follow his father to the ends of the earth. It was up to her whether she would go with them.

'Do you want to go talk to Dad together?' Grant said, his voice softening. 'We can clear this up. I know we can.'

'I'm sorry.' She ran to him and threw her arms around his neck. He lowered his face, nuzzling the side of hers. He was crying, she realized. 'I have to go.'

'Please don't.'

'I have to. I won't ever get past what I heard tonight.'

'Do you still love me, Marina?'

Marina pulled back so she could look at Grant. They held each other at arm's length, their fingers clasped tightly together.

'Yes,' she whispered. Tears dripped from her cheeks, and his. 'I do. I always will.'

'Then consider what you're doing. Think about the life we could have together. None of this has anything to do with us.'

'I wish that were true.' She pulled his hands to her lips and kissed them. Then she turned, and before she lost her nerve, she fled from the apartment. She scooped up her shoes and coat from the foyer floor and let the front door shut behind her. If Grant came after her, she was afraid she might stay. She pressed the elevator button hard and fast and was surprised when it opened right away. She stepped inside, barefoot, holding her shoes to her chest.

Annabel

Annabel cried until her throat ached and her head throbbed. Eventually, when she'd cried herself out, she peeled herself off the floor and forced herself to shower. When she emerged, the bedroom was cold and Annabel's wet shoulders shook as she stood in front of the bed. *Had they slept together more than once? Had he brought her here, to their apartment?* The thought made her sick.

Her eyes fell on the nail above the bed. On it used to hang the Marshall Cleve painting that Matthew had bought for her just before he died. Her breath caught in her throat. Where was the painting? Had they damaged it? Destroyed it? Taken it? The thought of that canvas torn, the thick silver frame cracked, broke her heart. As if it wasn't broken already.

She looked to the left of the bed, then to the right. There it was, tilted against the wall on one side was the painting. Annabel dropped to her knees and grasped the frame in her hands. It appeared undamaged. She wondered why someone had bothered to move it. *Perhaps they had been looking for a safe behind it*, she thought. She shivered. If it wasn't Jonas and Julian who had sent men to search her apartment, who was it? What had they hoped to find?

Annabel stared at the painting, her eyes misting over. Her fingers wrapped themselves around the frame.

You should own this, Matthew had said. *I want to buy you art. Your own private gallery.*

Had Zoe convinced him to sell client information to the highest bidder? Annabel couldn't believe it; but then, she wouldn't have believed that he had slept with Zoe, either, until she'd seen the pictures to prove it. And Matthew's appetite for wealth had always troubled Annabel. Now her head swirled with possibilities, all of them awful. Either Zoe was telling the truth and the photos were a setup, orchestrated by Jonas to blackmail Matthew into doing his bidding. Or Jonas and Julian were telling the truth and Zoe had convinced Matthew to betray the bank by selling client information. Annabel had never trusted Zoe, and the pictures hadn't helped. The question was: how much did she trust Matthew?

If ever anything happens to me, Matthew had said when he gave her the painting. Had he known that someone was trying to kill him? Annabel squeezed her eyes shut, trying to recall the conversation. *If ever anything happens to me . . .* what had he said next?

Her eyes opened.

There's value in the frame.

That's what he had said.

There's value in the frame. I want you to remember that.

At the time, it had struck her as an odd thing to say. But now . . .

Annabel popped to her feet. She let the towel slide off her body. She lay the painting on the bed and examined the frame. She let her fingers caress the edges of it, feeling for seams or small shifts in the wood.

Nothing.

It was a beautiful frame but not terribly distinct. Of all the things they owned, this frame was hardly the most valuable.

'Annabel?' Julian's voice drifted through the bedroom door. 'Are you all right?'

Annabel's head jerked up. Instinctively, she grabbed the towel from around her feet and pulled it up over her body. 'I'm fine!' she called out. 'Just got out of the shower.'

'All right. I was just getting worried.'

'I'm sorry. I'll be ready soon.'

'Take your time.'

Annabel flipped over the painting. She ran a hand over the backing paper. Along one edge, she felt a small ridge. Her eyes widened. She hurried to the bedroom door and, as quietly as possible, turned the lock on the door. Then she ran back into the bathroom. In a drawer, she found an old Dopp kit of Matthew's, crammed with odds and ends. And an old razor. Band-Aids. Antiseptic spray. Through the pipes, she could hear the muffled sound of Julian talking to someone in the living room. She was running out of time. Her fingers closed around what she was looking for: a small pocketknife.

She rushed back to the painting and slid the blade between the paper and the frame. Gently, she eased the adhesive on the paper until she was able to pull it back. There, taped to the inside edge of the frame, was a USB. Beneath it, a folded note.

Annabel pulled it free and, with trembling fingers, unfurled the note. Her eyes swelled with tears when she saw Matthew's handwriting and the slight smudge on the edge of the paper where his left hand dragged across the ink.

Beloved A —

If you are reading this, something has gone terribly wrong. Thank you for listening to me and remembering what I told you about there being value in this frame. You remain the cleverest person I know.

I am so sorry for everything. I never should have brought us here. Swiss United is a terrible place. They do terrible things for terrible people. I was, I'll admit, initially enchanted by the money. But it isn't worth it. I tried to get us out of it, but perhaps I acted too late.

If you are reading this, I am likely dead. Zoe may be, too. Bring this USB to Lorenzo Mora. I trust him to get it to the right people. He will explain everything.

Please know this, Beloved A — I loved you from the moment I first saw you. That love has never wavered. It has only grown stronger. I have made mistakes, and I take full responsibility for them. But I never, ever stopped loving you. If you believe only one thing, believe that.

Yours always,
Matthew

Annabel curled the note in her hand. Her eyes closed as she pressed it to her breast. Her tears fell to the floor. Her hair, still wet, dripped down her naked back.

'Annabel?' Julian's voice came again from the hallway. 'Jonas is anxious to get on the road. Are you nearly ready?'

'I'll be right there,' she called, her voice hoarse. She hurried to the closet, pulled on a pair of jeans and an oversize sweater. In her back pocket, she tucked the note with the USB.

In the drawer of her desk, she found a glue stick. It was old, but it would have to suffice. As quickly as she could, she dragged it across the back of the frame and, with the tips of her fingers, resealed the backing paper. Then, she propped the picture against the wall, sideways, just as she'd found it.

In a suitcase, she tossed together a few basic items: a cosmetics case, a hairbrush, a change of clothes. From a small box on her nightstand, she took a pair of pearl earrings that had once been her mother's and a bracelet that Matthew had given her on their first anniversary. Off the top shelf in the closet, she pulled out the box of notes. After a moment's deliberation, she picked out the note Matthew had written to her on the day he proposed, scribbled on a page he'd ripped out of a day planner. She kissed it, and then folded it and tucked it into her wallet. Everything else, she decided, she could leave behind.

Before zipping up her bag, Annabel picked up the pocketknife and slipped it into her cosmetics case. Small and dulled from use, it wasn't much of a weapon. Still, just knowing it was there gave her comfort. Where she was going, she'd need all the comfort she could get.

Marina

Twelve stories. All set to run the following day on the homepages of the most influential publications around the globe. Christophe Martin at the ICIJ had judiciously divided the stories among top journalists at the *New York Times, the Wall Street Journal*, the *Telegraph, Daily Mail, China Daily, El País, Financial Times, Le Monde, Süddeutsche Zeitung, the Moscow Times, Yomiuri Shimbun*, and Owen's website, the *Deliverable*. Collectively, the stories would demonstrate how Schmit & Muller had, for decades, funneled money from heads of state, cartel members, terrorists, corporate CEOs, arms dealers, financiers, tycoons, sheikhs, and other members of the global elite into numbered accounts at offshore banks like Swiss United and CIB for the explicit purpose of hiding those assets. The results would be devastating. Those exposed would be arrested, fined, disgraced. Several world leaders would be ousted. Secret relationships and business deals would be made public. Families would be split apart over the discovery of hidden assets, illegally gotten gains, evaded taxes, payments to mistresses and, in a few cases, second families. The stories were just the beginning. Owen and Christophe had selected these twelve stories to be released at once because they packed the biggest punch. But follow-up pieces would be rolling in for weeks, months, years. Vast quantities of data still remained inside of Maestra, unexamined. Owen sat at his office desk, nervously circling a pen between his fingers. As he dialed into the final conference call before the stories went to copy, he knew he was sitting on what was potentially the biggest story of them all. He just wasn't sure what to do with it.

'Owen Barry here. Sorry for the delay.'

'Hey, Owen,' Christophe Martin said. 'I think we're all on now. Any update on the Ellis story?'

'Yeah. That's why I was a few minutes late. I was hoping to have something for you all, but I don't think I do. We'll have to just go forward with the pieces we have.'

'We could delay another day or two if that would help,' Mike Sheeran at the *New York Times* piped up. 'The Ellis story is dynamite.'

'I'm concerned about our source,' Owen replied. 'He's been radio silent for twenty-four hours now. I don't think it's fair to him to continue to delay.'

'We agree,' said Sergei Ivanov, one of the Russian journalists from the *Moscow Times*. 'For us, a delay is too risky. Things are tense in Moscow. A colleague at our paper was attacked this morning with a knife in an alley outside his house. His laptop was stolen and he was left for dead. He's in critical condition; we're waiting to hear how he does in surgery. The police are saying it was a random mugging, but we don't believe that. We're concerned that word is spreading about an investigation into offshore assets. None of us are safe.'

'Have you left Moscow?'

'Yes. We're all right for the time being. But the longer we delay — '

'We feel similarly here,' Andres Gomez at *El País* announced. 'The Mora Cartel has eyes everywhere. We need to run this story now. We cannot sit on it much longer.'

'All right.' Owen tilted back in his chair, hands tucked behind his head. 'Agreed. The Ellis story can wait.'

Owen leaned farther back. Out of the corner of his eye, he saw the elevators open. Marina stepped out. A black skirt swirled around her hips; her white blouse was cut to reveal just a hint of her delicate shoulders. She pushed up onto her toes, looking for him. Owen swiveled his chair around, nearly toppling backward in the process.

'What the fuck?' he muttered, catching himself on the edge of the table.

'You there, Owen?'

'Yeah, sorry. Guys, I need to call you back.'

'We need to submit tonight or else — '

'Yeah, yeah. I get it. I'll call you back.'

Owen clicked off the call. He was still fumbling with his headset when Marina appeared in front of his desk.

'How'd you get in here?'

'Nice to see you, too.'

'Sorry, I figured when you slammed the door in my face you probably needed a few days to cool off before we could hang out again.'

'I'm sorry about that. I was upset.'

'Yeah, I got that.'

'You were angry, too.'

'Look, Marina, it's great to see you and all, but I'm on a deadline. Can we make up some other time?'

'I'm not here to make up. I'm here to help. Can I sit?'

Owen stared at her, assessing. Then he looped a foot around the empty chair at the cube next to him and kicked it over to her.

'If you're here to convince me not to run the Ellis story, you're wasting your time. And mine.'

'I'm not. I'm here to help you finish it.'

Owen let out a surprised laugh. 'See, this is why I'm not married. What the fuck happened? Did you have a fight with Junior or something? You've done quite the one-eighty on that family.'

Marina sighed. 'I understand that you're angry at me. And I'm sorry about that. We can talk about that later. When does this need to go to copy?'

'Five for the print editions, eleven for the websites. We want everything to be up by midnight New York time.'

'Okay. I think we can do this.'

'Only if you've got the smoking gun. Because I don't have enough to run a good story. All I've got is a paper trail linking Ellis to Swiss United and some transfers between shell companies that I think belong to Ellis and I think belong to Assad. But that's it and it's pretty tenuous. We need some kind of confirmation.'

Marina reached into her purse and pulled out her cell phone. 'Like a taped confession?'

'You're fucking kidding me.'

'Would I joke about something like this?'

'You talked to James Ellis?'

'I went straight to his house after I left your apartment. I wanted answers. I asked him about his accounts at Swiss United and his dealings with Assad. He admitted to both. And then he told me I would never tell anyone because it would ruin Grant's life — and mine — if I did.'

'He's right. It will ruin your life.'

'I know. And Grant's. And Grant doesn't deserve that.'

'So why are you here?'

'Because James had Duncan killed.'

Owen's expression turned from surprise to shock. '*James Ellis* had Duncan murdered?'

'Yes.'

'You have this on record?'

'Not on record, exactly. But he didn't do a great job of denying it. And I think I know how we can prove it. We'll have to work quickly, though. I need to get down to DC.'

'DC? Why?'

'Hunter Morse. Remember? At the Department of Justice. Duncan had his name circled in his day planner. He was supposed to go see him the day after he died. I think he's the key to this whole story.'

'You think he'll talk to you?'

'I don't know. But it's worth a shot.'

Owen checked his watch. 'If you leave now, you could be there by six.'

Marina stood up and pulled her purse over her shoulder. 'I'll send you the audio recording of Ellis from the car.'

'Hey, Marina?' Owen said, as she turned to leave his cube.

She looked at him, one perfect brow arched.

'Let's nail this guy to the wall.'

Annabel

Annabel stood at the window, gazing out across the expanse of Lake Geneva. The water glowed at this time of day, a mirror for the electric blues and celestial pinks of the brightening morning sky. In the distance, the craggy white mountains stood, silent and imposing, like sentinels beside the lake. The vertical rises and drops of their peaks were awe-inspiring. Annabel wondered how many people had lost their lives to those mountains. She thought of men with ice axes and crampons, buried beneath avalanches of snow. Of hikers who set off in the early morning light, never to return. Of her husband's plane, smashed to metallic chords on a mountaintop, a place so remote that it had never before been touched by any living being. She thought of Matthew's ashes, disappearing on the wind like smoke.

The room felt like a gilded prison cell. The walls were lacquered in a brilliant eggshell blue; the drapes were made of a thick, expensive-looking chintz. The bed was an antique four-poster. Like something out of Versailles, Annabel thought. Jonas and Julian had insisted that she stay here, at the Klausers' home in Cologny. It was for her protection, they said. They couldn't in good conscience let her stay in a hotel. So here she was, staying in a lavishly appointed guest room, with eighteenth-century furniture and a rug so soft it felt like cashmere, just ten feet down the hall from Jonas and Elsa. She'd never felt less safe in her life.

She hadn't slept. She hadn't bothered to unpack her suitcase, either. She didn't want to get comfortable here. She didn't like the idea of being naked in Jonas Klauser's house. She was vulnerable enough as it was. Within the hour, a car would take her to the airport. From there, she would fly back to London, where Khalid would meet her at Heathrow. He would give her Matthew's laptop and she would board a plane to New York. Then she'd board a train to DC and find Hunter Morse.

Jonas Klauser knew none of this, of course. Only that she was on a one-way flight home to New York. She couldn't stay in Switzerland any longer, she told him. It was too hard for her there. She just wanted to go home.

He had arranged for her flight. First class, nonstop. She had waited until he was asleep and then she had called the airline to change her ticket so that she had a one-hour layover in London. She changed the payment method, too, so that the charge would go on her credit card instead of his. She figured Jonas wouldn't notice. Even if he did, she hoped he would think she was just being polite.

Annabel heard a knock on the door.

'Annabel?' Elsa's muffled voice came from the hallway. 'Darling, your car is here.'

'Thank you,' Annabel called, trying not to sound as on edge as she actually was. 'Out in a minute.'

She gazed out the window for one last moment. The sun was rising above the horizon, bathing the mountains in light. She pressed her fingers to the glass. She felt its coolness against her skin. It was nearly freezing outside, she thought. The bright morning sun was deceptive, making the lake look inviting instead of deadly cold to the touch.

'Good-bye, Matthew,' she murmured, her eyes closing. 'I love you.'

Then she pulled away from the window, away from the view of the lake and the mountains beyond. It would be her last real glimpse of Geneva. She shut the shades and headed for the door.

Jonas and Elsa were waiting for Annabel in the hallway. Jonas moved quickly to take her suitcase. They seemed as nervous as she felt. Jonas descended the stairs, her suitcase in his hand. Elsa trailed behind, seeming unsure of what to do or how to be of help.

'I'm sorry you can't stay for breakfast,' she said. 'Can I send you off with something?'

'Oh, I'm all right. I don't want to overstay my welcome.'

'Don't be silly. You were hardly here at all.'

'Thank you. I'm eager to get home. It's time.'

Elsa looked troubled, but she nodded nonetheless.

'You could have taken my driver to the airport,' Jonas said. He frowned at the town car in the driveway. 'It wouldn't have been a bother.'

'Oh, no. You've done enough for me already.'

Now came the part that Annabel dreaded.

Jonas embraced her. She felt dizzy as his arms encircled her. She wanted to scream. Instead, she closed her eyes and waited for the moment to pass. Then, she forced a smile.

It's almost over, she told herself. *By this time tomorrow, Jonas Klauser's hands will be cuffed behind his back.*

'This is it, I guess,' Annabel said. She shivered involuntarily, as though her body itself was revolting against Jonas's touch. 'I'll never forget all that you've done.'

'Stay in touch,' Jonas replied. 'I'd like to know how you are doing.'

'Oh, I will. We'll speak again soon.'

'I hope so.'

Annabel nodded and turned away. Her heart was in her throat as she walked out of the Klausers' house and into the waiting car.

⋆ ⋆ ⋆

Once she'd reached the airport, Annabel felt her shoulders begin to release from around her ears. The hardest part was behind her now. Her departure from Geneva had gone smoothly. She had a plan; three more steps to go. She had to collect the laptop. Bring it to Hunter Morse. And then wait for the arrests to begin.

Jonas and Julian would be first. Then Fares Amir and the lawyers at Schmit & Muller. From what Khalid had told her, Matthew's laptop was filled with damning evidence against all of them, hundreds of documents that proved beyond a doubt that they colluded to hide the assets of

274

hundreds of international criminals, from Assad to Putin. Countless others would be arrested, too. Lawyers, accountants, bankers. People who Annabel had met and perhaps even liked. People who had attended Matthew's memorial service; maybe some who had considered him a friend. People who may or may not have made criminal decisions. Maybe they were just doing as they were told. Maybe, like Zoe, they had been naive enough to think that Swiss United was just like any other bank. Annabel was certainly guilty of such thinking. How wrong she had been. How wrong they all had been, these cogs in the wheel of a vast criminal enterprise.

Her flight was boarding. Annabel rose from her seat and headed to the gate. As she was about to hand over her boarding pass to the attendant, her phone rang. She stepped back, allowing the next passenger in line to move ahead of her. It was a number she didn't recognize, but from the country code, she knew it was coming from the United Kingdom.

'Annabel, listen to me. Where are you?' Khalid's voice was scratchy and faint, and muffled by what sounded like a passing train.

'Khalid?' Annabel pressed the phone tight to one ear and covered the other with the palm of her hand. 'I can hardly hear you.'

'Where are you?'

'I'm at the airport. Why? My flight is boarding. I'm on my way to you.'

'Annabel, you can't go to New York. Morse — '

'Khalid, you're cutting in and out.'

'I did some digging into Morse. He's getting paid by James Ellis. Ellis is a client of Jonas Klauser's. I think Ellis paid Morse off to tell him who the leak was inside of Swiss United. He can't be trusted.'

'Morse at the DOJ?' Annabel's head was spinning. The last of the passengers were boarding her flight to Heathrow. She watched as a red line appeared around the flight number on the board, indicating final boarding call.

'Yes. He's working for — '

Annabel heard a scuffling sound, a *thump*. Then, the line went dead.

'Khalid?' Annabel screamed. '*Khalid?*' But all she heard was dead air on the other end of the line.

People around her were staring.

'Are you all right?' a woman beside her approached, her face clouded with worry.

'Do you speak French, miss?' a man asked. '*Qu'est-ce qu'il y a?*'

'Madam, it's final boarding call for London, Heathrow Airport,' the attendant said. '*Dernier appel d'embarquement.*'

Annabel spun around. A crowd was gathering. At the back of it, she saw a familiar face. It was the man who bumped into her at the library, just as she was leaving the microfilm room. He had knocked the photographs out of her bag. When she made eye contact with him, he turned away and disappeared into the crowd.

She looked at the attendant, not comprehending.

'Madam, are you boarding?'

276

Annabel shook her head. 'No,' she said, her voice a whisper. 'No.' She picked up her bag and backed away, nearly colliding with the woman who had asked after her as she sprinted out of the gate.

Zoe

Zoe's shift at Café Hugo was ending. It was late afternoon, and the trickle of lunchgoers had dried up. The dinner crowd would start arriving in an hour or so, mostly fishermen and shopkeepers who came in for a beer and oysters after the workday. Zoe's uncle, Clement, liked to close the kitchen for an hour or two before dinner so he could smoke and play cards with his friends. Zoe was the only waitress on the day shift. Rose, the other girl, was supposed to come by four, but usually she didn't turn up until five. Rose didn't like Zoe; Zoe could tell. She showed her disapproval in small ways. Showing up late. Leaving food residue in the sinks. It didn't really matter. It wasn't like there was much work to do. This time of year, Café Hugo only needed a bare-bones staff. Tourist season was over. The terrace — Café Hugo's only real asset — was too cold to enjoy. Yesterday, Zoe had asked Clement if he wanted her to put the tables and chairs downstairs in the basement. '*Prochaine semaine,*' he said. *Next week.* That was Clement's answer to most things. Zoe had forgotten how slow people moved in Saint-Thérèse-de-la-Mer. Before, the snail's pace of things here had made her crazy. No one ever got anything done, she complained to her friends. They just went day by day; no real plans for the future. Before, she would have just taken the chairs downstairs anyway. It

278

needed to be done, and why wait? Now she just nodded and went back to wiping down the bar. Next week was fine with her.

She loosened the knot of her apron and slipped it over her head. She could hear laughter from the alley outside and smell the faint earthiness of Clement's hand-rolled cigarettes. She sat down at a table and began to count her tips. She made less money here in a week than she did in a day at Swiss United. But here, she could live on practically nothing. Clement was letting her stay in the apartment above the restaurant for free. He fed her, too, mostly leftovers from the kitchen. She couldn't live off his generosity forever, of course. But it was temporary. Eventually, one way or another, this would be over. She just hoped she'd be alive at the end of it.

Her tips were counted. Zoe looked up and was surprised to see a man sitting on the terrace. She hadn't heard him come in. He had chosen the table in the far left corner, the one with the best view of the sea. From his vantage point, he could see a swath of the glittering water from between the apricot-colored roofs of the surrounding houses. It was the best table at Café Hugo. Zoe wondered if he was one of Clement's regulars. Some of them remembered her from when she was a child. They would ask her about Geneva and if she was married now. They would ask her how long she was planning to stay in Saint-Thérèse-de-la-Mer. She was getting better at answering with nonanswers.

Zoe stood and slipped her apron back on. She

tucked her pencil behind her ear. She shivered when she opened the door; the temperature was dropping with the sun. A stiff cold wind sent the frayed awning over the terrace door flapping. The man didn't seem bothered by the breeze. He turned his head, put a cigarette to his lips. He cupped one hand around the lighter to protect the flame.

It wasn't until he tilted his head back that Zoe recognized him. His profile was unmistakable. Julian White had a sharp aquiline nose and a slender, almost feminine neck. He pushed his sandy blond hair off his forehead and closed his eyes as he savored the first drag. Then he crossed one leg over the other and slouched back in his chair. Clement's laughter drifted up from the alley behind the restaurant. Overhead, a gull squawked and swooped. Otherwise, they were alone.

Zoe's feet felt like lead. She had tried to prepare herself for this moment, when someone from Swiss United came for her. She stood still, rooted to the spot. *I should run,* she thought. But what if Julian saw her? Then he would know she was hiding something. If she ran, she was as good as dead.

Zoe forced herself to put one foot in front of the other until she was standing at Julian's side.

'Julian?' She conjured a smile. 'How funny to see you here.'

Julian looked up. The moment they locked eyes, she knew he knew. How much, she wasn't sure. But Julian White knew something. His visit to Café Hugo was neither coincidental nor was it friendly. Of course it wasn't. Zoe had been at Swiss United long enough to know better. No one at Swiss United would turn up here, at a café populated mostly by locals in a small fishing town in the South of France. Least of all Julian White, who, the last time she saw him, was complaining about the lack of caviar on the room service menu at Grand-Hôtel du Cap-Ferrat. No. Julian White was as calculated and deliberate as they came. He was here on business, and the business was her.

'Zoe,' he said, cool as the breeze. 'How nice it is to see you again.'

'And you. What brings you to Saint-Thérèse-de-la-Mer?'

Julian gestured at the sea. 'Oh, I love this corner of France. Look at this view. No wonder Van Gogh loved this town.'

'You're thinking of Saintes-Maries-de-la-Mer. On the other side of Aries.'

'Am I? Well, the coast is all lovely. You're lucky to live here.'

'Just for a while. My mother is ill.'

'Yes, I heard. I was sorry to hear that.'

'This is my uncle's restaurant. They needed the help.'

'Of course. How good of you to fill in.'

'Are you staying in town?'

Julian smiled. 'I don't know yet,' he said. 'I have some work in the area. I'm not sure how long it will take. Any recommendations?'

Zoe shrugged. 'Vila de la Mar is nice. But there are prettier places, in my opinion. Nice. Saint-Tropez.'

'Are you trying to get rid of me?'

'Of course not, no,' Zoe exclaimed. She felt her face flush with embarrassment. 'Here,' she said, thrusting a menu at Julian. 'The kitchen is closed, but — '

'I don't want to inconvenience you.'

'It's no trouble. Really. Whatever you want.'

Julian smiled. She felt his eyes slide down her neck and torso and linger on the gap between her thighs.

'Just a drink, maybe,' he said, after he had finished appraising her. 'Could you find me a nice bottle of red?'

'Of course.'

'Bring two glasses,' Julian called after her.

Zoe hurried back inside and slipped behind the bar. Her hands shook as she gripped the counter. She could sense Julian watching her through the glass. She bent down, as though getting something from a low shelf. When she was out of his sight line, she pulled her phone out of her pocket and texted her boyfriend, Arthur.

Julian White from Swiss United is here, she typed. What do I do?

Zoe waited for a response but none came. She grimaced and shoved the phone back into her pocket. She pulled a bottle of red out of the cabinet, placed it on her tray, and hurried back outside, hoping she hadn't been gone for a suspiciously long time.

'This is my uncle's favorite,' she said, holding out the bottle. 'Spicy and full bodied. From Corbières.'

'You sound like you know your wine.'

Zoe blushed again. 'No. Not really. Just enough to get by as a waitress.'

'Or to work at Swiss United.'

'I didn't realize knowledge of wine was part of that job.'

Julian laughed. 'Oh, but it is. You need to know about the finer things to work in private banking.'

'I was just an assistant.'

'Matthew didn't think so. He trusted you. Relied on you quite a bit.'

'I did my best to be helpful.'

'Sit. Have a glass with me.'

'Oh, no. Thank you. I have to work.'

Julian looked around at the empty terrace. 'There's no one here. You said the kitchen was closed. Have a drink with an old friend.'

Zoe sat. *At least it's daylight*, she told herself, as Julian poured her a glass of wine. *Clement is downstairs. Patrons will start to arrive soon.*

'You left right after Matthew's service. Why didn't you say good-bye?'

'I did. Well, to Annabel Werner, anyway. My mother was ill. It all happened quickly.'

'Your mother.'

'Yes.'

'It's funny, I thought I remembered Matthew saying that your mother had died when you were young.'

Zoe blanched. 'Yes. Well, I misspoke. It's my aunt that's sick. My mother died when I was a baby. My aunt raised me. I think of her as my mother.'

283

'Ah. And she owns this place?'

'Yes. With my uncle. He's the chef.'

'Where are you staying?'

'They lent me the apartment upstairs.'

'You should have said good-bye. To Jonas, at least. He was worried.'

'I — Yes, of course. I should have. I wasn't thinking so clearly after Matthew died.'

Julian nodded. He took a sip of wine and stared out at the sea. 'Terrible thing,' he said.

'Yes. Yes, it was.'

'You know, Matthew was my closest friend at the bank.'

She nodded.

'He was a terrific guy. Loads of fun. Before he died, though, I felt like something had changed. There was a darkness hanging over him. Do you know what I mean?'

'Perhaps,' Zoe said. She shrugged. She began to pull apart a cocktail napkin, rolling the paper between her fingertips into small, compact balls. 'It was a tough job.'

'Yes, that's true. Long hours and all that. But there was something else. I couldn't quite put my finger on it at the time.'

'What do you think it was?' Zoe asked.

'I think he was in some kind of trouble.'

'Trouble?'

'Yes. I don't know if it was financial trouble or what. But there were rumors.'

'Rumors of what?'

'That he was selling financial information. From inside Swiss United.'

'Matthew would never.' Zoe frowned.

284

'I agree. It seems out of character for him. But there was information leaking out of the bank. Some of it may have fallen into the hands of reporters.'

Zoe shivered. 'Reporters?'

'Yes. Jonas is aware of it. As you can imagine, he's quite upset. The idea that private financial information would leak out of the firm is devastating. Criminal, in fact.'

'And you think Matthew was the one leaking the information?'

'Well, that's the interesting thing.' Julian paused and finished what was left of his wine. 'At first, yes. I assumed so. But from what I understand, the leaks continue.'

Zoe gazed out at the gulls. There were only two today. Last week there had been more; the rest must have departed for warmer climes. They squawked and swooped over the alley behind the restaurant. Zoe could hear the rustling of the trash bags being changed, the creak and whine of the back door. The faint smell of bouillabaisse wafted up from the kitchen. One gull rushed by overhead, a crab claw in his beak. Victory. He would drop it on the stone steps at the end of the street. All the gulls did this. In the summer, the shopkeepers had to sweep them twice a day because of all the broken bits of shell and crab carcass.

'I have a hunch,' Julian said. 'Do you want to hear it?'

'Certainly.'

'Did you ever meet Arthur Maynard? At Schmit & Muller?'

Zoe felt faint. Before she could answer, Julian chuckled. 'Of course you did; what am I saying? I saw you together at the firm retreat in Zermatt.'

'In Zermatt?' Zoe whispered.

'Yes, last winter. You don't remember? You were coming off a chairlift together.'

'Oh, yes. I remember now. You have quite a memory.'

'I remember everything. One of my many quirks.'

'You were saying you had a hunch?'

'Oh, yes. A few months ago, I wondered aloud to Jonas if the leak was coming from Schmit & Muller. After all, they have access to many of our clients' financial records, as well as clients at CIB and a number of other banks.'

'And what did Jonas think?'

'That it was worth pursuing. We started keeping a close eye on all of our senior bankers, as well as the lawyers at Schmit & Muller with access to our clients.'

'And what did you find?'

Julian smiled. 'I think you know what we found.'

A tear slipped down Zoe's cheek. She didn't bother to wipe it away. Instead, she kept her eyes trained on the horizon, and the fading golden sky beyond it.

'Arthur and I are in a relationship.'

'He's married, you know.'

'He's separated.'

'His wife didn't think so. She's been very helpful to us.'

Zoe turned, her eyes blazing. 'What have you done to Arthur?'

Julian shook his head. 'Aren't you curious what Arthur did to us? Or did you know all along?'

Zoe began to cry. 'I don't know anything,' she said. 'Except that he's a good man, and I love him.'

'He was stealing confidential information from inside Schmit & Muller and feeding it to reporters in the States.'

'You have proof of this?'

'All the proof we need. And you know what I find curious?'

'What?'

'That these two men, Matthew Werner and Arthur Maynard, both decided to leak information at around the same time. Matthew went to the DOJ. Arthur, to the press. And there you are, in the middle of all of it.'

'Maybe they both came to their senses. After learning these firms did business with the Assads. Did you think of that?'

'I think it's impossible to believe that you didn't know these men were informants.'

'I've done nothing wrong. And neither has Arthur.'

'Well, we'll see. I think Jonas will be paying Arthur a visit shortly. He's in Paris, you know. At his flat there. His wife threw him out of their home in Luxembourg after she found out about you two.'

The door to the terrace clattered open. Julian and Zoe turned. There was Rose, late as always, busily knotting her apron at the back of her waist.

'*Je suis désolée*,' she was saying, as she strode toward Zoe. She paused when she noticed Julian. '*Excusez-moi*.'

'Rose,' Zoe stammered. She brushed her wet cheek with the back of her hand. 'This is an old colleague of mine, from Geneva. I'm sorry, Julian, but I need to get back to work. Our dinner shift is about to start.' Zoe rose to her feet, ignoring Rose's inquisitive look.

'Of course.' Julian stood as well. 'Good to meet you, Rose. Nice to catch up, Zoe.'

'Yes, such a surprise.'

Julian glanced at his watch. 'It's getting late. I think I'll stroll down to that place you mentioned — what was it called? — and see if they have a room.'

'Vila de la Mar.'

'Yes. That one. If I stay for a few days, perhaps we will see one another again.'

'Perhaps.'

'How much do I owe you? For the wine?'

'On the house.'

Julian nodded. '*Merci*,' he said. '*Bonsoir*.' He stuck his hands into his pockets and strolled to the door leading back inside. Before opening it, he paused. 'Oh, Zoe? One last thing.'

'Yes?'

'After Matthew died, no one could find his laptop.'

'His laptop?'

'Yes, you know. The one he used when he was traveling.'

'I imagine it was on the plane with him.'

'Maybe. I just thought you would know where

it was. It has so much confidential information on it.'

Zoe shook her head. 'I'm sorry.'

'Worth a try.' Julian nodded. 'Good night. See you again soon, I hope.'

Annabel

Khalid was dead. Annabel had heard him die. The idea of it made her physically sick. She'd thrown up twice — once at the airport in Geneva, once in the plane's tiny bathroom sink. She couldn't stop replaying their conversation in her head. His voice had been tense and labored, as though he was walking quickly while speaking to her. The sounds of the city blared in the background. Horns, wind, static, white noise. He cut in and out; she could hardly hear him. Had he been walking down a busy street in London? Was he at a train station? He said something she couldn't understand. Muffled sounds of a scuffle. Then nothing.

Had there been a gunshot? Annabel wasn't sure. At first she thought the thump she'd heard was the sound of the phone hitting the pavement. But it could have been a shot. Or a blunt blow to the head. It was her fault. If she hadn't taken the laptop to him, he would still be alive.

Ten hours after her conversation with Khalid, Annabel's plane touched down at Las Americas International Airport in the Dominican Republic. She felt faint from the heat. She'd dressed for November in New York, not a trip to the tropics. She pulled at her turtleneck as she waited for her suitcase. If the airport was air-conditioned, she couldn't feel it. She felt her back grow damp from the humid night air.

Her bag was the last to drop onto the carousel. Annabel collected it and glanced around the terminal. She hadn't eaten since Geneva. It was past midnight and the kiosks were closed. She walked to a vending machine and slid her credit card into it before realizing it was out of order. She sighed and stooped over the drinking fountain instead.

The rental car booth was at the far end of the terminal. The clerk behind it was chatting with a baggage handler. Annabel loitered by the drinking fountain until the baggage handler had waved good-bye and headed off in the other direction. When he was out of sight, she stepped forward and smiled at the clerk.

'*¿Habla usted Inglés?*' Annabel asked. She was too tired to communicate in another language. The clerk was young, maybe twenty-five at most. His hair was long and he wore earphones around his neck. The sign overhead indicated that he would be closing in ten minutes. He glanced at his watch before answering.

'*Sí, señorita.* What can I do for you?'

'I need to get to Isla Alma. Can you help me?'

The clerk frowned. 'Isla Alma is a private island. Do you mean La Palma?'

'No. I mean Isla Alma.'

'You'll need to go to the port in Boca Chica. It's thirty-five kilometers from here. Is someone on the island expecting you?'

'No.'

'The only way on or off that island is by a private boat.'

291

'There's no ferry? Or water taxi?'

The clerk laughed. 'To Isla Alma? No, señorita.'

The despair on Marina's face must have been apparent, because the clerk sighed. He gestured for her to lean over the counter. 'Listen. My cousin, he drives a limo. He's a good guy. He's done with his shift. He was just waiting around for me upstairs. He can take you there if you want. So you don't have to drive. You look tired. You shouldn't be on the road so late.'

'I am tired.' Annabel hesitated, but only for a minute. And of all the risks she was running, getting into a car with a stranger was probably the least of them. 'Okay. Thank you. That would be good.'

'He usually charges twenty-five dollars. You're American, right?'

'Yes. That's fine.'

'Okay. I'll go get him now. Wait here. He'll take you to the port in Boca Chica. After that, you're on your own. Isla Alma, it's not exactly a place where most people are welcome.'

'I'll take my chances.'

The clerk shrugged. 'Es tu vida.'

'May I use your phone? My cell phone is dead.'

'I'm not supposed to let anyone use the phone.'

'Please. I'll be quick, I promise.' Marina riffled through her purse and found an American twenty-dollar bill. She placed it on the counter.

The clerk took it and shot her a look.

'It's all I have. Unless you want euros. I'm sorry.'

He tucked the bill into his back pocket. 'Be fast, okay? I'll get my cousin.'

'Thank you.'

Annabel waited until the clerk was gone before pulling out Lorenzo's business card. Call me if you need a friend, he had said after Matthew's memorial service. She hoped he meant it.

The phone rang, once, twice, three times.

Please, please, please, Annabel whispered to herself. *Please answer the phone.* It hadn't occurred to her that she wouldn't be able to get to Lorenzo once she arrived in the Dominican Republic. Isla Alma was her refuge of last resort. From here, she had no other options.

'*Alo?*'

'Lorenzo?' Annabel's voice shook. She looked behind her. The clerk was across the terminal, talking to two other guys. His back was to her. She turned back, hunching over the phone.

'Who is this?'

'It's Annabel Werner. Matthew's wife.'

'Annabel?' Lorenzo's voice softened. 'Where are you? Are you all right?'

'I'm at the airport. Las Americas. I came to see you. I was going to take a taxi to the port.'

'I'll send my driver for you. Don't take a taxi. Be outside the terminal in fifteen minutes.'

'Are you sure? I'm sorry. I know it's the middle of the night and — ' Across the terminal, the clerk turned around and pointed at her. The two men stared. Annabel felt a wave of uneasiness. Something about the way they were assessing her felt wrong.

'I'm glad you called. Annabel?'

'Yes?'

'Don't talk to anyone until then. Don't use

your credit card. Just keep to yourself. Okay?'

'Okay. Thank you, Lorenzo. Thank you so much.'

'Be safe, my friend.'

Annabel hung up the phone and slipped away from the desk. By the time the clerk and his friends had returned, she was gone.

Zoe

In the darkness, Zoe loaded her suitcase into the trunk of her uncle's Peugeot. Clement warned her that the car was old and the tires were thin. It might not survive the seven-hour drive to Paris. Perhaps she could take the bus to Aries in the morning, and from there, the train?

Zoe couldn't wait until morning. She told Clement that Arthur, her boyfriend, was sick. The truth was that she feared he was either dead or would be soon. She hadn't heard from him since Julian's arrival in Saint-Thérèse-de-la-Mer.

It had been Zoe's idea to give data to Duncan Sander. Arthur had been against it at first. Yes, they needed to do something, he said. They couldn't stand by while their companies hid money for terrorists and drug dealers and war criminals like Assad. But what could a journalist do, except write a story? Words couldn't protect them. Words couldn't arrest Jonas Klauser, Fares Amir, the lawyers at Schmit & Muller. Words couldn't do anything. Arthur thought they should go to the police.

But which police, and where? Jonas Klauser was friends with the head of Fedpol. Zoe had seen them skiing together at a firm outing in Zermatt. That the federal authorities in Luxembourg were no different. The managing partners of Schmit & Muller had friends everywhere. It was the reason they had been able to operate for as long as they had in the manner that they did. Unlike Swiss United, which had legitimate clients and not-so-legitimate, Schmit & Muller's entire business was setting up shell companies for offshore banks. All their clients were hiding something. Bribing officials was a matter of course. Arthur suggested going to the Americans, but Zoe didn't think the Department of Justice would care about protecting either of them, since they weren't US citizens. They needed to find another way out.

Duncan Sander had contacted Arthur first. Tim Morris, a banker at Caribbean International Bank and a friend of Arthur's, was the connection between them. Duncan was looking for Morty Reiss, Tim said. Tim had managed Morty's account at CIB until Schmit & Muller abruptly closed it overnight, moving Reiss's money to Swiss United instead. Could Arthur help Duncan find him?

At first, Arthur ignored Duncan's calls. But then, Tim turned up dead. The victim of a freak boating accident, or so they said. Arthur was stunned. Zoe was not. *I told you*, she said. *They're ruthless, these banks. They'll do anything, to any of us.*

Zoe knew this firsthand. She'd known it when she'd accepted the job at Swiss United. Jonas had made it very clear: Zoe worked for him and him alone. She did whatever he told her to do. For that, she got paid eighty thousand euros a year, plus a healthy bonus if she did well. For someone like Zoe, it was a good offer. One she couldn't possibly refuse.

Matthew had been Zoe's first and only assignment. Every week, she was supposed to give Jonas a report: who Matthew met with and spoke to; any email communications of interest; where he traveled for work and for pleasure. Jonas wanted to know about Matthew's family and friends, and especially his wife. Jonas said he liked to keep close tabs on his junior bankers, particularly the ones he thought had promise.

It wasn't long before Jonas encouraged Zoe to sleep with Matthew. She knew that other girls at Swiss United did that, with both bankers and clients. It was just a way of getting closer to him, Jonas said. But Zoe knew what it really was: a means of leverage, should Matthew ever try to defect.

The setup had been easy enough. A weekend at the famously luxe Hotel Metropole in Monte Carlo. A reward for the top-earning bankers and their assistants. Lavish, alcohol-fueled dinners each night, followed by private rooms at the Casino de Monte-Carlo, all paid for by Swiss United. Some of the bankers brought home call girls; others rented sports cars and blew through hundreds of thousands of dollars on blackjack, roulette, craps. Zoe played her part, dressing in couture gowns and eye-popping jewels, all selected for her by Elsa Klauser. Dressed as she was, she could have had any man in Monaco. But she had her eye on Matthew. She was paid to.

Zoe had told herself that it didn't mean anything. She had slept with plenty of men before where it hadn't. And she liked Matthew.

He was handsome and kind and funny. Anyway, wasn't that really the reason she'd come to Swiss United in the first place? In the hopes of landing herself a rich banker as a husband? If she played her cards right, she could end up a banker's wife in Geneva. That was the plan. If someone had told her one year earlier that she'd be fucking a guy like Matthew in a suite at a five-star hotel in Monte Carlo, she'd have been thrilled. But this time felt different. This time, it was awful.

Maybe it was because she was being recorded. Zoe knew that a hidden surveillance camera had been installed in the room, just over the television. She'd been instructed to position herself in such a way that there would be clear shots of both her and Matthew.

Maybe it was Matthew's resistance that made it feel so wrong. Zoe got him back to her room by pretending she was too drunk to get there safely. When she reached up to kiss him in the elevator, he flinched and pulled away. It was only after another drink in the suite that she was able to coax him into bed. They hadn't even had sex. Just fooled around a little before Matthew passed out in a cold stupor. In the middle of the night, Matthew called out for Annabel in his sleep. When Zoe woke up, he was gone.

The next day, Zoe numbed herself with alcohol and Xanax. She feigned the flu so that she could sleep all day and avoid anyone from Swiss United. She couldn't shake the feeling that she'd been violated, though she had clearly been the aggressor. Matthew had been so out of it that Zoe suspected he'd been drugged. She wasn't sure that he even remembered what had happened. He had apologized, red-faced, a few days later. He seemed relieved when she told him he had nothing to be sorry for, and that nothing of any consequence had happened between them.

But something *had* happened. Zoe had changed. She became depressed and then angry. Self-loathing slowly morphed into rage. She hated Jonas Klauser with every fiber of her being. For what he had done to her, for the way he treated not just her but everyone around her. Zoe decided she would make him pay.

Slowly and carefully, she began to collect evidence against Jonas. It was easy enough to find it; she had access to all Matthew's files and emails, as well as most of the corporate database. The trick was not getting caught. Once she met Arthur, she realized the case she was building was far bigger than Jonas Klauser. The whole system was rotten to the core. But between the two of them, they could take it down.

After Tim died, Arthur agreed to reach out to Duncan Sander. Together, he and Zoe would provide Duncan with enough information to not only track down Morty Reiss but to blow the whole world of offshore banking wide open. It was the only way out, Zoe thought. Eventually all this would come crashing down around them, and there was plenty of evidence to land both of them in jail for a lifetime. This way, they'd be the first to jump off a sinking ship. All they had to do was stay alive long enough to see the stories in print.

After everything she'd done to him, Zoe couldn't stand to see Matthew go down with Jonas Klauser. He didn't deserve that. So one night, while walking home from the bank, Zoe told Matthew that there was a mole inside Swiss United. Someone she knew was leaking data from inside the bank to a journalist in the US. Soon, a story was about to be written that would incriminate them all.

Save yourself, she said. *Go to the authorities before they come to you.* That was how Matthew ended up cooperating with Hunter Morse, an agent at the Department of Justice.

Now Matthew was dead, and Duncan, too. And if she didn't get moving, Zoe knew she'd be dead before morning.

★ ★ ★

Once she was outside of Sainte-Thérèse-de-la-Mer, Zoe breathed a little easier. She turned on the radio. Her foot lightened on the gas.

When she reached the Vaucluse Mountains that she realized she was being followed. It was a feeling, more than anything. A prickling of her skin, a heightened awareness of the headlights behind her. It could be anyone, she told herself. But it was Julian. Deep in her bones, she knew it was him.

Zoe had chosen this route for a reason. The roads in this part of the country were winding and dangerous, particularly at night. At places, there were tunnels hewn from the rock, barely big enough to fit a compact car. Occasionally, the left-hand side of the road evaporated into thin air. If a driver was not careful, a quick or careless turn could send them careering off a cliff.

Even a seasoned driver had to have her wits about her. Zoe accelerated slightly; a test. The car behind followed suit. He wasn't hiding anymore. He wanted her to know he was on her tail. The two cars soared through the mountains, never more than thirty meters apart. It reminded Zoe of those magnetic cars her brother played with as a child. The bumper of one attracted the front of the other. But when turned around, the cars would repel each other, pushing each into opposite directions.

Rain began to fall. Light at first, then harder. The windshield wipers couldn't keep up. Zoe felt the tires, bald from overuse, slipping at each turn. She tightened her knuckles around the wheel, as though she could exert control over the car with sheer determination. A light blinked on Zoe's dashboard. She was driving so quickly and the turns were coming so close together, she was afraid to look down at it. Hopefully the light would go off on its own. Clement warned her that the car had peculiarities; so many, in fact, he hadn't bothered to enumerate them.

The light flashed insistently. Finally, on a relatively straight patch of road, Zoe looked down. To her horror, she realized the gas tank was empty.

How was this possible? The needle showed a full tank when she left Sainte-Thérèse-de-la-Mer. Now it had swung all the way to the left.

Maybe it was a mistake, she told herself. A quirk of an old car.

Or maybe the quirk was that the old Peugeot was less gas-efficient than she thought, and it didn't let you know until the very last minute.

There was no gas station for miles. The only car on the road was the one behind her. If she stopped moving, she was dead. Especially if he was armed, it would be easy for Julian to overpower her, drag her out of the car, and push her into one of the bottomless ravines all around them. No one would ever find her body. If they did, they might just think she'd jumped. With no job and not much family, no one would be surprised if Zoe Durand killed herself. She'd certainly considered it. If they killed Arthur, she'd have nothing left.

Now that she was confronted with the possibility of death, though, Zoe reacted like a scared animal. Her mind quieted and only one thought remained: survival. Her senses grew heightened, and she could feel every bump in the road beneath her tires. The sound of the rain faded away and was replaced only with the rush of her own blood coursing through her ears. She leaned forward, her eyes peering into the darkness ahead.

She knew exactly where she was. She'd driven this road with Clement plenty of times. Up ahead, fewer than two hundred meters, began the Gorges de la Nesque. Clement had told her that more than a hundred years ago, his relatives had worked on a railroad through the Gorges de la Nesque, but the project had been abandoned.

After that, his family had moved farther south, eventually settling in Saint-Thérèsè to become fishermen. Now, the D942, the narrow road on which Zoe was driving, was the only road through this canyon. She was about to reach the first of a series of low tunnels carved out of the mountain face. It was low, only two and half meters high. Not high enough for a truck or even an SUV to pass through. When Zoe was young, Clement had told her that trolls lived there. At the time, the thought had both terrified and thrilled her. She remembered the feeling of vertigo she'd experienced at a turnoff, when she'd glanced over the edge of the low barrier that separated the road from the sheer drop below.

The tunnel was an opportunity, she realized. She knew it was coming; Julian did not. Zoe could use this to her advantage. She accelerated as she approached the tunnel. The car behind her revved its engine, closing the gap between them slightly. Though she hadn't said a prayer in years, she murmured one beneath her breath. She needed all the help she could get.

As she turned the corner, the mouth of the tunnel appeared: a black hole in the ink-blue darkness. Zoe took a deep breath and slammed on the brakes. The car skidded, the rear of it flying outward, toward the edge of the cliff. Zoe shut her eyes, bracing herself for impact. The car had no airbags; the seat belts were threadbare and rusted at the clip. If she miscalculated, this would be it.

She flew forward as the car's front fender

smashed against the rim of the tunnel. Her arms went up just in time, protecting her forehead from hitting the steering wheel. The force of the collision thrust the tail of the car backward, so that the car now sat perpendicular to the road, blocking the tunnel's entrance. Zoe's head turned right and her eyes widened as she saw the car behind her barreling toward her. The headlights were blinding. She shut her eyes. A second later, the deafening sound of metal hitting rock exploded all around her. Zoe screamed.

A few minutes passed before Zoe's arms dropped from around her head. She lifted her forehead from the steering wheel. The first thing she noticed was the gentle sound of the rain against the windshield. Other than that, the world was quiet.

She opened her hands and flexed her fingers. Her shoulders dropped from around her ears. She moved her neck from right to left. Besides a dull ache in her shoulder, she was unhurt.

As if in a dream, Zoe unclicked her seat belt and opened the car door. She stepped out into the cold night air. Within seconds, her hair was slick against her scalp and her feet squished inside her boots. Her nostrils filled with the scent of umbrella pines soaking up the rain. She tucked her arms across her chest as she made her way around the car to the edge of the road.

There was a hole in the low stone wall that separated the D942 from the gorge. It was clean, no rubble around it, just the absence of stone. Like the spot where a tooth had been pulled from the gum, Zoe thought. She bent down and ran her hand along the gap.

Beyond it was nothing. A black abyss. Zoe leaned over the wall as far as she dared. Even though she couldn't see anything in the darkness, her body was shot through with chills, the way it had been when she'd first looked over this wall as a child. As though her body remembered this place, Zoe noticed the faintest spot of light deep inside the gorge. Two lights. Facing up toward the heavens, like stars that had fallen from the sky. His headlights. Zoe wondered if Julian was alive down there, trapped within the mangled metal body of the car. Perhaps he was unconscious, blood oozing from his head, his breath labored. Or maybe he had felt nothing at all. Maybe his heart had burst in the air, as she hoped Matthew's had when he realized his plane was going to crash. Maybe in those final seconds before his inevitable death, Julian had felt only a momentary weightlessness followed by a still, enveloping darkness.

Zoe walked back to her car. The key was in the ignition, the parking brake on. The engine hummed as it had before, and the red light blinked, indicating that she still had no gas. This fact no longer bothered her. As she slumped over the steering wheel, she felt a wave of relief well up inside her, and she began to sob. Julian was dead. For the moment, she was safe. Someone else would come for her again, and soon. But she would make it out of these mountains alive, and for tonight, that felt like enough.

Marina

It was dark by the time Marina arrived in the Adams Morgan section of Washington, DC. The cab pulled up to the curb of a quiet, tree-lined section of Kalorama Road, and Marina stepped out. Hunter Morse lived in a polite, redbricked Victorian town house that looked like all the other houses on the block. It had a well-tended patch of grass out front and a wrought iron fence, the gate of which was open. As Marina ascended the steps to the front door, she noticed a pile of packages on the porch. It had not, until this moment, occurred to her that Hunter Morse might be out of town. Marina's heart sank. She rang the bell anyway, hoping for a miracle.

Marina heard the scuffle of footsteps. She waited, wondering if she should ring again. As her hand moved toward the bell, there was a whirring of locks. The front door swung open. Behind it stood a pale, slim brunette. She looked not much older than Marina. Though it was early evening, she wore a bathrobe over black pajamas. Dark circles ringed her large, watchful eyes.

This woman wasn't his wife. Marina had done some research on Hunter Morse on her way down to DC, and as far as she could tell, Morse wasn't married. He had no social media presence. He had never written an article or given an interview. In fact, the only two places she saw his name were in an alumni bulletin for Columbia Law School and on a website devoted to amateur poker.

'What do you want?' the woman said, from behind the screen door.

'Does Hunter Morse live here? I was hoping I might speak to him for a few minutes.' Marina smiled pleasantly. 'Apologies for dropping by during dinnertime.'

The woman frowned. 'How do you know Hunter?'

'I don't. He was a friend of a friend. My friend passed away a few weeks ago.'

'Sorry to hear that.'

'Duncan was supposed to see Hunter the day after he died.'

The brunette paused. 'Duncan Sander?'

'Yes.'

'And you are?'

'Marina Tourneau. I worked with Duncan for almost ten years. He was a very close friend.'

The brunette opened the door all the way. 'Come in,' she said, waving Marina inside.

'You have some mail and — '

'Just leave it.'

Marina stepped into the house. The foyer was dark. The shades were drawn. As Marina followed the woman down the hall past the kitchen, she noticed a foot-high stack of mail on the counter.

'Is Hunter here?' she said, unable to control her curiosity.

The woman stopped and turned. Even in the semidark of the hallway, Marina could sense the woman's fear. She pressed a finger to her lips, and then nodded her head toward the back door. 'Outside,' she said, her voice low.

Marina nodded. She followed the woman onto a small brick patio with an even smaller plot of grass beyond it. The woman took a seat at a wooden picnic table. She dug a pack of cigarettes out of her pocket and lit one. Marina approached, unsure of whether to sit. The woman took a deep inhale and blew smoke in her direction. Then she gestured at the bench across from her.

'Smoke?' she offered, holding up the pack.

'Sure. Thanks.' Marina took one, placed it between her lips. She leaned in, letting the woman light it for her. 'Sorry, I didn't get your name.'

'Agnes. I work with Hunter.' She stared down at her hands. 'I'm also his girlfriend. As you can probably tell since I'm wearing his bathrobe.'

'Do you live here? It's such a lovely house.'

'No. It's Hunter's. I just stay here.'

'Is he — '

'He's gone. Went missing four days ago.'

'Missing?'

'Yes, missing. Went for a run. Never came back.' Agnes flicked her cigarette over a plastic cup that was evidently serving as an ashtray.

'Have you gone to the police?'

Tight-lipped, Agnes shook her head.

'Is it possible — '

Agnes let out a harsh laugh. 'That he ran away?'

'No, I didn't mean that. Maybe he's hurt or something. Shouldn't someone be looking for him?'

Agnes shot her a look of annoyance. 'You tell me. What happened to your journalist friend? He's dead, right?'

'Yes.'

'Home invasion? That's what they're saying?'

'Yes. So far, anyway.'

'You think that's what happened to him?'

Marina bit her lip. 'No,' she said quietly. 'I don't.'

'Yeah, well, Hunter didn't get mugged in Rock Creek Park, okay? They killed him. Just like they killed your friend. So.'

'When you say 'they' . . . '

Agnes sighed, annoyed. 'That bank. Swiss United. All the trouble started when Hunter started investigating them. He didn't want to, by the way. It was a case that he inherited. From a colleague who decided to retire at the age of forty-five and move to the Cayman Islands. Amazing coincidence, right? How everyone who investigates them disappears?'

'When did that start? The investigation?'

'About a year ago. At first, Hunter wasn't going to pursue it. All of us at DOJ have plenty on our plates. Inherited investigations end up going by the wayside most of the time. But then, on a whim, Hunt ran the numbers.'

'The numbers?'

'Yeah. How many billions of dollars are stored in offshore accounts. Except it wasn't billions. It was a lot more than that.'

'Thirty-two trillion.'

Agnes looked up, surprised. 'Exactly.'

'So the lost tax revenue is substantial.'

'To say the least.'

'So he decided it was worth pursuing.'

'Right. So he starts poking around and realizes that an alum of his law school now works at Swiss United.'

'Matthew Werner.'

'Yes. You know about Matthew?'

'I know that he's dead.'

'Plane crash.' Agnes rolled her eyes, as if to say, *Another accident. Right.*

'Did Hunter get Matthew to talk?'

Agnes sighed. She stubbed out her cigarette and lit another one. 'I think so. I don't really know. I know he went to New York to meet with him.'

'When was that?'

'About three months ago. After that, Hunter started getting really quiet about his work. At first, I thought he was breaking up with me.' She snorted. 'That sounds so stupid in retrospect, doesn't it?'

'He was trying to protect you.'

Agnes shrugged. 'I like to think so. Hunter wasn't perfect, though, you know?'

'What do you mean by that?'

'He had his stuff. He liked to gamble. It got him into trouble. We fought about it a lot.'

'Was he in debt?'

'Yeah. Up to his ears.'

'This is a pretty nice place.'

'It was his mom's place. He inherited it after she died. I wanted him to sell it. Both of us are on government salaries. The upkeep on a house like this . . . ' She shook her head. 'But we were talking about having a family. So that made him want to keep it. He said maybe he'd look for a job at a firm. He went to Columbia, you know? So he could have been making a lot more in the private sector.'

'Why didn't he?'

'He cared about his job. I do, too.'

Marina nodded. 'I get it. I'm the same. Journalists aren't exactly in it for the money.'

'About a month ago, Hunter said he had a solution to the debt.'

'Did he tell you what it was?'

'No. But I knew. James Ellis. That was his solution.'

Marina swallowed hard. 'The presidential candidate?'

'Yeah. He's a client of Swiss United.'

'You're sure?'

Agnes nodded. 'Hunter told me. He was disappointed. He was a fan of Ellis. As a candidate, I mean. He was worried that if it came out that Ellis had money stashed offshore, it would ruin his chances of winning.'

'Okay. So you think James Ellis paid him to keep the investigation under wraps? Is that what you mean?'

'Not James directly.'

'Someone who works for him?'

'His son.'

Marina sat completely still. She could hear the traffic on Kalorama, and the neighbor's porch door creaking. Someone was grilling outside. The heady scent of crisping beef filled her nostrils, and above her head, the paper-brown leaves turned in the wind.

'His son?'

'Grant Ellis. I thought Hunter was leaving me, right? So I went on his computer. I have his passwords and everything. I know that sounds terrible, but I really just wanted to know if he was cheating on me. Does that make me sound insane?'

'No. I've done it, too.'

Agnes's forehead relaxed. 'Right? I feel like we all have.'

'So what did you find out? About Grant Ellis, I mean.'

'He flew down here and had lunch with Hunter. A week later, a quarter million appeared in Hunter's bank account.'

'Are you sure the money came from the Ellis family?' Marina said each word slowly and carefully. There could be no misunderstandings now.

'Yes. From an LLC registered to Grant. Offshore, of course.'

'Did you ask Hunter about it?'

'Hunter told me an old acquaintance had offered him a side job. Some kind of consulting gig. He didn't tell me who it was. He didn't know I'd looked at his calendar. And, you know, at his bank records.'

'Maybe it was a legitimate consulting job, though. Right? Isn't that possible?'

Agnes raised her eyebrows. 'Two hundred fifty grand? That's four times what Hunter makes in a year.'

'Maybe it was for the campaign?' Marina could hear the desperation in her voice. 'Or maybe Grant was hiring him for his company? They need tax experts.'

Agnes frowned. 'Hunter had an inside source at Swiss United. He knew that Ellis had money there. Then Ellis pays him and a week later the source is dead? That doesn't sound like a consulting job to me. It sounds like Grant Ellis paid a government employee to tell him who his informant was.'

'And then Duncan comes poking around, asking questions.'

Agnes's lip quivered. 'That's the part I hate. Hunter wasn't a bad person. I really don't think he intended for anyone to get killed. I think maybe . . . maybe he just thought they wanted him to drop the investigation. That was all.'

'I know,' Marina said quietly. 'It's okay. I understand.'

Agnes's eyes welled up with tears. 'He's dead, isn't he? They killed him, too.'

'We don't know that.'

'Everyone else who's gotten within ten feet of this investigation is dead.'

'Maybe he got scared. Maybe he's hiding out.'

'Hiding out? What's he waiting for? Ellis isn't going away. He's going to be the goddamn president of the United States. He's going to get away with all of it. And you know what? The only person who knows — the only person who could destroy him — is Hunter. Of course they killed him. Wouldn't you?'

'Not the only person. Do you still have access to his computer? His bank accounts and everything?'

Agnes wiped tears away with the back of her

313

hand. 'So what? Do I go to the police? I don't trust the police.'

'Neither do I. That's why I want to publish all of this. Once this information goes public, Ellis will be arrested. So will the bankers at Swiss United. It's the only way we'll ever be safe.'

'If Hunter's alive, they'll arrest him, too.'

Marina nodded. 'Yes. They probably will. But arrested is better than dead.'

Agnes paused. 'Can you protect me?'

'I will try.'

'How? Why should I trust you?'

'Because of this.' Marina pulled the USB out of her purse. 'Duncan Sander had an informant inside a law firm called Schmit & Muller. The lawyers for Swiss United. Before he died, I met his informant in Paris. And he gave me this. I can show it to you, if you'd like. It's financial information from inside the bank.'

'So you're as dead as I am.'

'Basically, yes.'

'What do you need?'

'I need everything. His emails. Phone records. Calendars. And his bank statements. And I need it all now.'

Zoe

The red light was wrong. Though it blinked the whole way, Zoe made it out of the mountains without needing gas. The engine began to sputter as she approached Lyon. She pulled into a BP station off the A7, which, but for the man behind the register, was empty. Still, Zoe's heart thumped wildly as she stepped out of the car. Though the road had been clear since the mountains, she couldn't shake the feeling she was still being followed.

He's dead, she told herself. *You watched Julian White die.*

But there were others. There would always be others. Jonas Klauser had eyes everywhere. When she first started at Swiss United, the other assistants whispered about it; it was their version of an urban myth or fairy tale. *Corporate spies*, Jacqueline, the girl who sat in the cube across from her, had called them. *Watchers*, Matthew had said. Zoe imagined them to be men in ski masks who tapped phone lines, snapped pictures with telephoto lenses. Now she realized they were just everyday people. Your landlord. Your ex-boyfriend. Your roommate. The bank teller who, just moments earlier, allowed you to transfer the contents of your checking account to a bank in the Cayman Islands. For a price, anyone could be bought. And Swiss United had endless reserves, enough to pay that price without a second thought.

Zoe paid for her gas in cash. The waitressing job had been good for that. She'd been paid under the table, in small-denomination bills that she hadn't deposited in a bank account, but rather kept stashed in a duffel bag under her bed with the rest of her money. Over the past six months, she'd been slowly draining her bank account. A two-hundred-euro withdrawal here, a thousand there. Arthur had told her to do this. At first it had seemed paranoid, unnecessary. But now she was grateful. When she left Geneva, only eight hundred euros remained in her checking account. She could live without that eight hundred euros.

The guy behind the register was staring at her. Zoe felt his beady eyes lingering as she counted out the price of gas. Though it was cold inside the store, he was sweating through his shirt. Behind her head, a television channel was tuned to a local news station. A news anchor was saying something about a car accident, a hit-and-run. A child was dead. She glanced out of the glass storefront. The dent on the front of her Peugeot was clearly visible. She felt the man's eyes on her eyes, her cheekbones, the line of her nose. Maybe he was admiring her. Maybe he was checking to see whether she matched the description on the television. A few months ago, she would have dismissed it; men stared at her all the time. Now she couldn't afford to dismiss anything. The last thing she needed was for this guy to call the cops. She slid the cash across the counter without raising her eyes. She felt his fingertips brush hers as he took the money, and it sent an electric charge down her spine.

She sprinted to the car. Her hands shook as she put the key into the ignition. She was backing out of the gas station when her phone rang. It was a Parisian number, one she did not recognize. Inside the gas station, she could see the clerk on the phone.

'Hello?'

'Zoe, it's me.' Zoe's body shuddered with relief when she heard Arthur's voice.

'Where are you? I've been calling you and — '

'I'm in Paris. It wasn't safe for me in Luxembourg.'

'They know you're there. You can't go to your apartment. Jonas Klauser is looking for you.'

'I know. He's at my apartment.'

'How do you know?'

'I'm at the hotel across the street. I can see him in my window. He has bodyguards with him. Standing on the curb right outside. Where are you? Are you safe?'

'No.' Zoe began to weep. 'I'm driving to Paris. But Arthur, there was an accident.'

'Are you all right? Are you hurt?'

'Yes. I mean, yes, I'm fine. But — '

'Don't tell me now. Listen, Zoe, very carefully. I spoke to Owen Barry. All the stories are going to be published at midnight, New York time. That's in just a few hours. Once they are, it's only a matter of time before arrest warrants are issued for all the top people at Swiss United and Schmit & Muller.'

'It could be days before that happens. Weeks, even.'

'I don't think so. They won't see it coming, so they won't be able to run. Owen said it would happen within the day.'

'So what do we do? Until the arrests.'

'Stay alive.'

'I'm trying. Where do I go?'

'Owen said for us to go to the *Le Monde* office in Paris. Simon Cressy is there; he's working with them. He said we'll be safe there.'

'And you trust him?'

'We have to.'

'I'll meet you there, then?'

'Yes. I'm going to stay here at the hotel until Klauser leaves my apartment. He can't stay there all day.'

'Please be careful, Arthur.'

'I will. I love you, Zoe.'

'I love you, too.'

'I'll see you soon.' The line went dead. Zoe threw her cell phone onto the passenger's seat and took one last look at the gas station clerk. He was staring at her. Without bothering to fasten her seat belt, she shifted into reverse and slammed her foot on the gas. By the time she reached Paris, it would be getting light. The newspapers would be out on the stands. She had a full tank of gas and, for the moment, no one on her tail. She was almost home free.

Marina

On Kalorama Road, it was dark, illuminated only by infrequent streetlamps that let off an eerie, yellowish glow. Most of the neighbors' lights were out now. This was a quiet block, made up of single-family townhomes filled with young children. The few cars that were parked along the street were of a suburban variety: Subaru Foresters, Volvo Cross Countries, Toyota Siennas. Cars built for lacrosse sticks, juice boxes, weekend luggage. All except one. Directly across from Hunter Morse's house was a black sedan with tinted windows. Though she couldn't see inside, Marina was certain there was someone in the driver's seat. And just as she was watching him, she knew he was watching her.

Marina picked up her phone and dialed Owen's number.

'Hey,' Owen said when he picked up the phone. 'What's up?'

'He followed me down here.'

'To DC?'

'Yeah. He's parked outside of Morse's house.'

'Okay, Marina, you have to get out of there. Guy's a private detective. Used to be a cop. He's been on James Ellis's payroll for a while.'

Marina clenched her jaw. She stared out at the street. She wasn't surprised that James had her followed. But when he found out that she was paying a visit to Hunter Morse, things would get ugly, and fast.

'Hey, Owen?' Marina said. She stood on her toes, looking at the car parked next to the sedan. 'What if the neighbor was wrong? What if the car she saw was a Honda Element? I'm looking at one now. It's boxy. Looks an awful lot like a Kia.'

Owen chuckled. 'I'm way ahead of you there. My friend thought the same thing. Turns out there was a blue Honda with a New York plate, last digits 434, that crossed over from New York into Connecticut multiple times in the days leading up to Duncan's death, including the day he died. And get this: it was purchased at a secondhand lot by an ex-SEAL, Charlie Platt. Guy is a trained sniper. Haven't been able to tie him to Ellis yet, but — '

'We will. I know how,' Marina said, without expounding further. 'I've got to go. Ellis knows I'm here. Did you get the files we sent? All of Morse's emails and his calendar.'

'Yup. Story can be online in one hour. Christophe Martin is waiting for you at the ICIJ headquarters.'

'Thanks, Owen.'

'Be safe, Marina.'

Marina hung up the phone. Agnes was standing in the doorway, watching her.

'You sure you need me to go with you?' she said, looking hesitant.

'You can't stay here. It isn't safe.'

'But what if . . . ' Agnes bit her lip.

'Agnes, he's not coming back. At least, not right now. Okay?'

'I know. I know that.' Still, she didn't move from the door frame.

'Look, I don't want to scare you, but there's a car across the street. He's watching us. I think if we walk out the front door, we're in trouble.'

Agnes frowned. 'Are you sure? It could be anyone.'

'It isn't. Just trust me on this. Is there a way to get out from your backyard?'

'Not really. I mean, there's a hedge that separates us from the neighbor. Maybe there's a place we can crawl through?'

The car door opened. The driver emerged. He was dressed in all black, a black cap obscuring his face. Marina inhaled sharply and pulled away from the window.

'We need to go. Right now.'

She sprinted toward Agnes, pushing her back down the hallway. Wordlessly, the women ran through the back door and across the brick patio. Agnes tripped when she reached the steps and fell to her knees on the grass. When they heard the gentle chime of the front door opening and closing, Agnes let out a yelp of fear. Marina turned back and caught Agnes by the wrist, yanking her to her feet.

Marina saw what she thought was a gap in the hedge and she ran toward it.

'No!' Agnes hissed from behind her. She pointed toward the far end of the yard. 'There.'

'We have to go now!'

'Trust me. This way.' Agnes took hold of Marina's elbow, propelling them both forward into the darkness.

'Hurry,' Agnes whispered, and pushed Marina hard into the hedgerow. She felt a sharp pain as the pointed edge of a twig sliced across her cheek. She covered her face with her hands and, with the sheer force of her body, pushed through a small opening between the branches.

On the other side, she found herself facing a neighbor's screened-in porch.

Agnes ran up the steps and stooped at the back door, pulling up the corner of a welcome mat. From beneath it, she pulled out a key.

'He's a friend,' she whispered as she fumbled with the door. 'When he's away, he asks us to feed his cats.'

'Someone's in your backyard. Hurry.'

Agnes frantically shook the doorknob. Marina was about to run when she heard the door give way. The two women tumbled into the house. Marina pulled the door closed behind them, her hands shaking as she did.

'Is your friend home?' she called after Agnes, who was jogging down the hall. She glanced over her shoulder, but all she could see in the back-yard was darkness.

'Maybe,' Agnes said. 'Probably sleeping. But he always leaves his car keys on the front table.'

'You're going to take his car?'

'You have another idea?'

Marina froze. Outside she heard someone push-ing through the hedgerow. Branches snapped, the leaves rustled in protest.

'Go!' Marina barked. They fled to the front door, Agnes barely stopping to scoop a set of keys off the foyer table. Upstairs, they heard the muffled sound of footsteps.

'I'll explain this to him tomorrow!' Agnes called, as they jumped down the front steps. She hit a button on the key chain and the front lights of an SUV flashed across the street. 'There's his car. C'mon.'

Agnes hopped into the driver's seat. Marina skidded into the passenger's side, pulling the door shut as Agnes revved the engine. The SUV peeled out into the street, its tires screeching against the pavement.

Marina turned to look back over her shoulder as Agnes pulled out onto the darkened street. The man burst through the front door. He looked both ways, then zeroed in on their car. He sprinted toward them, nimbly jumping over a low fence like an Olympic hurdler. When he reached the pavement, he stopped.

'Gun!' Marina shouted, as the back window of the car shattered with a deafening pop. Her hand reflexively shot out, pulling Agnes down with her. Both women ducked and the car swerved. The tires hit the curb with a sickening crunch. Agnes jerked upright and yanked the wheel. The car bounced back into the road and she floored the gas.

'Fuck, that was close,' Agnes said, as they reached the end of Kalorama Road. 'Where did he come from?'

'I don't know,' Marina whispered. 'I didn't realize he followed me down here.'

'Wait — he was following you?' Agnes shot Marina a sidelong glance.

'Yeah. This might be a bad time to mention

this, but I'm actually engaged to Grant Ellis. Or was.'

'What?' Agnes shouted. A car honked as she ran a red light.

'Jesus! Watch the road. Let's just get to the ICIJ alive, okay?'

'I'm going to pull the car over right now unless you tell me exactly who you are and what you want.' Agnes's voice had a steel edge to it.

'I told you who I am. I'm a journalist. I worked with Duncan Sander. After he was murdered, I began investigating his death. That led me to Hunter. And, unfortunately, back to the Ellis family.'

'And that's it? You still want to write the story, even if it means that your fiancé will go to jail?'

'It's a story that needs to be written.'

For a moment, they were both silent. Agnes pulled to a stop at a light. Two blocks down, Marina could see the building where ICIJ was headquartered. She checked her watch: 10:45 p.m. When the clock struck eleven, Owen would upload the Ellis story. It would contain everything. James Ellis's millions stored in offshore accounts. His business ties to Assad. His blackmailing of a DOJ agent. And his hand in Duncan Sander's murder. The only thing Marina hadn't told Owen was that Grant was far more involved than she'd ever imagined.

'It's hard, isn't it?' Agnes said softly. 'When they aren't who you thought they were.'

'So hard,' Marina said, and she began to cry. She covered her face with her hands.

'You're brave. You're doing the right thing.'

The light turned to green. Agnes paused and looked over at Marina.

'Just go,' Marina said.

Agnes nodded. A small, resolute grimace appeared on her lips as she pressed her foot against the gas.

Annabel

Lorenzo Mora stood at the helm of a sleek twenty-two-foot Donzi, his black hair just visible over the boat's tinted windshield. Annabel watched as the boat approached the dock. Its low-slung hull cut through the darkness like a shark. The dock itself was poorly lit, but the moon was full. The light from it rippled off the water and illuminated the boat just enough for Annabel to read the name that was painted down its side: *Caballo Oscuro. Dark Horse.*

As he pulled alongside the moorings, Lorenzo cut the engine. In the passenger's seat was a large, bearded man, who hopped out of the boat with practiced ease. Lorenzo tossed him a dock line. Despite the heat, both men wore windbreakers. Annabel wondered if one or both of them were armed. She hoped so.

Annabel glanced behind her. Though it was past midnight, the port in Boca Chica was well populated. For the past thirty minutes, she had sat in the back of Lorenzo's chauffeured car, watching and waiting for Lorenzo to come get her. The faint dulcet tones of merengue filled the warm night air. The bar across from the port — a thatch-roofed space with plastic chairs and tables set out on the sidewalk — had a line of people waiting to be seated. It was high season here in the Dominican Republic. Couples strolled down Calle Duarte arm in arm. Most looked like tourists. The men swayed slightly from too many Santo Libres and were red-faced from playing golf in the sun. The women wore gauzy, floral dresses and sandals that had no place in their daily lives back home. None of them noticed Annabel. Some passed right by the car without so much as a glance. She felt strangely assured by their nearness. She liked to believe that if someone had followed her halfway around the world in order to kill her, they would have done it by now. And even if he was lying in wait, this would not be the place to do it. It was too public. Too obvious. Lorenzo's driver was armed. A trained killer would bide his time. When she was in a hotel room, perhaps. Or driving alone on a quiet road at night.

Now Lorenzo was here, and so for the moment, she was safe. It was dangerous, of course, to align herself with a man like Lorenzo Mora. But Matthew had trusted him, so she would, too. Annabel didn't have the luxury of thinking about the long-term consequences of her short-term decisions. She just wanted to stay alive until morning.

Lorenzo waved at her as she emerged from the backseat of the Mercedes sedan. Annabel noticed a few pedestrians staring as she strode down the dock. Lorenzo, she realized, must be a local celebrity of sorts. The Sugar King of Cane Bay. The Man from Isla Alma. She wondered how often he made an appearance on the local docks. She guessed not very often.

'Thank you,' she said. 'You're kind to come.'

'It's my pleasure. Annabel, this is Maurizio.

He can help you with your luggage.'

Maurizio nodded.

'Thank you,' Annabel said, handing over her suitcase.

'Did you bring a bathing suit? We have excellent snorkeling off the island.'

'I'm afraid I didn't pack for a vacation.'

Lorenzo laughed. 'I imagine you didn't. Hop in. We'll find some things to make you comfortable at the house.'

Maurizio offered Annabel a hand, and she stepped into the boat. Then he untied the dock lines and hopped in behind her. Lorenzo shifted the boat into gear and the engine whirred to life. Soon, they were out on the open water.

'Just a few minutes to the island,' Lorenzo said. It was so dark that Annabel couldn't tell where the water ended and where the sky began. The ambient light from the port was fading away. Overhead, the sky was littered with stars.

'I'm so sorry to arrive in the middle of the night like this,' Annabel said. 'You must think I'm crazy. I thought someone at the airport in Geneva was following me and I panicked. I didn't know where else to go.'

Lorenzo nodded. If he was surprised to see her, he didn't show it.

'I told you, you are always welcome here. Matthew helped me once, when I needed it most. In my culture, you don't forget that kind of thing.'

'May I ask you something?'

'That depends.'

'Did you know that Matthew was an

informant for the Department of Justice?'

Lorenzo didn't react.

'Maybe that's wrong,' Annabel corrected herself. 'He was talking to someone at the Department of Justice. I don't know if he gave them any information. He was supposed to meet this agent right before the crash. I think maybe he was killed so that the information never made it out of the bank.'

'How did you find that out?'

'I had his personal computer.'

'Do you now?'

'No. I left it with a friend.'

'A friend?'

'A friend in London. He's dead now.'

Lorenzo turned and stared at her. 'Your friend is dead? Are you sure?'

Annabel paused, considering. 'No. Not sure. Something happened to him, though. I was supposed to meet him at Heathrow on my way to the States. But he called me as I was about to board my plane. He told me that Hunter Morse — the agent who Matthew had been speaking to — was corrupt. He told me not to go meet him. And then I heard a thump and the line went dead.'

'When was this?'

'When I was at the Geneva airport. Right after, I saw someone following me. I knew I needed to leave Switzerland, but I didn't know where to go. Matthew told me I'd be safe here, with you. I saw a flight leaving for Miami, so I got on it.'

'You made the right decision.'

'Thank you. You've been very kind. Whatever debt you owed to Matthew, you're certainly repaying it now.'

Annabel could make out a dock and a well-lit beach ahead. Where the sand ended, there was a stone wall, and behind that, a thatch of palm trees. There were men on the beach, posted at regular intervals along the base of the wall. Even from afar, Annabel could tell that they were carrying automatic weapons. Annabel shivered. The wind off the water was stiff. She felt a light spray on her face and the taste of salt on her tongue.

Annabel had once read an article in *Town & Country* magazine about Cane Bay, the private club maintained by the Mora family on Isla Alma. According to the magazine, the club consisted of a main house and thirty villas dotting the bluffs over Cane Bay. The largest of the villas, Casa Blanca, was Lorenzo Mora's private residence. The other villas could be booked by members anytime and were said to be more luxurious than any hotel in the Caribbean.

Cane Bay's membership was secret, though it was rumored to include heads of state, celebrities, and international captains of industry. The guest policy was strict and few outsiders had ever been allowed access to the island. The pictures in *Town & Country* were the first to be printed in a magazine. Annabel still remembered the gorgeous two-page spread of Casa Blanca's stone-terraced infinity pool, its sparkling aquamarine water disappearing against the panorama of the Caribbean Sea beyond. In the picture,

330

Lorenzo lay on a white lounge chair, his feet crossed at the ankle, his hands behind his head. He was flanked on either side by two well-known actresses, who were not wearing bathing suits, but rather floor-length ball gowns. Lorenzo himself wore a tuxedo and a pair of black slippers emblazoned with the Cane Bay logo. He looked straight at the camera, a small smile on his lips. He was well aware of his own good fortune. At the time, it had reminded Annabel of a Slim Aarons photo: luxurious and elegant, a glimpse into a lifestyle that Annabel thought no longer existed. It never occurred to her that one day Lorenzo Mora would become her husband's client, or that she, Annabel, would visit this exquisite place. It had never occurred to her that Cane Bay was fueled by drug money and guarded by men with automatic weapons. At the time, Annabel had much to learn about the world of the ultrarich.

Annabel slumped back against the boat's leather seat. She let her eyes close. She felt the last of her energy slipping out of her. She had made it to Isla Alma. Her refuge of last resort. After this, she had nowhere else to go. A strange sense of peace set in. Maybe Lorenzo Mora worked for Jonas Klauser. Maybe she'd be dead in the morning. But at least she could stop running. She couldn't imagine running for one more day.

'You look exhausted.'

'I am. I'm sorry. It's been such a long day.'

'You'll be safe here. You should rest tonight. We'll talk in the morning. I think I can help you make sense of everything. First, though, welcome to Isla Alma.'

Annabel sat up. She felt the side of the boat knock up against the moorings. On the dock, there was a flurry of activity. Four men, dressed alike in cargo pants and dark shirts, helped Maurizio with the dock lines. One offered her a hand and hoisted her up. For a moment, she stood still, absorbing the view. The beach glowed in the moonlight, its powdered sand the color of pearls. Palm trees rustled and frogs sang. The stars overhead seemed brighter now, and the air smelled of jasmine.

This is paradise, Annabel thought. Then a guard with a gun slung across his back stepped forward.

'*Buenos noches, señora*,' he said. 'Let me show you to your villa.'

It wasn't a request. Annabel looked to Lorenzo, who nodded. 'Go with him. Get some rest. I'll come for you in the morning.'

Marina

It was 12:01 a.m. The stories were up, all across the globe.

Marina stood in front of a row of computer monitors at the ICIJ offices, reading the headlines. Agnes stood to her left; Christophe Martin, to her right. All three were silent. Behind them, a symphony of telephones were ringing off the hook.

'BIGGEST DATA LEAK IN HISTORY,' read the *Wall Street Journal*. 'INTERNAL LAW FIRM DOCUMENTS REVEAL TRILLIONS HIDDEN IN OFFSHORE ACCOUNTS.'

'LEAKED DATA FROM INSIDE A LUXEM-BOURG LAW FIRM REVEAL HOW CARTELS HIDE THEIR MONEY,' declared *El País*.

'PUTIN HIDING MILLIONS IN OFFSHORE ACCOUNTS,' read the *Moscow Times*. 'ILLE-GAL TIES TO BRATVA, OLIGARCHS, OTHER WORLD LEADERS.'

'MEET JONAS KLAUSER, PERSONAL BANKER TO THE ASSAD FAMILY,' read the *Financial Times*. 'AND FARES AMIR, THE HEDGE FUND MANAGER WHO LAUN-DERED THEIR MONEY.'

'DEATH OF TWO PRIVATE BANKERS EYED IN CONNECTION WITH SWISS BANK LEAK,' read *Le Monde*.

And then, on the last screen, the front page of *the Deliverable*.

'LEAKED SWISS BANK DOCUMENTS REVEAL LINKS BETWEEN JAMES ELLIS AND BASHAR AL-ASSAD,' it read. 'ELLIS A SUSPECT IN DEATH OF DUNCAN SANDER, JOURNALIST WHO ATTEMPTED TO UNCOVER STORY.'

Marina winced when she saw the picture beneath the headline. It showed James and Grant Ellis, walking side by side with a man Marina didn't recognize. She leaned in closer and read the small font: *James Ellis, in Geneva with his son, Grant Ellis, and Julian White, a private banker at Swiss United.*

'God, that's beautiful,' Christophe said. 'What a triumph of investigative reporting. In all the years I've been doing this, I've never seen something quite like this.'

From across the floor, a staffer gestured at Christophe. 'Chief of police is on the line.'

'Excuse me,' Christophe said, before turning to take the call.

'There's nothing here about Hunter,' Agnes whispered to Marina.

'Give it time,' Marina said. She put a hand on Agnes's shoulder. 'These are just the leads. There will be new stories pouring out for days. Longer.'

'When will they arrest them? The Ellises, I mean?'

'Soon. I'm sure they are working as fast as they can.'

'Won't they try to flee the country?'

Marina frowned. 'I don't think so. Ellis is a public figure. Where would he go?'

'What about Grant?'

Marina didn't have time to answer. Christophe walked toward them, a pained expression on his face. When he turned to Agnes, they both knew what he was about to say.

'No,' Agnes murmured.

'I'm so sorry, Agnes. They found Hunter.'

'What happened?' Marina whispered.

'He shot himself. Or so they say. He was in a friend's garage. The friend was out of town. I don't really know more than that.'

Agnes let out a wail, a guttural sound that seemed to silence the noisy office for a split second. Marina reached for her, and the women embraced. Agnes's whole body shook as she cried. Marina clung to her, holding her frame upright until the worst of it had passed.

'They killed him, Marina. They did it to him; they must have. He would never . . . Hunter would never . . . '

'There will be a full investigation,' Christophe said. 'I promise you that.'

Marina was silent. She didn't have the words. Whether Hunter Morse had pulled the trigger, Agnes was right. The Ellises had killed him. Just as they had killed Duncan. And she had a hunch they had killed Matthew Werner and Fatima Amir and Omar Khoury. And the banker at CIB. How many others were there? Marina closed her eyes. She felt her stomach roil in protest.

'Excuse me,' she murmured, and ran to the bathroom. She made it into the stall just in time to throw up.

When she had finished, she sunk to her knees on the hard, tiled floor and cried. The walls of the bathroom were paper-thin, and through them, Marina could hear the din of the office — the ringing of phones, the chattering of journalists, the buzz of television sets. If she could hear them, they could hear her. But she didn't care. She began screaming at the top of her lungs, and as she did, she pounded her fists against the metal stall door until the skin on one of her knuckles split open and she began to bleed.

Finally, when her fists were numb and her lungs were sore, Marina stopped. She pushed herself upright. She walked to the sink and splashed water on her face. She rinsed her mouth. She pulled her hair back, securing it with an elastic she kept around one wrist. She stared at herself in the mirror. Her skin glistened in the halogen light of the bathroom. She looked older than she remembered. Her cheeks were pale and hollowed against the bone. Deep creases had imprinted themselves beneath her eyes. She did not feel beautiful, but she did feel strong. Blood trickled from her knuckle, but she did not feel the cut. She rinsed it beneath the cold water of the sink and then walked back out into the office, ready to fight.

Zoe

Zoe pressed her forehead against the glass and looked out over the Tuileries. The trees were white with snow. They shone in the early morning light, illuminated like Christmas ornaments. If she craned her neck, she could see the Louvre to her left, its slate-gray roof disappearing into the dawn sky. To the right, the Eiffel Tower loomed, a single spike above the horizon. She wished she could go out onto the balcony. Zoe had always wanted to stay in an apartment in the 1st arrondissement. Preferably at Le Meurice hotel, which was just next door, in one of their grand suites with balconies that overlooked all of Paris. The kind of suites that lovers took, Zoe thought, on the sort of romantic liaisons that she and Arthur had only ever taken in cities where they knew no one and were therefore in no danger of being found out. Bruges. Ljubljana. Budapest. But never Paris, where Arthur had friends and colleagues, and where, more alarming, his wife had family.

Now Zoe wondered if they would ever stay in a hotel again. How long would they keep her penned up here, in an apartment paid for by the Department of Justice? When they had arrived, the guard outside the door had told them to stay inside. No going downstairs for a walk; no cigarettes on the balcony. Too dangerous. They were to stay away from the windows, even. As though there could be snipers hiding in the trees of the Tuileries, waiting for her to emerge. Zoe wondered if the guard was still out there. Joe something, a brutish American with a crew cut and broad shoulders and a ropey neck that bulged when he spoke. When they arrived, he was standing next to the door, hands behind his back. Maybe he had switched shifts overnight, replaced by another guard. No one had told them how long this would go on, how long they could expect to live like caged rats. It would be months, Zoe suspected, maybe even years. It was the price they would pay for what they had done. Instead of going to jail like the rest of their colleagues, they would testify against them. Zoe wondered now which was worse.

A knock came at the door. Zoe hesitated; it seemed too early for official business. Arthur was sleeping. They had arrived at the apartment well past midnight. It had been a last-minute solution. No one quite knew what to do with them. They couldn't stay at the *Le Monde* offices forever. Neither one could go home; it wasn't safe. They couldn't check into a hotel. Finally, Owen Barry had negotiated a protective custody arrangement with the Department of Justice. If the DOJ wanted Zoe and Arthur to testify, they would need to keep them alive.

Now the reality of what they had done was beginning to sink in. To the outside world, Zoe Durand and Arthur Maynard might be anonymous sources. But inside their companies, their covers were blown. They were the leak. And that meant that they would have targets on their backs for the rest of their lives.

The knock came again, more insistent this time. Zoe heard Arthur stirring in the bedroom. She strode across the living room and peered through the keyhole. When she saw that it was Simon Cressy, the editor of Le Monde, she opened the door.

'Good morning, Zoe,' Simon said. Behind him stood two men she did not recognize. 'I'm sorry to trouble you so early. Did you get any rest?'

Zoe shook her head. 'Not really. Please, come in.'

The three men entered the apartment. Zoe gestured for them to sit.

'This is Bill Holden from the Department of Justice,' Simon explained. 'And Mark Moyes from the Internal Revenue Service.'

Arthur appeared in the bedroom doorway. He wore the same clothes as yesterday: jeans and a rumpled button-down shirt. He had slept in those clothes. He would again tonight, unless someone brought him a change. He ran his hand through his hair, attempting to tame it.

'Sorry,' he said, and kissed Zoe on the cheek. 'Didn't realize we'd be having visitors so early.'

'Apologies for the intrusion,' Bill Holden said. He, too, looked like he had slept in his clothes. His shirt was creased and there was a light stain on one side of the collar. 'We took the red-eye here and we thought it was better to come straight to the apartment. To be blunt, Mr. Maynard, we're concerned for your safety here in Paris.'

'So are we.' Arthur let out a gruff chuckle. 'I

watched Jonas Klauser stake out my apartment with a pair of armed men less than twenty-four hours ago.'

'There is a warrant out for Mr. Klauser's arrest. But as you probably know, that doesn't mean you and Ms. Durand are safe to go about your daily lives.'

'I imagine we never will be again.'

Holden nodded. 'Your safety will depend on the cooperation of several governments, not just us. As you know, the rules are different in Luxembourg and in Switzerland. Mr. Klauser is a US citizen, but Hans Hoffman and Peter Weber are not.'

'I don't have much faith in law enforcement in Luxembourg,' Arthur replied. 'If I did, I would have gone to them in the first place.'

'We understand. Ordinarily, the Department of Justice offers this sort of protection only to people who come to us directly as whistle-blowers. But in your case, we know why you decided to approach the press instead.'

'It's not just the authorities in Luxembourg,' Zoe said. 'Matthew Werner went to the Department of Justice. He ended up dead.'

'Mr. Werner's tragic death was the result of the actions of one rogue Department of Justice employee. I assure you, we are doing everything we can internally to make sure that nothing like that ever happens again.'

'Has Hunter Morse been arrested?'

'Hunter Morse is dead. He killed himself.'

Zoe tightened her grip around Arthur's hand. 'That's awful.'

'Unfortunately, he wasn't the only one. Julian White's body turned up yesterday as well.'

'Julian White? From Swiss United?' Zoe felt his name catch in her throat.

'Yes.'

'What happened?'

'Car wreck. His body was found in a ravine in the Vaucluse Mountains.'

'Was anyone else hurt?' Zoe heard herself ask. She didn't want to keep talking about Julian, but it seemed like the appropriate response. She leaned in against Arthur, steadying her body against his. It hadn't occurred to her that they'd find his body so soon. She had hoped they wouldn't at all.

'No. He was alone in the car. We suspect it might have been intentional.'

'Intentional?'

'A suicide.'

Zoe let out a sharp exhale.

'That's terrible,' Arthur said.

'Terrible, yes. We haven't ruled out the possibility of foul play, of course. In either case. There will be investigations.'

'And what about Matthew Werner's death? Is that being investigated?' Arthur pressed.

'It is.'

Zoe closed her eyes. She felt Arthur's arm tighten around her.

'Are you all right, Ms. Durand?'

Zoe nodded. 'I'm fine. It's just . . . So many people are dead.'

'You worked in a dangerous business, Ms. Durand.'

341

'I know that now.'

'At this point, we think you have two options. The first is for you to enter the Witness Protection Program. We will give you new identities, appearances, passports. Your names will never appear in the press in connection with the leak.'

'Would we still have to testify? At trial, or before the US Senate?'

'Yes. But we could do it in a way that protects your identity.'

'Klauser already knows we're the leak. If he wants us dead, he'll find us.'

'In the twenty years I've been with the DOJ, we've never lost a witness in protection.'

'You've never had anyone like Jonas Klauser on trial.'

'We've had people testify against cartel members, mob bosses, you name it. That's what we do.'

Arthur let out a harsh laugh. 'Testifying against Klauser is the equivalent of testifying against cartel members, mob bosses, and terrorists at once. They're all his clients.'

'I understand your hesitation, Mr. Maynard. But let me remind you that you and Ms. Durand were part of this criminal enterprise. If you choose not to testify, you will be prosecuted along with the rest of your colleagues.'

'Even though we were the ones who leaked all the data?' Zoe asked, frowning. 'That seems unfair.'

Holden shrugged. 'I'm sorry you feel it's unfair, Ms. Durand. But in our country, we don't look kindly on people who aid and abet terrorists.'

'Would we be together?' Arthur asked. 'In witness protection, I mean.'

'It would be safer if you weren't.'

'We have to be together,' Zoe said. She looked at Arthur, pleading. 'Arthur, please. I can't be alone again. Not after everything. You're all I've ever had.'

'I won't leave you,' Arthur said, his voice stern. 'There must be another way.'

'There is one other option,' Moyes spoke up.

They both looked at him hopefully.

'You testify. But you do it out in the open. You give interviews. You go public. You become the Edward Snowdens of the offshore banking business.'

'That's crazy,' Arthur said. 'That will only put us in greater danger.'

'Will it? They know who you are. They know you were the leak. If you become heroes — celebrities, really — it makes it harder for them to kill you. And you could hire private security. You wouldn't be totally unprotected.'

For a moment, they were all silent. Zoe glanced back at the balcony. The sky was bright now, a clear, cold, cerulean blue. Soon, the shops on rue de Rivoli would fill with holiday shoppers. A line at the Louvre would accumulate. Tourists would walk through the Tuileries with hot chocolate and coffee. The big Ferris wheel at the Place de la Concorde would spin.

It occurred to her now that if she were to enter witness protection, she would never see Paris again. They might send her back to some small town like the one from which she'd come, except she'd know no one, have nothing, be no one. It was a heartbreaking thought.

'How would we pay for this private security?' Arthur asked. 'How will we survive? I won't ever be able to practice law again.'

'Here's the thing. If you are to cooperate fully — and that means giving us the names of every client you've ever spoken to, worked with, or were aware had money stored offshore — we believe the IRS will be able to recoup at least a billion dollars in fines and unpaid taxes.'

Arthur nodded. 'At least a billion.'

'Are you aware that the IRS will pay informants an award of up to thirty percent?'

'What?' Arthur leaned forward, as though he hadn't quite heard.

'You would pay us?' Zoe asked.

'If the information you provide to us leads to the recovery of funds, yes.'

'Thirty percent?'

'*Up to* thirty percent. To be frank, we've never had a recovery of this size, so we would need to discuss internally — '

'That's three hundred million dollars. Conservatively,' Arthur said.

'It could be far more,' Simon added. 'The offshore economy is in the trillions.'

'*Up to*, I said,' Moyes repeated nervously. 'And of course you'd need to pay taxes — '

'What about Annabel?' Zoe asked.

The men stopped and stared at her.

'Annabel?' Arthur asked. 'What about her?'

344

'She should get some of the money, too.' Zoe ignored the look Arthur was giving her. She turned to Bill Holden. 'Matthew Werner died because he was an informant for the Department of Justice. He was doing the same thing we are, except he trusted the wrong person. His wife should get his share of the money.'

'Annabel Werner will be well taken care of, I assure you,' Bill Holden said.

'Where is she now?'

'We — we're not sure.'

'You're not sure? Is she safe?'

'We don't know. But rest assured, we're looking for her.'

'Find her. And when you do, make sure she goes into protective custody. Whatever award we get, she gets a third. I won't have it any other way.'

'All right, Ms. Durand.' Bill Holden offered her a tight smile. 'You have my word. I will do everything in my power to ensure that Annabel Werner is safe.'

'So which is it, then?' Moyes asked. 'Do you want to be in protective custody? Or do you want to be heroes?'

'Heroes with a nine-figure bank account?' Arthur smiled. 'Absolutely.'

'Arthur, are you sure? The money would be there either way.'

Arthur turned to Zoe. He took her hands between his hands and pressed them against his cheeks. 'Zoe,' he said. 'I love you. I can't live without you. I won't. I'd rather take our chances together.'

Zoe felt tears well up in her eyes. Arthur leaned in for a kiss. It was a deep, slow, sensual kiss. His mouth on hers, his hand pulling her body against his. Zoe closed her eyes and felt a lightness in her body that she hadn't felt since she first fell in love with Arthur.

Holden cleared his throat.

'Sorry,' Arthur said, as he pulled back. He looked at Zoe, his fingers interwoven with hers, and they laughed. 'Heroes?' he said.

'Heroes.' She nodded.

'All right, then,' Moyes responded. 'We'll still need you in protective custody before and during the trials. And you'll need to give an interview. The sooner, the better.'

'Marina Tourneau,' Arthur replied. 'I want it to be with her.'

Holden hesitated. 'Not the *New York Times*? Or the *Wall Street Journal*?'

Arthur shook his head. 'With Marina Tourneau. At *Press* magazine. We wouldn't be here if it weren't for her.'

'Fine.' Holden nodded. 'Marina Tourneau. I don't know who she is, but she's about to win the goddamn Pulitzer for reporting. And you two are about to become the most famous sources since Deep Throat.'

Zoe smiled. She pushed up onto her toes and whispered into Arthur's ear. 'Mark Felt, I love you.'

Arthur smiled at the reference. It was the name he'd given to Duncan Sander when they had first started talking, back when Duncan was looking for Morty Reiss. Duncan had gotten the

Watergate reference right away and had laughed. He'd never once pressed Arthur for his real identity, something for which both Arthur and Zoe had been grateful.

Now Zoe felt a small wash of sadness, as she realized that Duncan would never learn his sources' real names. He would not see this monumental story in print, or Morty Reiss, the man he had been chasing for so many years, finally taken to task for his crimes.

Zoe squeezed Arthur's hand.

'Are you okay?' Arthur whispered.

Zoe nodded. 'I'll be fine.'

After these men were gone, she thought, she'd go out onto the balcony. She'd gaze out over the Tuileries. She'd kiss Arthur where the whole world could see them. And that would be worth everything. Even if it lasted for only a second, it would be worth it all.

Marina

A knot of journalists stood outside her apartment building. Marina saw them as the cab pulled up to the curb. It took her a moment to realize they were waiting for her. Her name had not appeared on the bylines of any of the stories. Marina had made sure of that. She didn't want to be part of the takedown of the Ellis family. She was, publicly, anyway, still Grant Ellis's fiancée. Reflexively, she touched the ring finger of her left hand. It was bare. The ring was in the dish on her bedside table. She would never wear it again.

It was too late to escape them. The crowd had spotted her. A reporter named Martin Wilkes, a friend of Owen's from the *Wall Street Journal*, called out her name.

Marina put on a pair of sunglasses and stepped out of the cab. As the reporters crowded around her, she kept her eyes trained to the curb.

All around her, they were shouting questions. When she reached the entrance, the doorman, Hugh, stepped protectively in front of her.

'I'm sorry, Ms. Tourneau,' he said. 'I didn't see it was you. Are you all right?'

'I'm fine, Hugh,' Marina replied. 'Thanks.'

Martin called out, 'Marina! How does it feel to be a part of the biggest news story of the year, instead of reporting on it?'

Marina turned. She looked him in the eye.

'It feels like I'm on the wrong side of things,' she said. 'Now, please excuse me.' She lowered her head and pushed her way inside.

'Is Grant home?' Marina asked Hugh.

'Yes, ma'am.'

Marina swallowed and nodded slowly.

'They arrested his father early this morning. I saw it on the news.'

'Yes, I know.'

'I'm so sorry, ma'am.'

'Don't be. It's not your fault.'

'Mr. Ellis is such a good man. Grant, I mean. Always polite. Knows my kids' names and asks after them.' He paused and then added, 'Not that his father isn't a good man. I just meant — '

'It's okay, Hugh. I know what you meant.' Marina gave him a small smile. 'I should go upstairs.'

Hugh nodded. He held open the elevator and pressed 12 for her. When the doors slid shut, Marina collapsed onto the bench at the back of the elevator. She'd been on her feet for more than twenty-four hours. Suddenly, she felt as though she couldn't stand up for another minute.

The doors pinged open. Marina stood and peered out. The twelfth floor was empty. Marina was grateful not to have run into any of her neighbors. She hurried down the hall, her heart racing. Her hands shook as she pushed open the front door.

'Grant?' she called out, as she placed her key on the foyer table.

'Look who's home.' Grant was sitting in an

349

armchair in the living room, his legs casually crossed. His hair was ruffled, and it looked as though he hadn't slept. He was wearing some kind of uniform, all blue with white stitching on the front pocket.

Marina walked toward him. She stopped short when she realized what was in his right hand: a .45-caliber pistol, resting on his knee and pointed directly at her.

'How was your trip to DC?' Grant said, his voice cold. 'I hope you sent my best to Hunter Morse.'

'He's dead, actually.'

'Is he? That's too bad. I liked the guy. So helpful.'

'You bribed him. To give you the identity of the whistle-blower inside Swiss United. And then you killed the whistle-blower.'

'Don't get ahead of yourself, Marina. All I did was have lunch with the guy.'

'How stupid do you think I am?'

'Not stupid at all. Too smart for your own good, as it turns out. To think, all this time I thought you were actually with me for the right reasons.'

'I was!' Marina snapped, exasperated. 'Do you really think I wanted this? This is hell for me, Grant. I trusted you, I loved you.'

'Then why did you do this?' Grant shouted. He rose to his feet and pointed the gun at Marina's heart. 'You've torn apart this family.'

Marina shook her head angrily, 'No. I've been protecting you all this time. I believed your father when he said you weren't involved in all

350

this dirty offshore business. I believed him right up until I learned that it was *you* who paid off Hunter Morse, and it was your old military buddy Charlie Platt who murdered Duncan.'

For one uncomfortable moment, they stared at each other in silence. Then Grant said, 'He deserved it, Marina. He turned you against me.'

'He did no such thing.'

'I heard your conversation in Paris. He was telling you to meet someone from Swiss United. Don't deny it.'

'That had nothing to do with you.'

'Like hell it didn't,' Grant snarled. 'That bastard never liked me. He was using you as a way to get inside our family. It was disgusting. The man had no boundaries. No sense of family.'

'And so you had him murdered.'

'You're damn right I did!' Grant shouted. 'And I should kill you, too, for what you've done.' Marina flinched as Grant waved the gun in her direction. For a split second, she considered running. But what good would that do? Grant was an expert marksman and he was only fifteen feet away. She'd be dead before she reached the foyer.

She put her hands up. 'You don't want to do that, Grant,' she said slowly. 'Just put the gun down.'

Grant kept it trained on her. 'Give me one reason why I shouldn't pull the trigger right now.'

'Because you'll get caught. There's a throng of reporters downstairs. Don't be stupid.'

Grant snorted. 'Please. Why do you think I'm wearing this? Hugh lent it to me this morning.' He kept the gun trained on her as he reached in his back pocket with one hand and pulled out a cap, which he put on his head. Suddenly, Marina recognized the outfit: it was the building mechanic's uniform. She was close enough now to read the stitching on the front pocket: 'Mendoza,' it read. The building address was beneath it. 'He's a good guy, Hugh. He realized I might need to make a quick exit.'

'And where will you go? They'll be waiting for you at the airport.'

Grant laughed. 'That's the nice thing about having a private plane and a new passport. Plenty of sunny countries out there with weak extradition policies.'

'You're just going to leave and let your father rot in jail? And Charlie Platt, too?'

'Oh, no.' Grant frowned in mock seriousness. 'You've wildly underestimated Charlie. He's one of the best spooks we had. He's terrific at disappearing. He's probably on the beach already, sipping a mai tai. Thanks to me, he's got enough cash in a Swiss bank account to last a lifetime. As for Dad, he'll be fine. You don't get to where he is in life by rolling over every time you hit a bump in the road.'

Grant turned his wrist and checked the time. 'This has been fun, Marina, but I've got a car waiting for me in the alley behind the building.'

He raised the gun, cocking his head slightly as he took aim. She knew she should run, but she was paralyzed with fear. She opened her mouth to protest but no sound came out. Instead, a shot reverberated through the apartment. A sharp pain exploded in her shoulder. She felt herself falling. Then everything went dark.

Annabel

Annabel peered out of the small, round window of Lorenzo Mora's private plane. Through the clouds, she could make out the brilliant blue of the Pacific Ocean and the craggy outline of the Baja coast. She didn't know where, exactly, she was supposed to land, only that it was a private airstrip, owned by the Mora family, somewhere north of Cabo San Lucas. But for the pilot, she was alone on the plane. Lorenzo had offered to fly with her, but Annabel declined. He had done enough for her already.

The plane circled and then began its descent. When the wheels touched the earth, Annabel felt a wash of relief. She was here. It was over.

The plane door opened. Annabel hurried down the stairs onto the tarmac. She blinked, her eyes adjusting to the bright light. The Mexican sun was at its apex. She shielded her eyes with her hand and glanced around.

There, beneath the shade of the single-story structure that served as an airport terminal, was Matthew. He had grown a thick beard and his skin was deeply tanned. He wore a linen shirt, blue jeans, and sandals. As he stood, Annabel noticed that he even carried himself differently. His hands were in his pockets, his stance relaxed. He bore only a fleeting to his former, suited self. But to Annabel, he was instantly recognizable.

'Matthew!' She dropped her bag and flew into his arms.

'Annabel,' he murmured, and buried his face into her neck. She felt the familiar crush of his forearm around her waist as he picked her up, spun her around.

They held each other for a long time. Then Annabel pulled back, admiring her husband. 'You have a beard,' she said, finally. They both laughed.

'You like it?'

'It's a good look for you. Relaxed.'

'Well, I've been forced into early retirement.'

'You picked a nice spot for it.'

Matthew glanced around. 'I didn't have much choice, but I'll take it. Good fishing and the sunsets are spectacular. I think we'll be happy here.'

Annabel burst into tears. Matthew pulled her close again, pressing her face to his chest. 'Shhh, it's okay now. We're okay.'

'I thought you were dead.'

'I know. I'm so sorry. I can't imagine what it's been like for you.'

'We had your funeral.'

'I know. It was the only way, Annabel. I didn't want to put you at more risk until it was over. As long as you didn't know I was alive, I had to believe they wouldn't hurt you.'

'Is it over? Will it ever be over?'

'I think so. It's the only story on the news now. They've arrested Jonas. Julian's dead. There's a manhunt under way for Fares Amir.'

'Where is Fatima?' Annabel hadn't thought about her until just now. 'And the pilot?'

'I don't know. I know they're safe. All of us are under CIA protection now. In fact, there are two men I want you to meet.' Matthew nodded toward the open door to the terminal building. Inside, it was un-air-conditioned but pleasant. A fan whirred overhead. In the corner, two men sat on folding chairs at a plastic table. One had neatly groomed hair and wore a crisp pair of white linen pants and loafers. Aviators sat on the bridge of his crooked nose. The other, a large, red-faced man, was sweating profusely in the heat. When he waved in greeting, damp patches appeared under his arms.

'Annabel, this is Thomas Jensen and Alexei Popov. Mr. Jensen works for MI6. Mr. Popov is CIA. They orchestrated everything. Because of them, I'm alive.'

Popov extended his hand, but Annabel threw her arms around him instead. The Russian let out a surprised laugh. He patted her uncomfortably on the back before pulling out of her grasp. She grabbed Jensen next.

'Thank you,' Annabel said, a fresh set of tears welling up in her eyes. 'Thank you for saving my husband.'

'Your husband is a hero,' Thomas Jensen said. He removed his sunglasses and placed them on the table. 'Because of him, we've been able to shut down Fares Amir's money-laundering operation. Mr. Amir has been the single biggest supplier of funds to Syrian terrorist organizations in the UK. We knew it, but without proof, we were unable to do anything about it.'

'And that's just one example,' Popov added.

'For years, the CIA has been looking for a way into one of the offshore banks. If it hadn't been for Mr. Mora, your husband never would have found his way to us, and we would have never found a way to take down Swiss United.'

'Does Lorenzo work for the CIA?' Annabel asked. 'I don't understand how he got involved in this.'

Popov and Jensen exchanged glances. 'He doesn't,' Popov said. 'But he has been a good resource for us. We needed an asset close to Jonas Klauser. It was too risky to approach employees of the bank. So we decided to send in a client instead. Mr. Mora is exactly the kind of client Jonas Klauser wants. Extremely wealthy and very definitely corrupt. Lots of assets needing to be hidden offshore. And since he's part of a known criminal enterprise, Klauser would never suspect that Mora was a CIA asset.'

'Mr. Mora's brother is facing money-laundering charges of his own in the UK,' Jensen explained. 'So we offered him a deal. He helped us get inside Swiss United and the Amir Group, and his brother stays out of prison.'

'During a meeting, Jonas told Lorenzo that he had a source within the Department of Justice who had identified me as a whistle-blower,' Matthew explained. 'He suggested that Lorenzo cut off communication with me. Lorenzo offered to take care of the problem, but Jonas said he'd do it himself. So Lorenzo went straight to Jensen and told him that there was a whistle-blower inside the bank who was in danger.'

'We had to work quickly,' Jensen said. 'We knew we had to extract both Matthew and

357

Fatima, who had been informing MI6 about her brother's dealings with Assad. We thought it would look suspicious if they both disappeared at the same time, so we decided to orchestrate the plane crash. There were so many people who wanted them both dead — the bank, the Assad family, Schmit & Muller — that we reasoned that they would all assume someone else had caused the crash. It was ingenious, really.'

Popov laughed. 'It was your idea.'

'And that's why MI6 values me as much as they do.'

Popov rolled his eyes. 'You were the wild card,' he said to Annabel. 'We didn't know if you'd have the wherewithal to investigate. But you did. And I have to say, you were quite resourceful. I couldn't believe you found those photographs of the crash at the library.'

'How did you get the Fedpol agents to give me fake photographs of the crash?' Annabel asked.

'Agent Vogel worked for us. Agent Bloch worked for Fedpol until we came knocking. Now he's with us permanently.'

'That man who was following me that night — was he CIA?'

'No. He was Klauser's man. He was just keeping an eye on you, to see if you knew anything. Fortunately for you, you didn't.'

'Why did you let me twist in the wind for so long? It's been two weeks. Once you had Matthew in protective custody, why didn't you arrest Jonas and the rest of them?'

'That was unfortunate. Matthew had been downloading financial data onto his personal computer for weeks. He also carried on with Hunter Morse at the DOJ, so we could have evidence that Morse was indeed feeding information to Klauser. But then we heard chatter about a hit man, hired by Swiss United. We needed to extract Matthew and Fatima, but we couldn't take the risk that Fares would look through Matthew's computer. So Matthew left it with Zoe Durand. We hoped to retrieve it from her, once Matthew and Fatima were safe.'

'But she gave it to me. And I gave it to Khalid.' Annabel winced. 'Is Khalid — '

'Safe,' Jensen said. 'A black eye, I'm afraid, but otherwise intact. We staged a mugging to remove the computer. We thought that if he was being followed and seen turning over a laptop to an MI6 agent, our cover would be blown. So, instead, we arranged for some thugs to take his bag outside the tube station.'

'Oh, thank God. I thought — '

'He's fine.'

'He must be terrified. Can you tell him I'm safe? Please? After everything he did for us . . . '

Popov and Jensen exchanged glances.

Jensen nodded. 'I'll let him know you are safe.'

'Thank you.'

'So you recovered the laptop, then.'

'We did. But as it turns out, we didn't need to. Zoe took matters into her own hands. She had been leaking information to a journalist all along.'

'Zoe?' Annabel's mouth dropped open in surprise.

'Zoe warned me that an article was going to come out about the bank. That's why, when

Morse called me, I decided to cooperate. I was trying to save my own skin,' Matthew said.

'Zoe and her partner, Arthur Maynard, had been communicating anonymously with a journalist in New York for months. Arthur was a lawyer at Schmit & Muller, so he had access to information from several offshore banks, not just Swiss United. And Zoe had access to most of Swiss United's files. Biggest data leak in history, they're saying.'

'Oh my God. That's why it's all over the press.'

'Yes. And the good news is, this will make it a lot easier for you two to disappear.'

'Because everyone will think that Zoe and Arthur are the source of all the information — and the cause of the arrests.'

'Precisely.'

'What will happen to them? Are they safe?'

Popov sighed. 'Well, no. Their cover is blown. But they have the benefit of being public figures now. They are being lauded as heroes, crusaders. So that makes them slightly more difficult to kill.'

'Also there's a matter of the money,' Jensen added. 'To the extent they need protection, they'll be able to afford it.'

'The money?'

'The reward. From the IRS. Up to thirty percent of reclaimed funds.'

'How much — ' Annabel looked at Matthew.

'We won't know for months,' Matthew said. 'But the conservative estimate is three hundred million dollars.'

'Wow,' Annabel whispered. 'Three hundred

million in recovered taxes?'

'No. The reward is three hundred million. Before taxes, of course. And split three ways.'

'Three ways?'

'Between Zoe, Arthur, and me.' Matthew grinned. 'So call it fifty million. Not a bad retirement fund.'

'I'm sorry,' Annabel said, shaking her head. 'You're telling me that the IRS is going to give you fifty million dollars.'

'Give *us*,' Matthew said.

'Give us,' Annabel repeated, dumbstruck.

Jensen reached for a briefcase, which he laid out on the table. He popped it open and, from it, pulled out two manila envelopes. He handed one to Matthew and the other to Annabel.

Annabel opened hers and reached inside. The first thing she pulled out was a Canadian passport. She opened it and was surprised to find her own picture smiling back at her. It was an old photograph, from her days in New York. Her hair was short, cropped close around the ears.

'I always liked that look on you,' Matthew whispered. She smiled as he pressed his lips to her neck.

'Josephine Ross,' she read, and nodded. 'I like it.'

'Elegant,' Matthew said.

'Who are you?'

'I'm your husband. I'm the man you married.'

'I know you are,' she said. She took his hands and kissed them. 'Whatever I call you, I know you are.'

'You can call me Nathan.'

'A wealthy entrepreneur from Toronto,' Jensen explained. 'You fell in love with this area while on vacation. And purchased a big house with a wraparound porch overlooking the sea.'

Annabel's eyes lit up. 'How did you — '

Matthew shrugged. 'I had a few requirements.'

'There doesn't happen to be an art studio?'

'Of course.'

Annabel threw her arms around Matthew. 'And you. You'll be there.'

'We'll never be apart again.'

'Would you like to see it?' Jensen asked. He pulled a car key out of his pocket.

Matthew nodded toward Annabel. 'Up to her.'

'Yes!' Annabel laughed. 'Of course.'

Jensen tossed her the keys. She caught them with one hand and then offered the other to Matthew. They walked together out of the airport building, Jensen and Popov trailing behind. When she got to the small parking lot, she stopped and laughed. There were two cars: a Jeep and a silver Porsche convertible.

'What?' Matthew shrugged. 'I told you there were a few requirements.'

She held up the keys. 'I'm driving, though.'

'Whatever you want, Josephine.'

Matthew opened the car door, and she slid behind the wheel. As she put the car into drive, she felt Matthew's hand fall to her thigh. The top was down and the breeze tousled her hair. She would have to cut it all off again, she thought, as she picked up speed. Especially if she was going to drive this car, on this open highway, beneath

362

this endless blue sky. The thought of that made her glad. She tilted her head back and laughed. She would follow Thomas Jensen's Jeep south for another twenty minutes before pulling into a long, private drive that someone would miss if they weren't looking for it.

This was it, Annabel thought, as they pulled up to the house. For the first time in years, she was home.

Epilogue

TWO MONTHS LATER

Marina could feel someone watching her. She opened her eyes and blinked in the late afternoon sun. A book lay on her stomach, pages splayed open. She must have fallen asleep while reading. When she sat up, she felt a sharp pain in her shoulder where the bullet had entered and then exited her body. The wound was just four inches from her heart. She'd been lucky. If Owen hadn't called the FBI as she was heading to her apartment to confront Grant, an agent wouldn't have burst through the apartment door just as Grant was about to fire at her. If the agent hadn't fired first, the bullet would have lodged in her heart.

Grant was still in the hospital. His lawyers were working out a plea agreement for, among myriad other charges, attempted murder. He would spend at least a decade in jail, she was told, for what he'd done to her. Charlie Platt, Grant's military buddy, was still in the wind. If they found him and got him to implicate Grant in Duncan's murder, there would be no deal. Grant would go to jail for the rest of his life.

Marina winced and lay back, chastising herself for putting weight on her left hand. Two surgeries later, Marina was mostly stitched back together. She was still doing physical therapy, though, and would be for several more months before her left side was fully functional. She might not ever get there, the doctors said. The muscular damage had been substantial. But the doctors didn't know how tough Marina could be when she set her mind to something. She wasn't about to let a weak shoulder slow her down. She had work to do.

'Careful, there, sleeping beauty.' Owen stood over her, holding out a cocktail. He wore a bathing suit and a linen shirt. It was an icy concoction, garnished with a wedge of pineapple. 'I was going to get us champagne, but . . . ' He gestured at the white powdered sand and the turquoise Caribbean Sea beyond it.

'When in Rome.' Marina eased into a sitting position, letting her feet swing over the edge of the hammock. She reached for her drink. 'How long was I asleep?'

'Who cares?'

Marina nodded. 'Good point. I keep forgetting we're on island time.' She took a small sip of her drink, and then another, longer slurp. 'God, this is delicious.'

'First drink in how long?'

Marina laughed. 'Two months? Alcohol and pain meds don't mix, you know.'

'Well, we have to celebrate. I have a surprise for you.'

From behind his back, Owen produced a magazine.

Marina sat up fully. Her eyes gleamed. 'No,' she breathed. 'You didn't. How?'

'I have my ways.'

'But it doesn't hit the stands until tomorrow. And I had to fight the front desk this morning to get me yesterday's *New York Times*.'

'Island time. It's good for you.'

Marina laughed. 'To be one day behind the news? On a remote island with terrible cell reception?'

'You needed a break.' Owen shot her a stern look. 'Anyway, connectivity is a small price to pay for a weekend away with the handsomest guy you know.'

Marina tipped her glass. 'Cheers.'

'You're dying to see it, aren't you?' Owen dangled the magazine in front of her, teasing.

She lunged for it. He snatched it away, but she was too quick for him.

'You have good reflexes for an old man.' She laughed. 'But not good enough.'

'I got distracted by that very low-cut bathing suit you're wearing. Unfair advantage.'

'I do what I need to do to get the information I need.' She shrugged as she paged through the magazine. 'It's why I'm so good at my job.'

'You are good,' Owen said, his voice suddenly serious. 'It's an incredible interview, Marina.'

Marina didn't answer. She was too busy reading. Her interview with Arthur Maynard and Zoe Durand was a full seven-page spread, one of the longest lead stories ever published by *Press*. She had written it mostly from her hospital bed, dictating the words to Owen as he sat beside her with a laptop. Though she had yet to meet Zoe and Arthur in person, Marina felt as though she knew them. She had spent nearly twenty hours

Skyping with them. It was the most challenging — and rewarding — interview she'd ever done. Of everyone she had spoken to over the past two months, she was most impressed with Zoe. At first glance, Zoe was quiet and young, still traumatized from her experience at Swiss United. But the longer they spoke, the clearer it became to Marina that Zoe had been the instigator of the leak and the mastermind behind the theft and dissemination of 2.5 terabytes of information that had, to date, led to more than a hundred arrests, the dismantling of several drug cartels, money-laundering operations, and one significant terrorist network. Not bad for a small-town girl from the South of France.

After Marina was finished, she paged through the rest of the magazine in reverent silence. The entire issue was dedicated to the leak that was now known worldwide as the Swiss Files. There was a piece on the arrest of James Ellis and the plea deal taken by Grant Ellis, as well as the suicide of Hunter Morse. Another story detailed the Americans who had been indicted for tax fraud, including three senators, two congress-men, two federal judges, and several CEOs of major corporations. There was an article about Fares Amir and his connection to the Assad family, penned by a *Press* correspondent in Europe. At the very end, there was an article about Morty Reiss. Two weeks after the collapse of Swiss United, Reiss had been arrested in Argentina. He had been living under an assumed name, pretending to be a retired real estate developer from Miami. The article detailed how

Reiss had avoided detection for eight years with the help of offshore banks like CIB and Swiss United. It was cowritten by Marina Tourneau and Duncan Sander.

Finally, she flipped back to the front cover. She bit her lip as she studied it, willing herself not to cry. It was one of her favorite photos of Duncan, a black-and-white shot of him from the Met Gala, four years earlier. He looked slim and dapper in a tuxedo, his hair trimmed short and combed neatly back with gel. He was standing at the center of a group of beautifully dressed and powerful women. Anna Wintour stood at his side, laughing at something he had just said. In his hand, he carried a small leather-bound diary, in which he wrote down not only engagements but snippets of interesting conversations he planned to use later in stories. If one looked hard enough, one could see a silver pen in his left hand, poised over the notebook. Marina knew it was the pen she'd given him after the Darlings story. It was emblazoned with the date of their first story together.

Beneath the photograph, in simple white lettering, read: *In Memory of Duncan Sander, Editor in Chief, May 1, 1958 — November 11, 2015.*

Press's art director had fought Marina about the cover. Marina knew she was in the minority; most of the staff thought the cover should feature Zoe and Arthur, the faces of the Swiss Files leak, not a photograph of Duncan. But Marina had overruled them. It was not something she planned to do often, but in this case, she felt it was of vital importance. To her, Duncan would always be the face of the Swiss Files leak. After all, he had launched the investigation. Zoe and Arthur were his sources. Without him, this issue — this story — wouldn't exist. It was one of the few perks of being the new editor in chief of *Press*. It was a title she wasn't totally comfortable with, at least not yet. But in this case, it had worked in her favor.

'The cover is great,' Owen said quietly.

'Thank you. Not sure anyone else agrees, but I love it.'

'Duncan would have loved it.'

Marina nodded. 'I know,' she said. 'And he deserves it.'

'That he does.'

'Thank you for getting this to me. It means a lot to hold it in my hands. I mean, I've seen it. But it never feels real until you see the final copy, right?'

Owen smiled and nodded. He understood. He picked up her drink where she had left it on the sand and handed it to her. Then he leaned behind the hammock and pulled a beer out of an ice bucket. He cracked it open, tossed the opener on the sand. 'Toast,' he said, raising his beer. 'To Duncan.'

'To Duncan.' Marina nodded.

'To the story of our lifetimes.'

'He said it would be.'

'He was almost always right.'

Marina tipped her glass, its frosty edge clinking against Owen's bottle. They both took a sip and stared out at the sun, which was dropping low on the horizon.

'What should we do tomorrow?'

'This?'

'We could. Or, if you're getting bored, I've been kicking around a story for a while. It would require a short boat ride over to the Dominican Republic. It's just there — do you see it?' Owen pointed at a dark mass across the water.

Marina sat up a little straighter.

'Are you suggesting we work on vacation?' She cocked her head, looking nonplussed.

Owen laughed. 'Let's not call it work. Let's call it exploring. You in?'

'You know I am. But tonight we celebrate. Right?'

'Tonight we celebrate.'

They clinked their glasses together. The sun was beginning its slow descent into dusk. Marina could make out the white form of a yacht out on the ocean. She watched it growing smaller and smaller, until finally it disappeared in the direction of the Dominican Republic. Tomorrow she would be there, too. Tomorrow, she reminded herself. Not tonight. She took a long, slow sip of her drink and lay back in the hammock. Then she pulled open the magazine and began to read in the fading evening light.

Acknowledgments

I am deeply indebted to the following people: Sally Kim, Danielle Dieterich, Karen Fink, Alexis Welby, Ashley McClay, Emily Ollis, and the entire team at G. P. Putnam's Sons; Alexandra Machinist, Josie Freedman and their colleagues at ICM; Pilar Queen; Andrea Katz; Ann-Marie Nieves; Julie Miesionczek; Todd Doughty; Anne Korkeakivi; Jovie Perkins; Elyssa Friedland; Leigh Abramson; Lauren Brody; Charlotte Houghteling; and Josephine Alger, all of whom were instrumental in the writing of this book. I am humbled and grateful for your help, support, and love.

This book is dedicated to my husband, Jonathan. He has taught me what it means to be a partner. I am lucky he is mine.

We do hope that you have enjoyed reading this large print book.

Did you know that all of our titles are available for purchase?

We publish a wide range of high quality large print books including:
Romances, Mysteries, Classics
General Fiction
Non Fiction and Westerns

Special interest titles available in large print are:
The Little Oxford Dictionary
Music Book
Song Book
Hymn Book
Service Book

Also available from us courtesy of Oxford University Press:
Young Readers' Dictionary
(large print edition)
Young Readers' Thesaurus
(large print edition)

For further information or a free brochure, please contact us at:
Ulverscroft Large Print Books Ltd.,
The Green, Bradgate Road, Anstey,
Leicester, LE7 7FU, England.
Tel: (00 44) 0116 236 4325
Fax: (00 44) 0116 234 0205

THE BLAME GAME

C. J. Cooke

Helen and Michael Pengilly are on a dream holiday in Central America with their children, Reuben and Saskia. But a sinister stranger is watching them — and on their way to the airport, a horrific accident devastates the family, leaving Saskia fighting for her life. Terrified as she recovers in hospital, Helen's memory is dragged back to a decades-old tragedy, while other pieces of the fugitive life she and Michael have lived for so long start to fall into place. A slashed car tyre. The night Helen was followed home in Kent. Silent phone calls at 3 a.m. Two bouts of severe food poisoning. To protect their family, Helen and Michael both said they would forget what happened. But there's someone who will stop at nothing to make them remember . . .

THE GIRL IN THE WATER

A. J. Grayson

The first body in the water was a woman's . . . the last body in the water would be mine. Amber adores her husband David and their dog Sadie, and her job working at a local bookstore. But when the body of a young woman is found in a stretch of river near their house, her world begins to collapse. The headaches she has been experiencing start to intensify, and she struggles to maintain a shaky hold on her own thoughts and memories. When Amber makes a chilling discovery in her home, she starts to doubt her husband and everything they have built their lives on. And as she probes deeper into the identity of the dead woman, the answers she uncovers will plunge her into a terrifying world where nothing, and no one, are what they seem . . .

LINE OF FIRE

Andy McNab

Backed into a corner by a man he knows he cannot trust, ex-deniable operator Nick Stone strikes a devil's bargain. In exchange for his own safety, he is charged with locating someone who doesn't want to be found, currently hiding out in one of the remotest corners in the UK — and this time Stone is not operating alone. But he and his team don't find just anyone: they find a world-class hacker whose work might threaten the stability of the western world as we know it. Before Stone finally sees which way to turn, the choice is ripped out of his hands. Most people might think of home as safety, but Nick Stone isn't most people. For him and his team, it's just another place to get caught in the line of fire . . .

STILL LIVES

Maria Hummel

Revered artist Kim Lord is about to unveil her most shocking show yet: *Still Lives*, a series of self-portraits in which she impersonates the female victims of America's most famous homicides, from Nicole Brown Simpson to the Black Dahlia. As celebrities and rich patrons pour into L.A.'s Rocque Museum for the opening night, the attendees wait eagerly for Kim's arrival. All except Maggie Richter, museum editor and ex-girlfriend of Greg Shaw Ferguson, Kim's new boyfriend. But Kim never shows up to her party — and when Greg is arrested on suspicion of murder, it seems that life is imitating art. Has Kim suffered the same fate as the women in her paintings? As Maggie is drawn into an investigation of her own, she uncovers dark and deadly truths that will change her life forever . . .